More praise for
A Piece of Heaven

"In this beautifully written ode to family bonds, the author presents an in-depth view of what truly matters in life-lasting relationships. . . . Readers should have their handkerchiefs ready and prepare to be enchanted."
—*Booklist*

"Beautifully drawn but deeply wounded characters populate the pages of this exceptional romance. Seamlessly combining the dark issues of abandonment, betrayal, infidelity, and alcoholism with a compelling love story, Samuel has written an intense, multi-faceted tale of relationships, family, and healing love."
—*Library Journal*

Acclaim for
No Place Like Home

"A lyrical novel of family, loss, and redemption, beautifully written, beautifully told."
—Jennifer Crusie

"If [you] yearn for a happy-ever-after ending, *No Place Like Home* is a novel for you."
—*The Denver Post*

Also by Barbara Samuel
Published by Ballantine Books

NO PLACE LIKE HOME

A Piece of Heaven

Barbara Samuel

BALLANTINE BOOKS • NEW YORK

A Ballantine Book
Published by The Random House Publishing Group

This book contains an excerpt from the forthcoming hardcover edition of *The Goddesses of Kitchen Avenue* by Barbara Samuel. This excerpt has been set for this edition only and may not reflect the final content of the forthcoming book.

www.ballantinebooks.com

ISBN 0-345-44568-6

Manufactured in the United States of America

First Hardcover Edition: February 2003
First Mass Market Edition: January 2004

OPM 10 9 8 7 6 5 4 3 2 1

This one is for Meg Ruley,
warrior, champion, wise woman,
and all-around wonderful human being.

ACKNOWLEDGMENTS

It's impossible to express how much some people helped with this book. My deepest thanks go, first and most deeply to Sally Pacheco and Adolph Chacon, because the book was born in their backyard on a summer night when someone started talking about holy dirt—and the help didn't stop there. Thanks to both of you for so generously sharing your world. Thanks to Sally for leading discussions, especially for sharing your mother and your insights on certain things. Thanks to Adolph for teaching me little things, all the time, words in Spanish and the way things were done in the old days and a million other things I can't possibly name.

Thanks to Mary Francis Pacheco, Sally's amazing mother, who shared stories of her life and times and made them live for me. Thanks to Krista Barber, Jennifer and Willie Chacon, who gave me an entirely different view of Chimayó. To Christie for a perfectly timed and insightful critique, to Holli Bradish, for a great artist's date down at Chimayó and Taos, a day I will always remember as magical and rare, and to the gang—clients and employees alike—at SCCCS. I had no idea, when I walked in those doors, how much my view of life and love and the universe was about to change, and I'm grateful.

And thanks to Rita Valdez, class of 1977 Doherty High School. Thanks, girl, for standing up for me all the time with those big, bad girls.

A Piece of Heaven

Sins become more subtle as you grow older: you commit sins of despair rather than lust.

—PIERS PAUL READ

Prologue

Abuela

Placida Ramirez knew she did not have much time. There was old in her bones, not like it had been when she was sixty and her knees got stiff after a rain, or when she was seventy-six and sometimes fell asleep in her chair, half-shucked corn still in her hands when she woke up.

No, this was an old that went deep, deep. She was the oldest woman in an old, old town, and even the littlest ones called her *vieja*.

And it would not be so bad to go on now. She'd outlived four of her children and two of her great-grandchildren, not counting the ones that never really came. Her husband had died so long ago she had lived longer without him than she had with him.

There was only one thing keeping her, and Placida had to fix it before she could go. So it was that she gathered herbs and incense and candlesticks that she had not used for a long, long time. And she waited till the moon was right—full and bursting with the light of women— and she cast her petition to the Madonna, the Virgin, the Mother.

Prayers did not always work. But this time, Placida felt a rush of warm wind over her old bones and through her heart. For a moment, she scowled at the candle flickering over the carved wooden robe of the statue of Guadalupe, thinking maybe this was just going to bring her more energy to see to things herself. "No," she said, and poked a finger toward the candle. It fell over.

With a small cry, she grabbed it up, but it was too late. The flame on the old altar cloth sped right for the thin muslin curtains over the window. They went up in a shiver of smoke. With her gnarled fingers, she could not unfasten the knots of her apron as fast as she wished, and in despair, she turned and took up the kitchen towel, trying to beat out the leaping flames. With sharp, disappointed movements, she slapped at the fire.

That was the trouble with saints and prayers and spells. A person had in mind a perfectly reasonable plan, but the tricksters always seemed to take it as a challenge.

Filler from *The Taos News*:

Full Moon Facts

The full moon is the phase of the Moon in which it is fully illuminated as seen from Earth, at the point when the Sun and Moon are on opposite sides of the Earth. The full moon reaches its highest elevation at midnight. High tides. Names for the August and September full moon: Full Red Moon, Full Green Corn Moon, Full Sturgeon Moon.

One

It was a good thing for Placida Ramirez that the moon was full when she set her house on fire at three o'clock in the morning that August night. Because it was the moon, shining like a searchlight through her bedroom windows, that had awakened Luna McGraw. Technically, it was a dream about her long-gone father that yanked her out of sleep. It was worries about her daughter's arrival tomorrow that kept her awake.

But the moon, so coldly white in the summer sky, took the blame.

Dragging on a pair of shorts beneath her sleeping shirt, she got up to make some coffee. It would make her mother crazy to know Luna was making coffee in the middle of the night. Why not a cup of tea? Something soothing and relaxing?

Not her style. Once upon a time, she would have poured a hefty measure of gold tequila into a water glass and sipped that. A part of her still wished she could.

At least coffee had some bite. Measuring out Costa Rican Irazú into her new Krupps grinder, she counted

out the seconds to twenty-one. Perfect grind for a latte.
Perfect grind for her, anyway. The world was entirely
too full of coffee nazis these days—coffee was about in-
dividual taste, and no one should let anyone else tell her
what to like. She liked hers strong enough to stand and
walk by itself, with steamed milk and a pound of sugar.
As drugs went, it wasn't bad. Also, a good latte took
some detail work. The measuring. The grinding. Now
she pressed the grounds, the color of good earth, into a
tiny metal basket, and clicked on the machine. While it
was heating up, she poured one-percent milk into a
giant ceramic mug and waited, yawning, for the steam
to be hot enough to make a froth.

The actions and the smell of coffee eased some of her
restlessness, and she found she could stand there with
one bare foot over the other without twitching too
much in nicotine withdrawal. Or wondering why it had
suddenly seemed like such a brilliant plan to quit smoking right now, when her daughter was coming to live
with her for the first time in eight years. Maybe, she
thought with resentment, it would be better to try again
in a few weeks, when there wasn't so much at stake.

But of course, Joy was the reason she had decided to
try. The reason she could stick with it for a few more
days. Joy hated cigarettes and Luna hated feeling like
such a failure in front of her daughter. Not smoking
seemed like a gesture of earnestness.

And really, she needed to quit anyway—everybody
had to quit, right?—it stunk and made you wrinkle
faster and it was bad for your health, and it was nearly
impossible to go out and have a long, lazy dinner with
anyone these days unless you wanted to keep a patch
handy, which was almost as sick in its way.

Primary reasons, she said to herself, an old habit. A
note taped to her cabinet said it: SMOKING STINKS. Never

mind dread diseases or wrinkles. She hated the smell of cigarettes on her body and in her hair, in the air and on her hands. Yuck. The way things smelled mattered to her—perfumes and incense and flowers, herbs and morning on the desert. Coffee brewing in the middle of the night.

The machine started to gurgle, and she stuck the steamer into the milk, bringing a fine foam to the top, then poured the finished espresso into the mug, added three packets of turbinado sugar, and stirred it all together.

Now what? There was a button that needed sewing on her best blouse. A novel, lying facedown on the kitchen table, could be read. In the workroom off the kitchen an assortment of crafts, including a half-painted table, waited. Luna went and stared at it—the wildest one yet, a blooming pink rose with a bleeding heart at the middle of it. Her mother hated it, said it was scary, and while Luna didn't agree with her, she wasn't in the right mood to work on it, either.

Tobacco. Tequila. White zinfandel. A long Marlboro, red pack.

At least they would be something to *do*.

With a half-bored, half-agitated sigh, she carried the mug outside to the porch. The cold moon burned overhead like an evil omen. Luna glared at it, settling into a metal, motel-style rocker she had painted with a kitschy, smiling Virgen de Guadalupe in a pink dress and lime green cloak and a Barbie-doll face. Guadalupe Barbie, she told people who wouldn't be offended. Even people who really loved her—and frankly, what was there not to love about 'Lupe?—were pleased by the rendition. Sitting there eased Luna, like sitting on her mother's lap.

But still that searchlight of a moon blazed over Taos. In the canyons of her mind, Luna's demons howled at it.

She could see them, with their greenish lizard skin and long claws and ears like bat wings, dragging out all the forgotten sins of a lifetime, the little and the big. All the sorrows that ordinarily stayed safely buried, the tattered bits from childhood, the protected velvets of things she couldn't bear to look at. One demon plucked out a bracelet made of copper links, machine-stamped with thunderbirds, and hearing her gasp of surprise and outrage, ran off cackling with it.

Night sweats, her mother called them, but that seemed to be understating the case a bit. Especially when Kitty had them, she was probably thinking about things like the time she swore at her boss, or the night Luna and her sister Elaine saw her grabbing a boyfriend's rear end on the way out. Kitty had just not done that much she'd have to regret.

Unlike Luna, with her AA pin and the daughter she'd lost custody of and the career she'd destroyed.

Oddly, though, none of those things were the ones haunting her tonight. Instead, she'd awakened thinking of her father, who'd left home when Luna was seven and never came back. She dreamed about him once or twice a year, so it wasn't particularly unusual. Sipping her latte, holding the sharp, milky taste in her mouth for a moment, she did think it was amazing how long you could miss a person, especially when he didn't deserve it.

Sitting now in Guadalupe's lap, with a smooth wind blowing over her face, Luna heard the trained therapist in her head, Therapist Barbie, who wore big tortoiseshell glasses and her silver hair in a French knot, point out the truth: *Not too surprising you should dream about him tonight, when your own child is coming to live with you. That drags up a lot of old issues, doesn't it?*

Bingo.

She was wide-awake in the middle of the night trying not to smoke cigarettes because her fifteen-year-old daughter was coming to live with her for the first time in eight years. More than life itself, Luna wanted to get it right.

A smooth wind, warm from sunbaked rocks high in the Sangre de Cristos that circled the town like a ring of sentries, blew across her face and knees. It smelled of the fields of chamiso and sage it crossed, fresh and utterly New Mexico. She'd missed that scent more than she could say when she'd left home at sixteen. Tonight there was a hint of woodsmoke in it, and Luna imagined a pair of honeymooning lovers curled before a kiva-shaped fireplace. The picture eased some of her tension, some of that crawl of nicotine need.

It helped so much, she did it again, just breathed in the night, hearing crickets and the faint howl of the wind, or maybe *La Llorona*, the famed weeping woman of legend who was said to walk the rivers here, looking for her lost children.

Lost children.

Bingo, said Barbie, dryly.

It was perfectly normal to be nervous, especially because there was quite a bit of murkiness surrounding the sudden change in custody agreement. Joy had been in a little trouble the past year, but it hadn't appeared to be serious. Luna had flown down to Atlanta twice, a hardship financially, but hadn't made much progress. Joy's appearance had shifted, her attitude was sometimes hostile, and her grades were slipping, but there were no signs of drugs or other substance abuse. Still, Luna had been uneasy, and asked her former husband to consider letting Joy spend a season or two with Luna in Taos. He'd adamantly refused.

Things had grown worse over the spring and early summer, during which Joy had been forced to stay in Atlanta instead of coming to Taos as she usually did, thanks to flunked classes. And then, suddenly, Marc, Luna's ex, had called to say Joy could come live in Taos. Luna, suspicious of a trick, had asked Marc to put it in writing. He had agreed. Even stranger.

Something was afoot. But whatever Marc's ulterior motives, Luna had a chance to make sure her daughter was all right, a chance to see her and be with her every day, a chance to find out what had caused such a dramatic change in her behavior over the past year. A chance, as the old *Quantum Leap* show said, to put right what once went wrong.

She'd painted the second bedroom, framed the thick-silled window with gauzy curtains, brushed up on the nutritional aspects of cooking for a child, even shifted her schedule at work to make sure she could be home after school. Friends teased her about it—no fifteen-year-old particularly cared if mommy was home after school, they said—but Luna just smiled. Her own mother had worked nights to be at home for her daughters after school, and it had meant a lot to her.

The crickets went utterly still, as if a giant hand had squashed them. Luna straightened, hearing a gust of wind gather in the distance. It rolled toward her, and she covered her eyes and put a hand over her mug just as it slammed into the little porch. It wasn't cold, just dusty, and Luna waited, eyes closed tight, for it to pass.

Smoke.

Not cigarette smoke, which she would have gladly inhaled to the very deepest part of her lungs. And not the gentle wisps of a honeymoon cottage. This was full-bodied, almost a taste, the thick smell of a fire that was pretty full of itself. When the gust of wind died, fast as it had come, she peered into the darkness, wishing that moon wasn't so bright so the flames would show. The summer had been painfully dry and fires were burning all over the Four Corners. The ancient neighborhood, surrounded by fields of dry grass and sage, was particularly vulnerable. Even a small fire could be disastrous.

She put her cup down and dashed out to the road, turning in a circle very slowly to see if she could see it, breathing in the strong smoke smell for clues to direction.

"Oh, shit!"

The fire wasn't at all distant. Bright orange flames poured out of the window of the very old woman who lived two doors down the street.

Charged with adrenaline—and likely caffeine—Luna dashed inside, phoned in the fire to 911, and then dashed back out, up the dirt road on bare feet, then up the grassy, prickly expanse of yard toward the old woman's house. A goathead bit her arch and she had to stop to pull it out, hands shaking. Fire danced through the kitchen window, licked at a pine that stood sentry near the back, threatened to burst, any second, through the roof.

Thinking with a sick feeling of the old woman, Luna leapt onto the porch and yanked open the screen door. "Hello!" she cried, pounding with her fist on the door. "Hello! Are you in there?"

Nothing. She tried the door and found it locked. "Hello?" She pounded harder. No answer, and smoke thick enough it was making her want to cough. She tried the window. Locked.

There was a flowerpot thick with chrysanthemums sitting on the step. Luna grabbed it, smashed the window, unlocked it, and stuck her head in the smoky interior. "Hello? Is anyone here? Grandma!" Maybe Spanish would be better. *"Abuela!"* she cried. *"Hola!"*

The smoke, sharp and acrid, stung her eyes. An ache of some primal terror burned in her chest. For a moment, she hesitated. The firemen would be here any second. They were trained for this. It was arrogant of her to think it was her job to try to save someone, wasn't it?

But then she thought of the wizened, tiny old woman, and there was no way she could just walk away and live with herself in the morning. Before she could chicken out, she ducked into the house through the window, dropping to the floor in some remembered bit of lore. The smoke wasn't so thick down there, and the air felt cool. Crawling on her hands and knees, she made her way through the dark. Living room. Door to a bedroom, closed.

Her heart was skittering so fast that she felt shaky. The fire was beginning to crackle and breathe, an animal gathering power. *Get out, get out, get out.* Luna resisted the terror. Coughing, she opened the bedroom door.

The room was blissfully free of smoke, at least for this second. She stood up and checked the bed. Empty.

From the back of the house came a loud, cracking noise, and a strange groan. Luna almost choked on her fear, imagining the beams of the house coming down. But faintly, she heard a yell—not a scream, but some kind of curse—and she dashed out of the room, pulling up her T-shirt to cover her nose and mouth. Her eyes watered profusely, but against the hellish light of the kitchen, she spotted a wizened figure moving, a shadow in the light.

Bracing herself for a millisecond, Luna took a breath through the fabric of her shirt, then dashed down the hallway to the heart of the fire. The old woman was in there, slapping a wet towel at the flames that danced up the walls. Hacking, coughing, sometimes nearly doubling over, she still kept swinging.

"*Abuela!*" Luna cried. "Come *on!*"

Giving Luna a look of fury, the old woman backed away, her foot nearly into the flames, and uttered a spate of Spanish that Luna didn't understand. Heat singed the hairs on her face, and it took everything she had to reach out, venture more deeply into the inferno, but she did it, connecting however she could with the old woman, who slapped at Luna's arms and wiggled her legs when Luna picked her up around the waist and tossed her over her shoulder. She could hear the fire engines now, close and coming closer.

"No! No!" *Abuela* cried, smacking at Luna's head and back, kicking her hard in the stomach. Luna grimly hung on and ran outside with more power than she would have believed she owned. When they were safely on the grass, Luna dumped her struggling bundle, taking an elbow to the eye for her trouble. At the influx of cool, mostly fresh air, she coughed hard and wiped the tears from her eyes, wondering if she'd be bruised tomorrow. Her cheekbone ached.

The old woman made a break for the house.

Luna grabbed her by the back of the dress. "You'll kill yourself in there!"

For a long moment, the old woman stared at the flames with an expression of purest fury. She said something in Spanish, and tried to yank her arm away.

Luna held on. "Are you going to try to get back in there again?"

"No," she said proudly, and slapped at Luna's hands.

"All right."

With narrowed eyes, *Abuela* took three steps back, watching in something like disgust as the firemen tramped up with their hoses, first hitting the old pine with a good soak, then addressing the fire licking up the roof. "How did it happen?" Luna asked her, finally.

Abuela glared. Then she spat out something Luna didn't understand, and waved her hand at the fire. She clamped her lips together and wouldn't say another word.

Thomas Coyote was not sleeping when his phone rang. He was sitting at the kitchen table doing nothing much of anything, just sitting under the glare of the overhead light in the unbreachable silence of late night and loneliness, his hands folded in front of him. He examined them minutely. Big hands, even for a big man, which he was. They were brown, both from nature and the sun, a kind of reddish brown. The crayon color burnt sienna, which was what he always used to color faces when he was a boy, making them the same color as the people around him. Burnt sienna and brown and another one he couldn't quite name just this minute. The one called peach he'd saved for ribbons or dresses.

The house was big and silent, though not empty. Sprawled across the threshold to the dining room was his dog, Tonto, a young and foolish Akita mix with a patch of black over one eye. His paws twitched as he chased a dream squirrel or rabbit. On the windowsill over the sink sat a fluffy black cat, Ranger, his tail swishing back and forth, back and forth, as he stared at the moon-bright landscape. In an upstairs bedroom slept Manuel "Tiny" Abeyta, one of his best workers, who'd appeared on Thomas's doorstep six weeks before with a black eye, the just-out-of-jail hair greasies, and a beaten look around his mouth. Three months on an ankle bracelet for domestic violence, and a two-way restraining order—Tiny couldn't approach his common-law wife and she could not approach him. His wife, too, was under restraint, facing a similar stretch of anger management classes. They were halfway through, and Thomas frankly didn't see much improvement, but you never knew when the turnaround might come. Tiny didn't have anybody but Thomas just now.

Tiny wasn't the first one to take the bed in that room, and he wouldn't be the last. It had made his wife crazy, these strays Thomas found, people as often as animals. Or animals as often as people. The stray part was the bit that had bugged Nadine.

At the back of his mind, a niggling vision of his ex-wife tried to rise, and resolutely, he went back to his hands. Nails oval, neat because he filed them regularly while he was watching TV. Couldn't stand raggedy nails. His work as an adobe layer meant there were inevitable bangs and nicks and cuts, and the clay sucked every bit of moisture out of a man's skin, but every night after his shower, he rubbed them with Bag Balm to help the cuts heal and keep the skin soft, a trick he'd learned from his grandmother, who told him when he was eighteen and getting ready for a date that no woman wanted to feel rough hands scratching up her *chichis*.

The memory made him smile, and he rubbed his hands together easily, liking the strength and flexibility in his long fingers, flat palms. Hands that had weighed a good number of *chichis* in their time, though not for a very long time. Maybe wouldn't anymore. It made him tired to even think of it, all the trouble and turmoil that went along with women.

The phone, shrilling into the stillness, made him jump, and he stared at it, a green phone hanging on the wall, for a long moment. Middle of the night phone calls were bad news. On the third ring, he got up and yanked the receiver off the hook. His hello was gruff.

A woman's voice said, "No one died or anything, but is this Thomas Coyote?"

"Yeah." A ripple of worry crossed his belly. "Is it Placida?"

"She's fine," the woman said. A good voice. Anglo, but western Anglo, with a little softness at the end of words. "But she . . . uh . . . had a bit of an incident tonight. She set her curtains on fire and the kitchen is damaged?" The voice rose on the end of the word, as if in a question, and he knew she was a native of the general area. He grunted acknowledgment, and the woman continued, "She's going to need to stay somewhere else tonight."

"I'll be right there."

It was a little less than two blocks, one block east and one downhill. He loped it easily, seeing the fire engines he'd heard and dismissed. A chill touched his chest. What if . . . ?

His grandmother, technically his great-grandmother, stood in huffy silence to one side of the yard. She was dressed in an ordinary flowered housedress, her hair in a long braid down her back. Her skinny arms were crossed over her chest, and light caught on the thick glasses that distorted her eyes. Soot covered her in streaks, and her hair carried a layer of fine ash. A cold sweat touched him. Damn. *"Abuela!"* he said, censure and worry in his tone. He didn't need to see her eyes to know she was irked, and that somehow, the woman standing beside her was—right or not—taking the blame.

"Grandma," he said, bending to put his arm around her shoulders. "What happened?"

She made a pishing noise, dismissive. In Spanish, she said, "You could see. I caught the curtains on fire."

He responded in English. It was their pattern. He spoke English. She spoke Spanish. The only time she ever used English, it was in a whisper. "How? Why so late?"

Placida Ramirez was old, but not feeble. "That's my business."

The woman standing on the other side of his grandmother made an amused little noise and he raised his head, gathering impressions. An air of sturdiness and directness, a headful of wild brown and blond curls, strong-looking legs. She'd obviously been inside the burning house—soot was smeared along her chin and the front of her shirt. One knee was scraped and dusty and she had a streak of blood on one arm. "You went in?"

"I broke the window," she said. "I knew she was really old, and it scared me that she might be still asleep."

"You know you're cut?"

She frowned and looked down, not seeing it at first, then lifted the sleeve of her T-shirt. "Ah, it's not bad. I'll be all right."

Her voice was smooth and green, like a pond in a forest. He looked at her muscled legs below her shorts, the looseness of breasts beneath her shirt. Rubbed his palm against his thigh. "You sure?"

She backed away. "Yeah. Now that she's safe, I'll just go clean up."

"I'm Thomas Coyote," he said, and extended his hand. A way to hold her another moment. "Thank you."

She hesitated and put her hand into his big one, and

he liked the sensible feel of her fingers. Strong palm, a good grip. "Luna McGraw."

His grandmother snorted and let go of an annoyed stream of Spanish, none of it complimentary. Thomas glared at her, letting go of the woman, feeling her flee the second he let her go. He thought it would have been neighborly to tell her they'd have her to dinner in order to thank her. Something. But he didn't. He settled his face into a frown and watched her cross the street, breaking into a simple, athletic lope as she passed the house next door, then cut across the lawn to a house he'd often noticed, a small, well-tended adobe with a pretty yard full of flowers. She ducked inside. A moment later, light brightened a set of long windows to the back.

His grandmother cursed next to him, and he couldn't make it all out—his Spanish was not that good—but he gathered it had something to do with the Anglo and the trickster. "She saved your life, *Abuela*," he said.

Placida scowled up at him.

He knew she wasn't trying to kill herself. It was a mortal sin, for one thing, and if she was anything, it was a good Catholic. But whatever she'd been doing, she wasn't talking now. "C'mon, let's get you home and in bed. You'll be too tired tomorrow to do anything."

Saints' Lives—Santa Rosa de Lima:

Born as Isabel to <u>Spanish</u> immigrants to the <u>New World</u>. A beautiful girl and devoted daughter, she was so devoted to her vow of chastity, she used pepper and lye to ruin her complexion so she would not be attractive. Lived and meditated in a garden, raising vegetables and making embroidered items to sell to support her family and help the other poor.

Two

Maggie's diary

17 Agosto 2001,
Sta. Joan de la Cruz

Dear Tupac,
  My name is Maggie and I just bought this notebook to write in a couple of weeks ago, because there is no one here to talk to anymore and I'm going crazy. This one time, a teacher told us you could write stuff down and it's almost like talking, and she told me I was a good writer, that it would probably make me happy to do this, and I guess it's better than nothing. I asked her who I'd be writing *to* and she said, just make somebody up, like this Jewish girl, Anne Frank, did. Somebody you think will listen to everything you say and want to hear it. So I picked you. Maybe if you're really dead you don't have anything else to do so maybe you won't mind.

I haven't started till tonight because I couldn't think what to say, but tonight, there's something to write about. Tonight, this is what happened.

There's a *bruja* who lives behind me. That means witch in Spanish. Her house is across the field, and when it caught fire, I was sitting in the window of my room, wrapped in a blanket, my feet hanging out over the ground two stories below. My mom used to hate it when I did that, but she doesn't notice anymore.

I don't do it to be dangerous. It's really not all that dangerous, though I guess a little kid could fall. I'm not little anymore, already fifteen, though I didn't have my *quinceañera* like I was supposed to last June because my dad died and everybody forgot. Well, I didn't forget, but everybody else did and I guess I understand. I'm not sure if you could have a *quinceañera* at, like, sixteen, but I've known the priest since I was born so maybe he'd let me. We'd already gotten all the stuff, too, really pretty napkins and things from Mexico, kinda too pink if you know what I mean, but I still liked it.

Anyways, I wasn't asleep because there was this really, really bright moon. It woke me up and I heard all these weird howling noises outside along the creek, and it scared me, made me keep thinking of *La Llorona*, who is a really scary ghost who steals children and drowns them, so I got up because usually that's all I have to do to feel better, just stop lying there, scaring myself. Because of course there's no ghost on the creek. I could see that once I looked—and not even a ghost could have hidden in that bright light. Might as well have been day, only it was cold.

So, anyways, I was telling you about the *bruja's* house catching fire. I wasn't looking that way, because my windows look out toward Taos Mountain, but when

I heard the fire trucks so close by, I went down to the backyard to see what was happening. Flames spit out of the back of the house like something on TV, bright orange against the night sky, beautiful when they popped up out of the roof, dancing and twirling along the edges of the wood. I stood there on the porch, blanket around my shoulders, watching the firemen with their hoses spray water on it.

The *bruja* is a skinny old woman who looks like an owl. She grows all the old plants in her garden, and my mom goes there for herbs for a cough or a charm for somebody or to ask about a dream she had.

I don't believe in any of that stuff. Charms, saints, spells, prayers—like anything can keep you safe, right? Didn't even keep the old woman safe, did it, because there was her house, burning down right before my eyes. I hate to tell you, but that made me a little bit happy. I didn't want her to die or nothing, but she gave me the creeps with her big old eyes and hands like claws.

"Magdalena!" My mother's voice, rough from sleeping, came out of a window behind me. "What are you doing?"

"The fire trucks woke me up," I told her. "I came to see what happened."

My mom came out on the porch in her bare feet, her hair all long and dark on her shoulders and back. Pretty long now. She had on a plain white nightdress, and under that awful moon, I thought she looked dead, her eyes all hollow, her skin pale gray. I guess my mom doesn't always sleep that well either, though you'd never know it in the daytime when she has on all her makeup for work. Everybody says then that she's really pretty and doesn't look her age, which is thirty-six.

Now she came outside like it was totally normal to be

wide awake in the middle of the night. She lit a ciga-rette. The smoke drifted out in little clouds, and she coughed. "D'you see Placida anywhere?"

"Yeah." I pointed to the shadow-people standing in the yard. "Somebody got her out."

All glassy-eyed, my mom says, "I gotta see her. Been having dreams again."

I told her, "Mom! I'm sick of your dreams!" I yanked my blanket around me. "Not every dream means some-thing you know!"

"Not every one, h'ita, but some do." She petted my shoulder and I wanted to move away because I was mad, but I also kind of liked the feeling of her strong hand. She's crazy most of the time now, which really isn't fair, considering. A person should get to keep one parent the same if she's only fifteen and still needs them.

But like somebody wanted me to know that she was big-time crazy, my mom said, "The dreams about your dad were real. I didn't want to think so, but I saw all that coming a long time before it did."

I rolled my eyes. "I'm going back to bed."

"Night, baby," was all she said. I looked at her through the window and she was just sitting there, shoulders hunched, smoking in the dark, all alone. It made me want to smash something, like when I went loco at school last year and tore up this classroom be-cause nobody would listen to me and I was so upset about my dad and they all wanted me to act all normal, when I wasn't. Now I wanted to smash the windows or one of the big glass bowls she used to like to collect. Now they just sit there, getting all dusty like every-thing else in the house. Like everybody here is dead, not just my dad. Pretty soon, spiders'll start building webs over things.

Well, I don't want to be dead. And I don't want her to be dead, either. I didn't even want to smash anything, really, because to tell you the truth, it didn't help all that much. Maybe for three minutes I felt better, and my dad was still just as dead.

I just want us to get on with things. Have normal supper at the table again, and laugh sometimes and just sit around and watch TV. That's all I want. It just doesn't seem like that much.

That's enough for now. My hand is tired and I've filled up four pages.

Love,
Maggie

Coffee Facts

1453: Coffee is introduced to Constantinople by Ottoman Turks. The world's first coffee shop, Kiva Han, opens there in 1475. Turkish law makes it legal for a woman to divorce her husband if he fails to provide her with her daily quota of coffee.

Three

When Luna was little, they didn't drink coffee. Nobody did. Her mother and grandmother drank tea, and Luna and her sister, Elaine, drank it with them, strong and hot and sweet, with milk in it, or iced and sweet. No milk, of course, though Luna guessed that was the idea behind chai, which she liked almost as much as a good latte. Almost.

Luna discovered coffee on her own, when she started working in a restaurant in town at the age of fifteen. All of the other waitresses and cooks drank it. It smelled so good it tempted her for a long time before she fell to its call. And once she fell, there began a love affair of great depth, and she was a person given to deep passions. Coffee had outlasted nearly all of them.

In spite of all the excitement overnight, or maybe because it distracted her from everything else she'd been worried about, Luna fell asleep immediately upon returning home after the fire incident. She awakened just after dawn, the kind of grumpy but indelible awake that wasn't going to turn back to sleep anytime soon. She got up and pulled open the freezer to look over her choices in coffee beans. Something bracing and full-bodied this morning, maybe a little spicy. From the seven bags of beans on the shelves, she chose a French roast they blended specially for her at a local coffee shop, ground it for the auto drip—a much coarser grind than for espresso—and stumbled into the shower. She washed the smoke out of her hair and soot out of her pores, then dressed in a pair of shorts and a light pink man-style shirt that she liked for its ambiguity, and also because it made her bust look a teeny bit bigger to balance out her not-so-flat rear. She combed her hair while it was still wet, before the curls turned to tangles.

And even drawing it all out, she was finished before the coffeemaker, which was what she'd wanted to avoid, because then she had to stand at the back door, looking up at the sky, wishing for a cigarette.

No, *wishing* hardly said it. Luna *ached* for a cigarette. For the ritual of tapping one out of a fresh pack, taking out one of the tiny lighters she liked, setting flame to the end, and inhaling deep. Deep. Then tilting back her head to blow the smoke toward the sky.

Instead, with a cranky scowl she tried to loosen and couldn't, quite, she yanked open the drawer in the kitchen and took out a new patch. The instructions said you could leave them on overnight, but she wanted to hasten the exit of nicotine from her system, so she took them off. She tugged up her shirtsleeve and saw the raw mark left by the adhesive from the day before, pulled up the other sleeve and saw the remains of the red square from the day before *that* and got the creeps a little bit. Disgusting to think what the drug had been doing to her body all these years if skin contact could do that much damage in a few hours. She'd read somewhere that a few drops of pure nicotine in a reservoir could kill an entire town. Or maybe it was a tube full.

Whatever. It wasn't much.

Behind her the coffee machine gurgled as it finished its cycle. *Coffee, cigarette, morning begins.* She stared at the Band-Aid colored patch with dull fury for a few seconds and wondered what the point was. She'd die of something anyway. Why aim for another ten years of life if every second was misery?

Stop. That was the voice of addiction. Taking a deep breath, deep, deeper, deepest, into her lungs, she held it and blew it out just like it was a lungful of smoke. It helped a little and she did it again. Something else she read—this was not her first attempt to quit—said smokers forgot to breathe deeply.

Just breathe.

The tension started easing out of her chest and she slapped the patch on her side. By the time she fixed a cup of coffee, the patch was starting to sting and tingle a little.

But it was still impossible to just sit on the porch and watch the neighborhood wake up, especially because she downed two cups of coffee in no time. Joy's plane didn't arrive in Santa Fe until after noon. A lot of time to burn.

So to speak.

From the porch, she could see Placida's house and decided to get a bottle of water and go take a look at the damage. Clouds hung low on Taos Mountain to the east, lending a deep quiet to the morning. The neighborhood, mostly old, square, small adobe houses—some old, some new—was built low along an acequia, an irrigation ditch that ran alongside the narrow dirt road. There were no large farms here, but it was rural enough—most people at least grew some beans and corn and maybe some melons or potatoes. Some people kept a few animals; a rooster crowed in the mornings, but Luna had never seen him. She imagined him to be a cock of some importance, with deep red feathers.

It was a great neighborhood and she loved it. The main thing was the quiet. Just now, there was only the sound of cottonwood leaves rattling against one another, water chuckling through the ditch. The Medinas' goats heard Luna's feet crunching on gravel and rushed their fence, bleating softly, sticking their gray and black noses over the top to see if she had anything good. A lot of people didn't like goats—thought their eyes were creepy—but Luna found them happy creatures, and patted all of their heads in turn, paying special attention to the kid, who leapt along the fence as far as he could.

She left the goats and angled across Placida's yard, rounding the herb gardens filled with almost indecently healthy plants, to take a look at the kitchen from the back.

It was bad. Early morning light shone on a gaping, charcoaled hole where the window had been, and showed another, the size of a truck tire, on the roof. Feeling a faint, wavery echo of her terror the night before, she walked along the side of the house, looking at it, sipping her water, and went around to the front. Someone had taped a big piece of cardboard over the shattered window. She climbed the steps to the porch and tried to look inside. Light came in from the east, but there was so much soot on the glass it was hard to see anything.

Maybe it was smelling the faint odor of wet, burned wood, but suddenly Luna thought it very, very lucky that she'd been awake. The old woman had not been about to come out of that house. Stepping back, Luna wondered what the heck she'd been doing lighting candles in the middle of the night.

A dog barked and she glanced over to see a big tan

and black dog loping toward the house. Young and well muscled, with a black spot comically circling one eye, he bounded up on the porch and nosed Luna's hand like they were old friends. She laughed. "Hey, guy. Where'd you come from?"

He sat down politely at her feet and grinned, his tongue lolling. "What a cutie!" She knelt to put her face on a level with his, scrubbing his head. "You're a doll."

"Good morning."

The voice.

The voice of Thomas Coyote, the old woman's grandson. Luna rose slowly, trying to cover the sudden shyness that overtook her. "Is he yours?"

"Yeah, the rascal."

She kept her hand on the dog's head, an anchor, finding it hard to look up at the man himself, able to take only little glances. He was a very attractive man. Not handsome or beautiful or anything like that—his skin was a little rough from a long-ago case of acne, and he carried a little extra weight around his middle—but very *present*. His presence colored the air, made it almost shimmer.

Truth be told, she'd had a distant sort of crush on him for months. It was a small town, and there weren't that many eligible men past a certain age. Too many *artistes* in Taos—writers and photographers and painters, all who took themselves so seriously that a woman was an afterthought, a convenience. Thomas was . . . not ordinary, never that . . . but *real*. She saw him around a lot, at the Dairy Queen on hot nights, in a café, eating dinner by himself as he read the newspapers from Albuquerque and Denver. Mainly, she saw him at the grocery store where she worked as a florist. He bought Tide detergent and a lot of Chef Boyardee canned ravioli and frozen corn on the cob.

Silence stretched, longer and thicker with every second. Tucking a lock of wild hair behind her ear like it might help, Luna managed a question. "How's your grandma?"

"Seems to be fine. She's sleeping this morning." He lifted his chin toward the window. "How's it look in there?"

"Not good."

He came up the steps and Luna instinctively kept a wide circle of empty space between them, watching as he repeated her gesture of a few minutes earlier, wiping the glass as if to get rid of the soot that was on the inside. She stood back safely, noticing that his hair, braided tightly into a single rope that fitted into the hollow of his spine almost to his waist, was still wet. It dampened the fabric of his blue-and-white striped shirt, a shirt that was tucked neatly into his jeans, the sleeves rolled up on powerful-looking forearms tanned the color of cinnamon.

Now he turned. "It looks worse than bad," he said gruffly, and shook his head. "I can't imagine what she was up to." From his pocket, he took a set of keys and unlocked the front door. "You want to hang around a second in case I go through the floor or something?"

"Sure."

"Stay," he said when the dog would have followed him into the house. The dog whined, but obeyed, all but sitting on Luna's foot. Thomas raised an eyebrow. "You, too."

She smiled a little, looking beyond him toward the burned kitchen. "I don't know that you ought to chance going in the kitchen. Those beams look pretty bad."

"Yeah." He walked slowly, looking up at the ceilings covered with black swirls. He stopped on the threshold to the kitchen. Without stepping on the charred floor, he bent and picked something up, then dropped it with a yelp, shaking his fingers. He looked over his shoulder at her.

"Hot?"

He made a rueful face. "Not the smartest thing I ever did." From his back pocket, he took a folded white handkerchief—how many men in the world still carried handkerchiefs?—and picked up what he'd dropped, carrying it back to where she stood. "Look."

It was a heavy metal candlestick holder. "Why would she be burning candles in the middle of the night?"

"A ritual, prayers of some kind." He turned it over, but it was the same all the way around. "Guess I'll take it to her."

Luna's eye caught on a curve of black hair against his brow, and she backed away a little jerkily. It was slightly humiliating to have to admit the whole crush business to herself and she really hoped he didn't pick up on it. "Good idea," she said.

Then she turned and went back out to the porch and opened her water bottle to take a long drink. He came outside, too, and she didn't look at him, choosing instead to focus on the blue rounds of mountains all around them. "Guess I'd better get going," she said.

"How's that scratch?" he asked.

She touched it. "A little raw, but nothing important."

"Do me a favor." He took a small notebook out of his pocket, along with a stub of a pencil and a pair of reading glasses, which he perched on his nose before he scribbled something on the paper. "My phone number," he said, "in case you need to see a doctor."

With the glasses on, he looked like a professor, somebody who'd be teaching ethnic studies or American Indian literature at UNM. For reasons she didn't examine, they made him seem more approachable. She could look directly at him as she took the paper.

It was a face both more and less than she'd thought from a distance. Unmistakably Indian, long and raw-boned, dominated by uncompromising cheekbones and a wide mouth. It was hard to decide what nation he belonged to—she didn't think it was Taos or even Pueblo, but one of the Plains nations—Cheyenne, maybe, or Lakota. His long dark eyes were somehow sad, but maybe that was something she added because of the lonely grocery items.

Stop mooning, will you?

Right. Luna took the piece of paper he held out to her and the air changed, like the barometric pressure had dropped all at once. It made her want to yawn to pop her ears. His aggressive nose had a glow of sunburn on it, and he smelled like something she couldn't quite name.

Suddenly, she wanted a cigarette.

Life was good. Life was excellent, as a matter of fact. "I'm sure it'll be fine," she said, edging away from him. "See you around."

He raised his head. Stood there holding his glasses, with his mouth turned down a little at the corners, and something in his expression made Luna realize that she wasn't alone in her attraction, that while she'd been thinking about that hair, he'd been noticing things about her, maybe lips or eyes or breasts, whatever his thing was. It gave her a pang, made her want all kinds of things she'd told herself she could live without.

Thomas inclined his head, and she waited for what might come next, but he said only, "Let me know if you have any trouble with that arm."

"Hope your grandma's okay."

He nodded, his eyes serious on her face.

There was nothing else to do, so she turned back toward her house and tried not to think about him looking at her backside. She couldn't help wishing, as she tried to walk normally, that she had a nice flow of waterlike hair to swish around, or nice long legs, or something else to watch, something really good.

Joy would be arriving in Santa Fe at two. Since she had a little time, Luna ducked into an AA meeting, just to be safe. The thoughts of tequila and wine had been quite powerful the night before, and maybe the cigarette struggle was bringing up some of those old demons. It was a good move. She emerged an hour later fortified and stronger.

She walked to her mother's house from the church basement where the meeting was held. It was still and quiet on the hill as she approached the house. This neighborhood, too, was built low, the dun-colored adobe blending into the landscape.

But these adobe villas ran to the millions of dollars. Cottonwoods and discreet plantings of native shrubs cushioned any noise that might offend, and hid the windows of the super-rich and even celebrity sorts who retreated here. Far below, children cried out in some game, and an airplane droned above the cloud cover.

As Luna approached the gate of the graceful courtyard and let herself in, she noticed a handful of leaves on the cottonwood were edged with gold, the first sign of autumn. It seemed too early, as if time was rushing too fast, and she fingered the leaves as she waited for her mother to answer the door.

"Luna!" her mother said. "You're early!"

She's the only one who called Luna by her real name. Everyone else just called her Lu. It was such an odd name, Luna as paired with McGraw. Luna came from her father, who was charmed by her white skin and pale hair. Her mother was charmed by her father, so she did not protest. It suggested a certain magic to her, a child named for the moon. And if Jesse Esquivel had not disappeared when Luna was seven and her sister five, she would have been Luna Esquivel, which made some sense.

With a stab of surprise, Luna felt her demons from the night before suddenly rise up and start to howl.

She put a hand to her chest. There were things a person didn't get over. No amount of therapy, journals, art, or rituals could take away the pain of some wounds. Period. Some of them lived on forever in big messy scars that were so tender they could bleed without much provocation at all. Luna's father leaving home left a scar like that. On Luna, on her sister Elaine, on her mother.

Standing in the courtyard of Kitty's luxurious home on a Saturday morning, Luna said, "Give me a minute, Mom."

Kitty cocked her head, but then she nodded. "Come in when you're ready."

Luna moved away from the door, pacing ten steps out and ten steps back. One of the things she learned in recovery was to acknowledge emotions as they arose, instead of trying to stuff them behind a wall. Not that she was always particularly good at it.

The dream hadn't been notable. Just her father and her, just before he left, in a tourist shop in Albuquerque, where he'd bought her a copper bracelet machine-stamped with thunderbirds.

Go with it, Therapist Barbie said.

Jesse Esquivel had left home one morning wearing a hard hat covered with football decals and a white T-shirt tucked into his jeans, and never came back. Luna remembered his arms, dark brown and bulging from his work, so strong that the sisters had swung on them like they were iron bars. He had loved them, their father. It was that fact that had made her wait, night after night, knees in the back of the couch so she could stare out the window, trusting that the smell of supper and her mother's perfume would bring him home. She waited in perfect expectation, every night for what seemed like years but her mother said was only a couple of months, for him to come back through that front door.

And she knew just how it would happen, too. He'd just show up some evening, maybe one of those back-to-school nights when the dark was starting to swallow up playtime in nibbles. He'd come in at the usual time, and the girls would leap up from their play and screech, "Daddy!" like they always did, and barrel into his sturdy legs, and he'd roar and laugh and let them swing on his arms. And then, drawn by the excitement, Kitty would come out, wiping her hands on a cup towel. She'd be wearing the nubby blue dress he liked so much and she'd kiss him on the lips and then the whole family would go sit down to the supper Kitty had made, and it would never be spoken of again.

The fantasy had never come true.

Standing in the courtyard of her mother's elegant home some thirty years later, remembering, Luna could still ache for that little girl. Luna had worn the copper bracelet for three years, never taking it off. Once a week, Kitty took a toothbrush to the green staining her wrist from it, but never insisted Luna remove it.

One early morning in the third grade, Luna slipped off the merry-go-round before class, and the bracelet caught on a screw that was just a tiny bit loose. It nearly wrenched her hand from her arm before the metal gave way in a twist. She still had the scar beneath her thumb.

The bracelet was not repairable, but somehow, she'd managed to keep the pieces all this time.

"Luna, sweetie, are you okay?" Kitty said from the door.

"Fine." She smiled to show she meant it. "I dreamed about Daddy last night. Made me a little sad, I guess."

A flicker of something went over Kitty's face, but she never spoke of Jesse, and she didn't now. With a little smile, she came over and hugged Luna in a breathless whirl of perfume and cosmetics, then pulled her inside with one arm because she had a shoe in the other. "I'm almost ready to go. Made some sweet rolls, so have one before we get out of here." She limped into the kitchen on one turquoise sandal, and waved toward the cof-feemaker as she leaned on the counter. "Help yourself. Caramel, just the way you like them."

"You are so evil," Luna said, knowing the last thing she should indulge in was a caramel pecan roll made from her mother's store of wicked treats. Her clothes were getting ominously tight as it was—the other down-side to giving up cigarettes.

But she took a china plate from the cupboard and served herself one anyway, knowing Kitty would not in-dulge, but she would drink the coffee. Luna poured two cups of the pale, watery brew. Sitting at the carved southwestern-style table, she watched Kitty struggle with the strap of her sandal, bracing her trim little butt against the counter. The angle showed off a generous amount of cleavage at the gold-adorned neckline of her turquoise blouse. Diamonds the size of walnuts glittered on her fingers. "Where's Frank?" Luna asked.

"Golfing," she said, finally getting the buckle caught around her pretty ankle. She shook down her trouser leg and tip-tapped over the saltillo tiles of the kitchen floor to the window over the sink. "We can probably see him if you want to. He wears a red hat so I can spot him anytime." With a girlish lean, she strained to see, and lifted a hand like he might see her waving. "There he is, on the seventh hole!"

Luna smiled. Impossible not to adore Frank, who adored her mother. A widowed Texas oilman, he'd met Kitty at the track where she worked as a cocktail waitress and pursued her kindly and relentlessly for six years before she agreed to marry him. She kept telling him it would never work, a waitress and a rich man, and he kept disagreeing and she'd finally given in with a collapse of tears and yearning that ripped his heart right out of his chest. Luna was there, living with her mother in the first, tender days of recovery. It was the only time in her life that she ever saw Kitty cry over her father.

All Frank did was take her in his arms, a big man with a paunch and a pate and the kindest, bluest eyes Luna had ever seen, and tell Kitty that he would cut off his own dick before he'd let her down. Which made her mother, the bawd, laugh so hard she kissed him.

That had been four years ago, and he'd made an art form of spoiling her. Kitty was finally learning how to enjoy it. He'd bought her the big Mediterranean-style house, and drowned her in jewels and took her on all the cruises she had dreamed of for two decades of what had to have been excruciatingly difficult financial times, raising two daughters alone.

Luna had no idea how she'd done it.

"Are you excited?" Kitty asked now, her eyes bright.

"Yeah. Maybe a little nervous, too."

"Of course you are, but you remember that you're a wonderful mother and trust your instincts. I am so excited to have our baby with us for the whole year!"

And Joy adored her grandmother. At least there was that. "I know. Me, too."

"Let's get moving, then, girl. Is your sister coming up tonight for the dinner?"

"Yes. Can she stay with you? She hates sleeping on my couch." Luna didn't say it, but she hated to have Elaine stay with her. She'd gone evangelical Christian about the time Luna turned to alcohol for her troubles, and it was a strain to listen to Jesus injunctions for more than a couple of hours.

"Oh, you know I don't mind. We have tons of room." She fastened an earring more securely and brushed her blond hair out of her eyes. She smoothed her slacks, picked up her turquoise leather purse, and said, "Ready?"

"As I'll ever be."

Thomas put off the phone call to his brother as long as possible. He avoided it by doing all kinds of Saturday chores—groceries for his expanding household, sweeping the floors in the halls upstairs, cleaning a bathroom, washing the animals' dishes. He wasn't allowed to get out his woodworking tools, however, until he actually made the call.

Finally, he went to the living room. Once it might have been called the sitting room or the parlor in the anomaly of a Victorian house in adobe Taos, a forgotten leftover that was still mostly shabby. He'd fallen in love with the house one morning on a walk, and talked Nadine into it. Another one of his failed projects, he guessed.

But the room was quiet and still just now. Sun came through the thin, old glass of the big front window and fell across the pine floor in bright swatches, caught on the breakfront Thomas had carved of cedar and the matching small table upon which the phone sat. This one was white, what once had been called a Princess line. He picked up the receiver. The dial tone buzzed in his ear.

For a long minute, he listened to it, feeling vaguely seasick. He wouldn't ask his cousins to keep doing his dirty work for him. But he prayed, as the phone rang in Albuquerque, that only the message machine would pick up.

Instead, it was a woman's voice. Bright and cheerful, called from some pleasant task, it said, to listen to pleasant news. For one long, agonizing second, he could see her clearly—the heavy weight of black hair around her shoulders, the tilt of her exotic dark eyes, the line of her long neck. Too young for him, he'd thought when they met. She chased him, as his mother would say, for over a year before he'd even agreed to go anywhere with her.

"Nadine," he said, "it's Thomas."

"I recognize your voice, Thomas. You don't have to introduce yourself every time."

"Yeah. Uh. I hear congratulations are in order. A baby in December?"

A half beat of silence. "How'd you hear?"

"James told me."

"Yeah. Well, thanks."

Thomas's eyelid started twitching. He put the tip of his finger to it. "Is my brother around?"

"He went to the store. Do you want me to have him call you?"

"No. Just tell him that Placida set her house on fire last night and she's all right, but she's staying with me for now."

"God, Thomas, is she all right?"

"I just said she was fine." It had always annoyed him, this habit she had of repeating things. "I just didn't want him to worry."

"Thomas," she said, "are you okay? I know how

much you wanted a baby and this couldn't have been—"

"Don't, Nadine." He hung up. His hand was sweating so badly that he nearly dropped the receiver.

He was fine. Just fine. Right as rain.

Grimly, he joined Tiny and Placida in the kitchen, a room he liked for two reasons. One, it was enormous. Big enough to hold a table, one Thomas had made himself from a beautiful slab of maple, and eight chairs. Two, it was filled with light all day. One big window over the sink faced south, and a whole wall of smaller windows in a line looked east, down the hill and across the city.

But those were the only good things about it. It had been remodeled in about 1920, upgrading the plumbing, installing tin cupboards that someone, somewhere over the years had covered with Con-Tact paper in wood tones. Judging by the peeling, even that had been twenty years ago or better. The floor was covered in worn linoleum in a pattern that had faded to an indistinguishable muted gray. He kept meaning to do something to it—he could at least expose the floor underneath, see if it was worth saving.

Just now, it was a room filled with the richness of chiles and pork and the subtler scent of fresh tortillas browning in an iron skillet. Placida stood at the stove happily cooking for the man curved around the table like a comma. Thomas stopped to nab a fresh tortilla and smell her stew. "How are you this morning?" he asked, touching her skinny back. "You feel okay?"

"Good, good," she said in Spanish. She lifted her chin to Tiny, happily devouring her cooking. "Your friend, he's hungry. I cooked."

Tiny grinned. "It's good, too. Better than old bachelor cooking, eh?"

Thomas nodded, reminded with a punch to the gut of the phone call. "Pack some of that up, *Abuela*," he said. "I'm gonna take some to your neighbor. Put it in the fridge and I'll take it to her later."

"No." She didn't look at him. "You stay away from her."

He raised his eyebrows. "She saved your life."

Stubbornly, she looked up at him. "No."

"No, she didn't save your life or no, I can't take her some chile?"

"Both." She raised her chin. "Tiny could take it to her."

Thomas reached for a tortilla from the stack on a plate. "Nope."

To avoid further argument, he ambled out on to the wide porch around the old house, tearing the warm tortilla into strips to eat. In one corner were his woodworking tools, and with a sigh of release, he picked up a twelve-inch block of soft pine with a few marks carved into it, and a chisel, and let the wood speak to him, take him away.

Placida's family had boasted two talents, valued highly in the old world. Her father had been a weaver from Chimayó, and her husband had been a *santero*, a woodcarver who devoted himself to saints. Among her children, then her grandchildren, the weaving had continued, and Thomas had a cousin who was getting rich exporting blankets to tourist markets.

The carving had gone wanting. None of Placida's sons were interested, and none of the grandsons until the very youngest, Thomas's *Tío* Hector. And then Thomas, whose mother had often said he was born with a stick in his hand. She'd brought him up to Taos often as a boy, letting him spend the long, soft mountain summers with his great-grandmother and her grandson Hector, who took care of her, and her goats and sheep. Hector had taught him by day how to work with adobe, how to make the bricks and how to build things with it so they lasted; by night, they carved saints and skeletons and other sacred objects.

He liked that his life contained this smooth continuity. That he could lose himself in the shape of a foot coming out from beneath a robe. That he could care for his grandmother after Hector died. That he'd turned his uncle's fading business into a roaring concern over the past five years. His house still needed so much work because he had no time to devote to it, not because he had no money for it. There was a lot of money in Taos these days, and a lot of it flowed into Thomas's pocket via adobe. Straw into gold.

Which somehow made him think of the woman who had rescued his grandmother. Her hair was straw and gold mixed together. Her eyes were dark. Wary. Almost as wary as his own must be. A rustle moved on his nerves, and he nodded. He would take her the chile no matter what Placida thought of it. It was only right.

From *Astrology Magazine*:

The Impact of Eclipses

Solar eclipses are something to notice and watch for—because they always signal the time for a change. This month, there are two major solar eclipses to look out for. This is a time of endings, of upheavals, of any kind of change that impacts human lives. Hold on to your hats! It's going to be a rocky road.

Four

The flight was late, of course, because Luna was so anxious to see her daughter. Kitty occupied herself with a pile of magazines, tearing out pictures every so often, pictures she would take home and glue into a spiral notebook she kept. The pictures weren't of window treatments or garden ideas she liked; they were just pretty—as likely to be a bottle of perfume as a stained glass window. She'd done it for as long as Luna could remember, long before the current wave of "be kind to yourself" trends had come along.

Luna, never able to sit still for long, bought a latte from a vendor and carried it up and down the hallway, trying not to think of hijackers or broken engines or any of the other awful things that could happen to planes. As she paced, her daughter's name rang through her mind like a song—*Joy, Joy, Joy.*

From the moment Joy lifted her calm, inquisitive gaze to Luna's face in the delivery room, Luna had been completely transformed. Ready to kill or die, ready to sing and dance, a willing, hungry servant to the siren of motherhood.

Which made what happened later so much worse. She took a sip of her latte and blinked against the memories. Not today, she said to the demons threatening to slip out of their caves. Not now. Maybe seeking the calm of her own mother, she settled beside Kitty in one of the sculpted plastic chairs.

Kitty put down the magazine. "Is Joy happy about coming for the school year?"

"She seems to be. It's hard to know with her the past year. I can't get a good read on her." It had been nearly six months since they'd been together, and though they talked on the phone and through E-mail a few times a week, it wasn't at all the same. "She's had some trouble in school, and Marc is really irritated."

"What a surprise," she said mildly. Kitty did not gossip—ever—and didn't allow it in her presence, but even she found it difficult to be charitable toward Luna's ex. And Marc was one of the few people in the world who wasn't charmed by Kitty—one of the worst fights Luna ever had with him had resulted after Marc cuttingly said Kitty was about as charming as a Las Vegas streetwalker. "I bet poor Joy will be delighted to get out of that house while he runs his campaign. I'd just hate to have reporters in my face all the time, and you know they will be if they haven't been already."

"I'm sure." Luna suspected that it was the campaign that had led to the change in custody agreement. A sulky teen might spoil a lot of photo ops. With Joy safely out of the way, Marc and his second family—scrubbed and blond and shiny—could pose as the all-American family at every event.

Not that she could say any of that to Kitty, and she was probably right: thinking that way never did anyone any good. But truth be told, Marc was a shallow, social-climbing bastard who'd seriously wounded Luna at a very vulnerable time in her life—and done it in the most manipulative, cold ways imaginable. At times, she'd had revenge fantasies that would have made Attila the Hun's blood run cold, and he'd deserved every single one and more.

Not that she ever would have indulged them. Even at her very worst, she'd never done anything to harm Joy, although the judge had seen it differently.

The flight was finally announced. Luna jumped up, and Kitty squeezed her hand. "Remember, sweetie, all a child needs is love."

Luna nodded, her heart swelling up in her chest. They jockeyed into position with the others in the waiting area, straining for a glimpse of Joy.

She didn't even see her until she stood right in front of her. "Mom. It's me."

Luna blinked at the pierced, Kool-Aid–dyed red- and black-haired ex-blonde who stood before her in a fishnet shirt, bell-bottoms, and black fingernails. A glittering blue stud shone from beneath her lower lip. Luna blinked, a thousand things rushing through her mind—mainly wondering what to say and how to handle the new look and what had brought it on. But they were all crowded out by the stinging swell of love and relief—she was really here! Here!—and the genuine, unmistakable happiness in Joy's pale blue eyes.

Flinging her arms around Joy, Luna squealed a little in happiness, loving the feel of thin arms around her neck, squeezing hard. "Oh, I'm so glad to see you!" she cried.

Joy clung a long time, fiercely. "Me, too," she breathed. "Totally."

When they got back to Taos, Joy was wiped out, and Luna led her to her new bedroom. She seemed to genuinely like it—Luna had painted the walls a vivid turquoise and found some kitschy Day of the Dead accessories, a lamp made of a grinning skeleton and a mirror framed with bones and skulls.

"I'm sorry it's so small in comparison to what you're used to," Luna said, opening the closet to show her the shelves inside, "and I know you'll want to add your own tastes, but the windows are great. Look." Yanking aside the curtains at the east window, she showed her the view of Taos Mountain, rising above a tangle of scrub oak. And to the north, a view of the creek.

"It's perfect, Mom. Really. I love the Day of the Dead. You're so artistic." Joy rubbed her fingers over a distressed dresser. "I'd love to be able to do this stuff."

"It's easy. I'll show you. For now, why don't you have a little nap. *Everybody* is coming to see you tonight."

"Good." She yawned and sank down on the bed. Luna headed for the door.

"Mom," she said, and Luna turned, smiling. "I am so glad to be here. Thank you."

Luna blew her a kiss.

In the kitchen, she turned on some quiet music to keep herself company as she made a potato salad. It was the only thing in the world she put together that rivaled the stellar skills of her friends and relatives. The particular recipe had come from one of Marc's elderly aunts, a southern treat. As she minced celery and onion, boiled potatoes in their skins, and chopped eggs, Luna hummed along with the CD, letting it repeat as she worked.

She had just slipped the bowl into the fridge and was thinking of a quick shower when a knock came at the door. Expecting Allie, her best friend, she had a tease about impatience on her lips when she opened the door.

But it wasn't Allie—it was Thomas Coyote. "Oh," she managed brilliantly, and stood there with the door handle under her right palm, staring at him. There didn't appear to be any other words currently available for speaking, not anywhere in her brain.

And the only thing that made that okay was that he didn't seem to have any words, either, so they stood there, staring at each other for what seemed like five minutes.

Luna had forgotten how it felt, this piercing kind of attraction. Forgotten the funny, loose need to gather in a thousand details of a man's person and hoard them for later remembering. She greedily absorbed the look of his neck at the opening of a white Henley, a triangle of dark smooth skin where the buttons had been left open, the crown of his head, tossing arcs of whitish gloss from the dense blackness of his hair, his mouth, wide and unsmiling . . .

"Uh, hi," she said, and it came out a little froggy. "Sorry. Brain lock. I didn't expect to see you."

Duh. She closed her mouth, stepping back to gesture him in.

"I just came by to thank you properly," he said, and it was only then that she noticed he carried a canvas tote bag, the kind the market paid customers five cents apiece to use for groceries. "I brought you something."

"Please, come in." She stepped backward into the living room, acutely aware of her bare feet, of the rumpled look of the blouse she'd been wearing all day. She couldn't even imagine how bad her hair probably looked—she'd reined it into a scrunchy to get it out of her way for cooking, but it had a mind of its own and didn't much like to behave. She forced herself not to raise a hand to it. "You didn't really have to do that."

He hesitated before crossing the threshold, as if her living room was the part of the map that warned, "There Be Dragons Here." Gingerly, he stepped inside. Luna ducked her head and noticed the shape of that long, sturdy thigh beneath his jeans and thought how muscular his work probably made his body. As he passed, a silver hoop peeking out from below his hair caught her eye, and beneath it, the round of a burly shoulder beneath cotton. When he stopped in front of her, she tried, really tried, to avoid looking at his hair, but there it was, a heavy black braid she wanted to unlace, spread apart, see how it fell when it was free.

He halted in the middle of the living room, next to the coffee table, and he looked enormous in contrast to her things. "Would you like to sit down?" Luna asked. "I have some soda in the fridge."

The bag hung at his side and he looked around the room, slowly, taking it in. Luna wondered what he thought of the colors a lot of people thought were too strong, if he liked the paintings, if he would be comfortable on the couch. She found she was twisting her fingers together, but it was somehow comforting and she didn't stop. He looked up at her. In that wonderful, husky voice, he said, "You really smell good."

"Oh, it's probably potato salad. My daughter has just arrived and I've been cooking."

His mouth didn't do more than twitch. "I'm pretty sure it's not potato salad."

Luna finally laughed, let her twisting fingers go. "Sorry, I'm being an idiot. In case you can't tell, I . . . uh . . . well—" She took a breath and raised her head, looking at him like a grown-up. "I've seen you around all over the place. I'm kind of flustered to be actually talking to you."

"Me, too." There was a directness, a relief, in the way they looked straight at each other finally, eye to eye, wondering what it might mean, letting it just be there. "I'm divorced," he said suddenly, and then as if aware how bald it sounded, "So you don't get the wrong impression."

"How long?"

Thomas ducked his head, looked inside the bag he carried. "Two years come October."

"It gets easier."

"It's not hard now." He lifted a shoulder. "It's my second divorce. I got the whole thing figured out now."

She nodded, seeing with a little sinking feeling how hard it wasn't, seeing it in the rigidness of his mouth trying not to frown, the blankness of eyes that didn't want to show how sad they were. "Not your choice, I take it?"

A shrug.

Mmm. Maybe it was better this way. The last thing she needed was a great man to show up just when she had other things to take care of. A man on the rebound was a dangerous thing indeed, and one of Luna's unbreakable rules was no one still in love with an ex. Not to mention he had *two* ex-wives. That didn't look good on anyone's résumé. And a really bad choice for her, when she had her goals so firmly in hand.

She took a step back. "Why don't you come in the kitchen and have a soda, Thomas? It's the good stuff." To lighten the tension, she added, "My favorite is the vanilla cream, but I'm betting you're more of a root beer kind of guy."

Light came back into his eyes, appreciation of the subtle, silly joke. "Vanilla, huh?"

Beautiful eyes, she thought with regret. Such a velvety brown. "You betcha."

Thomas followed her without really intending to, dutifully lugging the canvas bag of green chile stew he'd ladled out of the pot his grandmother had cooked on his stove today. Luna's was a very old house, a territorial adobe with a jutting bench circling the set of windows at the east end of the kitchen. There were striped turquoise and purple and yellow pillows lined up along it, and a low pine table. "Nice," he said. "You've done a lot of work in here."

"Thanks. Yes, I have. It took me almost a year to get it ready to live in."

In the background, some music played quietly, and he frowned, trying to place the notes. "Hey, I know this. 'White Bird.'" He narrowed his eyes. "*It's a Beautiful Day*, right?"

Genuine pleasure lit her face. "Right."

The music, exotic with violin, changed the spirit in him, gave him a sense of possibility, but didn't erase his awkwardness. He put the bag on the table and for something to do, took out the plastic bowl of chile and a thick foil package of tortillas, watching Luna move around her kitchen in her baggy shorts. He noticed again that her legs were very muscular. No bulging thighs or anything, but the long thin ropes across calf and knee that showed in every movement. She took glasses out of the cupboard—purple glass with yellow rims—and swung around to get ice. When she bent, he didn't quite have the strength to avert his gaze from the shorts riding up on her thighs. She gave him a fizzing glass full of root beer and he smelled it happily, letting the spray touch his nose before he drank of it, deeply. So good.

"What'd you bring me?" she asked.

"Chile." He put the offerings on her counter, remembered his *abuela*'s reaction to his bringing it over. "I gotta ask what you ever did to my grandmother."

"I don't know that I ever talked to her before last night." She made a face. "She was furious with me then."

"She wasn't going to let me bring this over."

"I thought she was going to beat me up in that kitchen, I swear. I don't know why, but she did not want to come out." She pulled off the lid from the Tupperware container of green chile stew and inhaled deeply, closing her eyes. "Wonderful." Picking up the foil package beside it, she put that to her nose, too. "And homemade tortillas." He liked the way she said it, not a question, a statement.

He nodded.

"God, I can't think of anything I like better. And the chile's still warm." She opened the package and peeled off a soft, fresh, thick tortilla, rolled it up, and dipped it in the bowl, then bent to catch it in her mouth without dripping it on her clothes. "Excellent."

Thomas watched with an almost helpless sense of attention. He stared at her mouth and spied her tongue and watched as she chewed, and looked at her breasts beneath her simple, pink button-up shirt and at her thick, riotous hair captured barely at all in a ponytail.

She looked up at him. Soberly. Like she knew something.

"How long you been divorced?" he asked roughly.

"Ages. Another lifetime."

"Your daughter lives with her dad?"

"Until now. It was for the best at the time." She brushed a lock of hair out of her eyes. "Do you have kids?"

"No." And then he added something he hadn't told anyone else. "She's pregnant now, though. My ex. Gonna have a baby in December."

"Bet that's kind of hard."

Thomas breathed in. "I don't think about it."

"Mmmm." She smiled, the slightest bit skeptically. "Is that so."

He relented. Told the truth, which was a strange thing to do these days. "Guess I haven't had much chance, really. You're the first person I've said it out loud to."

She put her hand on his. Thomas, without knowing why, turned his palm upward to meet it. "You know," she said, meeting his eyes, "I'm sure you think you'll die of the pain sometimes, but it gets better eventually. Just takes time."

They were standing closer together than was usual for strangers and he wondered why she didn't move away. The air changed around them, just like that, in a second, and it was so heavy it should have been dark purple. He noticed the curve of her neck and wanted to smell it.

Even as he was bending toward her, he knew he would regret it. But he did it anyway, leaned in and bent down far enough to kiss her. He didn't close his eyes and neither did she. It wasn't long. It wasn't tongues or even any movement, just the press of lips, so intimate and yet not. And for one tiny space of time, he felt hope—it smelled like potato salad and hung like the possibility of violin. But then he saw her eyes, deep and dark, large and round, not long and slanted—and pulled back with a jerk, feeling like an idiot. "Sorry."

"You're just lonely, Coyote." She patted his hand like an auntie, making him think he was the only one who'd felt that crackle in the air.

"Yeah," he said gruffly. "I guess." He turned toward the door. "See ya." He made it to the door, the tatters of his pride trailing from his stiff neck. What the hell was that, anyway? On the porch, he stopped to breathe in the air.

Luna spoke behind him. "Thomas."

He turned.

She pushed open the screen door and braced it against her shoulder, then held out her right hand. It trembled visibly. She put the other in front of her and it was shaking, too. "I don't need anything in my life," she said in a voice so husky he nearly had to lean over to hear it, "that can make me feel like that. Okay?"

And that, he understood. He nodded. "Good night, Luna."

"Everybody calls me Lu," she said, waving a hand.

"No," he said, "it's supposed to be Luna."

After a quick shower, Luna sat on the front porch with a wide-tooth comb and a bottle of spray detangler, working on her hair. Not the easiest task in the world, but she managed to get it into a semblance of order by the time Alicia Mondragon pulled up in her battered red Fiat, a completely impractical car she nursed along through hundreds of dollars of monthly minor and major repairs. She waved one thin arm at Luna and turned off the radio, then the car—if the radio was on when she tried to restart, it might overload the delicate electrical system—and climbed out. Her dog Jack, a mixed-blood German shepherd with an unabashed sense of his own lovability, leapt free and raced across the lot, happily nosing a neighbor's black cat who'd been visiting, then licked both of Luna's wrists and dashed back to Allie. Luna laughed.

Allie came up the walk with a giant blue bowl in her hands. A tall, wispy woman with long, dark hair, she wore a batik print skirt with a plain, V neck leotard and several hundred pounds of silver jewelry including a heavy silver pentagram set with a gorgeous moonstone. Alicia was Wiccan. She ran a little candle shop not far off the plaza, a narrow shop said to be haunted by the ghost of a Spanish woman who killed herself in the back over a lover who'd gone astray. Lots of those kinds of stories around Taos.

"Ooooh," Luna said as she came up the steps, and pointed to the pent. "That's new."

"Cost a fortune," she said, "but worth it, don't you think? I had to have it." She lifted the bowl. "I brought fruit salad. They had everything fresh, fresh, fresh at the farmers' market this morning."

"Excellent." Luna took the bowl and accepted a kiss on the cheek. Allie smelled of violets. "My mother is bringing spareribs, and Elaine is doing dessert."

"Yum. That turtle cheesecake she brought last time was to die for." She held the door for Luna. "One thing you have to admit about your sister is that she's a *great* cook."

"Yeah, too bad we have to pray over it all for two hours."

"All paths lead to one place," she said with a shrug.

Luna laughed, carrying the bowl into the kitchen. "You fake! The pent is just an accidental oversight, huh?"

She winked. "That medieval cross she had on last time was just a teeny bit obnoxious."

"Oh, she's had it a million years. Avon."

Allie trailed into the kitchen, where Luna tried not to look at the spot where Thomas had been standing twenty minutes before, but it seemed she could still smell him, and if she looked there would be ghostly footprints where he'd been. "I'm the first one here, huh?" Allie asked, going straight to the bowl of chile on the counter.

"You knew you would be."

She opened the lid on the Tupperware container and inhaled deeply. "Who made the chile?"

"Um." Luna picked up a dishtowel to twirl around in her hands. "This guy brought it over as a thank you. His grandmother set her house on fire last night and I called the fire trucks."

"Wow. What house? What happened?"

Luna told the story, watching as Allie tore off a section of a tortilla and dipped it in the bowl. "You want me to heat some of that up? Maybe I ought to go ahead and put it on the stove, warm the tortillas. Everybody will be here soon."

"Wait a minute," Allie said suddenly, eyes narrowing. *Busted.*

"What guy was this? Old, young, good-looking? What?"

It was hard to think of a way to answer her, because suddenly, Luna was thinking about the way he had tasted, the way he felt next to her, and it was almost tactile, as if some piece of him had stayed behind in the kitchen.

"Grandson," Allie said. Her mouth opened wide and she lifted her brows. "Oh, my God. Really? It was *him,* wasn't it? TC—The Crush?"

Luna twisted the towel into a tight coil. "His name is Thomas Coyote."

Allie's eyes glittered. "Is he as sad as he looks?"

"'Fraid so." She fished a saucepan from beneath the counter and put it on the stove. "Divorced, twice. The second one just a couple of years ago, and the ex is about to have a baby."

"Damn." Allie leaned on the counter with a sigh. "I

really thought he might have been one of the good guys, taking care of his grandma like that." She dipped a tortilla up and down in the pool of chile. "And damn—he is *so* hot."

Suddenly, she straightened and dashed around Luna. "Hey, there's my girl!" she cried, and hugged Joy, who was just coming out of the bedroom. Luna grinned, seeing by her daughter's faint blush that she was a little embarrassed as always by Allie's exuberance, but loved it nonetheless.

"Hey, Auntie," Joy said. Her hair was pulled back into a butterfly clip, with artful pieces drifting down here and there, but she'd changed into an oversized plain T-shirt and jeans, and she'd left out the lip stud. Thank heaven. Her feet were bare, showing toenails painted black.

Allie pulled back to examine her. "Wow," she said without falseness. "New look, huh?"

"Yeah." Joy shrugged and one hand went to her multi-pierced ear.

"I think I like it. Rebellious." She leaned in close. "How many times are your ears pierced?"

"Eight to the left, seven to the right."

"Oh! One for each year?"

Joy laughed, shooting her mother a very pleased look. "D'you know that you're the first adult to get that?"

"Some would say that's because I'm not an adult." Allie laughed. "What else? You have any others?"

"Belly button." She lifted her shirt to show a jewel in her navel. "And I had one in my eyebrow, but my dad made me take it out and it closed."

"Ow," Luna said, touching her eyebrow. "Didn't that hurt?"

"Not that much." She pointed to the one at the top of her ear. "That one hurt. It took forever to heal, too."

Giving her mother a cautious glance, she asked, "Are you mad?"

Luna shook her head honestly. When there was time and privacy, she intended to find out what was behind the flurry of body mutilations, but mad wasn't the right word. "Any tattoos?"

She looked away. "Uh. Well, one. Small, though, and hidden."

"Do I want to know where?"

Joy turned and lifted her shirt again, to show a small, colorful Celtic knot on the small of her back.

"Now, that's very nice," Luna said. "Excellent work and a good spot. It won't wrinkle."

"Eww!"

"It's true, though," Allie said. "I can't even imagine how all you kids are going to look at seventy, with your tattoos dripping. You made a good choice."

Luna glanced at the clock and jumped into motion. "Everyone is going to be here soon. I need to get the table set."

"I can help," Joy said.

"No, sweetie. You're our honored guest and get to sit around talking tonight. No work, period." She kissed her cheek and Joy didn't seem to mind it, giving Luna a smile as Allie took her hand and pulled her into the corner so she could capture all the details of Joy's past eight months.

At Joy's home in Atlanta, a dinner party meant eating in a room with a crystal chandelier, at a table that could seat sixteen with all the leaves in it. There were matching crystal glasses for water and wine, silver bread baskets lined with linen napkins, white china with little fern patterns, and silver candlesticks with white tapers burning politely at intervals. If there was music, it was something like Chopin or Mozart. Joy always felt strangled in that room.

Walking into the dining room of her mother's new home in Taos, she wanted to twirl around and spread out her arms to take it all in. It was Luna's first home of her own, and it had taken her a long, long time to save up for the down payment. The thing Joy loved the most about it was how different it was from the house in Atlanta. Everything there came in colors like champagne and ivory and oak, with maybe a little forest now and then. The rooms were long and square with windows framed in two layers of curtains—drapes and sheers.

This room had a long, antique table, banged up in the best possible way, and wooden chairs Joy's mother had painted with moons and stars, coyotes and skeletons, roses and crosses, all in really bright colors. Two sets of long doors opened out on to the smell of evening and chamiso coming in on a breeze from the patio. One plain adobe wall was hung with photographs of people—all the people Luna loved, she said with a happy smile—and there were fat candles all around the room, and an iron candelabra Luna showed Joy the first time they'd come here, when the house was so trashed Joy had privately wondered if her mother was insane.

Now she understood what her mother had said that day—that the iron candelabra was a connection to another time, like the wooden floors that were uneven in places from so many people walking on them over the years. The wide wooden boards were dark with age, but now they had a nice coat of something shiny on them, and a big plain rag rug kept you from slipping around too much.

It was kind of crowded, too, but in a good way. Joy squeezed between her Grandma Kitty and Allie, glad that she didn't have to sit in the chair next to her aunt

Elaine, who was really fat and sweating, and she was
nice, but sometimes she complained too much. Her
mother said Elaine was still in denial, whatever that
meant.

"This table is too big for this room," Elaine said.

Luna passed cloth napkins around. "So you've said
ninety-seven times." She held out her hands and everybody else joined hands and Luna said, "Elaine will you
say grace for us?"

Next to Joy, Allie muttered, "A short one, please goddess," and Joy had to bite her lip to keep from laughing, because it was totally true—Elaine could pray for a
really long time. Joy glanced up to see if she'd heard,
but it didn't seem like it. Elaine and Allie weren't crazy
about each other.

Elaine said, "God Almighty, King of Heaven and
Earth, Conqueror of All Evil, we come together tonight
to welcome Joy and praise your name."

Joy, still tired from flying—it was a lot scarier to fly
than it used to be—drifted on the up-and-down sound
of the prayer. A smell of sage and water came through
the doors, and it just felt so good to be here, where the
music was an old kind of rock, but at least not classical,
where the food sent up steam smelling of so many different things. It was good, too, in a way, to be with a
group of only girls.

Elaine said "Amen" a lot faster than Joy expected and
she looked up and caught her mom's eye. She winked.
Joy winked back.

They all dug into the food then, and this was different, too. Sometimes, the butter came the wrong way,
and everybody talked at once, to one another, joining in
conversations this way and that, making this big wave
of sound and happiness Joy loved. Allie made everybody—even Elaine—laugh really hard with a story from

her store, about a tourist kook who'd been sure Allie was an alien, like himself, from the Pleiades. "I have to say I've heard some strange come-ons in my time," she said, "but that takes the cake."

Even that was different. Joy couldn't even imagine any of her stepmom's friends talking about a man coming on to them. Of course, they were all married. That probably made a difference. At the thought of April, a tiny pang ran over her heart, and she pushed it away.

When they were cutting into the turtle cheesecake, Joy leaned into her grandma, who'd been very quiet most of the night. "Are you okay, Gram?"

She patted Joy's hand. "Fine, sweetie. How about you?"

"I'm so happy."

Kitty took her napkin out of her lap. "I vote we do sing-alongs."

"Yeah!" Joy cried. She loved it when they did that—put on old albums and danced and sang. Everybody got to pick their favorite, and play it like it was karaoke.

"Mom, not everybody jams like you do," Elaine protested.

"Elaine, darlin', you're the best singer of all of us."

Allie leaned her hand on her chin, looking to Joy like an Afghan hound who lived next door in Atlanta, sleek and pointy and elegant. "I could do tarot card readings."

Elaine shook her head. Joy felt sorry for her all of a sudden—and she realized that Elaine was a lot like April in a way. They were always trying to be safe.

Maybe Luna had noticed they were teasing her a lot, too, because she reached out and took Elaine's hand. "What would you like to do, Sissie? Scrabble, maybe? Trivial Pursuit?"

Elaine said, "I think we should ask Joy."

Joy straightened. "I think . . . ," she said, looking at Allie, then Kitty, then Elaine and her mom. Elaine was the greatest at Trivial Pursuit, but Allie was tense, too. "Let's play Trivial Pursuit, but only if Allie will give me a tarot reading after. Will you?"

Kitty's hand snaked out and touched the back of Joy's neck, and the touch made her feel important and special. Joy smiled at her.

"Tarot is black magic, you know," Elaine said. "Every time you give the devil power—"

"Elaine," Kitty said quietly, sipping from her cup.

Elaine went quiet. Luna said, "Pass another slice of that cheesecake down to Allie, Elaine. She's been talking about it all day."

Kitty winked at Luna across the table. Joy beamed.

It was so good to be home.

7–9 P.M. Coffee House Gathering, *alcohol-, drug-, and smoke-free concert for the whole family with music by Dan Ingroff, Charlie Whaler, and special guest Blade; coffee, tea, punch, and dessert at the San Geronimo Lodge, 1101 Witt Road, $4, 555-3776.*

8 P.M. The Goddess Babes, *belly dancing performance at The Mad Hatter's new location across from Smith's, 229 Paseo del Pueblo Sur, $5, 555-5196 or 555-0632.*

7–9 P.M. "The Burmese Harp," *Taos Mountain Sangha's Friday Night Film Series continues with discussion following film, $3–5 donation suggested, no one turned away for lack of funds, Taos Mountain Sangha Meditation Center, 107C Plaza Garcia, 555-2383.*

If Taos Mountain likes you, times will be good and that which you seek will be found here. If it doesn't, you'll be spit out like the used shell of a piñon nut.

Five

To get Joy settled and registered for school, Luna had a few days of vacation time, and she threw herself into the pleasure of having Joy with her, really *living* with her. It was not uniformly easy. Luna discovered that she hated Joy's music, headbanger-loud, a fact that amused Joy quite a lot. "If it's too loud, you're too old, Mom." Luna didn't tell her the expression had been around since she was a teenager. Wincing at the sound of bands with names like Slipknot and Disturbed and Mudvayne,

Luna did veto a poster that made her feel vaguely sick to her stomach—a collection of white dreadlocked boys with fake blood all over them. And to think people had once thought the Rolling Stones were bad boys.

Joy also could not believe that she had to connect to the Internet in the living room—because that's where the phone connection was. "Haven't you ever heard of privacy?" she complained. She was triply horrified to discover that Luna connected to the Internet with something as primitive as a modem and phone line. "You don't have cable or DSL or *anything*?"

Luna laughed. Gently.

They also discovered better things, such as the fact that they watched nearly all the same television shows, and loved to watch movies with a big bowl of popcorn between them. They liked the same foods and neither one much liked to talk first thing in the morning.

The best part was the house. In Luna's old apartment, they'd always been cramped together during Joy's visits. Luna had managed to win financing for the house eighteen months before, but it had needed so much work before she could move in—it was over two hundred years old, after all, and had been sorely neglected—Joy had not yet had a chance to stay there. It wasn't a huge place—living room and dining room, a long narrow kitchen, two bedrooms with a bath between, but it gave the two of them space enough that they could each have some privacy and escape options.

Before school started, they shopped a little. While they were buying the basics—spiral notebooks (black) and pens and a backpack (black)—Joy asked about school clothes. Her father had sent money for them—to her, not Luna—and she wanted to know the best place to go.

They were standing in the school supplies aisle at

Wal-Mart, surrounded by packages of pens and note-books with pictures of tigers and cartoon characters Luna didn't recognize. She reached for a folder with a big-eyed girl and a faintly exotic look to her, remembering yellow folders with line drawings of sports figures. Had there even been a choice then? She couldn't remember. "Who is this?" she asked.

"Mom." It was a faintly aggrieved tone that asked what cave she'd been living in. "That's Sailor Moon."

"Oh! I've heard of her." She flashed her daughter a smile and put the folder back. "You'll need new clothes, I'm sure—I bet you don't have much that's warm, do you?"

"Not really. How long till I need them?"

"A month, maybe two, depending on how soon it snows." She hesitated, wondering if this might also fall into the clueless category, but how much did certain things ever change? "Maybe it would be better if you waited until after the first week of school is over, so you can see what everybody else is wearing. They might have different styles than what's popular in Atlanta."

Joy played with the stud beneath her lower lip, sucking it in, then letting it go as she thought about it. Luna worried that Joy might take it the wrong way—she was big on "no game playing," as she called it. Her weird hair, multiple piercings, and the henna tattoos she drew around her wrists and ankles were a badge of honor. An identity flag.

Which Luna understood in a weird way. She'd grown up in the seventies, after all. Not exactly a normal decade.

Joy let go of the stud. "Good idea. Not," she hastened to add, "that I'll change anything. But I might want to see, just in case they're wearing something good."

Her first day of school was Luna's first day back to

work—August 28. They'd registered the Thursday before, and Joy had waved to a kid who'd lived next door to the old apartment. An auspicious sign, and one that seemed to make Joy feel pretty comfortable.

They shared a part of the walk that first day, since Luna had to be at work at seven. Although she didn't kid herself that this would be a long-term bonding ritual, it was still pretty good. The morning was bright and cool. Joy wore her fishnet shirt (black) with a red tank beneath it, a pair of bell-bottom jeans (black) that covered her feet in their combat boots (black), and a flowered scarf over her head. She looked as beautiful as a blue jay against the backdrop of pale green fields.

"Are you nervous?" Luna asked. She herself was wearing jeans and a simple scoop-neck T-shirt and walking sandals. She carried her work smock over her shoulder so it wouldn't get sweaty.

"Kinda."

"If you need me, don't hesitate to call."

"Oh, it's not that bad!" She shrugged. "At least this isn't dangerous. In Atlanta, sometimes it was."

"It was?"

Joy widened her eyes. "Yeah," she said in that "duh" voice. "Don't you read the papers? The most dangerous kids in the country are spoiled little rich boys with access to guns."

Luna chuckled. "I forgot." She paused. "Um . . . don't underestimate the gangs here. They might not be spoiled little rich boys, but they've got their own set of angers."

"Mom."

"What?" She didn't grow up with these kids. She was an outsider. Luna worried about it. There would be girls who would challenge her—tough girls who didn't have anything to lose. "Girls," she said. "I'm talking about girls, not boys."

"I'm fifteen, not six."

"I know." She smiled, lifting a shoulder. "And I trust you. You'll make friends fast."

At the main drag, they parted company, Joy going off to school, Luna heading to the Pay and Pack grocery store. On the way in, she nodded to Ernesto and Diane, smoking outside on the park bench management had put in the shade. "Still off?" Ernie asked.

"So far so good." Lifting her shirt sleeve to show the patch, she said, "Seventeen days."

"Goll, that's good," Diane said. She was nineteen and Hispanic and had the longest eyelashes Luna had ever seen. "I'm just too weak, I think."

"You'll do it." Luna lifted a hand and went in, suddenly very jealous of the fact that they were smoking and she wasn't. Not fair.

Luckily, because she'd been gone, there was a lot to do. Another woman, Renee, filled in when Luna took time off, but she generally made a mess of things. Or not a mess, exactly—she just didn't do things the way Luna liked them done. Tying an apron over her shirt, she got to work cleaning up, checking the displays to see what was offered for sale, what sort of bouquets Renee had made up, and what might be left; checking the water level in the potted ferns and dieffenbachia and English ivy—a real pain in the neck in the dry climate; they always fell prey to spider mites. Luna tried to talk people into buying pothos, instead. Finding them all dry as a bone, that was the first priority. She fitted a narrow green hose to the sink in back and turned on the water, drawing the hose behind her as she made her way around the plants and buckets and coolers, filling them all up.

It wasn't exciting work. It wasn't particularly challenging. It was, in the lingo of AA, a Job. She'd taken it when she'd been sober ninety-three days, and at the time, it seemed like God himself had ordained it. It was peaceful. The flowers, the coolness of the water, the smell of the plants and earth and carnations and roses. She loved putting her hands in dirt, and not having to dress up for work. She adored making bouquets from the big tubs of flowers that were delivered twice a week from a greenhouse in Albuquerque. Within a year, she'd taken over the department from the desultory administration of the former manager, and profits went up 23 percent the first six months.

So she stayed. The salary was decent and there were medical benefits, a little profit sharing, a retirement plan. Enough for her needs. She never had to take it home and worry about it, as she had so often with her clients. And there were fringe benefits to working in a grocery store—people she worked with and people who came into the store. It was possible to help someone every single day, and no matter how grumpy she felt when she came in, the flowers never failed to cheer her.

Lately, her mother had started to ask if Luna was planning to stay in the store forever, or if she might be thinking about going back to counseling. If it were anyone else, Luna would have said it was simple snobbishness talking, the idea that one sort of work was more valuable than another, that a florist was less valuable to the world than a psychologist, but it would never even occur to Kitty to rank jobs like that.

Luna had had no answer for Kitty that day. She still didn't. Every so often, she considered the idea of returning to counseling, and then just as quickly rejected it. The flower business was just fine.

But this morning, she discovered that not even a shipment of narcotically scented freesias could distract her from the difficulty of not smoking. It was rough. She'd never smoked on the job, per se, only in the break room in the old days, and then outside—which actually gave her a little more freedom, since there was a door right between the counters and the big metal sink.

She kept thinking it would get easier. In some ways, it was getting harder. She was discovering all the ways she'd used cigarettes in her life. At work, she'd used them a lot—as a reward and a retreat, to give herself a break or get away from an annoying or difficult situation, or—well, a million reasons. Get the bouquets finished, go outside. Get through a meeting with her control-freak boss, have a cigarette.

She also used the breaks as an escape, usually when her assistant was going on too long about her latest love affair—of which she had many. Jean, twenty-three and pretty, with trendy clothes and hair that came down over her forehead in a plastered, plastic kind of way, came in at ten. Before she even had her apron tied, she started talking. "I met the most *amazing* guy last night," she said. Her cheeks were flushed pink. "We sat there and talked, you know, like we'd known each other forever, I swear." She paused to wash her hands, scrubbing at a mark from a nightclub. "We talked movies and work and then"—she shook her hands and took a paper towel from the white metal dispenser on the wall—"we talked art. Art with a capital *A*."

Jean had come west from some grimy town in the northeast, studying art at the University of New Mexico in Albuquerque before fleeing to Taos, where she spent her days at the store, her nights alternating between painting oils of coyote skulls and drinking heavily with other aspirants to the O'Keeffe crown. She didn't even notice that Luna had said not a single word to her. "He just had such deep eyes, you know?"

"Mmm."

"We drank until three, can you imagine? I almost couldn't get up this morning."

In spite of herself, Luna smiled. Those were the good old days—party all night, sleep three or four hours, work all day and be ready to do it all again the next night. "Sounds interesting," she said, muting Jean's voice as she trimmed the stems of some aging chrysanthemums. Needed to put them on special today, she thought, running her index finger along the deep rust-red flowers, getting lost a little in the shape, the color, the tiny, tiny curls of the petals.

"So," Jean said behind her, "you think I should see him again?"

"Mmm." Luna glanced at the clock: 10:15. Usually, she'd gone out for a cigarette at this time, both to escape Jean and to breathe some fresh air on the patio that overlooked the Sangre de Cristos. "Why wouldn't you?"

"Well, I just told you, there is a little bit of something weird about him. Maybe he's like a serial killer or something." She crossed her arms. "Or maybe he's just creative, right? Like me."

A sensation like someone snapping a rubber band across her forehead made Luna turn from the sink almost violently. "I'm going outside for a few minutes. If Josh comes by, tell him I'll be back in twenty."

"You aren't smoking are you?" Jean smoked, but she was—as she'd told Luna often enough—young enough to get away with it.

"No," she said, and almost ran for the door.

Outside, she sucked in big lungfuls of air. It smelled of someone else's recent cigarette, and she forced herself to walk away from the patio, out to the road beyond. She'd walk ten minutes out and turn around. Maybe work off some of the tension.

One of the books she'd read on the process of quitting had suggested that cigarettes were a way for some people to avoid saying things they were afraid to utter, and the urge to smoke was a signal to pay attention to what you were trying not to say. So as she stomped down the road under the hot, midday sun, she thought about it. What would she say to Jean, beside the obvious: *Leave me alone, will you?*

Thinking that eased a little of the pressure. Hmmm. She tried it again. *Stop talking so much. I took the job to have silence, not this endless, mindless chatter.*

A tangle of nerves eased. Very interesting.

Okay, then, what else? Both intrigued and bemused, she dug a little deeper. What else might she say? *Please don't tell me about your love life. It makes me lonely and it makes me worry.* Even better. The roar really started subsiding. Was there more? Luna thought about it, remembering to breathe deeply as she walked. Sweat started trickling down the back of her neck, and she reached up to tie her hair in a knot around itself.

A new thought came up, and she said it out loud. "Jean, please stop drinking so much. You're going to take home the wrong guy one of these nights and get hurt or worse, you'll end up drowned in a ditch. In fact, I really wish you'd stop picking up strangers. It's dangerous."

Nearly every bit of the urge to smoke was swept away. Luna didn't know if it was the walking or the talking, but either way, it was a relief to lose it. Swinging her arms hard to loosen the muscles of her shoulders and neck, she wondered why some people could keep their thoughts to themselves without resorting to smoking or drinking, while she had used both. What was she so afraid of?

And how weird was it that she was headed into middle age—okay, it had arrived—with a master's degree in psychology, and had spent ten years as a therapist without ever knowing this about herself?

Best Friend Barbie, who wore jean shorts and a halter top and her dark hair in a ponytail, said, *Well, you always had your shields in place before now, right?*

Good point. Cigarettes had been doing a lot of work. Maybe, she thought with a frown, she didn't really want to give them up when there was so much she needed to do right with Joy. Maybe some people just needed the chemical barrier in order to manage the world.

Oh, please, said Barbie, *addict as delicate flower?*

"Thank you," she said aloud, smiling a little in spite of herself and the heat and the scritching annoyance on her nerves. Funny how the tapes all played the same way. Addicted to nicotine, addicted to alcohol, addicted to overeating . . . the voices calling you back all said the same things: *You aren't like everybody else. You're special. You're different, you need this.*

Barbie licked an ice-cream cone and dangled her feet in a small green stream. The only sensible action for such a hot morning. *You're gonna make it, Lu.*

Yeah. A breeze washed down from the mountains, cool as dawn. It rattled cottonwood leaves, swept over her hot neck. She thought of Jean again, of her skein of boyfriends—one loser after another, all of them tortured *artistes* without a penny, and nothing to offer but egocentric pain. But what did Luna know, really? It wasn't like she'd made great choices in men, either. Maybe Jean's focus on lots of great sex was better than trying to do everything by the rules. Either way, there were bound to be broken hearts.

And wasn't Luna just a little bit . . . well, *jealous*? Sex had not exactly been in plentiful supply the past couple of years. She didn't get out a lot. And even when she did, there was that problem of the man situation in Taos. There weren't that many worth sleeping with. It got to be too much trouble—pretending to be interested in his novel or his sculptures or his rambling tale of finding himself—to come to Taos just to get laid.

As if her thoughts of sex were written in a bubble over her head, a low whistle rang into the bright yellow day. Luna raised her head, sure the whistle was for someone else, but there wasn't anyone else but her on the road.

Except the whistlers—an adobe crew sitting in the shadows before an ancient, rambling farmhouse that had probably cost well into six figures with the water rights. There were four or five men in the shade of a giant cottonwood, the younger ones shirtless and tanned the color of rawhide, their jeans smeared with mud. She smiled distractedly to show her appreciation and kept walking.

The whistle rang out again. As a young woman, she'd found attention of this nature alarming or infuriating. It had seemed an enormous intrusion, an irritation. These days, she recognized the game and liked it. It was animalistic, probably, but what the heck. Still, she didn't look their way the second time, just kept walking. She *was* alone on the road, after all.

"Luna!"

Thomas.

She paused, thinking of his truck, loaded so heavily with tools and frames, and saw that it was parked to one side. A figure detached itself from the deepest shadows, and she stood where she was, anticipation and worry winding themselves around her lungs as Thomas stepped out into the light.

Even at fifty yards, he was something to see. A stillness all around him, a kind of envelope that separated him from everything else. Now that she knew a little of his history, she figured it was probably a protective bubble.

She wouldn't have minded having a bubble of her own just then. He was as dusty as the others, though he wore his shirt—thank God!—and it didn't matter. She felt like her feet were at the wrong angles, that she should do something with her hands, and she tucked them in her jeans' pockets. Even with the dust dulling his hair and adobe on his jeans, what she'd thought of was the split second he'd reached out to put his big hand over hers on the counter.

He halted about three feet away, standing at the end of the drive. "Hi," he said.

"Hi." Not content with her hands in her pockets, she crossed her arms, aware of the sweat on her neck, the sun burning into the part of her hair.

He looked away. "I just . . . uh . . . wanted to tell you that . . . um . . . I'm sorry for being so forward with you the other day." With an effort that cost him, he raised his chin. "Hope I didn't offend you."

Luna's mouth opened and said for her, "I did kiss you back, you know."

He quit looking everywhere but at her face, and met her eyes. Neither of them said anything. The sun beat down from the hot blue sky, melting the pavement beneath their feet. Luna kept thinking that she ought to just give him a little smile and walk away, but she wanted to stand there. Looking at him. Feeling it—her heart thudding and skittery, her throat dry with anticipation, her skin rippling because he was close. It had been so long since she'd felt this.

And he looked back, those deep eyes so compelling—bravado and appreciation and a big helping of wariness. It was the appreciation she liked.

He said finally, "You want to go get a drink with me later or something?" He wiped his forehead with the back of his wrist. "Back up a step, maybe?"

Baldly, she said, "I'm an alcoholic." That should do it, push him away. "I don't drink."

But Thomas Coyote only nodded, and she saw him put a little piece of her life in place—the daughter had lived with her father. Ah. "How about a sundae, then?" he said in that smooth, rich voice. "I'm kind of an ice cream-aholic, but they let me have a little now and then, see if I can handle it."

Only the barest of smiles touched his mouth, but the glow of it was in his eyes. Luna fell in love with him that very second. It swooped through her, burning, and sailed away so fast that she didn't recognize it. "Hot fudge?"

"Absolutely." He narrowed his eyes, looked at the sky. "Say, seven-thirty, at the DQ?"

"Okay," she said, and suddenly wanted to cry. Hastily, she backed away, touching her watch. "I have to get back to work."

"See ya," he said, and for one beat, looked at her with something like promise, then turned and walked back down the drive, big as a bear, with shoulders she wanted to touch.

Her hands were shaking as she turned back the way she'd come, and she reached for her cigarettes and lighter before she remembered they weren't there. "God, Lu, this is such a bad idea," she said aloud. "He's horny and on the rebound and you do not need any complications in your life."

But she didn't even consider not showing up.

At lunch, Joy sat alone in the courtyard of the school, watching everybody. They all knew one another. Three of the girls were talking in a knot over a table, looking around in that way that said they were gossiping about everybody else. One girl sat by herself in the shade, her back against the wall, and nobody talked to her. Joy thought the girl might live close by, that she'd seen her at the little park at the end of the street that nobody went to except the neighborhood kids. It wasn't much of a park. Worn-out grass, a few benches, a really old slide, some trees for shade. The teenagers smoked dope there, and though Joy didn't do that, the way she dressed made everybody think she did, so they didn't worry about her. She left them alone and they left her alone. Cool.

Joy was used to being alone when she came to Taos. She'd made a couple of friends in her mom's old neighborhood, a white guy named Derek who was pretty nice, but always wanted to put the moves on her, and a girl a little younger than she was who showed Joy how to put on eyeliner. But neither of those kids was around here today.

She watched the other girl out of the corner of her eye, wondering if she was new or something, too, like Joy, or if she might have done something the other kids knew about and they left her alone for it.

But it was too bright and boring outside and the worst that could happen was the girl would be a bitch. Kitty would tell her to be friendly and everything would be all right, and though Joy had learned that wasn't always true, it wasn't exactly untrue, either.

She stopped at the soda machine and bought a pop and carried it over to the girl, who looked up warily from a notebook she was scribbling in. "Hi," Joy said, and opened her Coke. She leaned on the wall, looking out at the other kids.

"Hi," the girl said without much interest. But she closed her notebook. After a minute she said, "You're new here."

Joy nodded. "I came here from Atlanta to live with my mom."

"You miss him, your dad?"

"No." Joy lifted a shoulder.

"My dad died in the spring," she said. "That's why nobody talks to me here. They think I'll be crazy again, like I was then."

Intrigued, Joy slid down the wall. "What'd you do?"

The girl shook her head slowly, her dark eyes distant, like she was looking backward. "A lot of stuff. I'm not proud of it, you know." She shook her long hair out of her face. "What's your name?"

"Joy. You?"

"Magdalena, but you can call me Maggie." She looked right at her. "Do you smoke? I have cigarettes."

"Yes! My mother quit and I haven't had any since I got here. Where do you go?"

Maggie stood up. "Come on. I'll show you."

Just for today *I will try to live through this day only, and not tackle all my problems at once. I can do something for twelve hours that would appall me if I felt that I had to keep it up for a lifetime.*

Just for today *I will be happy. This assumes what Abraham Lincoln said to be true, that "Most folks are as happy as they make up their minds to be."*

Just for today *I will adjust myself to what is, and not try to adjust everything to my own desires, I will take my "luck" as it comes and fit myself to it.*

Six

The only thing Luna thought about the rest of the work day was Thomas. It wasn't conscious thought, exactly, more like wisps of him that floated around her little space—his tilted dark eyes occupying the space over the sink, his wide mouth smiling there by the phone, his long, dark, beautiful hands in the general area of the cooler. She wanted to kiss him again almost as much as she didn't. The promise of him followed her home, a tickle on her spine, and she wondered what they'd say to each other.

But when she saw Joy curled up in a little ball on the couch, asleep, reality vaporized the fantasy. What kind of mother went out on a date the first day of school? She'd forgotten. What good mother would have let something so momentous slip her mind?

With some regret, she realized she should have

planned a good supper, too, so the two of them could sit down and chat a little without pressure. She'd meant to, and had forgotten.

Guilt chattered upward from her solar plexus as she looked down at her sleeping daughter. The thick hair spilled over the side of the couch, exotically colored but still as glossy as ever, and her skin was so dewy it was almost heartbreaking. At Joy's age, Luna's skin had been annoyingly prone to zits. Joy didn't appear to have had a pimple in her life.

She smelled, distinctly, of cigarettes.

Luna scowled. Surely Joy, Miss Cigarettes Are Disgusting, would not be smoking?

Interestingly, the odor did not make her want to rush out and have a cigarette herself. In fact, it was something of a miracle that she could pick up the scent on someone else, and it made her feel slightly smug, even as she considered the possibilities of why Joy might smell like that. It was possible she'd stopped at a house where the parents smoked, or she had made a friend who smoked. No jumping to conclusions.

Joy opened her eyes suddenly, with that wide-open, surprised startle. Sleep glazed her pale blue eyes and she blinked. "Hi."

"Hi. Been home long?"

She stretched luxuriously, and Luna noticed again that she had inherited Kitty's abundant bosom. "About an hour I guess."

"Hungry?"

"Very. School lunch is disgusting." She yawned. "I would have made something myself, but I just crashed for a while. Do we have any of that Cajun turkey left?"

"Sure." Luna dropped her bag on the coffee table and waved Joy into the kitchen, where she started taking things out of the fridge—the thin-sliced deli meat, broccoli sprouts, half a tomato, and the Dijon mustard they agreed made the sandwich heavenly. "Pita or black rye?" she asked, taking a knife from the drawer and two plates from the cupboard.

"Rye, please."

In quiet, they fixed enormous sandwiches, piling on veggies and condiments. Luna sliced a couple of apples to go with it, and pulled out some tortilla chips left over from the party. Admiring the colors of black bread and white corn chips and red apple against blue glass plates, she said, "Now that's pretty."

"Very patriotic." Joy snorted. "I think we should cut the apple into stars."

Luna laughed softly, settling on the stool to dig in. The walk home always seemed to leave her famished, and it appeared that Joy was the same way after school. "You don't mind eating dinner like this, do you? We can snack later if we're still hungry."

"Are you kidding? I love this."

"I'll try to remember to do sit-down dinners more often. Maybe a little closer to the real dinner hour, too, if you want."

Joy rolled her eyes. "Mom. No teenager in the world likes the family dinner hour, trust me." She shuddered for effect. "And besides, this is a sit-down dinner."

She nodded, thinking maybe some avocado would go well with this mix next time. "You'll tell me if you start wanting pot roast and potatoes and things like that, won't you?"

"I'll tell Grandma."

"Low blow," Luna said, but she grinned. "We will have dinner there on Saturdays, you know, so when you start getting mixed up in the local social whirl, remember to schedule stuff later on Saturday nights."

"Starting this week?"

"Do you have plans already?"

"Well, no, not exactly. I met this girl at school—she lives, like, right behind us. We talked about doing something maybe. But no way I want to miss Grandma's Saturday suppers. Maybe she'll do fondue."

"Maybe so." She made a mental note to request fondue. Her mother would be delighted to accommodate Joy's tastes. Or Luna's, for that matter.

The tradition had started when Elaine and Luna were small. Kitty worked as a cocktail waitress and didn't have to be at work until nine on weekend nights. Saturdays were her big tip night, and as a way to make all of them feel better about her absence those hours, she came up with the supper thing. Often in those younger days, the special supper had been something like Belgian waffles topped with strawberries and whipped cream, or French toast and link sausages. They loved breakfast for supper. It seemed somehow decadent to be eating pancakes as the sun set.

As they grew older, Kitty discovered all kinds of treats for them to share—cheese fondues and homemade pizzas, whatever food had caught her exuberant imagination. They'd put on the Beatles or The Doors or the Rolling Stones—Kitty was the original rock 'n' roll baby—and dance while they cooked and ate. Sometimes, she'd put their hair into fancy styles or they'd paint one another's nails. And when it came time for her to get ready, the girls went with her into her bedroom and helped pick out her earrings and bracelets and which eye shadows and lipstick colors she should wear. It was always Luna's job to decide the perfume, and it was a ritual to spritz it over the polished and beautiful Kitty just before she left them with their baby-sitter. The smell of it lingered in the room long after she'd driven away.

Luna smiled now, remembering it. "There's nobody like your grandma, you know it?"

Joy grinned. "She's so cool. Do you know she has like ninety-seven bras and all these girdles and stuff? She showed them to me last time I was here. Zebra prints and velvet and everything."

"Me and Elaine used to sneak into her drawers and try it all on." Something about bras made her remember Thomas and she jumped up, looking around madly for the scrap of paper he'd given her the morning at his grandmother's house. "Dang. I have to call this guy, right now."

"A boyfriend?" Joy asked with a lift of her eyebrows.

"No, not exactly. I just met him." The number was on the fridge, stuck beneath a magnet in the shape of a chili pepper. "But I told him I'd meet him for ice cream tonight, and I'm sorry to say that I forgot when I agreed to it that it is the first day of school."

"What difference does that make?"

Luna carried the number over to the phone and picked it up. "I just think it would be nice to be here."

Joy got up and pushed the button down. "Wait a second, will you?"

"Okay." She hung up the phone.

"Do you have a lot of boyfriends or guys you see? Do you go out on dates a lot?"

"Not hardly."

"That's what I thought. Grandma's always saying she wants you to get out more." She, seeming far the older, folded her hands on the table. "A woman needs male companionship. I think you kinda like this guy, because your cheeks are red."

Which made them redder, of course. "He seems nice."

"Mom." Joy leaned on her elbows. "I'm living here now. You don't have to be somebody else, you know, you can just have a normal life. You don't have to be somebody's idea of a perfect mother with me—I already have that back in Atlanta, and she drives me crazy."

"Perfect, huh?" In spite of herself, she was a teeny bit wounded.

"I don't mean that as a compliment, dude. She's always, like, chirpy." Joy did a valley girl thing with her head, back and forth. "And she's always got, like, perfect hair and perfect makeup and she wears a size three. Most of my friends don't even wear a size three, you know what I mean? It's stupid."

Laughing, Luna said, "So, I should feel better because my hair looks like I stuck my finger in an outlet, and I wear a size twelve on good days, and I rarely remember to wear lipstick, much less anything else?"

Joy's face was serious. "I know you're just kidding around, but that is what I mean. You're real. I mean, Grandma's real, too, even though she's all into how she looks. With April, it's like she's doing it because she's scared. Sometimes, I wanted to just see her get really mad, throw something or yell at someone, or just one time, eat a whole piece of cake instead of just taking a bite out of somebody else's." Her mouth tightened. "I never want to be like that. Never. It's like Dad's her god, and she'll do anything to give him what he wants, but he never even notices all the things she does."

A tightly bound bundle of emotions rolled down some internal slope and smashed into Luna's diaphragm. She reached instinctively for Joy's hand, and the bundle exploded on impact, scattering pieces of memory all over the place: she saw April, tense and tight, smiling perfectly, not a blond hair out of place, as she sat in on the trial. Saw her, three tiny tears running down her peach-soft cheeks, as Joy started screaming, "Mommy! Mom-MEE!" Saw April, brittle and stiff, trying to win love from a man who had no idea what it really meant or how to deliver it, and she felt painfully, deeply sorry for her.

"Thanks, Joy," she said roughly, and swallowed her emotionalism with a wry grimace. "You know, you've always done this, been so brutally honest it shocks people. I'm so glad you didn't outgrow it."

Joy turned her hand so she could hold her mother's, and rubbed her thumb over her knuckle. "Well," she said, "not everyone appreciates it."

"I know. But it's you, and you can't go around changing yourself for other people. It never works."

"Like April."

"Not exactly. April is naturally that person—she's a southern belle, and it might be time to get rid of that kind of model, but she's doing what she thinks is the right thing." Luna took a breath. "I was really remembering myself. Can you imagine me trying to be a southern belle? I tried so hard." Laughing, she shook her head. "It was just not a good fit."

Joy shuddered and used the action to pull free. "Just go out with this guy tonight, huh? I'll be fine."

"I'll be home by eight-thirty."

"Okay." She stood up and started to clear the plates away. "I have some homework to do, anyway." At the sink, she turned wickedly. "Don't forget to carry condoms. You know how guys are."

"Joy!"

She cracked up. "I'm only kidding, Mom."

"You are so much more grown-up than you were a year ago."

"It happens," she said, and that faint bitterness crossed her lips. She turned the water on in the sink, staring down into the forming bubbles with a distant expression.

Carefully, Luna focused on the task of screwing on the lids of condiment jars. "Joy, did something happen this year?"

"What do you mean?"

She retied the baggie of turkey, snapped on the top of the container that held sprouts. "Something upsetting."

"You mean because I look so different?"

Luna met her eyes. "It's a pretty big change."

A loose shrug, laced with disappointment. "Lot of things happened, but no one hurt me if that's what you mean. Nobody molested me or stalked me or anything like that, and I haven't started doing drugs, so don't worry about that, either, okay?" She snapped off the water and leaned her thin hip on the lip of the counter. "I won't lie—a lot of my friends do drugs and I look like a freak, so they offer, but I'm not interested."

"Okay," Luna said easily, and smiled. "You still say 'freak,' huh? That's what we used to say." She tucked the jars and bags back into the fridge, and plucked a dishrag out of the water to wipe down the table. "But here's the thing, Joy, there's really a uniform between groups, and it's like you went from Army to Navy. There had to be a reason."

"Freaks don't ask you to be anybody but yourself," she said. "I really got tired, Mom, of all the . . . crap . . . my friends were doing. Like one girl almost committed suicide over failing a test. She's like sixteen and she thinks her life is over? That's bad."

Luna had a sudden thought. "Does it have anything to do with April, the way she likes everything to be?"

A flicker, something dark, crossed Joy's face. "No." She bit the word off. Anger was in her eyes when she looked hard at Luna. "You know what? I love April. She's a good person. And she never gives me a hard time about all this.

In a way, she kind of likes me looking wild—she thinks I'm brave not to care what people think."

Listening between the lines, Luna asked, "How does your dad feel about it?"

Joy smiled, almost bitterly. "He hates it."

Ah. "What's going on with you two?"

A shrug. "Nothing." She opened her mouth, closed it, shook her head. "Nothing. We're just really different people and I don't like his values very much."

Luna nodded. Taking a breath, she forced herself to stop there. A little at a time was better. "How was it at the new school today?"

"Not bad." She tugged some rubber gloves over her hands—one of her vanities was very long, black fingernails. "I made a friend, which is nice. She lives right across the field, over there. Her name is Maggie. Her dad died in a car accident last spring."

"I know who she is. That was really sad—he wasn't very old. Is she okay?"

Joy shrugged. "I guess. I mean, how all right could you be when you lose your dad?"

"Right." She hesitated and added, "Well, I used to be fairly good at this stuff, so if it seems like she might need someone to talk to, I'm here."

"Thanks. I thought of that, too."

Luna got the broom, and Joy rinsed the dishes. "Mom," she said after a while. "Why did you quit? Even Dad says you were a really good therapist, even when . . ." She colored.

"Even when I was drinking?"

She nodded.

"I don't know," Luna said honestly. "It seemed wrong, all of a sudden, to be trying to help other people get their lives together when mine was such a mess."

"But you've been sober for four years."

"Yeah." She shrugged.

"Don't you ever miss it?"

"Drinking or counseling?" She smiled to take the sting out.

Joy's eyebrows rose. "Both, I guess."

Luna straightened and met her eyes. "Yes." She took a long, deep breath against the very small nudge of cigarette hunger rising in her lungs. "Drinking was a great escape, you know? And life gives us a lot of reasons to run away. So, sometimes when things are hard or scary, I still think about a nice shot of tequila. But I go to a meeting or I call my sponsor or I take a walk or"—she waved a hand to the back room—"or go do some crafts." She paused. "Do you worry about it, me falling off the wagon?"

Joy met her eyes. "No. You know, it was kind of unreal. I never saw you drink, so it's not like something I ever think about."

"I'm glad."

Joy pulled the basket out of the drain and emptied it in the trash. "What about counseling? You miss that?"

Luna swept a pile of mess from the floor into the dustpan, considering. "Yeah, I do. Every now and then, I give some thought to art therapy, using creativity to help women find out more about themselves."

"Why don't you do it, then?"

"Honestly, I don't know. One day at a time, huh? I think I'm where I'm supposed to be right now."

Joy nodded, and put the basket back in the sink. Luna settled the broom by the wall.

"Mom?" she said.

She turned.

"I'm glad I can talk to you. It means a lot to me that

you just tell the truth." She was blinking against a sheen of tears. "Thank you."

"You're welcome," Luna said.

It was a fairly long hike to the Dairy Queen from her house, so Luna got dressed early—tossing through about six different shirts before Joy helped her settle on the turquoise peasant blouse. "Makes your shoulders look sexy," she said. "And I think you should put up your hair, just let a little bit of it trail down your neck." She piled it up to illustrate. "See?"

So she wore it the way Joy pinned it, feeling like she was getting a special blessing for the date as she headed toward town. It was a gorgeous evening. The air was dry, cooling now as purple rain clouds ambled in from the southwest, turning the mountains a deep, dark blue. Sunlight poked through the clouds here and there, falling like solid golden needles in some places, liquid as orange juice in others.

It was those kinds of views that had haunted her in her years away. Whenever people would sigh over a beautiful sky or landscape, she had to bite her tongue to keep from saying, "Yeah, it's nice, but you should see my hometown." Hard to tell people that their landscapes are beautiful, but . . . well, not quite like this. She sometimes felt drunk on all that color, wanting to eat it, rub it all over herself, save it in jars and paint it on her clothes and ceilings.

Most of her walk was quiet. She walked past small houses with wide expanses of field around them. Once in a while, she heard a goat bleat, or a dog rush up to a fence. For the space of a quarter mile, a cheerful stray Border collie with a bandana collar trotted along beside her.

The quiet changed when she hit the main drag, of

course. Tourists clogged the streets with RVs and BMWs and motorcycles. They walked the sidewalks in groups of two and three and four, sporting sunburns and T-shirts with pictures of aspen trees and Indian pottery. Luna fell into the swarm, suddenly nervous when she spied the DQ sign up ahead. In a moment of panic, she ducked into the coffee shop and ordered a double latte on ice, buying herself a little time along with the infusion of caffeine courage. Carrying the paper cup, she drank of it deeply, undissolved sprinkles of turbinado sugar landing like heavy stars on her tongue as she walked the last block to the DQ.

Thomas was there already, and he didn't see her right away. She slowed down, taking him in, marveling with a little smile that she was actually going to sit down with him. Talk with him. Eat something with him. How often had she eyed him at the grocery store, peeked through her windows at him as he carried bags of supplies into his grandmother's house?

Passersby noticed him. His body was angled to the west so that the purple and orange light illuminated the craggy size of his nose, the high brow, and unkindly lit on the small curve of belly over his belt. He looked calm and dangerous with his hair loose on his shoulders, and she realized that he probably knew a certain sort of woman would like that hair a lot.

He saw her and raised his chin, crossing his arms over his chest in a loose way. The edge of a welcoming smile touched his mouth and it made Luna feel so wildly beautiful that she wanted to giggle. Toss her hair. Something.

"Hey," he said, quietly.

She took a sip of her latte and moved closer. "Hi," she said, feeling small next to him. He wore boots with a good heel, and her head only came to his chin.

"Did you walk?" he asked.

She nodded.

"You have no car or you like walking?"

She met his eyes and told the truth. "I don't have a driver's license."

"Drinking?"

Rare that anyone just came out and asked. Luna found it made it a lot easier to say simply, "That's right."

"Maybe you can tell me that story sometime."

She let go of a laugh that sounded a lot more bitter than sweet, and it embarrassed her. "I'd have to know you a whole lot better."

A heartbeat of a pause, during which he looked steadily at her face. "Okay." He tipped his head toward the window beneath the list of goods and prices. "You want to go in or stay outside?"

"Oh, outside definitely. With that sky?"

She felt she'd won something when he smiled. Together they walked to the window, where a painfully thin brown boy waited in an ill-fitting uniform to take their orders. Thomas looked at Luna. "Hot fudge?"

"Yes, please."

"Banana split or sundae?"

She looked at the boy, wavered, conscious of her greed and the fact that those shorts had been so tight last night. "Sundae."

"Nah, that hesitation was way too long." To the boy, he said, "It's our first date and she doesn't want me to think she's a pig. You know women."

The kid was starstruck in three seconds, giving Thomas an abashed smile at being included in the knowing-about-women thing. "So, a hot fudge banana split, then?"

"Two banana splits, one hot fudge, one normal with

nuts and whipped cream. The works." He pulled money out of his front pocket and peeled off several one-dollar bills he tossed on the counter, then looked at Luna with a wink. He patted his belly. "I'm a guy. We don't have to go easy, even when we get big as cars."

She grinned. "It would be good to be a guy at times."

"It's always good to be a guy."

Something about the spread of his strong, square hand gave her a jolt of greed—a flash of those fingers on her body, his mouth on hers, a shockingly intense kind of thought. She found herself flushing, and looked over her shoulder for a place to sit down. "I'll get the napkins and spoons. That table look good to you?"

"Sure."

She gathered supplies and settled at a picnic table at the far end of the concrete apron. On the horizon, the clouds were darkening. Erratic, distant threads of lightning wove through them, but there was not yet any smell of rain.

Thomas joined her and didn't sit across the table as she had expected, but right beside her, and not at a decent distance away, either. His thigh touched hers, bringing back her greed. She shifted a little away, took her banana split, bending to inhale the scent of chocolate for a moment. "Ah, thank you," she said. "It's very wicked."

"Yeah—my mom keeps nagging me to eat better, but she doesn't live here, so I'm safe." His grin was wide and winning, showing big white teeth and crinkles around his eyes. "I wasn't kiddin' about being an ice cream-aholic, either. I'm crazy for it."

"I used to see you here a lot last summer."

Something stricken crossed his mouth. "Hard summer. First one, you know, I was divorced." He dipped his spoon into strawberries and vanilla ice cream, lifted it up.

Damn. He was *so* not over his divorce. "Sorry to remind you of the bad times."

He shrugged. "You remember that, don't you, going through the rituals by yourself?"

"Yeah," she said. "I left town—but it was a little different for us. I hated my ex by then, and I was afraid of what I might do if I stayed." Especially since she'd been drinking at the time. Drinking a lot. Late at night, her fantasies had been very dark indeed.

Interest glittered in his eyes. "Like what?"

"Oh, lots of things. I made up so many revenge strategies they would fill a book."

"Tell me one."

"Hmmm." She swirled chocolate and vanilla together, admiring the preciseness of thin chocolate threads in the white. "Okay. One favorite was putting a bunch of rattlesnakes in their house one night—but of course, Joy lived with them, right, so that wouldn't work."

"Them? So it was an affair that broke up the marriage?"

"Yep." She sighed. "They're still together, so I guess it was true love or something."

He snorted. "Or something. Tell me another revenge fantasy."

"It's been a long time." She had to stop and think. "The usuals—sugar in the gas tanks, slit tires, breaking windows. I knew my ex would hate the mess eggs would make on his car, and I came very, very close to doing that." She took a bite. "Oh, I remember one— ants in their bed. Kind of the same category as snakes, though, I'm afraid. I ran to comic book tortures." She inclined her head. "Now you tell me one."

"I didn't have any."

"Not a single one?" Much as Luna tried to repress her, Therapist Barbie perked up. *How interesting,* she whispered. "Why not?"

Very simply, very roughly, he said, "I loved them both." Putting his attention on his dish, he cleared his throat. "She left me for my younger brother."

"Oh, this just gets better and better," Luna said, and it really did feel like her heart sunk—the lump in her chest dropped all the way to her belly. "Your brother."

He nodded. "Sucks, huh? He's always been a player, but I trusted him with my wife. Bad idea."

"No, it wasn't bad for you to trust them. It was bad for them to betray you." He did need a revenge fantasy. "Did you know, in some African cultures, the adulterous couple is buried up to their waist in the ground? Then they're starved, then the tribe"—she paused for effect—"cuts pieces of the lovers off and makes the other one eat it. Like cut her breast, make him eat it. Cut off his dick, make her eat it." She gave him a bright smile.

That twinkle burst in his dark eyes. "And you look like such a mild-mannered type."

"Beware what lurks in the hearts of women."

He didn't say anything for a while, and she figured she'd probably said enough. They ate in silence, their thighs somehow touching again, his arm sometimes brushing hers. In the far-off distance, thunder rolled softly.

"It would be so much easier if they were miserable together, wouldn't it?" he said.

"Definitely. If they had to make us feel so bad, they could at least have the decency to suffer for it." There was nothing left of her ice cream, unless she wanted to lick the dish. Wiping her hands with a napkin, she shifted a little toward Thomas, leaning with one elbow on the table. "My daughter was talking tonight about her stepmother. God, I hated her so much once, it was like a work of art." She could see it in her mind, something shaped of copper in the heat of rage and pain. "Truth is, though, I just feel sorry for her now. At least I escaped the bastard."

"Eventually," Thomas said slowly, "my brother will break Nadine's heart. He's just like my father—he'll leave her. And then," he added with a sigh, "she's gonna show up on my doorstep telling me how sorry she is."

"And what will you do then?"

"I don't know." He put a hand on her thigh and she jumped, which made him smile. "Are you afraid of me, Luna?"

She raised her head, daring herself to look right in his face. Nodded. "Not of you exactly," she said, not reaching for him in return. But they eased closer, millimeters at a time, and the air thickened again. It swirled around her, around him, and they were just looking at each other. His hand didn't move on her leg.

"I'm kinda scared of you," he said in that evening-song voice. "Tell me who you are."

His bare forearm rested on the table in front of her and there was no hair on it at all. It made his skin look smooth and silky, and she wanted to put her hand on it. It seemed bold, and considering what she'd learned here, a long way beyond unwise, but she did it anyway, settling her palm over the angle of elbow, sliding her middle finger into the crook neatly. "What do you want to know?"

Emboldened by her touch, he reached for a measure of her hair, twirled a curl around one finger. "What kind of shampoo do you use?"

She laughed. "Herbal Essence. You?"

"My grandma makes yucca shampoo. It's good

stuff." He quirked one eyebrow. "But I usually use whatever's on special."

It had been a very long time since Luna had been with anyone. Even longer since she'd been with someone who made her heart race. His hair fell in a curtain, hiding them from the rest of the customers, and she had a sense of his slanted cheekbone, the inky line of his eyelashes, before he bent in and kissed her.

And this time, she met him more easily, knowing it wasn't wise, but sighing in relief that he'd done it. His lips were hotter than they should have been, and smelled of pineapples, and Luna tasted bananas and syrup and something much deeper on his tongue. She kissed him as thoroughly as he kissed her, sampling lip shape and texture, and found that it was better than she remembered. She discovered that he was one of those rare men who like to kiss, who kissed as she did, angling with her, slowing and breathing and pausing, savoring what was, before a more complete opening.

Bad idea, said a voice she squashed by moving her hand on Thomas's arm, rubbing her palm over a bicep that was as powerful as it looked. He pulled her into him, pressing their bodies closer, his hand sliding around her neck. It suddenly seemed very intense, as if they were on the verge of embarrassing themselves in public. He must have felt it, too, because he pulled back a little, saying words over her mouth. "Let's go somewhere."

She pushed away, coming to her senses. Thinking of Joy with a sudden sense of danger and regret, she said, "Uh, no. I can't do that." She frowned at him. "I can't do *this*." She stood up. "Thanks for the ice cream."

Then she was bolting, as plain a case as she'd ever seen, because what she wanted more than anything was to turn around and take his hand and tell him to name the place. She imagined him naked in some tawdry room, imagined herself naked and plastered against him, and the lure of it was not some light little scarf of a vision, it had teeth—it pulled hard on her spine, nape to buttocks.

She set her shoulders, tossed hair off her hot face, told herself this was starting off all wrong, with the wrong messages, the wrong timing, the wrong everything.

"Luna!" Thomas spoke out of his truck window, which was right in front of her.

She veered around him. "I'm sorry," she said over her shoulder. "I've given you the wrong impression. I'm not the kind of person you think I am." Glancing over her shoulder, she crossed the street to get away from him. To get rid of that thick feeling in her chest, she broke into a slow jog, heading down the hill. The clouds were thick and dark overhead, the wind smelling of rain any second, and she'd have to run most of the way if she was going to miss the storm. Damn.

The truck door slammed behind her. She ignored it, feeling her breath come hard as she picked up her pace. But he was taller and longer-legged and he caught her by the elbow before she made it a half block. "Luna, please listen for one second." When she tried to keep walking, he said, "Please."

She halted and looked up at him, afraid everything would show on her face. Wanting too much, as always.

"Shit," he said, and put his hands on his hips. His hair lifted on the wind, making him look like a painting. "I don't do this, okay, go around fucking everybody, all right?"

The language felt like sharp rocks. "We don't have to—"

"Look at me."

She did.

Thomas kept his hands on his hips. "I get really

greedy around you, Luna. I don't know why. I wanted to fix this, not make it worse." He swallowed, lifted his chin. "I swear to God I won't touch you if you'll just come somewhere and sit with me, talk a little while." He raised a hand in an oath, and his eyes were sober and intense. Luna could see his hunger there. "When I look at you," he said, putting his hand on his chest, "I can breathe. It's been a long time since I could."

If it was a line, it was the best one she'd ever heard. "Yes."

He took her hand and led her back to the truck, and she liked being next to his big body as they walked up the road, feeling connected to him, wondering what people passing by thought about them. She climbed into his truck on the passenger side. It was clean and neat, with only a folder of papers on the bench seat he'd covered with a striped red set, the kind you could get at Wal-Mart for $29.95. He drove down to Rancho de Taos and pulled into a little café with windows facing the west. "This okay?" Thomas asked before they got out. "Just have some coffee?"

"It's fine."

It was far enough from the plaza and ordinary enough to be ignored by tourists, just a run-of-the-mill Mexican food café called Betty's Burritos. It had a black-and-white linoleum floor and plain vinyl upholstery. A mural of a Native American fancy dancer, painted crudely but with much love in tones of red, blue, and green, adorned one wall. A handful of tables were filled—an older Spanish couple, neatly dressed, glasses of beer before them; a family with little kids in the corner booth; a single overweight Native American girl at the counter, eating pie. A beaded sheath gathered her wealth of hair into a single tail that swept past the bottom of the stool.

The single waitress, a skinny Hispanic woman in her forties, came out of the kitchen at the sound of the bell over the door. "Hi, Thomas," she said. "Coffee?"

He nodded, pointed toward a booth by the window. "Do you want coffee, too?"

"Sure. It never keeps me awake for some reason."

It was served in heavy ceramic cups with little plastic pots of chemical cream. Luna asked for milk instead. She and Thomas were silent as they waited for the waitress to return, as if they were here to discuss something weighty—two parents with a troubled child, maybe, or friends with a big project. She hated the tension. "You look like a calendar," she said, noticing the way the light came through the window to wash over him.

He chuckled. "Maybe I could sell it on the Internet, huh?"

"The Lone Coyote."

"What's that?"

"It's from a Joan Baez song," she said. "I'll play it for you sometime."

He nodded, picked up his cup. "So, where're you from?"

"Right here. Taos. I was born in Albuquerque, but my mom grew up here, and we moved back when I was little. You?"

He cocked a thumb toward the south. "Same. Albuquerque. Mom's from here, too, though. Wonder if they know each other? How old is your mom?"

"Sixty-two."

"Mine's older. Seventy."

"Oh, well." Luna rubbed her fingers over the pattern on the Formica table, tracing the gold veins through the black. "When did you come to Taos, then?"

"Used to spend all my summers here when I was a kid. When my grandma had a heart attack, there wasn't anybody taking care of her the way I thought they should, and I was divorced"—he made a rueful expression with his mouth—"the first time, licking my wounds, so I came here. It suits me."

"Yeah, me, too," she said. "When I was a kid, I could not wait to get out of here, see the real world." She shook her head, smiling without humor. "I graduated from high school when I was sixteen, and was out of CU with a master's degree before I was twenty-two."

He whistled. "Overachiever, huh?"

"A bit." She relaxed a little, sipping coffee, her spine finally touching the back of the booth. "Can't think now why I was in such a hurry."

"We all think we know everything at that age."

"What did you know?"

"How to be a real Indian." His expression didn't shift, and she wondered how she knew he was poking fun at himself. "Not like all those fake Indians at the Pueblos and on the reservations, no sirree." His eyes glittered. "Went off to Los Angeles, enrolled in community college, got myself a card in AIM—you know what AIM is? American Indian Movement?"

"Sure."

Thomas let go of a breath, shaking his head in memory. "Nothing like a young fool to carry on, especially a young half blood."

"I've noticed."

He, too, relaxed, kicking out his legs beneath the table. "So," he said, "how long you been sober?"

"Well, that gets right to the heart of it." She blinked, thinking of all kinds of things related to being sober, getting sober, finding her way back. There was no reason not to tell the truth. "Four years last March."

"And still not driving, eh?"

The only way through most of this stuff was just

through it, and a sense of humor could be a big help. "Something about that third DWI—under suspension, I might add—just pissed that judge off."

He laughed appreciatively. Gaining big points from Luna.

"I'm not proud of it, you know," she said. "But sometimes you have to learn to live with things."

"Hurt anybody?"

"Nobody but me, by some miracle." She pulled up her sleeve and showed him the surgery scars. There were pins in three places in her elbow.

"Was that the last one?"

"Yeah." She looked at the scars, marveling as she always did that it looked just like the outline of a rose. An echo of something moved in her heart, little pings of regret that led nowhere. "Hit bottom." She pulled her sleeve down. "Now you," she said. "Tell me about the first wife. Was that in California?"

He nodded, his mouth turning down at the corners. "It was . . . volatile." As if making a decision, he pushed back the hair covering his neck and showed her a scar of his own. "She tried to cut my throat and I decided maybe it wasn't going to work out."

It was her turn to laugh. "Good call."

The waitress came by and poured more coffee. "Thanks, Debra," Thomas said. "How's your mom doing?"

"Good days and bad days. We're trying to get her back to work here, but she keeps saying it's just not the same without my dad."

"You keep trying. Tell her I asked about her."

"I will." Debra swung around to the other tables, pouring coffee from the right hand, iced tea in a clear plastic pitcher from the left.

"Her mom's a new widow," Thomas explained. He

added a dollop of her milk to his coffee. "What do you do for a living, Luna McGraw? Art?"

Startled, she said, "No! Not at all. Why did you think that?"

"Your house, all those bright colors, the weird Barbie dolls. The chairs. It looks like an artist's house."

"Oh," she said, waving her hand, pleased in spite of herself that he'd noticed the Barbies. "Those are just my hobbies. What I do to keep busy."

He narrowed his eyes faintly for a minute. "You don't do *any* art professionally?"

"Nope. I work the florist department at the Pay and Pack."

"You took a master's in horticulture?"

"Psychology. I was a therapist for ten years."

"Complicated."

"Not so much, really. This is the real thing." She spread her hands to indicate now. This minute.

Rain splashed against the windows suddenly, as if a child had thrown a handful of pebbles. "Here it comes," she said, inhaling in hopes of catching the scent through the plate glass.

And it came indeed, the rain that had been inexorably moving toward town for an hour. It closed them, her and Thomas, safely behind the plate glass window, enfolded by the warmth of the well-lit café. It lent a sense of coziness she wasn't entirely sure she liked.

Again, she wanted to photograph Thomas, or rather the scene itself—the quality of yellow against the wall behind his head, the smeary look of the water on the window, his strong brown hands clasped around that plain cup. The sight of his knuckles felt both too comfortable and too enclosing, and with a sense of rising panic, she looked at the rain and wondered how long it would last. How long could two strangers just make small talk?

"Penny," he said.

She bowed her head with a wry smile. "Small talk is painful."

There was a gruffness to his voice as he leaned over the table. "Maybe we should just skip it, then."

"How?"

Their feet bumped together. From speakers on the ceiling came a plaintive Spanish love song, and rain slapped at the window. "Maybe," he said, "we just talk about the real stuff, instead of all the filler."

"That's kind of scary."

He nodded.

She took a breath. Looked at him. "All right. You come into the store all the time. You buy canned ravioli and frozen corn on the cob and you eat Total for breakfast. Probably with bananas."

His eyes crinkled at the corners. "Had your eye on me, did you?"

" 'Fraid so. Scare you?"

"Nope. Wish I'd been paying attention." He moved suddenly, made a tent of his big hands, and put it over hers. "I really like looking at your face."

"I swear incessantly," she said.

"Even the *F* word?"

She laughed. "Especially that one."

His thumbs moved on her fingers. "I might still be in love with my ex-wife."

"I know." She turned her hands upward, meeting him palm to palm. "I can't afford to let anything happen that interferes with this chance with my daughter."

Blue heat built between their hands, and as if it grew too hot for him, Thomas rubbed her wrists, her forearms. His eyes, dark as molasses, rested on her face, unflinching, as if he wanted to see inside her head. She didn't look away.

"What if," he said, "this is a chance and we don't take it?"

"That's the other side of it, I guess."

"Willing to risk it?"

"Risk what?"

He put his hands on the outside of hers and pressed her palms together. Four hands at prayer, his surrounding hers. "Hope."

The much-washed softness of his collar against his neck made her feel tender. "I might have a little left in the bottom of my bag."

"I have a little extra, if you need to borrow some."

Luna laughed. "I might take you up on that."

"So you'll go out with me again?"

"I will."

"Tomorrow?"

"Not until the weekend. I need to spend my evenings with Joy."

"Fair enough. How about Saturday night?"

"Friday would be better."

"Okay. A movie, maybe something to eat?"

"I like that idea," she said. "A lot."

"Can I pick you up?"

She hesitated. "Maybe I can walk up to your house and meet you. Then we can go from there?" She lifted a shoulder. "I'd rather keep Joy out of things."

"Understandable." He leaned back and his hair slid over one arm, extravagant as mink.

It made her greedy again, and she looked away, to the rain outside, waiting for that urgency to fade, but instead of receding, flashes of wet mouths and naked bellies and sweat blinked over her vision. When he brushed one finger over the back of her hand, she jumped.

"Ready to go?" he asked. And she nodded, collected her bag. He drove her home in the rain that wasn't going to let up anytime soon. They didn't speak. Or kiss.

She just said, "Thanks, Thomas," and then hopped out of the truck, dashing through the rain to the front door.

From the Internet:
Reasons to Believe Tupac Shakur Faked His Own Death

Tupac always wore a bulletproof vest, no matter where he went. Why didn't he wear it to a very public event like a Tyson fight? (Because he wanted to make it seem like he could be shot.)

In most of his songs he talks about being buried, so why was he allegedly cremated the day after he "died"? And since when do they cremate someone the day after death without an autopsy? Furthermore, it is illegal to bury someone who has been murdered without an autopsy.

Tupac's alias is Makaveli. Though the spelling is different, Machiavelli was a sixteenth-century Italian philosopher who advocated the staging of one's death in order to evade one's enemies and gain power.

In Machiavelli's book Discourses Upon the First Ten Books of Titus Livy, *in Book 2 Chapter XIII, he says, "a prince who wishes to achieve great things must learn to deceive." This is Machiavelli's main idea and is the connection between Tupac and the writings of Machiavelli.*

The title of the new album by Makaveli (Tupac) is The 7 Day Theory. *He was shot on September 7th; and survived on the 7th, 8th, 9th, 10th, 11th, 12th, and "died" the 13th. Hence the title* The 7 Day Theory.

Seven

Maggie's Diary

10 Septiembre 2001,
San Nicolás T

Dear T,

I had to go with my mom to the *bruja*'s house tonight. I hate going with her, and it was totally creepy out. The sky made me think of an orange that was going moldy, half purple and half orange. Thunder banged around over the mountains and I hate storms and I didn't want to go nowhere, but my mom had that weird look around her eyes, kinda glassy, and it seemed more important to go with her.

My mom's been dreaming again and needed to see Mrs. Ramirez—that's the *bruja*'s name—so we walked in the wind to a tall, old house, where she's staying with her grandson. And like she was from a horror movie, the *bruja* came to the door just as the wind and thunder whirled themselves into rain. Her brown claws curled around her shawl, holding it in place as she gestured for us to come in, and we followed her down a hall to the kitchen without talking.

I have to say the house was cool in a way. The *bruja*'s old house always smelled kind of funny, but the grandson's didn't—it was nice, really, like wood and supper and something kinda salty that makes you know a man lives there. The floors were plain wood with no carpet. My mom's shoes made a *click-click* noise over them.

A man was in the big kitchen, talking on the phone. He was mad at whoever it was, yelling in a quiet way until he saw us, then he hung up real quick and he took off into another room, talking under his breath. I couldn't hear what he said, but you could tell he was mad at a woman or maybe his boss.

My mom and Mrs. Ramirez went to sit at the table, and I petted a black cat with long fur and then a big, goofy dog came out, too, and we all sat by the wall while my mom and the *bruja* started talking in low voices. My mom had brought cards, which she wanted to spread for Mrs. Ramirez, but I could see they made the old woman afraid, and she told my mom in Spanish to put them away. She crossed herself, which surprised me. My mom started to cry.

I was shocked to see the cards, to tell you the truth. My dad didn't like that kind of stuff, at all, and he would have thrown tarot cards in the trash. It made me mad that my mom had them now, like he didn't even matter.

And I wish she'd stop crying all the time. It's just sickening.

The dog was silly and *too* cute. I let him put my wrist in his mouth like he was going to chomp on it. He didn't, of course, just slobbered and panted all over it until the cat got grossed out and took off, shaking his ears. The dog got a big grin on his face like he was proud of himself then, and I laughed.

It made the ache in my chest feel a little better. Sometimes lately I think my mom is just going to keep getting thinner and thinner and thinner until she turns into a ghost. And if that happens, what will happen to me? Where will I go?

The dog jumped up suddenly and raced through the house, barking at someone coming inside, and I heard a man's heavy feet on the floor. He stomped and made a noise of cold. "It's raining like Armageddon out there," he said.

Then he came in the kitchen and right there, I saw something amazing. My mother, who makes me think of a corn husk most of the time, shone for a second, like the soft husk around a tamale. It was only the smallest time you can think of, but for a second, I remembered her hair all black and rich like it used to be, and how red her mouth was, how it sounded when she laughed.

I looked back to the guy. He was taking a pitcher out, pouring red Kool-Aid into a glass. He was big, with a working man's hands, not like my dad at all, but that was okay with me. I guess he was okay for an old guy, and I really wouldn't care if he was as ugly as a troll if he could make my mom look like that. Make her want to live.

I have a plan, but I don't want to write it down yet in case it would curse it. Maybe that new girl will help me. She seemed pretty cool.

That's enough now. Thanks for listening.

Maggie

Get answers to questions about love, career, finances, health, de-
parted loved ones, much more. Native American and Spanish, a
Wiccan teacher and master-level tarot reader, Alicia Mondragon
will be glad to ease you through difficult or nagging questions in a
half-hour tarot reading from the deck of your choice. Choose from
the classic Rider-Waite, Angel Cards, Enchanted Tarot, and many
others, and then take some time to browse our wide selection.

Eight

Just before she awakened on Thursday morning,
Luna dreamed of her father sitting at her dining room
table with Joy, playing a board game. He said to Luna,
"She's a great kid, isn't she?"

Not much of a scene, but packed with enough emotion, it yanked her awake. The sun was only a Maxfield
Parrish glow behind the mountains, but she was des-
perately glad to see even that much light. Something else
the not-smoking did—interfered with her naturally
good sleep patterns, gave her wild dreams. Weird to
have two dreams of her father in so short a time.

With the sun on the horizon, she could get up and
take a walk, leaving a note for Joy in case she awakened—fat chance, since she had to be bodily hauled
from her bed at seven—and set out with a bottle of
water in hand.

The craving for a cigarette was very painful this
morning. It lay on her lungs like a weight. Even when
she tried to breathe deeply and give herself those big pep
talks, it just sat there, aching. It made her want to

scream. Cry. Throw things. She wasn't sure anyone who hadn't been there could comprehend the physical difficulty in giving up nicotine.

Instead of smoking or crying, she put one foot in front of the other, over and over, walking due west on a narrow gravel road in the half dark. She passed a small park, and a cow munching quietly in a field, a broken-down car with a tag on the door, and a willow tree standing by itself in a field, the leaves just beginning to be laced with yellow. It seemed to glow in the soft purple morning.

She walked all the way to the edge of the Rio Grande Gorge, the walls steep and carved, furred with greenery. A breeze, brisk with impending autumn, blew over her face, and she settled on a big rock, thinking of all kinds of things as she tried to pretend she wasn't wanting a cigarette.

Joy's new friend Maggie came to mind. Luna had had a nodding relationship with the family since moving in six months ago, and Jerry Medina, the neighbor who kept three goats, had told her the terrible story of Maggie's father's death. He had died on the bridge over the gorge, one of the senseless things that sometimes happen with no real reason—his tires slid on the icy road and he lost control, slamming into the guard rail. An oncoming truck, unable to stop, ran head-on into it, killing him instantly. The truck driver escaped with only bruises and minor injuries.

And that made Luna think of her own father again and how much she'd missed him as a girl, which somehow made her want a cigarette even more. It did cross her mind to wonder about what she wasn't saying, but it all boiled down to life sucks sometimes, and she wasn't in the mood.

A dog came leaping toward her as if he recognized her, a big tan one.

"Hey cutie!" she said, looking around for Thomas as she rubbed the head of his exuberant dog. He was quite a distance across the field, looking vaguely dangerous and exciting in a jean jacket, his hair loose on his shoulders. She waved. While she waited for him, she threw a stick for the dog—what was his name? Oh, yeah, Tonto. How could she forget?—who leapt and twirled and raced back to her, stick in mouth, with the joy only a dog ever really showed. Dogs and four-year-olds.

"We gotta keep meeting like this," Thomas said, then gave her a puzzled expression. "I mean, quit, not keep."

Luna chuckled. Tonto dropped the stick at her feet and she bent down to pick it up and throw it hard, away from the edge of the gorge. "Don't you wish you could be that happy again?"

"It's the thing you gotta love about dogs." He stood next to her, leash in hand. "What brings you out so early?"

"Not smoking," she admitted.

"Ah. Been there."

"Yeah, me, too. Maybe this time, it'll stick."

He only nodded.

"How 'bout you?" she asked. "What are you doing up so early?"

His mouth tightened. "Domestic dispute, early."

"Fighting with your grandma?"

"Nah, I got this guy staying with me—on the ankle bracelet for domestic violence, you know? Him and his wife aren't supposed to have any contact, but she snuck into the house this morning. They woke me up. Fighting. Then having sex." He wiped a hand over his chin. "Like I couldn't hear them? They're right next to my bedroom."

"Ah."

"So I left, making a lot of noise, so she can get the hell out of there. I don't want the legal trouble. Tiny is one of my best crew members, and I'm willing to help him out, but this is just crazy."

DV—domestic violence—cases had been Luna's specialty, once upon a time. Surprising to feel the surge of blood over it now. "Is he taking anger management classes?"

"Yeah, second time for him, third for her."

"Ugh." She sighed, unscrewed the lid of her water and took a long sip. "Not great odds for them, then."

"I know." He stared into the middle distance, maybe at the lone tree growing on the other side of the gorge. Abruptly, he squatted, rubbing his neck. "I can't give up on him yet." With a rueful glance at her he added, "This is one of the things that drove my ex crazy, taking in strays. The animals and the people, all of them. Even my house is stray."

She laughed.

He looked up and a shine came into his dark eyes. "It is," he said. "A big old house nobody else wanted. I had to take it on, take care of it. Like Tiny, and Tonto and my grandma and Ranger."

"Ranger is . . . ?"

"A black cat. Showed up on the doorstep one day, skinny as a rail. What could I do?"

"I see your point." It was a good quality in a man and she liked him for it. "So do you draw the line at a certain number of strays, or just let them multiply as long as you have room?"

"Not sure. Can't kick out *Abuelita*, eh?" He sighed. "And Tiny . . . he's a good man, you know? There's just a bad thing between him and his wife."

She settled on the rock she'd been sitting on before he showed up. "I believe you."

A very soft breeze swirled over them. To the east, the first gold fingers of light edged into the crack between the worlds, and she gazed at it for a moment in anticipation, her hands deep in the pockets of her jacket. "I did that kind of work for a while," she volunteered, "counseling domestic violence offenders. And victims. I was better with offenders for some reason. I did it for a long time, actually. Ten years."

His eyebrows lifted. "Why'd you give it up? Burn out?"

"Not exactly." She'd mainly given it up because her life collapsed, and then—oh, she didn't know why she'd never gone back to it. She cleared her throat and gave him a look—fill in the blanks, it said.

He nodded.

She thought back to the old house where female victims and their children were housed, thought of the bravado of some of the girls in the groups she counseled in jail. *He deserved it—he cheated on me.* "Sometimes, men behave so very, very badly," she said. "And sometimes, I'd hear a story and think—she's right, he deserved it."

"Really? Like what?"

"Oh, I don't know—the guy who used his baby daughter's dress to jack off?"

He winced.

"Yeah, gross—and she kicked his butt, honey. But"— she bent down and tugged a strand of grass from its sheath, and stuck it in her mouth—"if I agreed that a woman had a right to kick a man's ass once in a while— then did I have to admit that maybe sometimes women deserved it, too?"

"I see what you mean." Absently, he touched the scar on his neck.

"Why did she cut your throat?" she asked.

"We were drunk," he said, lifting a shoulder. "Just stupidly drunk, and fighting, like we always did. It was a toxic relationship."

Luna frowned. "I thought if you were in AIM you weren't supposed to drink."

"Right. For good reason. Alcohol has done more damage to Indian cultures than all the smallpox blankets and buffalo slaughters together." His mouth turned down at the corners. "But we ignored the alcohol rule. We didn't go to meetings much—it was a game for both of us, I'm afraid. We liked partying and fighting and making up with sex." He sighed. "And that's who I see when I see Tiny and his wife. I don't know how to help him, help her. They're both good people. They're just bad together and they can't see how to live apart."

"Not poking my nose into your business, but if they're violating the terms of their probation, you need to get in touch with their caseworkers."

He nodded, not happily, and drew on the ground with a stick. "I know. I just hate to be responsible for sending either one of them to jail. They've got kids."

"Yeah, well, kids are hurt worse by one parent murdering the other."

"Good call." Abruptly, he bent that big bear head into his waiting palms. Exhaustion.

She wanted, so much, to put her hands on his shoulders, offer that little bit of comfort. But even thinking about it, about him turning to her brought back the agony of cigarette hunger. So she just sat there. Quietly.

After a minute, he stood. "Guess I need to get back. I've gotta start work in a little while. You want a ride?"

"Sure." She stood up, tossing her hair out of her face, then stopped dead. "Oh, Thomas, look!"

The sun had come over the horizon and the whole world was suddenly ablaze, as if a thousand fairies had put a lamp inside every blade of grass, every plant, every leaf. Sage and plumes of long feathery grasses shone like they were painted with fireflies, the air itself a soft rose. Luna held up her hands. Light caught on the little hairs along her arms, gilding her, and across the field, an adobe house glowed like gold. Beyond was the town, tumbling through little hills and valleys, and it was on fire, too, like a fairy tale, as if it would disappear when the sun set.

It felt, standing there, as if she were lit up, too, as if all the dark things, all the bad things, all the sadness in the world was washed clean. She made a noise, something wordless and full of amazement, and looked at Thomas to see if he was enjoying it, too.

He stood close by. Looking at her. And before he moved, she knew he would kiss her. It was there on his face, a stricken kind of hunger, and she met it with light-struck lips, hoping some of it would flow out of her into him. His hands were tight on the small of her back, pulling her hips close to his, and she put her arms around his neck.

Wordless, they walked to his truck and he drove her home. He touched her fingers as she got out. "See you tomorrow?"

"Yes."

Luna took off work an hour early, stopping in the coffee place to pick up fresh beans, along with a tall latte and a grande chai. The latte was hers, of course, the chai for her best friend Allie, because Luna needed to stop and talk to her. Not the phone for stuff like this.

The shop, The Turquoise Goddess, was one of Luna's favorite places. It smelled of exotic incenses and candles, and there was always some New Age-y kind of music playing. Today it was melancholy Native American flute, Nakai or Gomez, she wasn't sure which. Appropriate to the soft clouds that were puffing across the sky, dimming summer sunshine for autumn storms.

Allie was busy with a customer, so Luna lifted the cups to show her that she'd brought a treat, then carried them to the back of the shop. A small table and two chairs sat beneath a beaded hanging lamp in colors of red and blue. She read tarot and Angel cards for regulars, and since she didn't take a fee, they brought her payment in goods and services—everything from oil changes at the local garage to tatted pillowcases. Judging by the small pile of goodies on the table, it had been a busy day. Luna sat down and picked up a pile of Angel cards, plucking one out at random. It was a little girl angel, about seven or eight, naked. *Self-Acceptance.* Luna put it down, rolling her eyes. "Tell me something I don't know."

"Hey!" Allie came over in a cloud of softly ringing bells, wrists and ankles, which she said chased away negative energies. Once, that had probably been evil spirits, but Wiccans didn't believe in absolute evil, and although Luna personally had some trouble with that idea, it wasn't such a bad thing to lay responsibility for behavior on humans themselves. "What a great surprise!" she said. "And you must be a mind reader, because I've been dying for a chai all day!"

"I'm glad."

"What's up?"

Allie meant the question casually, but Luna didn't have a lot of time. "I need help. I'm confused. Scared. The guy—Thomas."

Her dark eyes quickened. "Oooh, this is good. Tell me about it."

"I saw him the other day," she said, realizing only as she said it how weird it was that she hadn't told Allie before this. "We had a sundae, and then we kissed and then we ended up having coffee when it rained, and then this morning, I ran into him again, up at the gorge and he kissed me. So I've kissed him, like, three times and I really am not looking for a guy in my life, that's just too many complications and—"

Allie was smiling her goddess smile, and touched Luna's hand. "Slow down, baby."

"That's what I want to do!"

"Three times you've kissed? I only count two, one over ice cream and one this morning."

"Yeah. Well, the first one was the day he brought the chile, after the fire. The day Joy got here."

"First day? And you didn't tell me?"

"I was embarrassed, I think. I mean, I have this big crush on this guy for a year or better, and there he was in my kitchen, kissing me like we were fourteen, and I figured I must have done something to telegraph my crush, and so I didn't want to say anything in case he didn't come back."

"Oh, Lu. Why are you so hard on yourself all the time?"

Luna thought of the Angel card. She shook her head, took a sip of coffee.

"So, you want the best friend or the tarot lady?"

"Either one."

Allie inclined her head, as if listening. "Let's draw some cards, huh?"

"Yeah, okay. I guess."

"Pick a deck."

There were three lined up on the side of the table, the

Rider-Waite, the Enchanted Tarot, and the Angel cards, which were beautiful and very positive, always. But Luna was in the mood for getting the warnings out in the open, and the Rider-Waite was the deck for that. "This one."

Luna didn't necessarily believe in tarot or any of those other things—divination and astrology and all the rest. She wasn't sure what she believed in, except her mother and Allie and Joy, who were enough for her. Allie put great store in divination, however, and people said she was gifted, so Luna let her read when she suggested it. If nothing else, it helped focus the questions. Allie made her shuffle the deck, then cut it three times, then held the deck spread out while Luna picked three cards.

"Hmm," Allie said, laying the cards side by side in a row. "Well, now that's very interesting."

Luna's heart thudded hard three times. She didn't always know what the cards meant, though Allie had told her not to get worried over the Death card, which meant new beginnings. It was the Tower card that was scary. Or maybe not scary, but it meant big stuff coming and it was always wise to get your act together in that case.

At any rate, there was no Death card. Only the Ten of Wands, then the Lovers, then the Knight of Cups, riding his horse in a kindly, noble fashion across the road of her life. "What does that mean?"

"Probably a lot of what you think it does," she said, narrowing her eyes. Luna recognized the concentration face—they'd been reading cards and palms together for more than five years—and let her be for a minute.

With the extravagantly long copper fingernail of her left index finger, Allie touched each of the cards in turn and smiled. "I'm *very* happy about this!" She said in a bright, tinkly voice. "Here's the first card: tens are a time of transition and culmination. This one says you're dragging around a lot of burdens you don't have to carry. You need to learn you don't have to do everything yourself."

Well, that rang true. But it would ring true for just about any female in America, wouldn't it?

"Two—the Lovers. That's sex, for sure, but it also points to new developments, or a new level of development in your life. Usually something physical that leads to something spiritual." She wiggled her eyebrows. "Have sex with him. Soon and often."

"Allie!"

"I'm not kidding. That's what this card says. Do it. It's telling you to be open and vulnerable if you want healing. You won't be sorry. Finally"—she smiled like a cat—"the Knight of Cups. A good man, a responsible man. I like him."

"No warnings?" she said, feeling cheated.

"You want opposing forces?"

"Yes."

She offered Luna the deck. "Draw a card."

She pulled one out, and another tumbled on to the table. The one she drew and gave to Allie was the Queen of Pentacles. It was upside down. The other one fell face first on the table and she left it there.

"Let's deal with this one, first," Allie said. "A dark-haired, dark-eyed woman, full of passion. Probably someone who lives close to the land, or earns her living from it in some way. Because it's upside down, there's suspicion and manipulation involved." Allie grimaced, tapped her finger on the rabbit in the picture. "This makes me think of pregnancy. What's the ex look like?"

Luna shrugged. "No idea."

"Okay, well, one of the opposing forces is a woman, an earthy woman."

"Not like a female force, maybe?"

"Could be. I'm betting on a living woman. Gut feeling." She peered at it, then shook her head and reached for the other card. The bell over the door rang and a pair of young women came in. "Hi," Allie called. "I'll be with you soon."

She turned the card over. "Now this is interesting." It was the Emperor, reversed. Allie closed her eyes and her hands were outstretched. It embarrassed Luna to death when she did this and there were other people present, but the two girls didn't seem to care or even notice.

"A big man," she said. "A big dark man. Someone in a powerful position in your life. *Very* powerful. Ring a bell?"

There was no one in power in her life, not a man, anyway. She and Barbie, they were doing it on their own. "Nope."

"This is really not very clear is it? A woman and a man. Let me try something."

"Allie, it's okay—I was just playing around. Really, I've got to—"

"Shuffle," Allie ordered.

But Luna suddenly could not bear to be here, to think about her life in this way, the possibilities, the power of love or betrayal, the intense highs and lows that were always part of loving someone. "No. That's enough."

Allie raised her head, and Luna saw the surprise and curiosity there. She was about to speak when one of the girls said, "Excuse me, can we get you to pull out the rings?"

Luna seized the moment. She stood up. "I've got to get home to Joy. We're doing our nails tonight. Hers black. Mine . . . I don't know what."

"I'll call you."

Luna rushed out, glad there was a wind coming down from the blue mountains to blow away the silly sense of impending . . . excitement the cards lent. It would be ridiculous to let a random drawing of cards influence events, and she certainly didn't intend to worry about any of it, but the picture of the Lovers, hair flying in the breeze, kept surfacing.

When she got home, there was trouble waiting. Joy was on the telephone, her voice bright and brittle, tears streaming down her cheeks. "April, I'm doing great. Really! If he wants to know how it is, he should stay home to talk to me sometimes."

Luna put her bag on the table and started putting away the few groceries she'd brought home in a canvas tote bag—big black plums, a chunk of Gouda, sourdough bread, and some fresh glazed doughnuts for dessert. Joy listened for a minute, then started to protest, "I don't care about—" She went quiet, listening, and gave Luna a look she couldn't read. She dashed away her tears with an angry wrist.

The groceries that had looked so appealing in the store now looked pitifully picnicky, not at all the offerings a mother should give her growing teenage daughter. She imagined April's fridge filled with tender roast beef and carrots, hearty soups, gallons of milk, and sweet tea. Freshly baked cobbler for dessert. Opening the fridge to put away the cheese, she was embarrassed by how spare it looked—a few stalks of celery in the crisper, three tall brown bottles of Henry Weinhardt vanilla soda, a quart of milk, which Luna only used in coffee. She would have to ask her mother to drive her to the store for a real shopping trip tomorrow or the next day. Maybe even tonight.

"Tell him," Joy said distinctly, "that I'm not coming back to Atlanta." She hung up.

"What's up?" Luna said, offering a plum, wet from the tap water she'd just washed it in. April probably used that spray stuff you bought in a bottle.

Joy took the plum, took a bite, shook the hair out of her eyes. "My dad thinks my educational chances will be ruined if I go to school here. He thinks it's too risky for me to spend the school year here."

A hollowness hit her belly. "I see."

"I'm not going back there," she said. "Not. Going." Then she darted a look at Luna. "Unless this is too much hassle?"

"Oh, my God, no! I love having you here!" She sat down, relief making her knees weak, and reached for Joy, touching just her elbow.

"I don't know why he's doing this," Joy cried. "He couldn't wait to get rid of me and now he wants me back there? It doesn't make any sense."

"Joy," Luna said cautiously, "I've never been entirely clear about the reasons for the change in custody arrangements. Did you and your father have a fight? Was it your decision or his?"

Finishing the plum, Joy tossed the pit toward the trash can by the fridge. It missed, and she stood up to put it in properly. "I've wanted to come for a couple of years, but he wouldn't let me. Then, last year, I just got sick of all his game stuff and I decided I wanted to make my own life." She quirked her mouth upward in a half grin. Luna saw her sister in the gesture. "So I gave up the good life and found the freaks."

Luna laughed, partly in relief. Partly in amusement. "Okay. But you don't have to give up the good grades."

"No," she said, "I know. That was a mistake, last year."

"Changing the way you look won't hurt you in the long run, as long as you don't tattoo your neck or arms or—heaven forefend—face. But you don't want to do things now that will limit your choices down the line. It's just so hard to know what you'll want later."

"I know, Mom." She pulled open the fridge. "What else is there to eat? I'm starving."

"Ravioli? It'll only take a few minutes to fix."

"Okay."

She sat down as Luna got up. "You can learn to do this, you know. It's really easy."

"I don't particularly want to know."

"Better for you, though." She took a bag of frozen cheese raviolis out of the freezer and put them on the counter, and took out a medium-sized saucepan and filled it with water. "Bring the water to a boil first," Luna said, turning on the burner.

"Mom, you graduated early, right? Why did you do it that way?"

Because her life was the opposite of Joy's, she wanted to say—because her mother had to work way too hard to just keep them in jeans and Luna wanted to get out and get into a place she could help take care of her. "It was my ticket to the world," she said instead. "I was smart. That's what I had. I used it."

"Didn't you want to party and stuff, just be a teenager?"

"Not really."

She narrowed her eyes. "You didn't party at all?"

"Not then. When I got to CU, yes, but I didn't even get into it then until I was a junior."

"Yeah, everybody says Boulder's a big party school."

Luna crossed her arms, remembering Carol, her party-hearty roommate that year. Luna was finally eighteen, and had been in school for two years, away from home, made the dean's list every time, too. It was time to let down her hair—and boy, Carol had been the one to show her how. "Made up for lost time that year,

I'll tell you. It scares me to death to think of you doing those things."

She lifted a shoulder. "You know, Mom, if I wanted to, I could do any drug you can think of—anything. I'm not interested. Just seems stupid."

"Good." The water started to rumble and Luna glanced at it, then back at her daughter. "Do you drink?"

"Never."

"That's good." Waving her over to the stove, Luna opened the ravioli and poured some in, showing her how many for how much water, all the while wondering what had changed to make Marc want to bring Joy back to Atlanta.

Suddenly, it worried her that she was seeing Thomas. The first guy she'd dated in at least a couple of years, but would it make her look bad if she went back to court? No, that was silly. She took a breath. Women dated. Especially women who had been divorced for close to a decade.

But she couldn't help sending out a little prayer. *Not this time. Please.*

"I'll call your dad later, see what's up," she said. "In the meantime, don't worry about him forcing you to go back. He can't. We changed the custody agreements officially. You have to go at Christmas, but he has to send you back. Okay?"

Joy let go of a breath. "Okay. Thanks, Mom." She slumped against the wall behind the bench. "And Grandma's richer than my dad, even, isn't she?"

Luna laughed. "Frank is, but yeah. Your father is pretty much outclassed there."

"Grandma would fight for me, if it came to that." It wasn't a question.

"Yep."

"Good," she said. And again. "Good."

El Santuario de Chimayó, The "Lourdes of America"

by Robert Scheer

Thirty miles north of Santa Fe, New Mexico, on a hill near the Santa Cruz river, stands El Santuario (The Shrine) of Chimayó . . .

A small room at the back of the chapel is called El Pocito. *It is also known as the "Room of Miracles." There is a round hole in the floor, through which people scoop out some of the sand. Some kneel and kiss the earth; some rub it on their bodies or onto photographs of family members too ill to travel. Most people carry home a small bagful. Some even eat a little of the sand.*

Nine

Placida Ramirez woke up feeling winded. In the air she smelled burned sugar, the odor of trouble. Outside, she could hear the cry of ravens. Nobody remembered anymore that they could be warnings of trouble, but she remembered. She didn't have to look in the yard to know there were three.

Out on the porch, she found Tiny, who stayed with Thomas because he had no other place to go. Placida did not wish to like him, but there was an air of starvation about him and she couldn't help feeding him, and he had such deep sorrow around him it clung like a purple cloud, the color of bruises. His wife was the daughter of a bad line, and he should never have kissed her, because things started in motion right then to this, to him sitting here with his heart in his throat, his children running wild in the street. She made a noise and said to him in Spanish, "I need to go to the church in Chimayó."

He shook his head and lifted his pant leg to show her the black bracelet around his ankle. "This don't let me go nowhere."

Placida knew better and not through any magic. Her grandson Donnie had been tethered to the bracelet for a year the third time they arrested him for drinking and getting behind the wheel of his car. He could go for a few hours, now and then, long as he asked. "We'll ask 'em. And I'll make you a charm."

The sorrow around him thinned the smallest bit. Hope could do that. He frowned. "I got a car. I'll ask."

She waited with her hands in her lap, looking down from the deep shade of the porch to the town just below, peeking out from between cottonwoods. Her heart, none too steady these days, went into one of its racing spins. The ravens bickered over in the side yard, trying to get her attention, but she steadfastly ignored them.

Tiny came out, his back a little straighter, his keys in his hand. He helped her down the steps into his car, a pretty thing painted in a sparkly kind of purple, with an engine that sounded like thunder. He rolled the windows down for her and made her strap herself into the seat belt. It rocked and rumbled around her, the car, feeling powerful, and she patted the door happily. When he started down the narrow road out of Taos toward Chimayó, he didn't talk, but he turned the radio to the one with Mexican songs, and he knew some of the words. She remembered his father had sung for a long time. Maybe there was music in Tiny, too. She would see what she could do.

At the church, he stayed outside, the way so many people will do, as if he was afraid it would fall down on him, or he might fall down on his knees himself, his guilt and unhappiness turning him into one of the *penitentes* who still secretly scourged themselves in the mountains on holy days. Placida snorted to herself. So much noise they made with all their howling. The saints could hear a whisper. On those holy days, they had to be covering their ears in pain, like a mother with too many babies all setting each other off in wails that got louder and louder.

There were many pilgrims and tourists in the church, a lot of them clumped together in the room with Santo Niño in his little white stall, all waiting their chance to collect the holy dirt. Placida was in no hurry. She fingered the turquoise rosary Thomas brought her from a famous shrine in California, and went to look at Santo Niño. At his feet were the shoes of babies, and on the walls around him were written many names. Placida closed her eyes to hear the echoes of the prayers that hung in the space—one voice and then another and another and another until they swirled around one another and up to heaven.

When she opened her eyes again, the tourists had all gone but one, an old woman like herself, who had to take a minute to bend her knees good enough. Placida nodded to her and went into the tiny room, where the air was so cold, and knelt. From the hole in the floor where the priest had found the crucifix, over and over, she scooped out a healthy measure of holy dirt. As she did it, the smell of burned sugar filled the room, blotting out even the damp animal smell of the sand.

Trouble. She made her way back outside, her rosary swinging around her hand, and hurried up to Tiny, who was eating something out of a foil-wrapped package. He gave her a tamale he had bought across the street, and she took it, washing it down with a Coke in a big white cup, standing right by the car in the sun.

The quiet came over her then, like the church was in

the holy palm of God and nothing could touch it. Across the street, a young man with bright green eyes was selling spices. He had the look of the boy she had once believed she would marry, a boy whose family had grown the sharp red Chimayó chiles she loved. She said to Tiny, "I want to buy some of his spices."

Tiny gestured for the man to come over, and he sold them three bags of spices, two red and one green. Tiny gave him the money after wrangling. A good man, one who didn't make an old woman pay for a trifle like spices. He would have the first charm.

They went to get in the car, Tiny coming around the car to hold her elbow, as he should do. Good manners, this one. But just as she bent, she saw right there, panting heavily in the full heat of day, a black dog. Pregnant. Placida narrowed her eyes, holding tight to her jar, but the dog only watched them climb in and drive away.

Trouble, trouble. The air was nearly orange with trouble.

On Friday, Thomas arose a little earlier than usual to check the weather. It had been raining lightly when he went to bed and he'd had little expectation that the crew would get any work done today. His expectation proved correct. Peering out his second-floor bedroom window, he saw that the sky was dark, the ground wet. On his way downstairs, he tapped at Tiny's door and poked his head in. "No work today." Tiny mumbled a reply.

The stairs were dark and twisting, and he had to duck beneath the beams, smelling coffee and something meaty cooking. That was something good about having his grandmother here—long before the sun woke, she was in the kitchen cooking. He kept trying to tell her she didn't have to do it, that she was old enough she could just sit in a rocking chair if she wanted all day long, but she waved that away, the recommendation of a lunatic. She liked to be busy.

This morning, as always, she sat at the table in her flowered apron, the snaps fastened all the way to the neck. Beneath, a dark blue cardigan poked out. The radio on the counter was tuned to her Spanish station, the voices rattling out very quiet news and weather reports. "Mornin'," Thomas said, lifting the lid of a pot to smell the contents. It was a chicken cut in pieces, the skin still pink and cold. "Supper?"

She nodded, her attention on the task before her.

A pottery dish with a cover sat toward the back of the old stove and Thomas lifted the lid to find the fresh tortillas he knew would be there, along with a pot of beans she'd put on the stove to warm from the night before. He dished some into a bowl and poured coffee into a mug advertising Martinez Concrete, then settled at the table, looking over the arrangement of spices and cloth and something that looked like a bottle of dirt, and gold thread and tiny tin saint's medals. "Whatcha doing?" he asked.

"Making charms."

"For what?"

"Protection." She didn't look at him, her eyes focused on the needle and thread in front of a giant magnifying glass on a stand.

"Want me to thread that needle?"

"I could do it."

He nodded and swiveled in his chair toward the wall phone, thinking suddenly of Luna calling him on this phone the night Placida had nearly burned down the house. He picked it up and dialed the first member of his crew, delivered the news of no work, ate some beans, dialed the next and the next. Only two of the six numbers were busy so early, and he gave them a minute as he stood up to look outside. It was agreeably dark and a little chilly. Thomas opened the back door to take a breath of the sweet coolness of rain, standing there to feel a wind blowing rain across his face. Behind him, the dog clicked into the room, whining softly to be let out.

Thomas pushed the door open. Tonto stood at the door, sniffing and uncertain, balefully looking at Thomas as if he could turn off the drizzle. "In or out, dog."

The dog went out, hanging his head. Business was business. The cat, licking his chops over the chicken smell, settled his paws more firmly on the worn linoleum. *No thanks.*

The phone rang. Placida got up to answer it even though he waved her down—she liked knowing what was going on—and Thomas hung by the door, waiting for Tonto to come back. The dog was edging along the porch, trying to find a dry spot, his ears down miserably, and Thomas couldn't help but chuckle.

"It's you," Placida said in a disapproving voice, holding out the phone.

He took it, expecting one of the guys. Instead, it was Nadine's voice. "Thomas? Do you have a minute?"

No, he wanted to say, looking over his shoulder for rescue. "Not really. I gotta call my crew. What's up? Something wrong with my brother?"

"No . . . I mean, not really . . ." She burst into tears. "I just don't know who else to talk to."

"What is it?"

"I just . . . he isn't . . ." At the other end of the phone, she gulped and sniffled and was obviously out of control. Thomas frowned. This was the real thing, deep tears, sorrowful tears. His cheek twitched in memory and a feeling like panic came into his chest.

He didn't say anything, waiting while she gathered control. The dog came to the screen, wagging his tail, and Thomas looked to his grandmother to see if she'd let him in, but she'd gone into deaf-dumb-and-blind mode the minute he took the phone.

Women. Damn.

Trying to keep the phone line above the table, Thomas moved toward the door, using his right hand to keep the spiral cord aloft. "What's the problem, Nadine?" he said impatiently. "I really have calls to make."

He probably sensed the disaster coming, and if it had been anyone but Nadine on the phone, crying in his ear the way she'd cried on his table the night she told him she was leaving, he might have stopped it.

Instead, he was trying hard not to feel that night coming back into his body, gritting his teeth, bracing his bones, as Tonto leapt up on his back legs like a circus dog, waiting to get in. With youthful exuberance, the dog blasted through the first slight opening, wiggling into the kitchen. The floor was wet from blown mist, and Tonto's wet paws skittered. Thomas, still gritting his teeth against the soft, broken sobs in his ear, swerved out of his way, backed into the cold body of the fridge, as the dog tried to stop and couldn't, his momentum sending him into a skidding slide across the linoleum.

The cat, alarmed, leapt up on the table, knocking over a bottle, then a dish. Something broke with a crash, and Placida stood up, yelling, and caught the edge of the phone cord in her upraised hand, which yanked it out of Thomas's hand. The receiver went flying, crashing into the things on the table and the cat's head, who yelped and jumped off the table, landing too close to the dog, who yipped, turned, slipped, and slammed into Thomas.

Who went down flat on his ass, laughing, trying to

keep from landing on the dog or the cat, who both took one look at the furious Placida and the broom in her hand before departing—fast—for parts unknown. Thomas laughed until he was choking, knowing even as he did it that it was a reaction to that sound of grief in Nadine's voice, a way to let it go without losing his mind. It wasn't until he realized his grandmother was staring in dismay at the table that he stood up, extracted the phone from the mess, and said, "Gotta call you back," and hung up before she could say anything.

"Let me help you, *Abuelita*," Thomas said, reaching for an oval medal. There was a smell of roses and heat coming from the mingled powders. He saw a pinkish barklike substance he thought was incense, and chile spices, and dirt scattered together, pink and brick red and pale brown sand. He pinched a little of the mix and put it in his palm. The smell made him a little dizzy. "What is all this?"

She just looked at it, her gnarled hands loose at her sides. The radio poured out a chipper little salsa piece, heavy on the trumpet, and helplessly, Thomas picked out the medals, the lengths of gold braid, the broken bottle, a small plastic can of incense with a label that read, INCIENSO DEL ESPIRITU—INDIO PODEROSO BENDICION AL HOGAR. Spiritual Incense—Powerful Indian house blessing. The pile of sand suddenly made sense. "Chimayó dirt?" he asked.

She nodded, staring balefully at the mess.

"We'll get you some more. We'll drive down today if you want." A bag of ground red chiles bled into the piles of dirt and incense. He rescued it. "Do you have some more of this?"

Her eyes narrowed and she raised her old, sharp eyes to his face. "Was it *La Diabla* on the phone?"

He hated for her to call Nadine that, but nothing he'd

said had dissuaded her. He nodded, fingering the piles of charms in his palm. "What d'you want me to do with these, eh?"

She scowled, looking suddenly tiny and old and uncertain as she stared at them, her brow furrowed and pained. "Put 'em down."

"You want me to drive you down to Chimayó?"

Thunder shuddered through the sky and Placida jumped. "No," she said harshly. "No. Put them down, and go. Go. Out of my kitchen."

It didn't seem like the time to say it was his kitchen. Thomas put the medals down in a pile on his table, feeling sand sticking to the lines in his palms. He brushed at it, then backed out of the room. "I'll go down to Rosa's café for my breakfast. Tell anyone who calls to reach me there."

"Good. Go."

The phone rang as he left the room, but Thomas didn't bother to wait for it. He knew it would be Nadine and he didn't want to talk to her. He fled into the rain, the smell of Chimayó chile and dirt and rose-scented incense filling the truck as he started it and drove through the morning gray to Rosa's café.

The rain plagued Joy Loggia, too, as she stood miserably beneath the eaves of school, wondering if she should call her grandmother to come get her. It wasn't a heavy rain, just a slow, soft kind of grayness that would creep under the collar of her coat and down her back in a particularly icky way. But she didn't really want to see her grandmother right now. She was grumpy and her period had started during second hour, which meant she had to use the lumpy, thick pads they sold in the school machines, and feel yucky all day. Her grandmother would be all nice, but she'd fuss and Joy didn't feel like being fussed over.

Thunder rolled through the valley, low and deep, and Joy glared at the sky. Why didn't her mother have a driver's license like normal mothers?

The thought made her feel guilty, which made her chest ache, and that made her even more mad. It wasn't her fault her mom had lost her license, but who was paying the price today?

"Hey, girl. 'Sup?" Maggie, skinny and big-eyed, came up beside her. She had her notebook clasped close to her chest, like always. Her hair, long, long, long, curled all over in the wet, making her look like one of the dolls April collected. Maggie even had the pretty red mouth like those dolls. All she needed was a red flamenco dress.

"Hey," Joy said, and some of the irritation left her nerves. "What're you doing?"

"Nothin'. Wanna come to my house this afternoon? My mom's working." She lifted an eyebrow wickedly. "She has cigarettes there."

She scowled at the sky. "I guess you don't have a ride, either?"

"Nah. It'll be all right, though. We'll just get wet. No big deal." She shrugged, cocked her head. "C'mon."

"Ugh. I don't know. I started. No tampons. Maybe I oughtta just go home."

"My mom's got a tea from the *bruja* that'll make you feel better." She smiled, tugged on Joy's arm. "C'mon."

Joy liked being with Maggie. She liked even just looking at her. It was amazing that Maggie had no idea that she was one of the most beautiful girls in the entire school. The other girls knew it, and all the guys, but Maggie was just lost inside her head somewhere and didn't pay attention to the rest of the world. Joy didn't know why she liked that so much, but she did. It was easy to be around her.

Tucking her chin close to her chest, she followed Maggie on to the little road that led toward their houses. A mile away. "The rain is *cold* here."

"Nah, it's not cold!" She flung out her hands, and tossed back her head to let the rain fall on her face. "You'll see. Winter is cold. Snow is cold. This is nice."

"I can't help it if I have southern blood."

Maggie laughed. "Girl, you are *so* grouchy!"

"And you are too cheerful. Did something happen today?"

A car drew up beside them, with a guy around twenty driving. "Magdalena," he said, glaring at her, "what are you doing in the rain?"

"Ricky! When did you come home?" She danced up to the car and gave him a hug. "My mom know yet?"

He looked over Maggie's shoulder to Joy, lifting his chin in greeting.

"Hi," Joy said back. Her heart sped up a little. His eyes were long, shaped like cat eyes, and dark.

"I got in last night," he said. "You guys want a ride?"

Maggie laughed, light and girlish. "Joy's been crying all the way from the school about how cold it is, so I guess. This is my uncle Ricky," she said. "He's my dad's youngest brother."

Joy went around the car and climbed into the back-seat. It smelled like aftershave.

"Sorry," he said. "I drove from San Diego. It's a mess." He reached around and pushed some clothes to one side. Joy saw that his hand was dark and smooth, and wondered what he'd been doing in California.

"It's all right," she said.

He inclined his head. "What's with the hair?"

Joy flushed, touching it self-consciously. "Just something I did to piss off my dad the senator."

He grinned, and her heart flipped for real. His teeth were big and white in his angled face. "You'd be cuter as a blond."

"Mind your own business, *Tío*," Maggie said, slamming the door. "I like it."

"Yeah, well, you're a girl."

Joy wondered how old he was, all the way to Maggie's house, which wasn't really very far in the car. She thought he would come in with them, but he didn't. "Tell your mom I'll come over after a while. Got stuff to do." He looked directly at Joy. "Nice to meet you, Girl with Wrong Hair."

"Joy," she said.

He smiled with one side of his mouth. "I like that. See ya, Joy." He drove off.

Maggie laughed. "Oooh, Ricky was flirting with you big time, girl!"

"I'm sure he flirts with everybody."

"He does," she said, and Joy felt pricked. "But he still thought you were cute."

"He's old, Maggie. Way older than us."

She made a noise. "Nineteen, that's all. He had to go to San Diego to help his sister. Her husband is in the Navy and she's pregnant with twins and had to stay in bed. They wouldn't even let her fly home, can you imagine?"

Joy shook her head, still feeling strangely light. Nineteen wasn't that old. Not at all. She'd be sixteen in December.

They went inside and Maggie made Joy a cup of tea that smelled of cinnamon, then they went upstairs to Maggie's room. It was a funny house, tall and narrow and kind of dark, but Maggie's room was under the eaves and had a bunch of windows. They opened them all up and lit cigarettes. "My mom never notices because she smokes, you know," Maggie said, blowing smoke outside to the damp day.

"Better safe than sorry. Would she get mad if she knew?"

A quick shift of a shoulder. "I dunno." Her face brightened and she tapped Joy's knee. "But you know what? I think there's this guy who might, like, bring her out of it. He's the *bruja*'s grandson or something."

The tea gave Joy a sense of calm and well-being, what April would have called a zenlike calm. The smoke added to the sense of floating. All the pressure drained right out of her neck, pooling harmlessly on the floor at her feet. "You're matchmaking them, then?"

"Not exactly." Maggie stared across the fields. "I'm not sure how, you know?"

"Mmmm." Joy didn't necessarily think matchmaking was all it was cracked up to be. But she thought about her mom. "I think my mom has a new guy. She got all silly about him the other night."

"D'you ever wish your parents would get back together?"

"No *way*. My dad is such a jerk, I even wish my stepmom would get rid of him."

"How's he a jerk?"

Joy smoked for a minute, torn. She'd never really talked about this before and it made her feel disloyal or something. "He has a girlfriend." Saying it out loud made her feel kind of sick to her stomach.

"Oh, yuck. Did you see her?"

"No. He's pretty careful."

"So how do you know? Maybe it just seems like it."

Joy had tried to tell herself the same thing for months.

"No. He talks to her on the phone and meets her in other cities when he travels for business. He's been seeing her a really long time, too, like five years."

Maggie looked sad. "Does your stepmom know?"

That was the worst of all. "I don't think so. He's really careful." She tossed the butt out the window and fell back on the pillows. "April, my stepmom, is rich and she's like old southern money, so he needs her. This other person is just a nobody in some small town."

"Ew. How can he be so mean?"

Joy shook her head. "He did the same thing to my mom. He cheated on her and made everybody think she was a drunk and then he took her to court and left her for his girlfriend." She opened her eyes with a bitter smile. "Who was April."

"What a drag."

"Yeah." She sat up suddenly, embarrassed that she'd said so much. "Your room is great. Is that the Virgin of Guadalupe?"

Maggie nodded. "It was in my dad's car when he wrecked. She didn't do such a good job, but he loved that statue, so I brought it in here."

The statue, about twelve inches high, sat on top of Maggie's dresser with a bunch of other stuff—a candle holder and a box with glitter all over it and a shrine covered with glitter and roses. Joy couldn't make out the picture inside and stood up to get a better look. It was a black-and-white magazine picture of Tupac Shakur, his head down, his chest bare and showing all of his tattoos, his hands outstretched. A dollar bill with "Tupac Is Alive" written on it was glued to the bottom of the shrine. "Hey, I've seen these," Joy said, "these kits to make shrines for dead rock stars. Never saw one for Tupac, though. Where'd you get it?"

"It's not a kit," Maggie said, and she looked offended. "I made it myself, from things around here."

"Sorry, I mean, I just thought . . ."

Maggie inclined her head, the big dark eyes getting shiny and soft, and touched her index finger to the arch over the picture. "The day of my dad's funeral, my mom made me go to the store. It was really hot and I didn't want to walk, but she made me go get some ice for all the people coming over. That dollar was in my change."

Joy said, "Wow."

"It seemed like my dad was telling me something, that he was telling me to look for Tupac, you know?" She lifted her chin. "You probably think that's stupid."

"No," Joy said, and meant it. "I believe in that stuff, messages and all that. It sounds like you and your dad were really close. If he wanted to talk to anybody, it would probably be you, right?"

The shiny tears in Maggie's eyes welled up and spilled over, rushing over her smooth face in a streak of black eyeliner. "That's exactly what I thought." She turned back to the shrine, picked up some matches and lit a candle in front of it. "I want my dad to tell my mom that it's okay, too."

Joy took her time taking a new cigarette out of the pack. She didn't want it, exactly, but it wasn't like she had a chance to smoke at home and it was something to do to keep her hands and eyes busy. It seemed important not to say the wrong thing right this minute. When she fussed with the cigarette and got it going, she blew out a lungful of smoke and said, "So do you think Tupac is alive, like they say?"

Maggie took a new cigarette out, too, and lit it. She held it like an old hand, like she'd been smoking twenty years. "I don't know. Not really, I guess, but then why did I get that bill from my dad? Maybe I should be trying to find out for real."

"Maybe." Joy grinned. "It's something to do, anyway, right? Better than school."

They laughed at that, made a joke about one of their teachers, and then there was a slamming of a door downstairs. "Oh, shit!" Maggie whispered, and threw the cigarette out the window, tossed the pack under her bed and started waving her hand in the air. Joy followed suit, ducking and laughing when Maggie picked up a bottle of perfume and sprayed it all around.

"Magdalena!" her mother cried. "Come down. I have something to show you."

"Be right there!" She paused, as if listening, and said to Joy. "She sounds good today. I'm glad you can meet her."

Downstairs, Joy saw where Maggie got her looks. This was the thing about New Mexico that was different from Atlanta for *real*, the way women were beautiful. In Atlanta, everybody was into being a lady, like they'd just left a plantation tea. Around here, beautiful meant sexy or, sometimes, athletic. Maggie's mom was in the sexy category. She had long hair and even though she was wearing a business suit, there was some chest showing, and her nails were long and red.

"Hi," she said to Joy. "I'm Sally."

"This is Joy, Mom. I told you about her."

Sally hugged Maggie. "Look what I have." She held out her hand, and cradled in her palm was a little pillow of fabric. "Mrs. Ramirez made it for me, a special charm."

"Oh! Were you at her house today? Was her grandson around?"

"Yeah. She gave him one, too. Why?"

Maggie examined the packet very closely, then cut Joy a glance. "I just thought he was kinda cute for an old guy, that's all."

Sally grinned, touched her daughter's head. "Are you matchmaking, *h'ita*?"

"Nope." She put the packet back in her mom's hand. "We're gonna go to the store. Bye."

Joy paused. "Somebody named Ricky came by. He said he would see you later."

"Oooh," Maggie said, laughing. "Joy liked him, I think!"

"No, I didn't. I was just being polite."

Sally touched her arm. "Magdalena teases everybody she likes. Don't let her bother you. Come back, huh? Have supper with us some night."

"I will," Joy said, then Maggie was pulling her along, out into the rain, where she danced lightly on the porch and gave Joy a happy smile.

Milagros, or miracles, are small symbolic articles used to petition the saints for miracles. Someone who has a broken leg, for example, will offer a leg. Someone who has been unlucky in love offers a heart. Someone who has a sick or lost cow will offer a cow. Milagros are spiritual, magical, and full of powerful energy. In the Mexican Catholic church, one will often see statues of saints with their robes covered with the tiny offerings placed on the saint to ask for help or to express gratitude for a miracle.

Ten

Fridays were Luna's short day. She left work at noon to do her weekly shopping. As was her habit, Kitty picked her up, popping open the trunk when she saw Luna dragging a very full cart. She started to get out, but Luna waved her back. "No sense in both of us getting soaked!" She pulled her collar close to her neck to shield against the drizzle, and loaded groceries into the trunk. There were the usual items that were too heavy to carry on her daily walks—bags of potatoes and oranges and apples, since they were on special this week; olive oil and orange juice and two gallons of milk. She'd also really stocked up on meats to freeze, and frozen veggies and pizzas, and things like frozen waffles and bagels Joy could fix for snacks after school or late at night or for late breakfasts on the weekends. She ate lots of eggs, so Luna took home an extra dozen to boil so they'd be in the fridge, ready to go whenever she was hungry. Kitty said, "My goodness!" and patted Luna's shoulder. "I can see you've got a teenage girl in the house. Lord, the two of you nearly bankrupted me, I swear."

They stopped by Wal-Mart, where she picked up the rest of the school supplies Joy needed—a store of pencils and pens, extra spiral notebooks, a box to hold supplies for an art class—as well as the sundry paper products every household needed. It was always cheaper to stock up at Wal-Mart, much as the locals had protested when it was built, and it was a very long hike from her house.

"Do you want to have lunch?" Kitty asked.

"No, thanks. I think I need a little quiet time, actually."

"Perfectly understandable." She turned smoothly into the driveway. "Teenagers are noisy, aren't they?"

Luna kissed her cheek. "Thanks, Mom."

She put things away and cleaned up a little bit, running the vacuum and tackling the bathroom, gaining a rather motherly glow over the full larder and tidy home that would greet her daughter. In truth, she'd forgotten how much she liked that part of marriage—taking care of things, making a home.

By the time she finished her chores, she still had an hour of quiet time before Joy arrived home from school. The wet, gray day made her want a very special cup of coffee, and she took out her small French press and put the kettle on to boil. While it was heating, she measured out three-quarters Fancy Bourbon Santos and one-quarter Mexican Pluma Altura beans and ground them coarsely. When the water was almost ready to boil, she poured it over the beans in the press and stirred them with a chopstick she kept for the purpose, then let the mix brew for five minutes. When it was finished, she poured the coffee into her favorite oversize cup, painted with cats, and feeling luxurious, carried it into her "art" room.

The room, a strip of glassed-in porch behind the bed-rooms, held the washer and dryer at one end, her craft supplies at the other. The floor was plain, ancient linoleum, and windows ran side by side all the way around two walls. It was an especially lovely place on a rainy day like this, the sound pattering lightly against the glass, the clouds softening the light and granting a sense of coziness. Through the windows to the east, ris-ing above the scrub oak, showed a strip of Taos Moun-tain, his head buried in pillows of gray.

It wasn't, contrary to Allie and Elaine's recent nag-ging, the room of a real artist. More like the collection of a craft magpie. There was a cabinet filled with vari-ous kinds of paint, mostly acrylic, and brushes; plastic baskets of beads and feathers and even rocks she found on walks. One basket held nothing but *milagros*, the tiny cast metal things in shapes of fish or eyes or arms or whatever, used for all kinds of ceremonies and prayers and blessings. Another contained Barbie doll parts—shoes and belts and other accessories, but also spare arms and legs and torsos. There were whole dolls, too, but she wasn't interested in small work today.

Taking a smock out of the cupboard, an old work shirt now covered with every splash of paint she'd ever used, she put it on over her jeans, then carried a small bucket of selected paints—reds, oranges, pinks, and black—to a round metal table that would eventually complement the Virgin of Guadalupe metal chair on her porch. The table had a rose with a bleeding heart at the middle, the painting Kitty thought was so creepy. Luna inclined her head, disagreeing once again. It was lush. It was bloody and vivid, but not creepy.

Dipping her brush into a particularly intense metallic pink, Luna felt the pressure on the back of her neck give way suddenly. She hadn't discovered the whole craft thing until she was in recovery. Until then, she'd had no time to devote to it, and privately thought crafts were the desperate productions of women who had no meaning in their lives.

How life loved to play tricks! The early weeks and months of recovery had driven her insane with boredom, and in Kitty's sewing room one day, she found an unpainted plaster statue of a pair of children in a garden, and all the paints that went with it. Kitty set her up in the basement and Luna spent the next two days engrossed.

At peace.

There was something so calming about it, the small movements, the tight focus, the concentration and the colors. Contrary to popular belief, most alcoholics were control freaks, and that small, simple control of *something* was very healing.

So Luna and Kitty took to wandering craft stores, and Luna tried nearly everything they offered at least once. Anything that required too much close work ended up making her more irritable, rather than less; she rejected cross-stitch and miniatures for that reason. Kitty suggested she stick with paint-related things, and Luna tried decoupage, more ceramics, even some floral watercolors, but it was finally furniture that captured her. Well, and the Barbie dolls, but that had been a hobby for a long, long time. Several, in various stages of dress and completion, looked down benignly as she worked this afternoon in the quiet rain, as if approving the fact that she was close to finishing the table. So was she. Working on Joy's room had taken most of the summer, and although it had been very well received—and to be quite honest, she was inordinately proud of it—it wasn't something she could display. And despite her protests to the contrary, she loved people to look at her paintings and dolls and admire them.

From her perch on an unfinished chair, rickety but full of potential, Therapist Barbie said, *Do you think you might be an artist, then?*

Luna paused, brush in the air. Considered.

Growing up in a place like Taos, where every other person you met was an artist, made anyone think twice about any calling she might have. Or think she might have. Artists loved it, loved the support they found among one another, and even bad artists were unusually sensitive to shadows and light and the brilliance of color. They came to Taos and fell in love, over and over, each one thinking they'd discovered something new. She'd seen Taos Mountain drawn, photographed, painted in oils, watercolors, acrylics and tempera, sketched in charcoal and pastels, even crayon.

But so much of it was *bad* art—things people had slaved over, thinking they were original and fresh and real, and they weren't. They were just more recycled adobe churches and adobe doorways and quaint Pueblo renderings. Or more kitschy folk art, she acknowledged with a flush.

But the colors—how could a person escape them? They permeated everything. Growing up, Luna had not understood how the pink of Guadalupe's robes and the turquoise windowsills and the flash of dark summer thunderstorms and the drenching of sunlight, day after day, influenced her. In discovering crafts, she could let that color out, here and there, for her own pleasure, with no ego whatsoever involved.

No, she wasn't an artist.

But that didn't mean she couldn't play. There was something so sensual about it, about painting the plump, juicy rounds of a crimson drop of blood, something so transporting about losing herself in the curve of the brush against the surface. It was the only time she could stop thinking. She became the colors, the light, a prism through which something could be reflected, however poorly.

Delicately, she dotted Lowrider pink into the turn of a petal. Sometimes it was poorly done. But this was a good one.

Joy came in around four and carried a Coke into the room. "Mom, I wish you'd think about selling some of this stuff. It's really cool, and I don't think you're seeing it."

"Takes all the fun out of it." She wiped a smear of paint from her wrist with a rag. "How was your day?"

"Okay." They talked about Joy's art teacher, and the math teacher, whom she liked and had told her she should move up one grade, to Algebra II, and the biology teacher who was too young and not in control of the classroom, and the English teacher with a mellifluous voice—Joy really used the word *mellifluous*—who had read one of Joy's friend Maggie's poems out loud. "It was really, really good, Mom. I swear. So, so, so sad, with these great images in it—sometimes it seems like I can see everybody else's talents, things they can't even see, but I don't have any of my own."

"We all have talents, love."

Joy raised a shoulder, took a long swallow of Coke. "Well, I'm smart," she said, her left leg swinging over the edge of an armchair. "I'm very good with numbers and I can speak up, but I don't have any artistic talent of any kind. No music, no art, no writing, nothing. I'm okay at all of them, but not really good at any of them."

Luna grinned, and touched up the edge of a petal with

a thin brush filled with black paint. "Gosh, then, you might be a business whiz or something unusable like that, huh?"

She rolled her eyes. "Yeah, I'm such a business type, can't you tell?"

"Nothing wrong with business, Joy. There are business angles to creative work, too, you know. Maybe you can find something to do in that realm—run a gallery, or be a talent scout, or an agent. God knows artists need honest people in their corners. Most of them are not very good at that end of their work, and they suffer for it."

Joy turned her lips down at the corners. "Hmm. I never thought about it before. I wonder how somebody gets into those kinds of things."

"I don't know." Luna put her brush down and wiped her hands. "But you're in a good place to find out. Stop in and talk to the gallery owners. I think there are some literary agents in town, and I know there's a publisher or two. Gotta be dozens of people who'd be more than happy to share their experiences with you."

The phone rang and Joy leapt up to answer it. The phone was right around the corner and Luna heard her bright, expectant hello, then a long silence. "Dad," she said. "Dad, can you listen to—"

Luna felt that thud of dread, low in her belly, and thought of the freezer full of food. She raised her chin. Joy had gone silent, and Luna could hear the sound of Marc's voice coming over the line. She stirred her brush in a jar of water, watching thin clouds of paint disperse, like blood from a shark bite into the ocean.

Joy said forcefully, "Dad, listen to me!"

Luna stood, ready to intervene if necessary.

A complaint, then Joy said, "You know, I kept calling in the evenings, hoping to just have a conversation with you, and you couldn't even be bothered to talk to me for three minutes, now all of a sudden you want me to come home and live with you? *No!*"

She listened, then made a mewling protest. "That's not fair, Dad! I don't know how you can be so mean!" She paused, then, "It is not for my own good, it's for *your* own good, and you're mean and I hate you and I will never live with you again, no matter what you do."

Luna capped the paints spread out around her, a pulse of anger starting to pound in her temples. Joy started to cry. "Please, Dad, don't do this. Just let me live here. You have everything good out there already."

She started crying, harder. Luna asked quietly, "What's going on?"

Joy covered her eyes and handed the phone over wordlessly, running into her bedroom.

"Marc," Luna said into the receiver, "what just happened?"

"I want her home, Lu. She doesn't belong out there."

"You don't have any right to make that choice for her."

"That's where you're wrong. I'm her father and that's what I want for her, and since you—her mother— haven't been, shall we say, entirely *present* in her life, I'll thank you to stay out of it."

Luna laughed shortly. "We have an official custody arrangement that's now in my favor, Marc, and I made it formal because I suspected something like this might happen. I thought it would take longer than a week or two for you to change your mind, but I knew you'd start trying to control her the minute she left."

"Oh, please, spare me the melodrama."

Luna closed her eyes. Took a breath. "Stop hurting her, Marc. Think about someone besides yourself for once." She hung up, and went to her daughter's room.

Joy was facedown on her bed, crying in the hysterically broken way only a teenage girl could pull off. Luna sat down beside her, touched her back. "Honey, don't take it like that. Your father . . . is just who he is. You can't change him."

She flung her body over. "He always wants to control me! You know what he threatened on the phone? To take away my allowance! Just because he changed his mind?"

"It's rotten. It is." She folded her hands. "Maybe I can make it up. What's he sending?"

"No, that's not fair. He's supposed to take care of this. He promised me, and he's let me down so much, he can't get away with this."

Luna frowned. She chose her words carefully. "Joy, why are you so angry with him? I know he's kind of a jerk, but that hasn't changed much. Is there something you aren't telling me?"

Joy moaned and turned her face away, curling her body into a little comma. When Luna reached for her, she flinched away, and a sick feeling went through her. "He doesn't—"

"Oh, God, no." Joy turned over. "Nothing like that. He doesn't molest anybody, not me or anybody else. And he isn't a secret heroin addict, either. He's just a liar and a cheat and I hated finding that out about him, and I thought, all this time, that I was at least the one person he loved and cared about, but I found out now that I don't matter any more than anyone else." She pressed her face into the pillow. "Leave me alone," she said in a muffled voice.

"None of this is your fault, Joy," she said, then left her alone, closing the door gently behind her.

It was close to five, and she was supposed to meet Thomas at seven. She picked up the phone and dialed the number from the note stuck to the fridge. *"Hola?"* answered a woman. Probably Placida.

"Can I speak to Thomas, please?"

"He's not home. Call back later."

"Wait, wait," she cried, hoping Placida heard before she hung up. "Can you give him a message for me, or is there a cell phone I can reach him on?"

There was a sound of movement at the other end of the line. Then Thomas's voice said, "Hello?"

"Hi, Thomas. This is Lu McGraw. I'm so glad I caught you."

"Hi." He chuckled, and she could hear rapid, annoyed Spanish in the background. "She lied to you. I was sitting right at the table with her."

"She hates me!"

"Nah. You have to get to know her. What's up?"

"I have to cancel. My ex called and my daughter is really upset and I think I'd like to take her to a movie or something. Can we reschedule?"

"How's tomorrow?"

A sense of relief passed through her. "Sure." Then she remembered. "Maybe not. I have to go to a wedding reception at the VFW. Unless you'd want to put in an appearance with me and then we can go somewhere else?"

"I'm game. Should I pick you up?"

"No, I'll be at my mother's house. I'll meet you there at say . . . eight o'clock?"

"All right." A soft pause. She could imagine him standing in a kitchen, with the smell of food cooking all around him, maybe still in his work clothes. A whisper went over her skin. "I'm really looking forward to it, Luna."

"Me, too."

Thomas had no religion to speak of, not his father's or his mother's, though both had shown him their ways—

his mother taking him to Mass, his father the basics of sweat and earth. Thomas carved saints out of respect for the tradition, and he had built a sweat lodge because it was healthy and healing and he liked the dark, moist heat. And there was something about the lodge that made a man forget, disconnect from his life and his worries, give them over to the ... whatever. Great Spirit. Universe. Something. He had a sense of things being out there, but was never quite sure what.

Since his date had cancelled out on him, he decided it was a good time to sweat. He piled round river rocks into the pit outside the lodge, and built a hot fire over it, liking the look of the sparks flying into the gray afternoon. It took several hours, and he tended it between other duties.

It had been a long day, running errands for his grandmother, trying to make arrangements to have her house gutted and finished so it could be sold. He intended to have her live with him now. She was too old to be on her own.

Something he hadn't told her yet. Today, they'd gone to her house and collected some boxes of her things, and he'd been alarmed at the ennui that had come over her in those familiar rooms. She picked things up and put them back down, like a ghost brushing over the accoutrements of a life now gone. In the end, she'd only taken her clothes, unable to figure out what else she wanted with her. When they got back to his house, she had napped for hours.

She was so old. He didn't know exactly how old, but she told stories sometimes about riding a wagon into Santa Fe, and the days when Indians sold their wares alongside the road. Some of that had likely gone on into the thirties. But Placida also remembered Pancho Villa's raid in New Mexico, and he figured that put her into her early nineties at the minimum. It made him tired to imagine being so old. Once he'd made a comment about feeling too old to start again after Nadine left him, and she shook her head. "You don't know how many lives you lead in eighty years."

He was on life number three or four, he figured. The young man who warred; the broken one who came home to New Mexico, to Taos and his roots; the wiser, calmer adult man who became a husband who created a home and stability for a family that never came. Now, he'd been forced to start another new life, without the family he'd prepared himself for.

As he puttered around the big old house, feeding the dog and cat, washing dishes so his grandmother wouldn't do it later, sweeping the porch, tending the fire, listening to Tiny talk in a low, intent voice to his wife, he wondered how pathetic he was for wanting his old granny here with him, for adopting strays and lost men into his house so he wouldn't be alone. He paused to look out over the vista, down the hill into town, and then to the mountains beyond, wishing with a sudden sharp yearning for the children he didn't have. He had wanted them so much, sons and daughters spilling out of the rooms, filling the halls with their squabbling and laughter. They had tried and tried and tried, he and Nadine, and she had not conceived with him. Only with his brother.

She had left a message on his machine, an urgent plea to call her. He'd listened to it, then erased it. He was too tired to listen to her histrionics.

Behind him in the living room, Tiny cried out something in protest, and Thomas looked over his shoulder in concern. There was a bang through the open window. Thomas put aside the broom and went inside to check on him. Tiny sat on the couch, his head in his hands.

"Let it go, man," Thomas said. "Go take a shower. You can sweat it out."

It was nothing fancy, a small hut built of willow and canvas, with a traditional blanket over the door. Under cover of darkness, with little spots of spitting rain hitting their flesh, Thomas and Tiny stripped to their skins and ducked into the darkness. Thomas scattered sweet grass over the rocks and ladled water over them. The scent filled his head, traveled on steam to his sinuses and lungs.

The rule was silence or song, and Tiny had had some trouble with that from the beginning. Tonight, he sat resentfully across from Thomas, his body gleaming with sweat, rage coming off him in hot little explosions. Thomas said, again, "Let it go, man."

"I can't." He bowed his head. "If I think of her with another guy, it feels like somebody's clawing my heart out."

"I know."

"Goddamn it, bro, how d'you do it? And it was your own brother!"

Thomas sprinkled water over the burning hot rocks, building up steam. When it curled down from the ceiling to envelope them, he closed his eyes. He saw blips of himself, wild with rage, drunk in the White Horse and trying to pick a fight. "It didn't happen all at once. I felt the same way you do. Like I could kill somebody."

Tiny slammed a fist to his skinny, hairless chest. "If she's out there fuckin' around, what's that say to my kids, huh?"

"It's a rumor, Tiny. You don't know she's doing anything."

"She's a cunt, man. She is. She'll do anything."

The brittle violence was in his voice. Thomas knew the sound, knew how that could feel, shards of glass ripping along a man's nerves. "Don't," Thomas said. "If you love her, respect her."

"What about her respecting me?"

"She does. She loves you, too, Tiny. You love each other, and you made these kids together, and you've had good times." The steam and heat burned through the air, along their skin. Thomas wiped his face, leaning his back against the twiggy wall. "You've only got three more weeks of class and then the restraining order can be lifted. Don't do anything to screw that up."

Tiny did not speak. That was the thing about sweating, Thomas thought. Even against your will, it could take away the darkness sometimes. It leaked away through your pores. "I love her, man, that's all. I just never loved anybody else like this, never."

"Love is a good thing."

Another long quiet. "Yeah," he said, at last. "Yeah, love is good."

The weather was gorgeous Saturday night, so Luna told Kitty not to worry about picking them up—she and Joy would walk. Tucking her going-out clothes into a small canvas bag she carried over her shoulder, the delicate gold sandals and the white skirt that showed off her one really good feature, tanned, strong legs she gained by walking everywhere. The weather was cool and sweet, light with the coming of fall. "You've never spent a winter here," she said to Joy. "Think you'll like snow?"

"Are you kidding? I'm dying to ski. How often can I go, do you think?"

"I'll pay for once a month. The rest is in your court."

"That's all? Once a month? How am I supposed to get money?"

"Hmm." Luna pretended to think about it seriously. "I know! Get a job?"

But Joy was honestly annoyed. Maybe for the first time since she'd been here. "Doing what?" She put a little hit on the "what," a little gesture with her head Luna thought of as African American. "Washing dishes? Working at McDonald's? No one will *hire* a fifteen-year-old, for your information."

"Trust me, you can find work here. The tourist trade needs bodies. I'll be glad to put out some feelers to see what I can turn up. What would you like to do?"

Joy huffed. "I don't want to get all dirty with other people's slimy dishes, that's for sure. Or their food."

"Okay, retail, then." She frowned. "You'll probably have to change your hair back, or at least dye it just one color."

"No way!" She shook her head. "I can't believe I have to work to go skiing."

Luna laughed softly. "It's expensive, sweetie. Sorry. I just don't have it—and frankly, it won't hurt you in the least to work for the luxuries you want."

"Whatever. I don't want to talk about this right now."

"All right." She let the subject go, breathing in the evening. "I love the smell of fall coming," she said cheerfully. "Skiing aside, you have a lot to look forward to. There's a lot about winter that's magical."

"I guess." Joy tossed hair out of her eyes. "Are you planning to *ever* get a driver's license again?"

Good aim, said Barbie.

A scritch of nicotine craving broke on Luna's nerves, but she took a breath and said, "Probably. Is it causing you a problem?"

"Duh. I had to walk home in the rain the other day."

"Why didn't you call Grandma? She wants you to call under those circumstances."

"I didn't feel like being nice."

"Is that anything like now?"

She scowled at Luna. "I just think it would be sort of interesting not to have to walk everywhere all the time. It gets old."

Something to think about, getting the license restored. But the idea made her feel a little woozy for reasons she didn't bother to examine. The last time she'd driven a car . . . well, it hadn't been pretty. "I'll think about it."

They walked up the long, twisting hill to Kitty's house in silence. The sun was close to setting, and Kitty had lit a dozen hanging paper lanterns in the courtyard. The Beatles spilled through the open door, *Ob-la-di*.

"I wish she'd get some new musical tastes," Joy said.

"Okay, that's it." Luna grabbed Joy's arm. "What's with you tonight? Are you mad about me going out? Are you mad about your dad? What? You will not spend the entire evening flinging those barbs and trying to hurt people, do you understand me?"

Joy tossed that mass of hair around, adopting the long-suffering-teen expression every parent comes to know so intimately. "Fine," she said, as if it had been Luna, not her, who had been throwing darts.

"What's going on, Joy?"

Her head dropped, her hair falling forward around her face. "Sorry," she said. "I talked to April and the boys today and I just missed them all of a sudden. It's different here and sometimes that's hard. I miss my cat. I miss my friends. I miss things just being the way they always have been, even though that's why I wanted to change." She tucked her hair behind her ear, the black fingernails looking stark against her pale white skin. "It's not you, okay? I want to be here. But sometimes, I want April and the boys here, too."

Hard to hear that. Even after eight years, it was hard to think one nice thing about the woman who'd settled in to take care of her daughter and hadn't done such a bad job of it. Hard to admit to herself that she still wished for Joy to hate April. Which made Luna a not very nice person, and she hated that. "Not your dad?"

"No. I hate him. Especially now. I hated him before I came, too, but now he's just trying to get his own way like always and that's just mean." Raising miserable eyes, she said, "You know he couldn't even talk to me for five minutes on the phone today? I'm really mad at him about this and he needed to respect me enough to listen, and he wouldn't. He just blew me off. I hate that."

"I'm sorry, honey."

"It's not your fault."

The heavy glass door swung open. "I thought I heard voices," Kitty said. "What're you two doing out here? We're waiting for you." There was an edge of annoyance to her voice. Very unusual.

"Sorry, Mom," Luna said. "We were talking about something important."

But Kitty just distractedly turned and click-clacked down the hall paved with saltillo tiles. "Hey Jude" came on the stereo, and a little alarm went off in Luna's head. Heart. "Jude" was a song that meant Kitty was thinking of her long-gone husband, or thinking about how to not miss him. It was hot-wired into Luna from a hundred nights and afternoons when Kitty played it, over and over, trying to make herself be less lonely. She didn't cry. She didn't fall to drinking martinis midafternoon. She didn't start beating her daughters. She just put on the Beatles and tried to be brave.

The next song would be "Let It Be" and that was a song that broke Luna's heart to smithereens each and every time.

As they came into the kitchen, Luna flashed a questioning look at her sister Elaine, who wore a blank expression.

She shrugged, obviously as aware as she that something weird was going on.

"I have something to tell you, girls," Kitty said. "Elaine, there's iced tea in the fridge; Luna, I made your coffee the way you like it." She poured a giant white mug of it and passed it across the butcher block island where they all settled on barstools beneath the softly pink light overhead. The coffee smelled rich and hot in the air, deep as night.

Luna tasted it. "Excellent, Mom."

"Joy, sweetie, what would you like? I bought some cherry Coke. Or some Pellegrino?"

"Oh, how did you know?"

Kitty winked one turquoise-limned eyelid. "I make it my business to know things."

Once the drinks were served—Kitty pouring a rather large martini, which was not completely unheard of but definitely underscored the strangeness of everything—Kitty took a sip and said, "Girls, I have news."

Luna exchanged a look with Elaine. "Okay, we know that part. What is the news?"

"It's about your father."

Luna felt like someone twisted her spine, just a little bit, at the very base. Sickening. "What?"

"I had a letter a couple of weeks ago," Kitty said. "It was from a lawyer who wanted to find out if I was the Kitty McGraw who was once Kitty Esquivel, married to Jesse. I didn't know what he wanted, but I called and left a message with the secretary, then forgot about it.

"This afternoon, he called back. Your father left us— all of us—a parcel of land up near Trinidad. There's also an offer on the table for it from a development company that wants to buy it immediately."

"Left it?" Luna echoed.

"For a lot of money?" Elaine asked.

"Yes," Kitty said to both of them. With a French-manicured hand, she lifted her martini and took a big gulp.

"He's dead, then," Luna said, a lump in her throat.

"Brilliant, Sherlock," Elaine said. "Not that it matters, since we haven't seen him in decades."

"We need to make a decision," Kitty said. "The lawyer is mailing me some paperwork by express mail, and we can look it over together."

"How much land?" Elaine asked.

"Four hundred acres."

Elaine chortled.

Kitty said dully, "I guess we need to see it before we decide."

Luna thought of the dreams of her father. No wonder. She'd probably been picking up on her mother's thought of him. "Mom," Luna said, putting a hand over Kitty's. "Are you okay?"

She made a noise, an aggrieved little *tsk*, and took a tissue out of her pocket to press against her mouth. "No," she said. "I . . . I'm . . . it's just not fair. All these years without a word? Now this? After he's *dead*?"

"Yeah," Elaine said. "If he had enough to buy all that land, he was doing just fine while we barely made it."

"He's dead," Luna said again. "Now we'll never know."

"Know what?" Elaine asked with annoyance.

Kitty said it for her. "Why he left."

Since music is a language with some meaning at least for the immense majority of mankind, although only a tiny minority of people are capable of formulating a meaning in it, and since it is the only language with the contradictory attributes of being at once intelligible and untranslatable, the musical creator is a being comparable to the gods, and music itself the supreme mystery of the science of man, a mystery that all the various disciplines come up against and which holds the key to their progress.

—CLAUDE LÉVI-STRAUSS

Eleven

After Kitty's initial announcement and the first flurry of discussion, they all sort of let it drop. Luna discovered her thoughts skittering toward the reality—he's dead!—then away, over and over. But she lost herself in the Saturday supper ritual. They made Belgian waffles with fresh strawberries, and she pigged out on a whole one piled high with freshly whipped cream, even though she'd promised herself she had to get serious about not eating anything too awful for a while. As it was, the jeans she was wearing were so tight around the waist that she had to undo the button halfway through the meal.

She wasn't wrong about the next cut from the Beatles—it was "Let It Be." Thankfully, that was the last one. Kitty seemed to snap out of it after that. She put on Janis Joplin and they ended up dancing barefoot in the living room to *Cheap Thrills*, Kitty shaking and shimmying all over the place in her good girdle and push-up bra. Elaine, Kitty, and Luna knew every single syllable, and beat, and had millions of years ago worked out the routines. Joy threw herself into it quite creditably, and with her red and black hair and fishnet shirt, looked more Janis-like than any of the rest of them. Luna grinned at her, and by Joy's wink, Joy knew it, too.

But it was Elaine who was always so amazing during these impromptu wild night sing-alongs. She often protested them because she was shy about her body and dancing, but in her secret heart, Elaine had always, always, always wanted to be a rock 'n' roll singer. Luna remembered the posters on their shared bedroom wall, remembered Elaine belting out songs from the radio at school recess, just to surprise and shock everyone with the immensity of her voice.

Luna didn't know exactly where the dream had gone—it seemed to slowly disappear as Elaine started gaining weight in her early teens, and was completely hidden by the time she graduated from high school, weighing 220—but every so often, it surfaced again. "Piece of My Heart" was guaranteed to bring out the blueswoman living deep inside Elaine. Luna and Kitty slowed, exchanging a glance. Luna shot a glance at Joy and lifted her chin to indicate Joy should watch her aunt as "Summertime"—a nice version, Luna thought, but nowhere close to the Louis Armstrong/Ella Fitzgerald masterpiece—finished.

Elaine was already there, her own heart readied by the intro of "Summertime." She'd slowed all the way down, and her eyes closed, her body swaying and grooving, and she was right on the beat, like her body became the guitars and the drums.

Then she lit the torch of her voice. It was a hard song to sing, rough and high, but Elaine got around that by dropping it an octave and letting her deep alto ring out like a gravel road.

When the CD went into "Turtle Blues," Kitty and Luna both reached for their drinks, knowing that Elaine was on now. She started to sing, deep and wild, "I ain't the kind of woman who'd make your life a bed of ease," and Joy stopped in her tracks. To stare.

Kitty and Luna grinned at each other. No one got Elaine. The church secretary in her bad, short perm, her hair the most dull color imaginable—that bland shade between blond and brown that's neither one—wearing a T-shirt with little glitter butterfly appliqués across the chest, a pair of ordinary, old-fashioned glasses on her face, singing the blues like her bones were made of them.

Of the three of them, Elaine was the most damaged. Kitty got through because she had girls to raise. Luna was warped, undeniably, but she had a certain faith in things that never did go away. Elaine just had a hell of a time believing in anything, except her Christianity, and sometimes Luna thought Elaine used religion like a shield, something to hide behind. She was so afraid, all the time. All the time.

And when her sister sang like this, Luna wanted to cry. Cry for lost chances, for things that would never be, but Joy didn't have all that baggage. At the end of the song, she said, "Aunt Elaine, I can't believe you can sing like that and you're not out there doing something with it."

Elaine just laughed, getting a drink of water. "It's just a game."

"No," Joy said, fiercely. "That's a *gift*."

Looking a little abashed, Elaine said, "Thank you, Joy."

"You don't waste gifts."

Elaine blinked. "I'm not wasting it. I sing in the choir."

"That's wasting it," Joy said. "You're not singing the blues at church, are you?"

"Well, not—"

"It's a sin to waste a voice like that," Joy said, and dashed away a tear. "And I'm mad at you that I'm nearly sixteen years old and you never even shared it with *me*." She shook her head. "Anyone want anything? I'm going to the kitchen."

"No, thanks."

Luna raised her eyebrows at Elaine. "And a little child should lead them."

"Don't be ridiculous."

Luna spied the clock, and slapped her hands together. "Oh, God! I have to go right now! Mom, call me a cab—I gotta get out of here, and there's no time to both change and walk."

Kitty perked up. "Do you have a *date*?"

"Kinda. What I don't have is time to talk about it much right this minute." She rushed into the bathroom to change her clothes, rubbing lotion on her bare legs beneath the white skirt, putting on some lipstick from her mother's gigantic store. "Mom!" she called around the corner, "can I borrow this burnt raisin lipstick?"

"Take whatever you want, darlin'." Kitty clicked down the hall. "What are you wearing? Oooh, I like the gold sandals. Nice with your tan. And what a fine rear end you've got these days, girl." Kitty came up beside her and they looked into the mirror. Luna peered at herself, focusing on the things she liked—her round dark eyes with a little gold eye shadow, her mouth that looked pretty good with the lipstick—rather than the ones she didn't, which were numerous. Wildly numerous. She put a hand on her lower belly. "Too tight? I've gained a little weight without the cigarettes."

"Sexy," Kitty pronounced.

Luna touched her hair, careful not to do too much to it since it was halfway behaving, just kind of ringlets instead of the wilderness of frizz it could sometimes become. "What should I do with my hair?"

"Not a thing." Kitty inclined her head. "You are beautiful, Luna McGraw, and don't you ever forget it." She slapped her on the butt. "Come on, what do you know? Stomach in, chest out, chin high, sugar. And what are you saying?"

Luna grinned, sucking in her belly, throwing back her shoulders. "What man in his right mind wouldn't want me?"

Kitty winked. "There you go." A horn from outside. "Have a good time, sweetie."

Thomas waited outside the VFW for Luna, listening to the music spilling out the doors. It was a Spanish band, young, with a dusky-voiced singer. The music stirred him up, made him pace as he waited, and he wished for some of the calm of the sweat back again. He'd sweated out the sorrow of the day, but that seemed to just leave room for anticipation.

She came in a cab, stepping out with her wild blond curls falling down around her face. She wore a white skirt that showed her powerfully muscled legs, and a plain white peasant blouse that framed her shoulders and neck perfectly. There was much to like about Luna McGraw, but as she came toward him tonight, luminous and a little shy, he fell into her big dark eyes. Fell in. Reached out for her before she even spoke, taking her neck and bending down to kiss her full on the mouth.

She kissed him back with a little sound, pressing her body into his, and he raised his head. "Hi."

"Hi." She smiled up at him. "You pulled your hair back."

"I can let it down."

She inclined her head. "No, maybe it's better up."

"Better how?"

"You know very well. That hair is dangerous."

Thomas chuckled. "Yeah?" he said, and reached around for the end of the braid to pull off the rubber band. "Do you have a comb?"

"No, leave it. It's all right."

He grinned and unwove the braid, combing his fingers through it. When he got to the top, he shook his head a little. "Okay?"

"Allow me." She took a comb from her purse and he turned to let her smooth it for him, liking the tentative feel of her hands skimming through his hair. "It's so long," she said, and her palm traveled the length of it. His skin rippled, nerves popping awake after a long sleep.

When she stopped, he turned, ready to make a small joke to ease the tension, but she had not entirely loosed his hair, and she wrapped it around her wrist and looked at him, tugging lightly to draw him down to her. "I'm trying to be a grown-up here, Thomas," she said, "but you are the sexiest man I think I've ever seen, and all I really want to do is touch you."

They slid into a pool of shadow by the wall and he pressed into her the way he'd been wanting to since the first time he saw her, feeling her thighs on the front of his. Her arms curled up around his neck, opening her breasts to his chest. Their mouths meshed, opened, and her hands moved on him, down his back, along his sides, then down his thighs, exploring. And he explored in return, touching her surprisingly small shoulders, the softness of breasts, her ribs and strong hips.

Then they stopped kissing and he braced himself on the wall and they rubbed hot and hard together, wordless, letting their bodies speak for them. Chest to chest, hip to hip, her hands on his back restless and smooth at once. He bent his head into her neck and put his hands around her fanny, pulling her tighter, sighing at the press of her mouth to his throat. He thought he should maybe take it somewhere else, but it was good like this. Good when she pressed upward into him, made a soft sound of regret. "I guess we oughtta go inside," he said.

"I'll be in major trouble with everyone if I don't put in an appearance," she said, sighing. "Hold that thought, though, huh?"

He leaned in and kissed her once more. "I promise."

"Wait," she said, and peered up at him, pulling a tissue out of her purse and handing it to him, then taking a mirror and lipstick out of the tiny thing herself. "Wipe your mouth or everyone will know." She stepped into a pool of light, reapplied her lipstick, smacked her lips together and gave him a bright wink. "Better?"

"Gorgeous," he said, the skin on the back of his neck tight. What a sexy thing that was, the way women put on lipstick. The way she did it. "Am I good?"

"Perfect." She held out her hand, and tucked the tissue back in her purse. "Let's go. No more kissing until we leave."

He took her hand. "This all right?"

"Yeah," she said. "This is really good."

The reception was in full swing—the tables crowded with people in dress clothes, the dance floor full of couples doing a basic two-step. Paper streamers and balloons decorated the walls, and at the head table, the bride and groom were tucked together like a pair of swans.

The wedding was for Luna's coworkers, but as soon as they walked in, people started talking to Thomas, of course. He nodded to one table, stopped and shook hands with a man at another, and waved at another. An older man with a friendly, if slightly boozy smile waved back cheerily. "That's my cousin Victor, there. He used to sing all over, but he's worn out now. He's a good man. Give you the shirt off his back." Thomas smiled down at Luna. "He'll ask you to dance."

"I don't dance very well."

"He won't care."

"Then I'll say yes."

He took her hand gently then, and Luna felt as if she'd surprised him in some way.

She loved walking through the room with him. Women eyed him. Men respected him. They looked at her differently—and she couldn't remember if any of her coworkers had seen her with any guy before. She didn't think so. "Let's go say hi to the bride and groom," she said, "Then we can find a place to sit down."

A voice came from the gloom to her right. "Lu!"

Peering through the clouds of cigarette smoke, she saw Jean at a table with several other people, including a properly brooding and beautiful Byronic sort with a three-day growth of beard and limpid dark eyes. She introduced him as Gary, and waited for Luna to introduce Thomas. She didn't. "We're going to say hi to Linda," Luna said, moving away. When they were out of earshot, she said, "Hope that didn't seem rude, but she's a gossip and a nosy girl and I don't want to share any more of my life with her than is absolutely necessary."

"That's cool."

They greeted the happy pair, then nabbed a tiny two-seater right on the edge of the dance floor when another couple vacated it. "What do you want to drink?" Thomas asked. "I'll get it."

"Ginger ale," she said. "And Thomas, don't avoid a beer or something because I don't drink, okay?"

"Sure?"

"Yes. I'm very well aware that not everyone is an alcoholic."

"It doesn't make you want it yourself, to sit with somebody who's drinking?"

"Sometimes," she admitted, and looked around the room. There were a lot of things about drinking she missed, and this was one of them—she'd loved settling into a warm, friendly drinking establishment to fall into the bottle with everyone else. "But that's my struggle, not yours, okay?"

She liked the respect in his dark eyes as he nodded.

What about tonight? Therapist Barbie said. *Aching for a tequila now? A nice way to blur the edges so you could sleep with him without excuses?*

It was a thought. It would make it easier and she really wanted him and worried about the consequences. But drinking not only dulled the worry, it dulled the experience, and *if* she slept with Thomas Coyote, she wanted to be fully cognizant of every single, blessed minute.

No, she didn't want a drink. Not tonight. But as she sat there waiting for Thomas to come back, the same could not be said for cigarettes. She watched a woman smoking at a table not far away. Watched, almost mesmerized as she inhaled, paused, let go of a breath-softened cloud of blue smoke. Luna's sinuses quivered.

"It gets easier," Thomas said, putting the drinks down.

"What?"

He chuckled. "Smoking. You were staring at that woman like she was a hypnotist."

"Busted." She grinned, shook her head. Glumly, she stirred her ginger ale with the tiny blue and red straws. "This ain't my first rodeo. I've quit so many times it's ridiculous."

Thomas spied someone across the room. "Damn."

Luna glanced over her shoulder. "What's wrong?"

"Do you know that woman? Angelica?"

"Sure. She's a cashier." Not a bad position in the hierarchy of grocery store work. "What's the matter?"

"It's her husband who lives with me."

"The one who—Oh." Luna winced, watching as the woman kissed a man next to her. "And I take it that's not the husband."

He shook his head, his mouth grim.

"You aren't responsible, Thomas."

"Yeah," he said. "I know." He shifted in his chair, putting his back to her.

Luna looked at the woman. She was a little overweight through the middle, and her shirt was tight, showing off a lot of cleavage at the top. Her eyes were heavily made up. The guy she was with was nothing spectacular, the kind of man who was once a pretty boy and now didn't have anything to fall back on.

A twinge of something went through Luna, a kind of yearning, like catching the scent of a particular moment in time. For the space of a few seconds, she was transported to a plain room with fans blowing from two different corners over a collection of women pouring their hearts onto the floor in a spill of beauty and hunger, longing and pain, laughter and healing. It was sharp and sweet, incredibly fierce. *I could help her.*

A man stopped by the table, thin and rugged as a

long-used rope. *"Cómo está su abuela?"* he asked, his fine brown hand on Thomas's shoulder.

Thomas answered in Spanish, a language Luna didn't speak, even though she knew she ought to. She could gather the gist of it—*she's fine, the house is not so good, who knows why these things happen.* The old man liked Thomas for taking care of his family the way he should. Things like that mattered around here.

When the man moved on, Thomas said, "I'm going to have her live with me. Take care of her."

"She's pretty old."

"Yeah. She remembers Pancho Villa's raid in New Mexico."

"Amazing." Luna sipped her ginger ale, imagining a bandit man with a big mustache and ropes of ammunition in a cross over his chest. "How romantic."

"She doesn't think so. She said once he was nothing but a petty criminal with a good imagination."

Luna laughed.

Thomas leaned in. "I love the way you laugh," he said, taking her hand.

"Thank you."

He cocked his head toward the dance floor. "Ready to come dance with me?"

She thought of their kiss, the sudden rush of heat through her limbs, and felt a touch of it again. "I don't know if we should," she said. "I'm really a bad dancer. I will step all over you. I mean, hurt you."

"I'll take my chances."

If it hadn't been for that sweep of glossy hair gleaming over one shoulder, Luna might have been able to say no. But she really couldn't resist the idea of being so close to him, feeling his body, smelling his skin. "You'll be sorry," she said, but she stood up.

Spanish dancing in New Mexico was a very simple

thing. And Luna always thought it was utterly stupid that she hadn't really ever learned to do it, but it was a classic catch-22: it was so embarrassing that she was so bad at it that she couldn't seem to stick with actually learning it. Allie tried to teach her once and gave up because Luna nearly broke her instep.

So as much as she wanted to be next to the delectable Thomas, breathing in his smell, touching his body, the second they stepped out on the floor, she realized everyone would see her dancing badly with one of the most desirable men in the room and they would be snickering behind their hands for weeks. She could just imagine the teasing she'd get next week. "Oh, Thomas," she said, pulling at his hand, "no, I don't think I can do this. Never mind."

He snared her before she could flee entirely. "Luna."

The band started a new song, and he stood there for a second, listening. "Put your hand on my shoulder. The other on my waist. There you go. Now, let's just move a little bit."

Luna took a breath, trying to relax, and follow. But it was following that was hard. She couldn't seem to do it, and stepped on him twice, then nearly beaned a woman nearby with her elbow. She halted, looking at him miserably.

His nostrils quivered. "You really are bad, aren't you?"

"Yes."

"Come closer." He put his hand on the small of her back and pressed her hips into his. "This is a control issue, you realize that, right? You can't let go."

"Oh!" Made perfect sense. Not that it would make much difference.

"Feel me, all right?" Thomas said. "Catch the rhythm of the music, feel it come through me."

And it wasn't awful to feel him. Not awful at all. His

hand was broad across the small of her back, his thighs laced between hers. "Feel that in my thigh? Now feel the echo in my hand?"

She looked up at him. "I think so," she said softly.

Their eyes met, and that weird barometric pressure drop happened again. Luna could almost hear it. With it came a sense of overwhelming, almost shaky desire, and she felt the tremor in him, the small changes in his body. "God, I want you," he said gruffly.

A man in a crisp, purple-and-white striped shirt swung his partner around next to them, bumping Thomas, and said something in Spanish. The woman laughed.

To her surprise, the desire was shaken by the bubble of annoyance that burst in her. "God, that irks me," she muttered.

"What, the speaking in Spanish?"

"Yes." She shook her hair out of her eyes. "It's like whispering in front of other people—it's so *exclusive*."

"I barely speak any."

"But everybody speaks it to you, because you don't look white."

He laughed softly. "True. What's wrong, little girl, nobody inviting you to their parties?" His hand moved on her back and she realized they were just standing there, swaying the slightest bit on their little space of floor. Feet planted, hands roving the slightest bit, body heat building between their bellies. She could smell his shampoo—something with lime in it.

"My father spoke Spanish," she said before she knew she would. And a sharp sense of loss went through her, making her throat tight.

"Where is he now?"

"Dead." She clipped the word to halt that angle of discussion. "Are you going to show me how to do this damned dance or not?"

"No," he said, and catching her head in his hands, bent to kiss her. His eyes were open as he did it, and at the shock of his tongue, tasting faintly of tomato juice, a vivid, bright turquoise flash went racing down her nape, through her spine, into her buttocks. Her nipples pearled, almost embarrassingly so. "I'd rather get out of here, if you wouldn't mind."

"Where?" she asked, and grew aware of the people noticing them. She backed away and pulled his hand, making her way to the edge of the floor, near the door. She knew where she wanted to go, but didn't want to seem too—well, *slutty* was the word that came to mind.

But hell, they were grown-ups. Why bother with all that coyness when they both knew what they wanted?

Still, she let him say it. He eyed the band, holding her hand in his, rubbing his thumb over her knuckles. "We can't go to my house. Or yours, I guess."

Disappointment pierced her. She nodded.

"Um." He cleared his throat, bent close. "Don't take this the wrong way. If you don't think it's too tacky, there's a million hotel rooms in this city."

It made her blush, and he started to take it back. "Okay, sorry. I'm not . . . it's just—"

She raised a hand to his mouth. "The answer is yes, Thomas. Let's go."

His smile was positively dazzling, and Luna knew at least twelve women around them must have swooned dead in their tracks. She heard their breath sigh out of them and surround her with longing, the color of it a dusky purple. "My kind of woman," he said, and pulled her outside, where they stopped to do a little more heavy kissing, then climbed into his truck. Shocking, she told herself. But it wasn't.

It just wasn't.

• • •

Luna sat in the cab of the truck while he went in, her hands trembling just below the surface, trembling enough that she had to tuck them beneath her thighs. A sense of distant shock rumbled through her, but it wasn't enough to make her get out of the truck, make him stop registering. She watched him through the window, watched his hair move over his big shoulders, yellow lamplight shining on his hard, somewhat weary face, and her breath came a little higher and tighter in her chest.

Thomas.

Inside a room furnished with imitation Navajo blankets in red and gray, and touristy pottery, and fixtures with thunderbirds carved into them, Thomas turned on a lamp and locked the door, and then he came toward her, taking a condom out of his pocket, that he threw on the bed. "I got it in the bathroom at the VFW," he said, explaining. She could see it made him shy to say it, to think about it.

Which made her feel suddenly shy. Stupid. Slutty. She put her hands over her face and said in an agonized voice, "Thomas—"

"Please don't," he said, and came to her. "It's been so long since I wanted a woman." He put his hands on her shoulders, touched her hair.

And it was so good to be touched. It grounded something in her, something that always felt like it was flying out, threatening to take her with it. His hands were big and heavy and warm, and his thumbs touched her neck. She looked up at him, seeing with a little shock that it was still that weary, handsome face, that it was still his gentle eyes looking down at her, so dark and liquid. He kissed her, holding her face in that gentle way, and Luna swayed into him.

"Don't think, Luna," he said as her hands lit on his

chest. "This is good, this is now. It doesn't have to be anything else."

She felt dizzy on the scent of him, and when he tugged on the hem of her shirt, she raised her arms so that he could pull it off over her head. Then she reached behind her and unfastened her bra, not even minding somehow that her breasts were too soft to sit up high, and her stomach wasn't flat anymore—in fact there was a little indentation where the skirt waistband dug into her.

It didn't feel that strange to stand topless in front of Thomas Coyote, bathed in lamplight and his gaze, which flickered and flowed over her shoulders and breasts, over her belly and bare legs, touched her hair and her lips before he started doing it all with his hands.

Luna had spun a dozen half fantasies about this man, but none of them matched the reality of his strong dark hands curving to the round of her shoulders, then lifting her breasts. She couldn't close her eyes, didn't want to, because the sight of him was so good. His hands, his hair, the look on his face, so intent and reverent and hot. He took his time, touching what he could see, trailing three fingers down the middle of her tummy, tracing her ribs. He kissed her, touching her, and then reached around to the zipper of her skirt. Luna let it fall, then backed away and skimmed her panties off, too, and stood there naked and brazen and not caring. *This is it.*

Her bones were liquid as he stood back to look at her, sighing softly before he took off his own clothes with no grace. It wasn't a perfect body, either, with its little round of belly and scars. He had some tattoos she would examine later, and a nasty scar low on his right hipbone. She loved the colors of his skin, dark mocha on his hands and arms that faded to a soft tan elsewhere, and the pure strength in his shoulders and arms, and the look of that black, long hair trailing over him.

"Jesus," he said, and the word broke something waiting in her. Luna launched herself toward him and they tangled deep, the two of them, welcoming each other with lips and tongues, arms and hands and legs. Their skin skidded and slipped, elbows and teeth and knobs of knees getting in the way for a moment until they found a way to rearrange, fitting together again, finding ways to lace themselves into one.

It had been so long, and Luna had wanted this particular man so much that she found a great deep cry tearing from her throat as he entered her, all force and heat, his tongue in her mouth, his hands almost painful on her buttocks. The size of him around her, his hair falling over her, touching her face, her shoulder, the force of him . . .

She thought she might dissolve entirely in her orgasm, blown to bits by him, herself, the combination. There were times release could nearly hurt, and this was one of them, and she found herself holding on to him so fiercely that her entire body was one forceful muscle, and then he was starting to roar and growl in that guttural way, and they rocked hard together, until he curled his hands tight around her fanny and held her hard, pulsing, and she thought, her head falling back in purest nothingness, *Thank God*.

Tomorrow, she might feel like a slut. Tomorrow, she could beat herself up about it.

Tonight, she would simply take what he offered.

They kissed, gasping and sweaty, he braced on his elbows, his big hands on her head, their hips moving in faint delicious echoes of release. They kissed. And kissed. Luna dragged her fingers through his hair, letting it slide like silk stockings over her wrists and forearms; breathed in the smell of him, fire and sage, and drank of his mouth; reveled in the heft of him, the feeling of him around her, in her.

But he did finally get too heavy, and she shifted a little. "Can't breathe."

"Sorry."

Which meant they had to slide apart, pulsing in aftermath, and think of what to do next. A few minutes ago, Luna had wanted nothing more than for him to see her naked, to see if that was what he could want and enjoy. Now she thought of the cellulite on the back of her thighs and the almost-nothingness of her small breasts and the age showing on her belly.

"Be right back," he said, and as he pattered into the bathroom, she curled her arms on her chest, turning on her side to hide what she could, tucking her face between the pillows.

He came back, sturdy on his feet, carrying a warm washcloth and a towel. It unnerved her and she wasn't quite sure how to perform such an intimate act under his eyes, but when she reached for the cloth, he shook his head gently. "Allow me."

He washed her. She had to close her eyes. It made her heart hurt, his gentleness, the matter-of-fact way he didn't mind looking *there*, and when he finished it with a soft, light kiss—also there—she nearly burst into tears.

"Let's get under the covers," he said quietly.

Luna had to open her eyes, move her body, stand up to pull the covers back. He climbed in and lifted them up in a big tent for her. She dived under them, curled close to his big body, and he let the covers settle down over them, tucking her under his arm. "You okay?" he asked.

Not really, she wanted to say. She wanted to put on

her clothes and go home now, and think about this and why it made her chest hurt. But that wasn't the answer he was looking for.

Raising her head, she started to make a light, complimentary comment about his prowess, like how great he was, what a good lover, how he had pleased her. But the moment she met his eyes, it slammed her again—he was *there*, his long dark eyes so gentle, that faintly raised scar on his neck reminding her that he knew about the hard, dark places of life. She said. "No. You?"

He swallowed, then shook his head. Moved that big hand over her hair, his gaze on the curl he toyed with. "I knew you'd feel bad. I should have stopped you."

A wave of something came over Luna—sex and longing and a kind of wild, wild pain, like a wind howling down a mountain. It hurt and it swelled and the only thing that seemed available to help it was Thomas's mouth. So she bent over his face and kissed him. Lightly. Tasting the full lower lip, the sharply cut upper. She traced the line of his jaw, the surface of his face, feeling below her fingertips the faint roughness of his scars. It helped. The pressure in her chest eased, and she let the primary need of him rise up again. She needed to learn him, the smell and taste, his sounds and wishes. "Oh, Thomas," she whispered. "You scare me."

"Don't think," he said, his touch suddenly urgent. "Make love to me, Luna. That's all it needs to be tonight." His tongue touched hers. "Don't think."

From Placida Ramirez, who was taught by her mother:

Instructions for a Charm Using Chimayó Dirt

You will need holy water, holy dirt, a saint's medal for whatever the purpose of the charm is for, a length of fabric, thread and a needle, prayers, incense if you want. Gather everything together and pray over it, then cut the fabric into the size you need; a good cotton is best to keep the dirt inside. Dampen dirt with holy water and wet the fabric, thread, and needle with holy water, too. Make a little pillow with dirt inside, and the incense if you want it, and sew up three sides, praying as you sew. When you finish three sides, put in the medal and say the saint's prayer, then sew up the last side.

Twelve

Luna crept in around one, the back of her neck damp from a shower, her cheeks hot with spent passion, and found Joy asleep on the couch in front of the television. It gave her a pang of guilt—this was what she didn't want to do to Joy: be a party-hearty kind of mother of the sort that was becoming more and more common. Women lost and overwhelmed and so hungry for touch that they slept with any man who was halfway friendly. Luna had always understood the need, particularly among those women who were most harshly judged— the young ones who had no man and a passel of children. What else could make you forget like sex could? She knew why they needed it.

But life for a mother wasn't about what was good for *you*. It was about what was good for the child, and the hollow feeling in Luna's belly told her she wasn't thrilled with herself about this. She should be the one asleep on the couch, waiting for Joy to come home.

"Hey, honey," she said quietly, kneeling next to the couch. "Time to go to bed."

Joy moved her head, then one finger. Collapsed back into sleep.

"Joy," Luna said again.

"Go 'way," she said, shrugging her hand away. "I'll sleep here. I like it."

Half smiling, Luna nudged her daughter one more time. Joy had always been a champion sleeper. Luna could cart her anywhere when she was small, and Joy would just sleep—Luna would tumble her down wherever, and she'd slump into her cat-curl and sigh back to sleep.

Now, however, she was too big to carry. "C'mon, babe, get up. You'll have a crick in your neck in the morning."

"I don't care."

"You will."

Finally, Joy opened her eyes. Or one eye, anyway. "Okay, I'm going." She flung out one hand to let Luna haul her up, then stumbled into her bedroom, pulling off her shirt over her head as she went. The line of smooth, thin back, made whiter by the black bra across it, made Luna want to go lie down next to her, protect her forever from anyone who would see that back and not take proper care of it, not love it the way she did.

Joy's door closed, and Luna moved around the house, picking up some dishes and an empty bag of Fritos and a pair of shoes Joy had left in the middle of the room for no apparent reason. An open box of stationery was on the table, and two envelopes were addressed in Joy's girlish, looping hand. One was to April Loggia. The other was to Bobby and Bruce Loggia. The o's and g's had smiley faces in them.

It had to be killing her to be away from her brothers. She was devoted to them.

Even after she finished the straightening, Luna felt no closer to sleep than she had when she came in. Her body was soft with release, but she was also keyed up, wanting—something.

Tobacco. Tequila. White zinfandel. A long Marlboro, red pack.

Yeah. All of the above.

Instead, she made a cup of hot chocolate in the quiet kitchen and put some crackers and cheese on a plate and carried it all into the workroom. She didn't feel like getting all covered with paint, so she wandered over to the corner and picked up a Barbie doll she had bought at Toys "R" Us in Pueblo a while back. Teresa, Barbie's Hispanic friend. They didn't have Teresa back in the old days—choices had been limited then to blond, brunette, or redheaded, bendable knees and a twisting waist. Elaine and Luna had had lots of them, though Elaine had never been into them as much. At seven, Luna was serious about her Barbies. She had a carrying case with little hangers, and drawers for the shoes, and infinitesimal combs and brushes. She ironed tiny dresses and spent hours and hours and hours just making up things that were going on with the girls.

When she hit adolescence, girls didn't even wear makeup, much less play with fashion dolls, so Luna reluctantly put the dolls aside and they were eventually given away, along with the Colorforms and roller skates and chalkboard.

Best Friend Barbie said, *Didn't know how much you needed me, didja?* Her hair was in a ponytail, and her shirt was tied up under her breasts.

Au contraire. Luna sipped her chocolate. Somewhere between that reluctant giveaway and now, she'd managed to amass quite a collection. At first, she pretended they were kitsch for her dry dorm room—a cute one at a garage sale, a flea market, the toy store—Barbies of various ages, generations, occupations. She wasn't into Midge or Francie or any of the others, and in truth, she had a distinct preference for the standard perky blonde. The longer the hair, the better. This probably said something about her enslavement to a male-dominated society's standard of beauty, but what the heck. She could never get her own hair to grow past her shoulders and purely loved the idea of it swishing around her waist.

Unlike some serious collectors who tracked down original beauties from 1959, Luna's collection was not particularly notable. Sometimes she bought them new—especially the costumed ones, and some from the Dolls of the World Collection—but she didn't treat them with reverence or anything. They came out of their boxes and she posed them around the room and fussed with their hems and adjusted their hair. Beast Ken, out of his heavy Beast costume so she could see his cheerful face, was currently sitting on the windowsill with his arm upraised to Medieval Barbie, who was getting very dusty. Luna picked her up and brushed her off. Should take better care of them.

Most of the dolls were just ordinary ones from garage sales or thrift shops, dressed or decorated according to the mood of the moment. She picked up one in New Orleans once, a dark-haired '70s model with a few paint splatters over her feet. Luna hung *milagros* from her ears and fingers, and wrapped a turban of shiny blue fabric around her head, and a Copacabana kind of bra and skirt that she found right on the shelf of the local grocery store. She occupied a corner all her own in

Luna's bedroom—complete with a tiny blue crystal ball and some itty-bitty tarot cards that Allie and Luna spent a whole night making once.

She knew it was a silly sort of thing for a grown-up woman. But it also didn't hurt anything.

Tonight, she plucked at Teresa's skirt, touched her tiny shoes. She'd fallen in love with this one the first time she'd seen her—the long hair, her dusky skin, her pretty mouth. Teresa in all her guises was the exception Luna made to straight Barbie. This particular one was Quinceañera Teresa, a girl dressed up in a weddinglike dress for her fifteenth birthday celebration. Lots of girls around Taos still celebrated the *quinceañera* in the old way and she'd always had a sneaking envy for it. She wasn't clear on the details, since she'd never actually attended one, but the girls went to church and dedicated themselves to the Virgin, then had a reception afterwards. It appeared to have most of the accoutrements of a wedding—the dress and attendants and a cake.

Tobacco. Tequila. White zinfandel. A long Marlboro, red pack.

What was this about? She rolled her neck, rubbed a shoulder.

She wanted a cigarette. Badly. Had all evening. Being with Thomas, rich and wonderful as it had been, had not given her the peace she thought she might have been hoping for. The nagging pain, deep in her chest, was still there, and she brushed Teresa's hair with a tiny plastic brush, trying to pinpoint it.

It wasn't unfamiliar, the deep, hollow ache. As a young teen, she'd thrown herself into her studies to alleviate it, often falling asleep over a book. As an older teen, she discovered cigarettes helped. And then—oh, joy of joys—she'd finally discovered alcohol. Nothing eased that ache like a good shot of tequila. When she first started drinking, it was the first time in her life she'd been able to escape that eternal, endless, constant ache. She'd never known how it felt. The dark feelings were just—erased. She could relax. Breathe.

They don't call it self-medication for nothing, Barbie said.

Luna nibbled on a Ritz and brushed Teresa's hair and thought about the man speaking Spanish at the VFW. Thought about her rush to have sex with Thomas, even though they both knew it was too soon.

Thomas. Ugh. Was she nuts? It was insane to be sleeping with a man, letting her heart be captured, an inch at a time, by a man who was still maybe in love with his ex, a man so good and gentle and kind that he'd break her heart to pieces eventually. What kind of sane woman allowed herself to get tangled up in a relationship like that, especially when her life was coming together so well?

Hair fell in her face and she shoved it away violently. Self-sabotage was her specialty. And just looking at the whole thing objectively, that's certainly what this looked like.

Across the room, Barbie wiggled her foot with a knowing little look on her face. *Is that really why you're freaked tonight?*

"I have no idea," she said aloud, then picked up her cup and drained it. She'd go to bed. Just stop thinking.

Run, run, run away, sang BF Barbie from behind her. Softly, not meanly.

"Whatever," Luna said, and turned off the light. Sometimes retreat was really okay. At least if she was asleep, she wouldn't be thinking of the relief a cigarette might bring.

• • •

Thomas had not slept so well in years. He awakened with a sense of optimism, hearing birds twittering outside, seeing the bright dawn breaking over Taos Mountain. The house was asleep. He had only one thought in his mind.

Luna.

He had not showered when he came home, so he could sleep with the smell of her on him, and he raised his hands now, smelling her on his palms, and he wanted to see her. Make sure she wasn't regretful. So, without coffee, without anything, he set out in the cool of a September morning and walked the three blocks to her house. He heard himself humming "White Bird" under his breath.

Hope. God, it had been a long time. Even the sight of her house, that building that had the good fortune to rest over her head, gave him a faint rush of adrenaline, and that made him want to laugh, too. Flowers grew in wild profusion around the adobe, the grass long and starred with dew. Across the narrow street, a trio of longhaired goats bleated at him, and he said, "Good morning," before he turned to go up to her porch, trying to scent her. He did not want to wake her, but even more, he didn't want to wake her daughter.

Obviously, she rose early, since he'd twice seen her afoot before seven. So he sat on the porch and waited, watching the sun climb into a brilliance of blue sky, tipping cottonwoods with glittery color. And he thought of her. Closed his eyes, called up the look of her eyes and her mouth, open in panting hunger. His body was covered with tiny bruises and scratches and he wondered if she was marked, too.

The door opened behind him. "Thomas!" she said in surprise.

He leapt up. "I wanted to make sure you were okay,"

he said, coming toward her. He stopped, stricken, just a foot away. Her hair was unbrushed, tangled and wild, like spun light around those big dark eyes that hid and revealed.

"I'm fine," she said quietly, still staring at him.

He reached out a hand and pulled her closer, putting his hands around her face so she would look up at him. "Thank you," he whispered, and kissed her. She tasted like coffee and sugar, like something wicked and real, and he was all the way there in three seconds.

She pushed away. "My daughter!"

"Sorry." He stepped back.

They stood there looking at each other, and Thomas felt foolish and immature, his hands too big at his sides. The silence stretched an endless, agonizing time, like dead air.

He said, "I guess I—"

She said, "Thomas, I—"

They halted, waited, spoke together again. "I'm being so rude!" she said, as he said, "I'm sorry to have barged in like this."

Luna laughed and took his hand. "Come in and have some coffee, why don't you?" She led him into the kitchen, and he stood in the exact place where he had kissed her the first time, and the same, helplessly longing sense of wonder filled him as it did then. He wanted to bend his head into her neck, smooth a hand over her back, just be close again, chest to chest. The sensation was physical, a not-quite tingle on his chest, the front of his legs, his palms. She poured coffee into a big red mug and brought it to him.

"My daughter is asleep in the other room," she said quietly. There were shadows below her eyes and he raised a thumb to touch them.

"Did you sleep well?"

"Not really," she said, smiling a little. "You?"

"I did." As if there were invisible strands winding around them, he moved closer. "I woke up thinking of you."

She put a hand up, keeping him at a small distance. "Maybe this is too rash, Thomas. I haven't even *kissed* anyone in years. It feels too fast."

He put his hand around the side of her neck and bent closer, hungry to smell her skin. "I thought we were going to skip the small talk."

"That's not small." But the force behind her hand softened. Her face lifted.

"Too much talk is always small," he said roughly, and bent into the offering of her mouth, and it was no different this time than any other. Any sense of propriety or resistance dissolved in the union, and he pulled her into him, into the places on his body that needed her, against his chest, his legs, his mouth. He filled his palms with her bottom, his mouth with her tongue. She tugged on his hair with one hand, wrapping it around her arm, and leaned into the crook of his elbow, all of her soft and giving and receptive, and he lifted her up to the counter. "I just want to look." She nodded, and he opened her robe a little, and kissed the pale moons of her breasts, her throat, her mouth.

"Oh, God, Thomas," she breathed, kissing his ear, his eye, pulling him into her, wrapping her legs around him. "I want you so much again it's like a drug."

"When?"

"I don't know. I promised my daughter a picnic by the river today."

"I'll bring Tiny and meet you there. We'll sneak away."

"No! I can't do that," she whispered. Her face was troubled. "Not with my daughter there."

"I'll just go. We don't have to do anything. Please," he whispered like a boy. "Please."

"This is crazy, Thomas," she said, breathless, and rubbed her nose against his cheek.

"Yeah," he agreed, and sucked her lower lip into his mouth, not caring. Not caring.

She pushed him away, almost violently, bending, walking to the back door. She went out and stood on the patio, breathing in. "This is too much, too fast," she said.

He followed her, still lost in a narcotic golden haze, and touched her shoulder. "You need to stop thinking so much."

"Maybe for some people that's the right answer," she said. "I have to be careful."

There was such a depth of sorrow in her voice. "Of what, Luna?" he asked gently, brushing his fingers over her neck. "Not me."

"No," she said, raising her big dark eyes. He could see nothing in them, only a dim light of regret. "Myself, mainly. Being too rash. Making mistakes that hurt people."

"Drinking."

"Mostly," she agreed. She put her hand over his wrist, and it wasn't clear at first whether she would pull his hand off her, or hold it there. In the end, she let her palm fall over his knuckles, and met his eyes. "I just don't ever want to go there again."

"You're too hard on yourself," he said quietly. "There are a lot of alcoholics in the world."

"I was a drunk."

In spite of himself, he winced a little at the word.

Her smile was bitter. "It wasn't pretty, and I don't want it to ever sound prettier than that."

A breeze swept over them, lifting curls around her

face. They glittered like gold and silver, and he captured one corkscrew in his fingers. "Let me come to the river," he said quietly. "I'll be good, I promise."

For a moment, she didn't answer him, only gazed up at him. Then she shook her head with some bewilderment. "How is it that we've suddenly arrived here, Thomas?"

"I don't know," he whispered, bending down to kiss her once more before he left. "I'm glad."

A cool breeze fluttered through the kitchen and sniffed over the supplies scattered over the counter. Picnics were one of Luna's favorite things, and she kept a big wicker basket of supplies—plastic glasses with bright blue and yellow flowers, a set of inexpensive flatware, cloth napkins, and a big checked cloth to put on the ground. On top of those, she packed bananas and freshly baked devil's food cake, cheese and apples and celery sticks, a big box of assorted crackers, and a can of fake cheese for Joy to spray on them.

All the while, she was thinking of a cigarette. Lighting it, inhaling it, blowing it out. She'd put on her nicotine patch already, but then Thomas had arrived, tasting of himself and smelling of the motel room last night, and . . .

She exhaled, hard. Maybe she needed *two* patches to deal with everything that was stirring up.

The basket was packed, ready to go. Still only five minutes to seven. Joy had asked to sleep until eight or so, which wasn't unreasonable for a weekend morning, and Luna restlessly poured a second cup of coffee, a sharp blend that tasted almost too bitter. She carried it outside, where she breathed in the light mountain air, breathed it out slowly. Still the clutch of cigarette hunger clawed her nerves.

She took a tiny sip of coffee and wondered what she wanted to say that cigarettes would keep quiet. A part of it was that she was dying to call Allie and tell her about the night, say *Oh my God, he kissed me and kissed me and kissed me.* She would tell about how beautiful his hair was when it was down around his shoulders, and how gentle he was, and how he'd come over this morning to make sure she was okay.

But it was all too new and fresh and private just this moment. She wanted to savor it and walk around it some more first.

A bold, bitter, biting rocket of nicotine withdrawal went through her. Sudden. Inexplicable. It made her want to scream. It hurt. It tugged at every nerve in her body, little demon claws curling into the edge of her jaw and the back of her eyes and the base of her spine.

Putting down her coffee cup, she pulled the back door closed and headed down the road that looped in a long circle resembling a city block, but much, much longer. It wasn't enough to just walk hard, and after a minute, she bent down and broke into a little jog, then a faster one. The sandals on her feet were scant protection from the gravel on the road, but she welcomed that pain, welcomed the protest from her shins and ankles, and ran until she couldn't breathe anymore, and was sweating so much she'd have to take another shower before they left.

Then, sweating and breathing hard, she walked it off, shaking her arms and shoulders, circling one end of the loop. She walked around a wide yellow field broken only by a tuft of sheep clustered beneath a willow tree, the light skating over all of it like dew. The road headed down, and she could see her own house, sitting in its hollow back from the road. The Jacob's Coat rose was a smear of Monet-like color against the soft dun of the adobe, the grass verdant from the recent rains, and the sight eased her.

Better.

What couldn't she say? That she was afraid of Thomas?

A swelter of irritation. *That's not it.* She'd *said* that aloud, to herself and to him.

Was she afraid of the idea of involvement? This had the potential for seriousness, for serious love and serious hope, and because of that, serious pain.

Not it, not it, not it.

"Argh!" She breathed in deeply—and a hosanna might as well have gone up, because she smelled cigarette smoke. Close by. Narrowing her eyes, she looked around for it, and spied a woman standing in front of the house that belonged to Joy's new friend. The woman was standing in grass up to her ankles, her thick hair gathered haphazardly into a ponytail that hung down her back. She was much too thin. In her hand was a cigarette.

"Good morning," Luna said brightly.

The woman looked up, surprised but not startled. Gesturing with her cigarette to the yard, she said, "It's out of control."

Luna knew why she'd stopped and she didn't question it, didn't stop to think or ask herself if this was what she really wanted. The words spilled out of her mouth. "Look, I don't want to be weird, but do you have another cigarette? I've been trying to quit, but I just want one."

"Oh, sure!" Smokers were always helpful in this circumstance. Luna herself had always been more than happy to supply a fellow addict.

The woman reached into the pocket of her skirt, one that had fit much better once upon a time, and shook out a Marlboro from a red pack. Luna took it and bent into the flame the woman offered.

Smoke hit her throat, swirled into her lungs, and she closed her eyes to blow it out. "Oh. My. God."

The woman laughed. "Better than sex, isn't it?"

"Sometimes," Luna agreed, dizziness filling her head in the most pleasant possible way.

"You live right over the arroyo, don't you? By Placida's old house?"

"Yeah." Luna switched the cigarette to her left hand to offer her right. The woman had to do the same thing. "Lu McGraw. I think our daughters might be friends. Joy Loggia is mine. Weird hair, a thousand earrings?"

"Sure. I met her the other day. I'm Sally."

"She'll smell this on me when I go in," Luna said, and took another drag. Even better. But the shape of it seemed sort of wrong, too big, fatter than she remembered. And there was a certain awkward self-consciousness to the act of lifting it to her mouth, holding it there.

"Tell her you talked to me and I was smoking." She smiled, but it was the kind of worn-at-the-edges look to it that said she didn't do it much. "She knows I smoke."

"Good idea." Holding the cigarette, looking at it, she felt the fury and sadness and black-hole weight of whatever just dissolved. "Why does everything that feels good or tastes good have to be bad for you?"

"I know, huh?"

They stood there companionably, united in the quiet and the morning and tobacco. "Thank you very, very much."

"No problem."

Still, Luna didn't move on. Sorrow was etched in the sharpness of Sally's collarbone and the way her hair was tied in a ribbon at the back of her neck, not even brushed. Eyeliner from the day before was smeared below her eyes.

And the old therapist in her noticed other, little things—the way Sally kept her arms crossed over her middle, protectively. The way she looked at the yard, moved a foot, put it back down, like the task was too much for her. "It's hard, isn't it," Luna said, "taking care of a house by yourself?"

"My husband, he used to do it all. He took so much pride in it, too." Weariness crossed her face. "I just don't know. See, look I let his roses go."

"I know someone who can help you. He doesn't charge much." It was a lie. Luna did all the work herself, but surely there was someone who could be hired for basic lawn service and the like. "You want me to call you with his number?"

Sally nodded. "That would be good. Yes. Thank you."

"I'll get your number from Joy and call you tomorrow." Something made her reach up and touch Sally's arm. "Hang in there." She wanted to add something more, but could see the small kindness had unnerved her enough.

"Thanks."

Tiny Abeyta did not particularly want to go with his boss to the river. He wanted to stay home and see if he could reach his wife by telephone, maybe talk her into sneaking up to the house for a little while. His cousin had told him that Angelica was out with some other guy the other day, drinking beer at a café in Espanola. He'd tried calling her already this morning, but she sometimes went to Mass, and he figured that's where she was. He would hang around the house so's he could call her later and see.

But Thomas wouldn't give up, not even when Tiny protested that he was on the bracelet and couldn't go hang out whenever he felt like it. Thomas shook his head, knowing Tiny had Sunday afternoons for errands. So, stuck, Tiny helped Thomas load everything up. A gallon jug of iced tea he made from herbal tea bags, and candy bars and chips and roast beef sandwiches, all loaded into a cooler with pop. No beer, though Tiny was kinda hoping, even though Thomas didn't do a lot of drinking anymore. Less and less every day, seemed like. The guys gave him a hard time about it when they went to the White Horse after work on Fridays, saying he wore a skirt and he was getting old. They called him *viejo*, and one even brought him a cane one day.

But it was just like the whole thing of Thomas paying on Mondays instead of Fridays—nothing they said could change his mind once it was made up, and if he said he wasn't going to the White Horse, no amount of talk would make him go. It made it easier for Tiny in a way, he had to admit. He'd been doing real good not going to the Horse on Fridays, till that last time, and he wouldn't go anymore now, never.

Stubborn, that's what Thomas Coyote was. He kept nudging Tiny along with more things to put in the truck—blankets to lie on, and some fresh shoes in case they got wet, and fishing poles. He whistled the whole time, a cantina song about dancing. Cheerful. So cheerful, it kinda started getting Tiny in a good mood after a while, and he eyed the blue sky through the windows of the kitchen, and started thinking about the sound of the river and the smell of it, and he thought it might not be so bad to go. He could ask to bring along Ramundo, his youngest, who was only four and would like to fish with his dad.

But when he tried the house again, nobody answered.

He decided maybe Angelica was at her mama's house, and called there, but though he could hear the kids hollering about something in the background, Angelica wasn't there and her mother wouldn't say *where* she was, which meant it was someplace he wouldn't like. "I just wanted to take Mundo fishing with me," he said, "but forget it now."

It put him in a very bad mood, wondering where his wife was, and he slammed down the phone and glared at it, his mind racing, his stomach feeling sick and tight. He couldn't eat a lot these days. Every so often, he'd be real hungry and eat a lot, mostly stuff *Abuelita* cooked because she made things like his mom, who had died a couple years back. Usually, though, his stomach felt like this, sick or tight, and he couldn't get any food into it. He drank a lot of milk, just to keep up his strength for work, but he was losing a lot of weight.

Abuelita came into the kitchen then. He hadn't seen her in days and days—she was tired, Thomas said, sleeping a lot. When she saw him, she gave a little cry. "Manuel," she said, calling him by the name nobody ever used. "I got something for you for bringing me to Chimayó," she said to him in Spanish, and pressed into his palm a small packet. "It's for good luck. Keep you safe from the witches."

Thomas *tsked* at the word *bruja*s but Tiny was honored. He raised it to his lips and kissed it, taking her old hand into his. "*Gracias.*"

His heart felt lighter as he tucked the charm into his wallet, carefully, right behind his driver's license. Maybe, he thought, he could just go to the river for a while for himself, and just forget about everything else.

Maybe, just maybe, he didn't have to know everything all the time.

La Llorona

La Llorona is the legend of a woman who has lost her children, and who can be heard, and sometimes seen, weeping in the night. La Llorona (the name means "She who weeps" in Spanish) is in most stories said to be Mexican, although sometimes she is a woman who lived in the American Southwest. As with most urban legends, there are many variations of La Llorona, *but the central plot remains intact: The woman has lost her children, usually because she herself has killed them because she wants to marry a man who doesn't want any children. She is so anguished over the depressing circumstances that she kills herself as well, and is thus doomed forever to roam her native land, weeping and wringing her hands. Sometimes she is said to be searching for her children, and sometimes she is said to appear only as a warning to those who see her.*

Thirteen

When Luna went east as a young woman, the rivers had astonished her. They were mighty things, wild and deep and sometimes so far across you could barely see the other side. Unpacking the basket on the banks of the Rio Grande, she said as much to Joy. "This was the biggest river I saw until I was twenty-three."

Joy grinned. "And you walked uphill in the snow to school, right?"

"Both ways," Luna answered. "I'm not kidding, though. This was the mightiest river around."

"Pretty sad, Mom."

They both looked at it, a copper-colored flow that was moving fairly quickly, thanks to the rains of the past few days, but a very mild-looking creature indeed in comparison to the Savannah. Still, the power of it was evident in the gorge it had carved. "Don't forget, though, it's a mountain river and it has dangerous undercurrents."

"I wasn't planning on swimming." She pulled a T-shirt off to show her bikini top. "It's way too cold."

"True enough." That had been another surprise, to discover that water outdoors was not always just above freezing.

Joy took out a bottle of oil and buttered her skin. Her pale, thin, white skin. "How much sunscreen does that have?" Luna asked.

"I don't know." She handed over the bottle. "Not much. The whole point is to get a tan. Do you have any idea how white I look in that school? They're calling me fish girl."

Luna chuckled. "Fish girl? Who calls you that?"

"Oh, this girl named Yvonne. She's just a pain in the neck."

"Well, fish girl or not," she said, looking for the SPF number on the bottle, and groaning when she saw it was only eight, "you can't lie out in this sun without better protection than that. It's high altitude sun and there's no humidity to block any of it. You'll be burned to a crisp tonight."

"I only *brought* that one," she said, wiggling to get more comfortable.

"That's when it comes in handy to have a mom." Luna pulled out some hefty sunblock, and handed it to her. "Use this."

"Mom! It's SPF 30. I won't even get a tint!"

"Trust me, you will." Luna used some on her face—mainly to prevent more wrinkles than she already would get from living in the high altitude sun her whole life—but her arms and legs were pretty tan from walking everywhere and she didn't use anything on them.

Joy huffed, but she did as she was told. "I wish I had your skin tone instead of Dad's."

"Well, but you also got his straight hair, so count your blessings."

"I guess." She laid back down. "Now I'm going to be totally lazy."

"Fine with me." Luna put on her sunglasses and rested her arms on her knees, admiring the quiet view of cottonwoods with their shiny leaves and rugged, deeply grooved trunks. Scrub oak grew in tufts. The sky arched overhead in an exuberant deep shade of blue. It was a color that didn't exist anywhere else she'd ever seen, which made up somewhat for the wrinkles.

The fact of Thomas coming by prearrangement hung in the air, and Luna wondered how to best handle it. Should she just wing it, be surprised?

Never lie. If nothing else, it kept things a lot simpler. "Joy, that guy I went out with last night?"

"Mmm-hmm?"

Luna paused, feeling heat crawl up her cheeks in sudden realization. She'd made these plans to be with Joy, then had invited someone else along without even talking to Joy about it. And it was a guy she'd only dated twice, for heaven's sake. But she was stuck now. "He's coming by this afternoon."

"Okay."

That was it? Just okay? "I won't make a habit of it—"

"Mom." Joy opened her arms and lifted her long slim arms to shade her face. "You've gotta relax. It's not 1972 anymore. You don't have to wait until you're going to get married to introduce me to someone. I know they don't all work out. That's life."

"Maybe not," she said, feeling foolish. "I just don't want you to get the wrong idea."

Joy gave her a bewildered frown. "What idea?"

"That . . . well, that I—"

"Mom, you've been single for eight years, and I've been living with my dad and the woman he left you for." She spread her hands. "Okay? This isn't *The Brady Bunch*. Sex is all out in the open these days."

Luna flushed. Which made Joy laugh.

"I guess I don't want you to think your mother is hot to trot," she said.

" 'Hot to trot'?" Joy hooted. "Is that like *cut a rug, daddy-o*?"

"Oh, hush."

Her grin glinted in her aquamarine eyes. "You're really old-fashioned in some ways. Worse, even, than some southern belle."

"No way!"

"Way. The south ain't what it used to be. You'd be surprised."

Luna's memories of Georgia were so wrapped up in Marc and the disasters that had befallen her with him that she sometimes forgot how much she'd loved the place. "I liked it there. Being polite and courteous and everybody taking the high road. Mannerly."

"Repressed," Joy countered. "You can have it."

"You feeling better about the boys and April today?"

"I guess."

"It's okay to be honest, Joy."

"Is it?"

"Yes," Luna said, and meant it.

Joy sat up, dusting sand from her palms. "I've always tried not to talk about her much."

"I know," Luna said, wanting to reach out and tuck a

lock of loose hair behind her ear. "But it was a long time ago. I'm over it. Trust me."

Joy peered at her mother for a long moment, chewing the inside of her cheek. Luna's curiosity skyrocketed. "What?"

"All right—I'm worried about her. She sounds funny."

"Funny how?"

"I don't know." She grimaced. "Like her voice is coming out of a tube."

"Have you asked her what's wrong?"

"She says there's nothing the matter." Joy shook her head. "I'm not even sure why I think she's lying."

"It's usually a good idea to trust your instincts in something like that. Is there anyone you could call about her? Maybe her mother or a sister?"

"No." The word was quite final. "I'm sure it's nothing."

"Joy—"

"Let's not talk about this anymore. It's too weird for me." She twisted her multicolored hair into a knot and stuck a stick through it to hold it. "How're you feeling about your mom's big surprise last night?"

Blankly, Luna said, "Big surprise?"

"The land? The fact that your dad is dead?"

"Oh, that. I forgot."

"Forgot?" Joy echoed. "How could you forget that?"

Luna thought of the cigarette she'd smoked this morning.

Finally, said Psychotherapist Barbie.

"Lots of practice in denial," Luna said quietly. The weird, sucking hollowness that had been in her chest this morning came back. She looked at her daughter. "I guess I'm not doing that well, actually."

"Do you think you want to keep the land?"

"I'd like to at least see it before we make a decision."

"Better do it fast, because Elaine wants the cash bad."

Nodding, Luna dug her toes into the hot dirt at the edge of the blanket, feeling sunshine burn down on the tops of her knees. "The one I'm more worried about is your grandmother. She didn't take it particularly well."

"No offense, Mom, but I don't know why it would matter. Wasn't it like thirty years ago or something?" She said thirty like it was five hundred.

"Closer to thirty-five." Idly, Luna put her hands in the dirt beside her feet, and watched mica sparkling over her skin. A wavery vision of her father, bent over a shovel in the garden, came to her. "It's hard to explain," she said. "It might sound crazy to say that he was a good man. A kind man. He was good to us."

"He left you."

"Yes." She patted the dirt into a smooth square, using the side of her palm to make it absolutely flat and smooth, then picked up a twig and started to draw. "That's only the end part, though. Before that, he was always full of laughter and presents. He and my mom used to dance in the living room, and he was always there for dinner." She scowled, realizing that she'd drawn a thunderbird on the flat square of dirt. Irritably, she rubbed it out. "At least, that's how I remember it."

"You ever talk to Grandma about it?"

"She won't talk about him."

"Never? That's kinda weird."

Luna lifted a shoulder. "You know how she is—nothing negative, no gossip, all that. Maybe she doesn't have anything nice to say, so she's not saying anything at all."

"Did you ever just *ask*?"

"Sure. She always got really busy and forgot I asked the question."

Joy closed her eyes. "I wonder why he left."

"Yeah."

"There had to be something. Another woman, probably. That's usually it."

She wanted to protest: *No, there was nobody else. You didn't see the way he looked at her.* But of course, it was probably true. "More than likely," she said sadly, and stood up, brushing off the seat of her shorts. "I'm going to wade for a little while."

"I'll be right here in case you drown in the undercurrents."

Luna chuckled. "Thanks ever so."

"Anytime."

The sand was burning hot, and Luna wished for a pair of thongs but instead just raced for the waterline and sank her poor feet into the icy water. Standing there with it rushing over her arches and toes, she peered into the amber-shaded current and thought about smoking with Sally that morning. Amazing to think that her father hadn't even crossed her mind.

And with a shock, she realized she'd gone even further than having a cigarette to avoid her feelings on this one—she'd had sex with Thomas. Dramatically, intensely. Partly because she wanted him, but partly to get around thinking about that land and everything that had dredged up.

A magpie sailed overhead, flashing black and white feathers against the Lalique blue of the sky. Luna watched him, and into the quiet, Best Friend Barbie said, *So—what lie were you telling yourself, sweetie?*

Hmm. If it was so shocking to find out he was dead, maybe she had believed him to be dead all along. If he hadn't been mysteriously murdered—her own secret theory of his disappearance—then she had to deal with the fact that he'd chosen to leave them. Chosen.

Anger stung the edges of her heart, and she waded upriver noisily, thinking of her faithful vigil at the window.

Waiting for him to come home. Believing absolutely that he *would*.

Stopping suddenly, she closed her eyes and focused on that little girl on the couch, going back to her.

Blue curtains, dusty with desert air. The couch a nubby brown beneath her elbows. Something sticking her knee—a broken spring, probably—as she stared out the picture window. A forgotten Barbie lay beside the sidewalk to the house and somebody should go get her before she got messed up, even though it was one of the ugly ones with short hair and straight knees. Ancient.

Smell of supper in the air. Onions and meat and something sweet baking in the oven, a little extra.

Concentrate. See him coming up the walk. A tank top showing his big brown arms, tanned so dark, dark, dark. Jeans dusty with concrete. Black boots. A black metal lunch bucket in one hand, his hard hat in the other. Black curls stuck to his head with sweat.

Concentrate. He'd come in the door, whistle for the girls, and they'd rush out of their corners to fling themselves on him, and he'd drop his lunch box with a clatter and catch one girl in each arm, growling like a tiger as he pretended to bite them. He'd smell of sunshine and sweat and cigarettes, maybe a beer if he'd stopped somewhere on the way home.

Daddy.

Luna opened her eyes and let the tears come. That poor little girl! And her poor mother, and her poor sister. All waiting and waiting for the man they loved who didn't come home for thirty-five years. It made her furious, suddenly. Why did men do that? How could they just walk away from their families? What could be so important that it overrode the faith of a child?

Just down the bank, a woman with long black hair moved into sight, bending to put her hands in the water.

She wore vaguely hippyish clothes—a broomstick skirt and a long-sleeved red cotton blouse, open at the neck. Luna was smitten by the length of that hair, nearly to her knees, and by the graceful line of her back. Very beautiful, she thought, and remembered, barely, being that young herself.

"Mom!" Joy's voice came from bank.

Luna turned. There stood Thomas, and her heart stopped. An erotic vision of him, braced on his elbows as he moved in her, flashed over her memory, and a primal, deep tingle burned at the base of her spine. For the space of a few seconds, the only thing in the world were his eyes, long and dark and promising.

She realized she wasn't moving, just standing there staring, and with a little shake, moved toward them. Next to Thomas was a tall rangy man with black hair and an unsmiling mouth. She stuck out her hand. "Hi. Lu McGraw. This is my daughter Joy."

"Her name is Luna," Thomas said.

In a very soft voice, the man said, "I'm Tiny Abeyta." His hand was limp as seaweed.

"Joy," Luna said, gesturing to include her, "this is Thomas."

"Hi," Joy said.

There was a long space of awkwardness while they all measured each other—Joy looking at Thomas with no expression, Tiny eyeing Luna, Thomas and Luna carefully not eyeing each other. "Well," Luna said. "You want something to drink?"

"We're gonna unload the supplies," Thomas said, "then do some fishing."

"You're going to fish?" Joy asked, perking up. "What kind of fish live in this river?"

"Brown trout, mainly. Maybe a rainbow or two." A gentleness on his face. "You like fishing?"

"I don't know. I've never done it." She flashed her most impish smile.

"Never?"

Joy shook her head. "I really like eating it, though. That's the one bad thing about New Mexico. No good fish."

He nodded, lifting things out of the back of the truck. "I lived in California once," he said. "I remember the good fish. So fresh." He handed Joy a cooler. "Maybe we can get some fresh fish today to cook over the fire, huh?"

Joy smiled.

Watching them, Luna felt a ripple of disturbance. *Don't like him too much,* she wanted to caution her daughter. *He won't last.*

Sullenly, suddenly, she was very sorry that she'd agreed to let Thomas join them, and resolved, right there in the blaze of the hot September sun, to make sure to keep them apart in the future. The one thing that she could do for Joy was protect her from the hurts that were so obvious.

Thomas carried the fishing poles down to the edge of the river, and they all trailed behind him. Joy had the honor of carting the tackle box, a much-scarred, gray plastic thing that when opened revealed an entire sub-culture Luna knew nothing about. "Cool!" Joy said, picking up a bottle of something black and slimy. "Is this bait?"

"Yep." He pulled out another one, that looked like corn. "This works better, though, for trout. We probably won't catch anything today since we're fishing at the wrong time, but you never know."

He picked up the rods and explained the various parts to her, then illustrated how to toss the line in the water. It was just basic fishing, not fly-fishing, he told her, which was more complicated and took a lot of time to master. Joy's first few attempts were clumsy, but she didn't giggle in that self-deprecating way so many girls—and women—did, just gathered herself, concentrated, and tried again until she got it. Thomas said, "There you go."

She grinned at Luna over her shoulder.

Tiny and Luna sat on a flat rock in a patch of shade. Thomas looked at her. "You aren't going to try?"

"Nope."

He shook his head in mock disappointment. "And I bet you don't watch football, either."

"Good guess." A manly man, of course. Luna never attracted anyone anymore who liked to sip wine and listen to classical music on Sunday afternoons. Not that she was particularly attracted to *them*, either. Much as she lamented the football code, there was a lot to be said for a man being a man. She had women to do things with if she wanted New Age music or an afternoon at the opera.

Now she narrowed her eyes in consideration. "I bet you're a Raider fan."

Surprise winked over his face before he caught it. "How'd you know?"

Tiny let go of a little hoot of amusement. "She's got you, boss."

"Lucky guess," Luna said. "They're the most rabid fans of all."

"I'm not rabid," he said, casting his line.

Tiny snorted. "He never misses a game. Never."

"That's an exaggeration," Thomas said, focusing on the fishing line. "I'm missing one today."

"Not on television here," Tiny said.

Luna chuckled.

"Hey, I love football," Joy volunteered. "Only Atlanta, though."

Thomas turned his mouth down at the corners, nodding approval, and asked her about a draft pick Luna had never heard of. Joy gave her opinion in what seemed to be a very knowledgeable way. How did that happen, Luna wondered, then she knew. Joy had learned about football to have something to share with her dad.

"So," Luna said to Tiny, "I take it you're not a big fan?"

A quick shrug. "I like it, you know, but there's just so much stuff to do all the time. I got four kids, and a house—takes a lot of work to keep things nice." He pulled up his pants leg and showed her the thick, bulky electronic bracelet attached to his ankle. "This has messed me up, put me real far behind."

"How much longer do you have to wear it?"

"Six weeks."

She whistled. "Pretty expensive."

"Sheee. Tell me about it. Me and my wife both gotta wear 'em, so you know it's killin' me."

Luna thought of the wife last night at the VFW. How had she managed to get away like that? It made her think the monitoring center wasn't doing what it needed to do. "What's it up to now? Ten or twelve bucks a day?"

He took a cigarette out of his pocket. A short Marlboro, from the red pack. "I wish. It's fourteen-fifty." He bent his head into the cigarette, cupped his hand around the lighter, puffed to get it going. His licorice black hair fell forward, and he brushed it away as he exhaled.

Seeing her close attention, he said, "Sorry. You want one?"

She shook her head.

"Me and my wife, once we finish our classes, we could live together again. Two weeks."

Joy looked over her shoulder. "I *thought* I smelled a cigarette! Mom, it better not be you smoking!"

The patch stuck to the underside of Luna's arm tingled. "Nope."

"You're quitting?" Tiny said, and pulled the cigarette from his lips. "I'll put it out."

"No, don't," she said. "I'll just sit here and get a secondhand fix."

He grinned, and it erased some of the haunted leanness in his face. She could see the young man he had been, not so long ago, the one who had believed he would have something good, and instead was sitting here, too hungry for his family, aching to put things right.

"How's your counseling going?" she asked.

"It's all right, you know. They say the same things every time."

Luna just listened.

He smoked some more. "This guy's always saying that you need to think about the worst you could do. Like kill somebody. And then think maybe it's not so bad if you just let each other go." He looked at her. "I don't think that's right, you know?"

"What's wrong about it?"

"When you get married, it's supposed to be for life, not just till you don't feel like it anymore."

"That's true. And there's a lot of trouble caused by divorces. Especially for kids."

"God, I couldn't stand to be away from my kids like that. It would just kill me."

"You know, though"—Luna shifted, tucking her legs beneath her—"there are people who spend their whole lives making each other miserable. My grandparents did." She glanced at him to see if this was the right story, and he had inclined his head in interest, so she went for it. "My grandmother was very religious, totally Catholic, you know, and my grandpa—well, let's just say he wasn't. She wasn't a drag or anything, but just a very clean-living person, walked every day, ate right, all that. He was a drinker and card player and a smoker. I don't even know what they saw in each other to begin with."

He chuckled softly. "I know people like that."

"They couldn't be in the same room with each other without having a fight. Apart, they were fine; together, they turned into something evil. Their kids were all screwed up from the fighting, and one day, my grandma just left him. Just like that." She snapped her fingers. "She went to Albuquerque to work in the university cafeteria, and he stayed behind at his job, finally free to just party whenever he wanted—and he did, too. He loved closing down the bars, smoking cigarettes till he coughed his lungs out, chasing women."

Tiny smiled. "Sounds like a pretty wild guy."

"Absolutely. Here's the thing, though, Tiny." Luna touched his arm in a purely instinctive gesture. "My grandma went to Albuquerque and started working in the cafeteria, and going to a new church. She met this guy who was as sober as she was and they got married and they lived together for twenty years, very happily. In the end, they were both a lot happier. And so were their kids, because they didn't have to worry that one would kill the other."

He put out his cigarette and tucked the butt into the cellophane of his pack, something Luna liked him for. "I hear what you're saying, but it's not like that with me and my wife. I couldn't love anybody else."

"Really?" Something about his face made her feel airless all of a sudden. This one wasn't changing his thinking. He would never be able to let go, not without a lot more, very intensive counseling. His culture, his world, his methods all said he had to do things in a certain way, and a six- or twelve- or even a fifty-week class in anger management would never address the underlying problems. He needed one-to-ones—but who would pay for it? Not the state. Not him—he couldn't afford it. And Luna couldn't stand it. "Tiny, is she your first love?"

"Nah." He pulled up his sleeve and showed a name tattooed on his forearm: GLORIA. "I was with Gloria from the time I was thirteen to when I got out of the Army. We were gonna get married, but I caught her messing around with another guy and left her."

"Long time, then, you were together."

"Yeah." He pulled his sleeve down.

"Did it break your heart?"

"Yeah." He looked at her. "But it's not the same. I'm telling you, Angelica is special. She's my heart. She's the mother of my children."

"I admire your devotion," she said, and meant it, "it's rare. But Tiny—"

Joy whooped on the bank. "I caught one! I think I got one! Thomas, help!"

Tiny and Luna jumped up, watching as Thomas helped Joy reel in her fish, a flipping, fighting trout of some size. They reeled it in and put it on the bank, at which point Luna had to turn away. She hated seeing them die. It was just so unfair that they should be swimming along, minding their own business and somebody came and snatched them out and then they were dead.

Once it was properly throat-slit, Luna could go over there and congratulate Joy, who was jumping around like a little kid. "I caught one! I caught one!"

There was no chance to talk anymore with Tiny, but Luna saw him later, sitting on the bank, smoking thoughtfully. Maybe talking helped. Maybe not. You could only do what was right in front of you to do.

Joy loved catching her first fish. It left her feeling all cheerful and happy, and she helped Thomas build a fire in a little pit designed for that purpose. He showed her how to clean the fish, then wrap it up in foil with butter. While they waited for it, they grazed on sandwiches and cheese and crackers, drank lemonade and iced tea and big bottles of water. Thomas, Tiny, and Luna batted around politics and the good old days, when there weren't so many Californians moving into New Mexico, when you could buy a house for next to nothing. When the fish was done, they split it four ways, the succulent, steamed meat as buttery and tender as the day itself.

Joy wished that Maggie was with her. It wasn't so much that she wasn't enjoying the company of her mother and Thomas, she was. Just that grown-ups were always, well, grown-ups. All their boring discussions, like when they were young back in the ancient times, and they could even sit and be quiet for like twelve thousand years. The skinny guy, Tiny, ended up falling asleep on the blanket in a patch of shade, leaving Joy's mom and Thomas to sit, not quite touching, on a rock by the water. Thomas put his line in the current and put his hands on his thighs, and Joy saw her mother trying not to look at him.

It was so cute. Her mom even blushed. And Joy could tell that Thomas really liked her, that it was everything he could do not to gobble her up. His eyes were wild with it, and he took every little excuse he could think of to accidentally touch her. Fingers, hands, arm to arm. Joy couldn't wait to tell Maggie that her mom had a boyfriend for real.

"I'm gonna take a walk," Joy said after lunch.

"You want company?" Luna asked.

She lifted a shoulder. "Not unless I have to have some. It's safe, right?"

"Stay on the path so you don't get lost."

Thomas added, "And watch for rattlers."

"Rattlers don't scare me," Joy said, rolling her eyes.

"Really?"

"A snake that warns you? Please. You ever see a river full of water moccasins? Now *they're* scary."

His smile, Joy thought, was very nice. It crinkled his eyes. "Can't say that I have." He pointed to a dun colored path cutting between a pair of old, old cottonwoods. "There's some petroglyphs up that way. Look at the rocks as you go."

"Cool," Joy said, even though she didn't know what petroglyphs were. Something old, no doubt. There was always something old around here. One of these days, she wanted to get to Mesa Verde and see the cliff dwellings. It wasn't that far. A girl she knew at school in Atlanta went on vacation there and said it was really, really cool. She picked up a bottle of water and waved. "Be good," she said in a singsong voice.

Her mom blushed.

As she walked, she thought about them finally getting to kiss and wished for a boyfriend of her own. Like that cousin of Maggie's. Or uncle? Anyway, what if he was just out walking here today, and she came around the corner and there he was, all alone, sitting on a rock, looking up at the sky? She would be so startled, and he would give her that smile, that teasing smile with his eyes glittering a little bit. A warmth moved in her body as she thought about it. He was *so* cute. And not *that* old. Maybe he would notice her if she got her hair back to the right color.

There were some other people along the path—in fact, it was kind of busy. Two little boys barreled down the hill toward her, yelling at the top of their lungs, and she thought of her little brothers with a pang. That was the hardest part about this, missing them so much. She hadn't expected it—and sometimes she was afraid that she couldn't do it, couldn't live with her mom if it meant never living with her brothers again.

These boys were dark, and they said *"Hola!"* before they dashed by her, two sturdy little things in jeans and plaid shirts. They dipped through a break in the trees and she heard splashing, and decided to follow them. It was still and quiet in this spot, and she looked back the way she'd come, spying the picnic blanket spread on the bank. Tiny was gone. Joy's mom and Thomas were on their rock, locked in a kiss.

Joy knew she should look away, that she was intruding on a private moment, but there was something so electrifying about it that her cheeks got hot and something moved in her stomach, low and hot. Thomas was a big man, and he wrapped her mother up like a little doll, as if he would absorb her into his body. He kissed her with all his attention, his hand on her face, her blond curls scattering over his wrist. And her mother— her mother looked like she would happily die just then. As Joy watched, Thomas's hand moved down, covering her mother's breast . . .

Joy turned away, awash in a heat that humiliated her. Her body felt strange, like it didn't belong to her, and she stomped through the scrub oak, ducking into and out of the paths that led back to the mountain, blind.

What was *wrong* with her? Sometimes all she could think about was a boy's hand on her breasts. Sometimes, late at night, she'd lie in her bed and think about it, and her whole body burned. It made her restless. It made her reckless. She'd paid for it, too, and she still wanted it again.

It wasn't like it was easy to find guys who liked her. They thought she was too tall. Or they were afraid of her dad. Or she was a good girl. Or she wasn't their type. Or they were disgusted because she'd dated one black guy for two lousy months, and he turned out to be the biggest jerk she'd ever met. A friend had tried to warn her not to go out with guys who were that good-looking, but she hadn't listened. "Any guy," Tracy said, "who is that cute is going to be too much trouble." And he had been. Especially because there were a lot of boys still who wouldn't go out with a girl who had gone with a black guy.

Not that she'd want to be with a guy who would think that was bad.

It was so complicated!

She stubbed her toe on a rock. Hard. With a yelp, she hopped around, blinking back tears, and saw that it was starting to bleed. A bad stub. She turned around to go back to the river, and realized she was confused. Not lost, surely. There was a thin path—she hadn't gone off it, and she could still hear the little boys yelling and carrying on, and below their voices, the rushing sound of water.

Limping, holding her toe up as much as possible, she headed back toward the sound of the boys' voices, blood dripping down into the valley between her toes. It hurt, too, and suddenly, the sun seemed really hot, and the undergrowth kind of scary. She thought she saw the figure of someone up ahead—a patch of red shirt, and the swish of hair—and yelled, "Hey! Lady!" The woman kept moving, briskly, sun dappling over her shoulders. "Hey! Help!"

She came around a turn, feeling really sorry for herself and starting to cry—and nearly ran into somebody. She had to swallow a scream as she looked up, and it was Thomas's quiet friend Tiny. He looked confused. "Did you see a lady over here?" he said.

"Yeah," she said, "and her little kids over there, too, but look." She pointed at her foot, which was now covered in a truly gory amount of blood. The whole top of the toe was flapping with loose skin—not as bad as it looked, but pretty disgusting all the same. "Help me get to the water and wash it off."

"Eee, girl, that's bad. Lean on my arm. Hop."

Joy gratefully took his skinny arm. It wasn't far to the water. She carefully didn't look toward her mother, and was thankful when Tiny whistled, long and loud, to get their attention. Not that they'd be doing anything in broad daylight, of course, nothing more than a little necking, but she didn't want to even see that. She shoved her foot into the cold water, squeezing his arm a little and sucking in air over her teeth. "Oooh, that hurts!"

"Stop the bleeding, though." He looked over his shoulder. "You saw that lady, too, then, huh? She wasn't just my imagination?"

"No, I saw her. Really long hair? A red shirt."

"Yeah." He blew out his cheeks in relief and gave her an oddly appealing grin. "I thought it might be *La Llorona* and that I was in big trouble."

"Who's that?"

"You don't know her?" He inclined his head, making a *tsking* sound, and squatted. Joy recognized the stance of a tall tale and got ready to listen. "*La Llorona*," he said, "is an evil, evil ghost. She killed her children when her man disappointed her, and she spends all of her time wandering the river, trying to suck children into the water to drown them, or sometimes warning men they're going to die."

A bird cried overhead, right on time, and an involuntary shudder passed down Joy's spine before she laughed. "That scared me!"

He nudged her. "Me, too!" he said, and laughed.

"What'd you do, kiddo?" her mom asked, coming up with Thomas following behind. Her cheekbones were red, but more with sunburn than shame, and Joy was glad about that. She pulled her foot out of the water with a pitiful expression. "I got an owie, Mommy."

"Oh! I guess you did." She bent in to look at the wound, her hand around Joy's ankle. "You always have gotten the worst stubbed toes. Poor you!"

Sun glinted on the gold and silver in her mother's blond curls, and she raised dark brown eyes full of love to Joy's face, her mouth pursed in a half smile, half frown of sympathy, and Joy suddenly remembered being three and six and seven, coming to her mommy with these stubbed toes. Her eyes filled with tears of gratitude. "Nobody ever takes care of me like you do," she said, adopting a little girl voice so it wouldn't be so serious.

"C'mon, kiddo, I've got a first-aid kit in the car."

Thomas bent down and put his back to her. "Climb on. I'll give you a piggyback ride."

"I'm way too heavy!" she said, but Tiny laughed. "He's strong, *h'ita*," he said, so she climbed on. His braid was hot from the sun and smelled like the wind on a summer day. His shoulders were broad as a canyon, and even though her toe dripped blood all the way, she felt safe. Safer, she thought, than she'd ever felt in her life. How could that be?

Late, late in the afternoon, Thomas tugged Luna to her feet and they walked down a path through the trees. It was lazy and rich, just walking with him. Her body was limp with the lassitude of sunshine and peacefulness. A good day to be alive, she thought. Days like this made all the others worth living.

Thomas said, "I heard what you were saying to Tiny. Thanks."

"Probably none of my business. But he's in so much pain." She thought of Tiny's wife, sitting there so self-consciously last night. "So is his wife." She shook her head. "What's their story?"

He sighed. "I don't know. *Abuelita* says Angelica is from a bad line of witches."

That piqued her interest. "Really."

"She gave Tiny a charm this morning. And me, too." He pulled it out of his pocket and put it in her hand.

"What's in it?"

"Holy dirt, mainly. A saint's medal." He lifted a shoulder. "Who knows?"

"And what's it for?"

"Protection, I guess."

"Dirt for protection?"

"Ah, that's not just any dirt. It's holy dirt from Chimayó."

"I see," Luna said with proper reverence. "I've heard about it, but never been there. Have you?"

"Lots of times." He took the packet from her hand and hefted it, as if he was gauging the weight of magic it contained. "It's a holy place, but some of it gives me the creeps. They have these dolls in there—I don't like them. And Santo Niño—do you know him?"

"No. Baby Saint?"

He tucked the charm back into his wallet. "Baby Jesus. They say he walks around the countryside, doing miracles, and he does it so often they have to replace his shoes once a year. I was terrified of him when I was a kid."

"Why?"

"He's in this special stall in a side room, a big statue with clothes like a toddler in the eighteenth century or something. Inside the stall are a bunch of baby shoes, and people have carved the names of people—probably kids, mostly—into the wood around him." He quirked his mouth. "When I was little, I thought I could hear the whispers, and I always had nightmares about him coming into my room to tell me he'd seen me doing bad things."

"Yeah, that's pretty creepy."

They were only talking to avoid kissing, and Luna finally halted, putting a hand on his arm. "I think it's safe now."

He glanced over his shoulder. "Coast is clear." A hand came to her cheek. "Thank God."

Virgen de Guadalupe

Long, long ago, an Indian peasant named Juan Diego was crossing a hill when a vision of a beautiful dark-skinned woman, covered in golden light, appeared to him. She told him she was the Madonna, the mother of Jesus, and that she wanted a church built to her right on this very spot. Juan, much awed, carried the message to the bishop as requested, but the man did not believe him. Three days later, Guadalupe again showed herself to him, and made roses of Castile bloom in the middle of winter. Juan Diego filled his cloak with them and carried them back to the bishop. When he opened his cloak, the roses spilled out, fresh and beautiful, and the bishop was convinced. Even today, Juan Diego's sacred cloak still carries the image of the beautiful dark virgin who is, by all accounts, the queen of Mexico.

Fourteen

Maggie's Diary

17 Septiembre 2001,
San Roberto B

Dear Tupac,

My mom's getting worse and I don't know what to do. Yesterday, her boss called all pissed off and wanted to know how come she hadn't been to work in three days. Which I didn't know. I told him she was really sick with the flu and he said she had to call him. He was tired of her just not showing up. Enough is enough.

When my dad was around, Sundays were a big day in our house. We got up early and went to Mass, all of us together, at Our Lady of Guadalupe church, right in town. Then we'd go to a restaurant for lunch, then around somewhere. Sometimes we drove up to Pueblo to shop, or over to the Pueblo to eat some fry bread, out to the mountains somewhere, sometimes down to Espanola to visit cousins. Stuff like that. It wasn't always what I wanted to do, but it was still fun. Wish I hadn't complained so much then. It was good and I didn't even know it.

And every Sunday night, except when we went shopping, my mom cooked something good. A lot of times during the week, we only eat regular stuff like spaghetti or burritos because they're fast and my mom has to work, after all. But every Sunday, my mom did this big supper—pork chops, maybe, or a big roast or sometimes she bought tamales from the old ladies at church who sell them, and she'd make some green chile and we'd eat that.

So, this Sunday, today, I decided maybe that's what she needed. I called my uncle Ricky and he came and got me so I could buy some tamales. Then I called my grandma, my dad's mom, and asked her to come over for supper and told Ricky he could come, too, if he wanted. He said he would like to, and he's nineteen already, even though he's still got one more year at high school, so he's pretty grown-up. That made me feel good.

My mom was taking one of her long, long naps, so she didn't notice that I was in the kitchen all day. I used one of my mom's recipes, and it's not like I don't cook— I'm pretty good at it—so pretty soon the whole house was smelling good, filled up with these nice smells. The kitchen got all steamy, which made me feel cheerful, and I even turned on the Spanish radio station and listened to it, because it made me think of my dad. He liked the Spanish radio.

Late in the day, it got cloudy and that made it even

cozier. I set the table with the bright red and yellow plates my mom got from Pier One in Albuquerque, with pictures of roosters and sunflowers and teakettles, really loud stuff and silly, and that's what my mom liked about them.

My friend Joy called around five. "Whatcha doing?"

"Setting the table. We're having tamales. Want to come? Ever eat really good tamales?" I don't think they have stuff like that in Atlanta.

"I don't think I can. My toe is stubbed bad. It's totally disgusting."

"Your mom can't drive you?"

"No."

"It's only around the block—like half a mile. Put on some big shoes."

"It's too sore." Joy sounded like really disappointed, and I felt disappointed, too. "It would be so nice to get out—with somebody my age."

"Maybe my mom will come get you when she wakes up, okay? You want to?"

"No, don't go through all that. I should probably do homework anyway." The phone clicked and she said, "I gotta go. That's call waiting. See you at school tomorrow."

So right after that, it started to rain. Not the big rains we've been having, but soft. Colder. My grandma and Ricky came over and I wanted to get my sweater when I let them in! My grandma said, "Brr! Winter's coming." Then she lifted up her nose and smelled. "Oh, *h'ita*, it smells so good in here!"

I told her thanks and got them to come in the kitchen to see the table, which looked so cheery, and my grandma says, "So where's your mom?"

I told her she was sleeping. Grandma lifted up the pan lids and looked inside, and I was kind of nervous that it might not be good. She took a big spoon out of the drawer and stirred the chile, looking at it for about a whole minute, I swear, and I can never think what she sees in a pot—just a bunch of chiles and onions and specks of pepper and meat. "I didn't get the onions small enough, did I?"

"They're perfect." She took a bite and looked at the wall. "It's good, real good. You're gonna be a great cook." She turned down the heat a little bit and told me, "Next time, maybe leave the pork cooking while you go to church, then when you come back, it'll be real tender." She said it in a nice way, just giving me something new about cooking and I didn't take it the wrong way.

"You two get ready to eat," Grandma said. "I'm going to get Sally up."

Ricky lifted up the lid of the tortilla keep and tells me, "Not homemade."

"Duh," I told him.

He grinned at me to show he was only teasing, and took one out anyway. "You should have Grandma teach you, so then you know how when you grow up." He rolled it up and leaned on the counter, chomping it, and it made me think of my dad *so much*, especially when he did this thing, tossing a piece of hair off his forehead, that I got tears in my eyes all of a sudden.

Ricky's saying, "What's wrong, Maggie? What happened?" and I just shook my head, shaking my head so the tears wouldn't ruin my eyeliner. "You just look so much like my dad."

He came over and put his arms around me and said, "I'm sorry, *h'ita*. I know. I miss him so much sometimes. Every so often, I think of something I want to tell him, or I see a car he'd like, and then—I remember all over that I'm not gonna tell him anything ever again."

I didn't care about my eyeliner then. It was so nice just to talk about him. I told Ricky, "I miss him all kinda ways, like when the tomato plants were in the Safeway parking lot, and when they sing the Latin songs in church, or when I'm painting my toenails, because he thought it was funny that I liked painting them green."

From my mom's room came this big noise, like a fight, and my heart fell all the way to the floor. To the basement. I didn't know till then that my mom had took some of her sleeping pills. Now she wouldn't really be awake till morning. If we got her out of bed anyway, she'd be all hysterical and strange, and I just couldn't stand that, so I ran into the room and told my Grandma to leave her alone, come and eat, it would be okay. My grandma says, all outraged, "You cooked!"

I just took her hand and brought her back to the kitchen. "I'll save her some. I promise." But that extra plate on the table bugged me and I asked Ricky if he'd go get Joy, telling him about the stubbed toe and the reason she couldn't walk over here even if it was so close. And he was up for it. Just pulled out his keys and went to get her. So then we had a nice supper after all and I think Joy kinda liked Ricky.

My mom's not getting better though. I don't know who's going to help her. I don't know who to ask. My grandma tried to get me to think about coming to live with her, at least until my mom is better, but how can I do that? Just leave her with nobody? She'd die for sure.

I have to go to school tomorrow. Night.

4. *Made a searching and fearless moral inventory of ourselves.*

5. *Admitted to God, to ourselves and to another human being the exact nature of our wrongs.*

6. *Were entirely ready to have God remove all these defects of character.*

7. *Humbly asked Him to remove our shortcomings.*

8. *Made a list of all persons we had harmed, and became willing to make amends to them all.*

9. *Made direct amends to such people wherever possible, except when to do so would injure them or others.*

10. *Continued to take personal inventory and when we were wrong promptly admitted it.*

Fifteen

After Joy left, Luna found herself restless. Hungry. It was too wet outside to garden, but she put on a rain hat and started walking anyway, enjoying the soft drizzle that put moisture back into her desert-dried sinuses and lungs, dampened her face and eyelashes and lips.

Until her feet carried her there, she had not realized that she was going to walk by Thomas's house. See where he lived and what it was like.

Like a teenager. How *cute,* said Barbie, cooing.

Not very. But she was still glad she'd done it when she saw it. In the soft drizzle, it looked a little shabby sitting at the very top of a hill, the yard so steep that someone had created steps with railroad ties. It was a two-story Victorian anomaly with stucco walls and a porch that wrapped all the way around the front and one side. A woman would have hung flower baskets on the empty hooks, but the only flowers growing here were tall purple phlox and a giant stand of cosmos—plants that didn't need anything but a glance to thrive. She remembered that Thomas had said the house was a stray he'd adopted and she smiled, liking him for that. There was grandeur left in her, that big house, and a kind of serenity in the big front windows that gazed over the valley. The view had to be amazing from those windows. She had a moment of house-lust.

Since she hadn't known she was coming, she didn't know whether she'd planned to go to the door or just walk by, but the choice was taken from her when she spied Thomas himself sitting in the shadows of the porch roof. He sat in a chair, something in his hands, and his dog came leaping off the porch, skidding on the wet grass as he came toward her, happily licking her hand, then bouncing back toward the porch as if to say, "C'mon! It's so great to have a visitor!"

Thomas stood, not smiling, and Luna had a bad moment, thinking this had been an utterly adolescent thing to do and she ought to be flogged for not at least calling first. There just hadn't been that much thought involved—she was acting on instinct.

He gestured for her to come up there, and she picked her way up the steps carefully, water dripping from her hat, her cheeks flaming. "I wanted to see where you lived," she said, ducking under the shelter of the porch roof.

Thomas only looked at her for a long moment. "I'm glad you came—"

Tiny slammed out of the house, talking before he saw Luna standing there. "Hector Baca saw Angelica out this afternoon with some dickhead and I can't get through to nobody to find out what's going on. Thomas—" He saw Luna. "Oh."

Behind her, the heavens suddenly opened and water poured through the split, a river from heaven pouring on the ground. Blocking her exit.

"Hold on one second," Thomas said, putting his hand on her upper arm. "Don't go."

She nodded.

"Tiny, inside."

They started to go in, but the phone in Tiny's hand rang, and he answered it urgently, then shoved it into Thomas's hand. "It's your ex," he said, and it was plain he meant Luna to hear, that he wanted others to suffer with him. He banged back into the house.

Luna wished for an earthquake to suck her deep into the bowels of the earth, out of sight. A clap of thunder burst in the sky and she jumped.

"Nadine," Thomas barked into the phone, "what is it?" He didn't move away, and Luna thought he might be doing it on purpose to reassure her that it didn't mean anything, his ex calling.

She turned away, looking out over the valley. Eddies of mist made the fields of chamiso and sage look soft and furry, and the ankles of the mountains beneath the skirts of thick dark clouds were dark, dark blue. She tried not to listen, but it wasn't like he made a secret of it. "That's none of your business," he said. Then, "Nadine, what do you want me to do?"

A longer pause, filled with the rain crashing around the porch. Luna could hear the tinny voice of a sobbing woman at the other end of the line. Thomas's voice was gentler when he spoke again. "Maybe you need to go to

a counselor. If he won't go with you, go by yourself."
Captured by something in his voice, Luna glanced over
at him in time to see him drop a shoulder, hide a flash
of emotion on his face. "Nadine," he said. Then more
strongly, interrupting. "Nadine—"

I might still be in love with my ex-wife.

Cheeks burning, Luna walked down the porch a little
way, to give him more privacy. Through a window at
the far end, she saw Placida sitting in a rocking chair in
a big, old kitchen. Catholic radio played in Spanish, and
she worked a rosary along with the announcer, blue
beads spilling through her gnarled hands like hope.
Luna had a sudden memory of her father's mother, in a
house with turquoise linoleum and pink bathroom fixtures, kneeling before a small altar she kept at the end
of the hall. She had died when Luna was four, so the
memory was very, very old.

Placida didn't see her, and Luna stepped back a little
to make sure she wasn't staring rudely, but she couldn't
stop admiring the scene. It made her want to paint. A
light over the sink showed a big black cat on the windowsill, his tail flicking, and the pool of light almost
touched Placida. Her flowered housedress and the
amazement of her hair, still probably down to her hips
if she took it out of the braids she piled it into, mostly
gray, but with some black left in it. Luna thought of her
being on the earth when Pancho Villa was riding
through Mexico, and sitting in a wagon on the road to
Raton.

Close behind her Thomas said, "Nadine, I'm sorry,
but I don't think I can help you." He hung up and
sighed, bending over Luna's neck to plant a kiss there,
the gesture somehow familiar even though they'd
known each other less than two weeks. It was comfortable, and Luna found herself reaching for his wrist,

drawing his hand into hers, offering whatever he needed just then.

"I'm sorry," she said. "I came at a very bad time."

"No," he said, and tugged her closer, putting his chin down on her shoulder, his arms looped around her waist. "I'm glad you're here. Come sit down."

Luna settled in one of the chairs and he sat down beside her, picking up the piece of wood he'd been holding. A soft shape was emerging—a knee pushing at a drape of fabric, a foot. When he took up a knife, curls of wood drifted off the blade to dance into the air. "I think it's a Virgin," he said. "I haven't done one for a while."

"*Santos?*"

He nodded. "*Abuela*'s line used to have a lot of *santeros.*" He held it up, admiring it, and she loved the smoothness of his lines, the look of his dark hand on the wood. "Now I'm the only one."

She smiled, but her hands were clasped hard and she made herself release them. Forcing herself not to ask about the ex-wife.

As if he read her mind, he said, "Nadine, my ex, heard about you from somebody. She wanted to get on my case about hanging out with a white woman."

"Ah!"

"She's also pregnant," he added, "so she's a little crazy, and she thinks my brother is running around on her."

"Is he?"

He pursed his lips, gently shaping his thumb over the foot of the *santo*. "Probably. It's what he does. He's just like my father."

"Not you?"

He raised his eyes. "No."

The phone, sitting on the small metal table between them, rang, and Thomas looked at it with weariness.

"Sorry," he said and picked it up. "Hello? Oh, Angelica, he'll be really glad to talk to you."

Tiny was out on the porch before Thomas had a chance to move, and grabbed the phone and dashed back inside. Luna could hear his voice, rising and falling in the particular sound of relief. She touched her chest, the ache there, and closed her eyes. "God," she said quietly.

"Love hurts," Thomas said.

The rain was letting up, and she rubbed her hands on her thighs. "I guess I'll get back. Joy went to her friend's house and I . . . " She lifted a shoulder. "I don't know. My feet just brought me here."

"Joy's gone?"

She nodded.

"Your house is empty?"

Luna grinned. "Yep."

He was on his feet, pulling his keys out of his pocket in a half second. "I'll be back later," he called to whoever, and grabbed her hand, tugging her to her feet and out to his truck.

Thomas didn't even think. It took three minutes to drive to her house, another two to shed their clothes and fall into her big, extrasoft bed, piled with silky pillows in emerald and sapphire and gold. He pushed her, naked, into the piles of fabric and then just stood over her for a minute. She lifted her arms above her head and tilted her head sideways a little, as if offering all she was.

It slayed him. Outside, rain began to fall lightly, and the scent washed into the room, and Thomas could not breathe for looking at Luna. Her pale white flesh so bright against the vivid colors of her bed, the sparkle of an earring against her neck, the curve of belly that slid into thighs and the low triangle of hair, the bend of her knee suddenly revealing the secret between, her eyes so wide and steady and deep, fixed on his face. Everything in him was aroused—his eyes and the palms of his hands, his knees and the skin across his chest; there was a buzzing around his skull and his tongue. He couldn't think how to get them all on her at once, and tried one at a time instead.

First he looked at her, then bent over her and smelled her skin, then put his tongue on her shoulder and tasted it, nibbled her arm, pressed the flat of his tongue on the lower curve of her breast, making her breathe out in a soft gust as his hair fell around them, loose and trailing. His organ brushed her thighs, his knee bumped her calf.

"It's been so long, so long, so long," he said raggedly, using his nose to trace the line of her belly, his hands on her sides. He couldn't think of ever burning like this, the low simmer going all day and night now, every nerve alive, hungry, waiting for the next chance. "This is so good," he said. He put his fingers between her legs, wanting to make her cry out again, and he made it last, going so slowly so that he could watch her breasts rise and fall in the open while he touched her.

Her hands floated down his back, down his sides, over his buttocks. "Yes," she whispered, and kissed his chin, his eyes, his forehead.

They made love, slowly, so slowly, rolling into satisfaction rather than roaring into it, and then they were free to lie in Luna's bed, side by side, holding hands, which took away all the things he'd been worrying about, all the things he didn't want to think about. On her ceiling was a folklike painting of the galaxy, the background dark, bright blue, the stars childlike yellow and gold and white, the planets shaped like hearts and painted like bowling balls. "Did you do that?"

"Yeah. It was fun, once I figured out how to get up there."

"How did you?"

She grinned. "Rented a scaffold, Mr. Construction."

He laughed softly. "Good thinking." For a while, they were quiet, their bodies looped and tangled. "I love your house," he said.

"Me, too. I always wanted an old adobe and now I have one."

"How old is it?"

"Not sure, exactly. Around 1840."

He touched the wall, whistling. "Pretty old. Mine was built in 1891."

"That's old, too. Does it have a story?"

"A blacksmith built it. Nothing matches. None of the windows are the same size. The floors are crooked." He smiled. "Still love it, though. One of these days, I want to tackle the kitchen." He looked at her. "I should have taken you inside."

Luna lifted up on one elbow. "Wouldn't want to get cursed by *Abuelita*." She ran an open palm in a line from the hollow of his throat to the base of his organ, the exploration of a new lover.

He pressed her hand to his belly. "That's ice cream. I keep a store of it, just in case."

She kissed his belly button, her hair tickling his chest. "I love it."

It pained him a little, made an ache grow right in the middle of his heart. "Thought women all wanted six-pack abs."

"Overrated." She moved, pulling the covers over them. "We can't stay here long. Joy might come in early."

"I understand. Just a minute or two more, huh?"

She settled her head on his shoulder, and he found he liked the fit. Sleepiness from the long day in the wind and sun settled over him, a quiet he hadn't felt in a long time.

To keep himself from drifting off, he said, "I liked your daughter. She's a good kid—funny and open-minded."

"She liked you back." She turned her head. "I'm not crazy about the two of you spending much time together, Thomas. I don't want her to be in the middle of my relationships."

He felt a little prick of rejection, then realized how it would be to have to protect a child against the capriciousness of lovers who might be casual or serious—who knew, in the beginning, which would be which? "Okay."

"That doesn't hurt your feelings?"

"Yeah," he said. "But I'll live with it. You're right. We don't know, do we, where we'll be next week or next month?"

"Right." She curled into him. "For now, though, I like it."

"Me, too." He closed his eyes, covered her breast with his hand, thinking idly of carving it into wood, this particular shape, wondering how to create the soft heft. It made him chuckle. To explain, he said, "I'm thinking of the Virgin Mary's *chichis*. Think I'm in trouble?"

"I bet they all thought of them, all those sculptors who carved her breasts. They had to, didn't they?"

"Mmm." He curved his fingers around, memorizing it.

There was such lassitude in his limbs, such a sense of relaxation. His mind drifted, back to her daughter, the sweetness of the interplay between mother and daughter when Joy stubbed her toe. Joy. Luna must have loved her a lot to name her that. He spoke aloud the next thought. "Why did you leave her behind?"

Her body jerked the slightest bit at the question and he knew immediately it was wrong. "It was for the best at the time," she said.

Thomas had heard the words before, that first night

in her kitchen. He shifted to one elbow so that he could look at her. "Because you drank?"

"Yes." She pulled the cover up from their feet and over her shoulder.

"You don't like talking about it."

"No."

"Does that mean you won't?"

She took a breath and let it out. "Thomas, let's just not, okay? It was a miserable time in my life and I hate thinking about it. I really let her down." A shadow crossed her face, putting a frown between her brows. "This is probably more of the same kind of thing, too, but I can't seem to help myself."

"What is the same? Sex is the same as drinking?"

"Sometimes. And smoking and overeating and all those other compulsive things."

He chuckled. "So I'm like a cigarette? You want to suck on me, baby?" He leered and leaned in close, biting on her shoulder playfully.

Luna laughed and pushed at him. "You know what I mean."

"You take things too seriously."

"Sometimes, I do," she agreed, and raised her eyes. Guileless and wide and somehow wary, like a cat who'd been left in the alley, watching her owners drive away to their new home. "But with Joy, I'm not kidding around. I really want a second chance with her. A chance to show her that I can be the mother I should have been. And speaking of that—" She hopped up and threw his clothes at him. "You have to get dressed and come into the kitchen and we have to pretend to be civilized in case she comes home early."

He put on his boxers and his jeans, interested now more than ever in the walls she was throwing up. "What if," he said, buttoning his shirt, "I tell you the worst things I've done? Will you tell me how you left her?"

She whirled. "Why do you want to know this stuff? Can't we just start here?"

"We could," he said. "But I want to know more than that."

For a long moment, she only looked at him. "Come into the kitchen," she said.

Luna washed her face at the sink and dried it on a cup towel, then took two sodas out of the fridge and carried them to the corner, where Thomas waited. She sat down.

"So?" he said.

A flicker of anger licked at her nape. "You're kinda pushy, you know that?"

An unapologetic grin. "Yep."

She poured soda slowly into her glass, carefully so it wouldn't foam up too much. The vanilla scent of it wafted into the air. "I went to college when I was sixteen. I was just totally driven, straight As, landed a full-ride scholarship to CU. I met Marc there the first year. He was as working class as I was, only he was from Jackson, Mississippi, and the class structure there is a little more intense, I gather."

Thomas nodded to show he was listening.

"We didn't hook up right away, but we dated off and on for most of my undergraduate days, then got serious when we were in grad school. We got married when I was twenty-three and moved to Atlanta after he finished law school. We both had a lot to learn. How to dress, how to drink, how to have dinner parties for twenty-five, how to talk to people according to their societal rank . . ." A sense of pressure built over her sinuses. "It was such bullshit. I hated it. But as I said, we were both pretty driven, so I did what I had to do."

She took a sip of soda. "One thing that was required was a lot of drinking. Wine, martinis, scotch—all of it. I had a pretty high tolerance, which impressed Marc a lot; a woman who can handle her liquor in that crowd is an asset, let me tell you." She paused, remembering. "Man, they drank a lot, those people. If you put them in bars and put beers and shots in their hands, instead of martinis and scotches, they'd be drunks. Not in that crowd, though. I knew one lady who drank gin morning, noon, and night and the servants just went around quietly behind her, picking up the slack."

"Must be nice."

"Enabling."

"I guess." He frowned. "So were you working, too, or just doing the corporate wife thing?"

She raised her index finger. "First bone of contention. I found out in college that I loved working with people who didn't have many options. The money was never as important to me as being able to help people in some way, and in Atlanta, I found work with a clinic that specialized in counseling low-income families. The woman who ran it had landed a bunch of grants to get it open and she didn't pay much, but I loved the work." She looked at him. "If there was something like that here, Tiny could get the help he needs, instead of this crap the courts order."

Thomas nodded, his mouth grim.

"Marc wanted me to get my Ph.D. so I could go hang up a shingle and treat rich folks, but I stood my ground for once and stuck with the clinic. At least it was something that was mine, you know? Nothing else was, trust me. I'm pretty sure I knew it even then." She reached into a drawer and pulled out a photograph. "That's me on the left."

"Good God. What happened to your hair?"

"I straightened it in those days."

He handed the picture back. "I like you much better like this."

Luna looked at the woman in the photo. Her hair was restrained in a headband—pre-Hillary, the style had been quite popular with some women—and swung in a neat, ear-length bob. A demure blouse with a Peter Pan collar hid what had been a painfully thin frame, and she was laughing. Holding a martini. "Me, too," she said quietly.

"So, then . . . ?"

"So then I got pregnant with Joy. I quit drinking, quit the party rounds. I worked and gained weight and got ready for Joy. Marc hated it all—hated me not being with him at the parties, hated my body, hated my refusal to do exactly what he wanted when he wanted it done." She shook her head. "I was so miserable, but there I was—you know?"

"Sure."

"That's when he started sleeping around."

"You didn't cheat on *him*, though, did you?"

Luna, feeling vulnerable, attacked in her own way. "Are you in love with her still, Thomas? I think I need to know that."

He pursed his lips. Lowered his eyes. Not a great sign. "I don't know the answer, Luna."

"Then why are we doing this?"

"What? Finding out about each other?"

She met his gaze stubbornly. "You're finding out about me, not the other way around."

"I'm not trying to hide anything, Luna. I won't lie— there's a lot of shit left over from all that, but I'm not sure that I ever did love her. I never went after her—she was too young and she was too much trouble, too volatile, and I just wasn't all that interested. But she was pretty determined. And beautiful." He shrugged. "She's very beautiful. Exotic. Get a lot of points out in the world with a woman like that on your arm."

She nodded.

"I'm trying to sort through it all, Luna. What was real and what wasn't. The one thing I do know is that I wanted a family. She was available."

And she'd made one with someone else. "I'm sorry."

A shrug. "What're you gonna do?" He touched her hand. "I really want to know about Joy. Keep going."

Luna gave him a wry grin. "You're stubborn."

"So they say."

"The background doesn't matter all that much, really. I can blame a lot on Marc, but I brought it all on myself, Thomas. That's what you need to know. He was an asshole, but I could have made a lot of other choices than the ones I made."

"How?"

Suddenly, she wished they were still in bed, curled together. It would be so much easier to say all this if she didn't have to look at him. "Marc was a lot of negative things," she said. "But he was also a very good father. He really loved Joy and she really loved him, and I wanted to make our marriage work for her sake, so she'd have a mommy *and* a daddy. I didn't, you know?" Her throat threatened to tighten up, but she drank some soda and it opened again. "To make that happen, I had to lie to myself a lot. Pretend I had no idea the reason he was so late so often was that he was with other women." She scowled, ran a fingernail along the edge of the table. "That's not exactly right, either. In hindsight, I knew he was seeing other women because the evidence presented itself, but I had no reason to suspect him then. I'm sure I felt it on some level and just denied it."

"That's natural, Luna." He touched her hand, his fingers tracing the bones gently.

A sense of strangulation rose in her chest. "God, Thomas, this is so pathetic and awful. Why do you want to know?"

"It's not pathetic."

"Yes, it is." She swallowed and stood up, moving away. "I don't know that I—" She shook her head. She could have wild sex with him but she couldn't tell him why she left her daughter behind? That was a skewed kind of intimacy.

Behind her, Thomas said, "The only thing I wanted was to be a father. I'm good at it. I like kids, and there are so many of them who need somebody—and then I found out I was sterile. It was such a blow. Such a blow," he said more quietly. His face was open, and it was hard to look at him, see the pain there, in a face that once had been as full of energy and hope as hers had been, once upon a time, and know all that he'd come to lose. "It matters to you, the loss of your daughter. So it matters to me because I'm feeling something here and I think you are, too."

Luna met his eyes and said, "At some point, I decided I needed to go back on the party circuit. And I remembered how much better drinking made me feel. So it became a habit. A little more and a little more. I had a good housekeeper, a live-in, actually, who helped keep things running when I was hungover. I never drank around Joy, you know, not until she went to bed if I was home."

She braced herself on the counter a little more solidly. "Marc started to travel a lot, and I started to drink a lot more. I functioned, more or less. Worked and played with Joy, then got drunk every night." Tears always showed up at this moment, and she couldn't keep the shine away, but she could swallow most of them if she was careful not to speak too quickly. "When Joy was about five, Marc met someone else. Someone from an old southern family who would be able to smooth his way into that world he wanted so badly, and over the course of two years, he set me up. He collected a lot of photos and receipts and everything else you can think of, to show that I was a drunk, and then he filed for divorce and for custody of Joy. I pretty much lost everything. My job. My home. My family." She blinked. "My daughter."

"Damn."

"And that," she said with bitter humor, "is when I became a dedicated drunk. I came back to New Mexico and lived in Albuquerque. Close enough, I think, to my mother and sister that I could get help when I was ready, but far enough away that I didn't have to humiliate them." She paused, took a breath, and said the last part. "It took three years, but I finally hit bottom and called my mother, and she came and got me into rehab. I've been sober four years now."

He stood up and came over, putting his hands on either side of her, bending down to put his forehead on Luna's. "He should have helped you instead of helping you dig your grave." Very gently, he kissed the bridge of her nose. "I'm glad you survived it. That you're here right now. That you told me the story."

"I don't ever want to talk about it again, is that clear?"

"You're too hard on yourself," he said in that gruff voice. "People fuck up, Luna, they just do. It's part of the game."

"Not like that," she said. "Most people don't abandon their children. They don't get drunk and wreck cars. Three times, Thomas, I wrecked a car drunk. Most people don't—"

He kissed her. Lifted up her face and kissed her silent. "Stop," he whispered. "You were trying, trying to kill yourself and I'm glad you didn't."

Light caught unkindly in the scars on his cheeks, and she touched the roughness with her fingertips. "The real miracle is that I didn't kill anybody else."

"Or go to jail for a long time."

"Yeah. Lucky, I guess."

"Or white." He smiled.

"That, too."

"You need to stop being so cruel to yourself," he said, hands in her hair. "You lost everything and you went crazy. That's not so strange."

She realized she was crying, and she hated that, but he tasted like hope. She might hate that even more. There was honor in his touch, and compassion, and gentleness, and humor, and how could she love somebody again? Ever? "Let's talk about something else, okay?" she whispered. Then he was holding her and rocking her back and forth, and there was so much power and reliability in his body, in the way he held her.

His mouth was close to her ear, and his voice was low and gentle. "Let me tell you something, Luna-Lu. I haven't been able to take a full breath in two years. Since I saw you with my grandmother the night of the fire, I'm whistling." He pulled her closer, in that soft grind that was so suggestive, smiling down at her. "I didn't even want to jack off, to tell you the truth. Now all I'm thinking is when can we do it again?"

She laughed, shocked at the graphic phrase in spite of herself.

"Maybe," he said more seriously, "we'll find out we can't be together for some reason or another. It happens. We've both been around the block enough to know that"—he shook his head—"things come between people."

"Yeah."

"But for now, this is good. It's really good, me and you." He said it quietly, earnestly. "Let's just be with it while it's here, eh?"

She nodded, and weary, rested her head on his chest, just breathing him in, the scent of Thomas Coyote who held her as if she were a precious, precious thing. It had been a very long time.

Joy stood on her porch, awkwardly, surprised that Ricardo—"It's not Ricky," he'd told her, "only my family calls me that"—had walked her up to the porch, even though she told him she was okay, that she could limp that much, just not walk around the block. Truthfully, her toe was hurting now and she was really, really sleepy, like she'd been running around all day when it was only being outside. When she stood still, it was almost like she could feel the river in her veins, lulling her to sleep. "Well," she said, turning to hold out her hand to him. "Thanks."

He grinned at her, and his teeth were so beautiful, so white and big in the dark that Joy felt her heart flutter a little bit. His hands were in his pockets, but he made a show of taking one out, his fingers lacing between hers in a way that was so forward she shouldn't like it, but she did. "Can I call you, Girl with Wrong Hair?"

"Not if you call me that."

He laughed. "Okay, can I call you, Joy?"

"Yeah," she said, and that flutter came again. But she didn't want to seem like some dumb high school girl; she wanted to be more sophisticated than that, and she added, "Please."

He took a pen out of his back pocket and handed it to her, holding out his arm. "Write it down for me."

His forearm was dark and smooth and it gave her a

little jolt to put her palm on it, to write her phone number beneath the vein along the inside. She thought she could feel his breath on her shoulder, but when she looked up, he only smiled and took his pen back. "Good night, Joy," he said.

"Night, Ricardo." She went inside, and rested just inside the door for a minute so she could collect herself before she went to the kitchen, where she'd seen her mom's head a minute ago. And suddenly, it seemed so good to her, so rich to be in this house, to have her mom waiting up with a friend of her own sitting with her, that she rushed into the kitchen and flung her arms around her mom's neck. Luna caught her, laughing softly, and Joy smelled something strange and rich in her hair— maybe like the river, or Thomas, her boyfriend, or something. "Did you have a good time?"

"Oh, yeah. I mean"—she thought of how sad Maggie had been, but Ricardo had been so cute!—"yes and no. I'm worried about Maggie. Oh, it was sad over there tonight. Maggie cooked all this food and her mom didn't even get up. Just her uncle and her grandma and me to eat it, and I know Maggie did it for her mom."

"Is that the daughter of the man who was killed last spring?" Thomas asked.

"Yeah. You know her?"

"I think so. Her mother comes to see my grandmother for herbs and things like that."

Joy's stomach flipped over. "You're the *bruja*'s grandson?"

"*Bruja?*" He laughed. "Is that what they say about her? I guess so."

Oh, man, oh man, oh man. Maggie would be so mad at Joy when she found out that Joy's mom's new boyfriend was the same guy Maggie wanted for her mom! Still, maybe Joy could help a little. "You should tell your grandma that she's really sick, that Sally is really sick. She needs something. Not just that charm."

Thomas cleared his throat, frowning. "My grandma's not a psychologist or anything. She's just an old woman who prays."

Joy bit her lip. "I know. But I'm worried about my friend. She's been okay, you know? But she was like all sad tonight, trying to pretend it was okay, but it wasn't. And Mom, I didn't tell you this, but she has a shrine to Tupac and she makes offerings to it, like he's a saint or something. I think she doesn't know what to do."

For a long moment, Luna was quiet, then she said, "I'm not sure what I can do, Joy. I'd like to help because you care so much about this girl, but I'm not sure what you're asking for."

"Can I just bring her over sometimes, over here?"

"Of course."

"And maybe, Mom," Joy said, earnestly, just thinking of it suddenly, "you could just talk to her mom whenever you see her. Maybe you'll see something or whatever."

Luna nodded. "I can keep my eyes open."

"Me, too," Thomas said.

The phone rang, and startled, Luna answered it, worry on her face. A worry that cleared immediately. "Sure," she said, "Hang on." Lowering the phone to her stomach, she said with a smile, "It's for you. A guy named Ricardo with wonderful telephone manners."

Her tummy flipped. "I'll take it into my room. Good night you guys!" She rushed into her room and clicked on the remote, and heard Ricardo's voice pour into her ear. "What're you doing?"

From *GlamGal* magazine, August 2001:

Good Grooming As a Way to Inner Peace

The greats—Elizabeth Taylor, Sophia Loren, et al—have always known the way to inner peace is the care and tending of one's outer shell. Nothing can beat an avocado facial and a great manicure to make you look your best, and we all know when you look good, you feel good. Try these six (cheap!) tips for looking good this month: egg and avocado facial, mayonnaise hair treatment, sugar skin scrub, olive oil foot treatment, lavender-rose herbal spa bath, and our personal fave: lemon-peppermint alcohol spritz. Recipes below.

Sixteen

The road to hell was paved with good intentions. Luna truly meant to keep an eye out for Sally, the widow having such a hard time adjusting, but she simply forgot in the new world of juggling her life at a much more hectic pace. It was one thing to take care of herself and her life without a car; it was proving to be much more difficult with two of them. A small example was the milk situation. Joy drank a lot of milk, which meant bringing gallons home from work instead of the quarts she usually carted. She didn't mind walking with a bag of groceries, but a gallon of milk weighed a ton, and Joy drank about a gallon every other day.

That was only one small example. Luna hated it that Joy walked home in the rain one day, hated it one evening when Joy remembered, well past dark, that she needed a special set of pens for art class the following morning; even the night Joy had had a stubbed toe and wanted to go around the corner to Maggie's house. Not to mention, who wanted her daughter out after dark?

So there were the hassles of not driving and wondering why she still didn't. But even the difficulty wasn't enough to prevent the feeling of panic that filled her at the idea of actually getting behind the wheel of a car again. Kitty had bought Luna a car over a year ago—a sobriety/birthday present. It was a cute little blue Toyota, and Luna knew how thrilled Kitty had been to be able to afford to give it to her.

But Luna had climbed into the adorable little thing and had had a panic attack. A full-scale, all-out, can't-breathe, I'm-gonna-die panic attack. And that was the last time she tried. Kitty just patted her shoulder and said it would be in the garage whenever she was ready. Frank drove it sometimes, just to keep it in good condition, but it was Luna's car.

Whenever she was ready for it.

Beyond the driving headache, it was also insane at work—the back to school, end of summer rushes. People were putting up jam and veggies and acting like winter would mean not being able to go anywhere. And her head was crowded with thoughts of Thomas, whom she hadn't been able to see but once, for a very short, hot brace of kisses on Wednesday afternoon, and conversely, worries about Marc and what his next trick might be.

And then there was the problem of her mother. Or rather her father. Elaine had called Luna at work on Wednesday morning. "I think you need to go see Mom today," she said without preamble. "And realize we need to just sell that land because the whole thing is breaking her heart."

"Hi, Elaine," Luna said dryly, stacking vases.

"I'm sorry, Lu, but you're not thinking about this, and I think Mom is really handling it badly."

"What are you talking about?"

"Did you even know Frank is out of town this week? Do you ever go see your mother?"

Luna sighed. She always got aggressive when she was worried. "Of course I go see her. I see her all the time. It's just been busy this week and I haven't had a chance. Did you talk to her or something? Is there something wrong?"

"I think there is, Lu. She sounded weird last night. Like not really there, or something."

"I'll go this afternoon."

"What about the land?"

"I haven't even had a chance to think about it, Elaine. Let's not do anything rash, okay? I think we need to at least see it."

"I don't need to see it. Do you realize he was living not forty miles from me since I've been in Raton? That sucks. And then why'd he have to do it like this?"

"I know. It's not fair. But I'm not going to feel happy about selling it until we see it. Maybe not even then. Maybe it was his way of making up to us."

"I could buy a brand new house, Lu. You have one. I don't. I live in this crummy apartment."

Elaine made more money than Luna did, but she took a deep breath. "I'll think about it, I promise. Okay?"

"Fine. Call me about Mom."

"I will."

When Luna came in that afternoon, she said to Joy, "Let's go see Grandma."

Joy, stretched out on the couch with a paperback novel in her hands, sighed heavily. "Do we have to walk?"

"How else?"

"It's too far. I get sick of walking all the time. It's hot and my toe hurts."

"Fine." Hearing her sister's petty tone in the word, Luna bit back her annoyance, which was mostly directed toward herself anyway. More kindly she said, "Okay. I'll go alone. No biggie."

Joy huffed. "Are you ever going to get a driver's license?"

"I don't know."

"If I get a New Mexico license will you get me a car?"

"I already have one you can drive." She flipped through the mail, separating bills from junk from personal. Not that there was ever that much personal mail anymore. Everybody used e-mail. "It's a nice Toyota."

"How old do I have to be to drive here?"

"Sixteen. And you'll need a job, too, to support the habit. Gas, insurance, upkeep, all of it."

Joy flung herself back on the pillows. "Oh, like anybody could pay for any of that on five dollars an hour."

"It's pretty expensive, all right."

"What if I can get my dad to pay?"

Tempting. "Nope. It's your responsibility."

Another huff. "Forget it. I want money to ski." She sat up, very straight, horror on her face. "But if you don't have a car, there's no way to get there, is there?"

Stricken, Luna sank down in the chair. "Uh, no. Good point."

"Don't you think it's just a little bit immature of you to just keep avoiding the issue of driving like a normal person?" Joy flung one arm over her head, her bracelets rattling down her arms in a tinny wash. "Hitching rides with everyone, getting your mom to drive you to the store when you need a lot of groceries or you have to pick up your daughter from the airport?"

"Maybe." Luna shrugged. "Lots of people don't drive."

"Yeah, epileptics and old ladies!"

A prickly wave of irritation rose in her chest, whipped right through her shoulders to her arms, and she wanted a cigarette urgently. Why had she thought it would be a good idea to quit smoking just as she brought her teenager to live with her again?

What wasn't she saying? "I don't have to be what you want me to be, Joy. I only have to be somebody I'm comfortable with." She took a breath. "I was honestly thinking earlier today that it is hard on you that I don't drive and I need to think about it, but you have to give me some time."

Joy lowered her eyes, picked invisible stuff from her jeans. "Whatever."

Luna stood. "I really am worried about Grandma, so I'm going to walk up there. Do you want to go or stay? There's frozen pizza if you get hungry, and I'll be home by seven or eight."

"I'll just stay here. Maybe I'll go see Maggie after a while. And Ricardo said he might call."

"Do you have homework?"

"I did it already."

"All right." Luna popped a kiss on her head, even if she didn't want it, and headed out.

It was hot in the late afternoon sunshine, probably close to ninety, which was hot for September, but not unheard of. It wasn't more than a mile and a half to Kitty's house, but it suddenly did seem like a long way up those hills, crossing all those streets, and dodging cars on the narrow lanes in between. Feeling winded, she stopped, hands on her hips, wondering if she wanted to go after all. But the truth was, it wasn't about Luna. It was about her mother. She couldn't stand to think of Kitty sad and alone, and she wasn't the type to be able to ask for help.

Luna started walking. It wouldn't take more than a half hour and Kitty would bring her home later.

But . . . out of the mouths of babes. Why *was* she still avoiding driving? She could have reinstated her driver's license eighteen months ago, and instead, she'd just drifted along, walking everywhere. Why?

She didn't really have an answer, and still didn't have one when she rang her mother's doorbell, feeling sweaty and stinky and out of breath. As she waited for Kitty to answer, she noticed the cottonwoods that shaded the courtyard were really starting to turn color now, a cluster of bright yellow leaves standing out amid the green. It was always such a surprise, every year, to look up and notice fall.

Kitty answered the door in her bathrobe. She had on no makeup. Her feet were bare. A kindling of alarm went through Luna. "Mom! Are you sick?"

"No." She shook her head vaguely. "Frank had to go to Arizona for business and I'm just taking a couple of days to lie around." She pulled a crumpled tissue out of her robe pocket and wiped her nose. Her eyes were red-rimmed. Weary. "Come on in, honey. I'll make you some tea."

Luna took charge. Putting an arm around Kitty's shoulders, she led her into the kitchen, settled her in a chair, and said, "Stay." Kitty's Pomeranian came running in and whined pitifully, and Luna bent over and picked him up, dumping him on her mother's lap. "Give your dog some love," she said. "I'll make you something to eat. How long has it been?"

"I don't know."

"Did you eat breakfast? I don't see any evidence of it."

Kitty tucked her dog under her chin. The golden creature wiggled happily, but didn't get overly excited, as if sensing there was more going on here. "I don't know," Kitty said. "I think so."

Best Friend Barbie, braiding her hair, said, *Uh-oh.*

It's not that bad, Luna argued, pulling out eggs and cheese and butter and lining them up on the counter. *Just a little depressed.*

A little! When was the last time your mother went without her makeup? 1979?

Luna made coffee, heated butter in the heavy skillet, scrambled eggs with cheese, and sliced bread for toast, chattering lightly, asking simple questions Kitty could answer easily. As she put the plate down in front of her, Luna realized she was flat-out terrified. She had never, in all of her life, seen her mother like this. Nestling a fork next to the plate, she said gently, "Eat."

Kitty picked up the fork and robotically put food in her mouth, chewing like she'd been programmed, but Luna figured it didn't matter how it went in, as long as it did. She sat down opposite and petted Roger, the dog, drinking some coffee, wondering what she should do once Kitty was fed. In the bright light of the kitchen, she saw that her mother was getting old. The skin under her jaw was softening, and her eyelids were wrinkled. It pierced her.

When the eggs were gone, Luna edged the coffee cup over and Kitty picked that up, less robotically, and took a sip. "Let's take this out to the back. I want to smoke a cigarette, and Frank will kill me if he knows I've done it."

"A cigarette?" Luna started laughing. "Mom! You haven't smoked in fifteen years." Not to mention, Frank really would kill her. His wife had died of lung cancer. He hated cigarettes with a ferocity reserved for those who'd lost someone to the weed—and had been a major nag force in her drive to quit.

"I know. It's temporary." She walked down the hall in her swishy robe, still looking gorgeous for all her diminishment, and Luna loved her so much it was like a pain. Everything about her—the bravery in her shoulders that had had to carry too much, the vanity that kept her so beautiful, her absolute insistence upon believing the best of everything. There wasn't anyone on the earth like Kitty McGraw Esquivel Torrance, and Luna didn't know how she got so lucky as to be her daughter, but she was grateful.

They sat in the green and gold of evening on the deck that looked out over the blue sea of the valley. Kitty took out a Virginia Slim Ultra Light Menthol and lit it.

Luna reached for the pack and took one, too. "If you're smoking, I'm smoking, too."

Kitty looked at her for a minute, then nodded.

They sat back in guilty pleasure and smoked. Suddenly, Kitty said, "I slept with him the first time we went out. That's not such a big thing now, but it was then. I was a virgin, because girls were, good girls anyway, the ones who wanted to get something out of life." She looked toward the horizon. "And I was a good girl. Ambitious, but good." She smoked, blew out a ladylike plume of smoke. "The first minute I laid eyes on Jesse Esquivel . . ." She trailed off.

Never, ever did Kitty talk about Luna's father. Not anything about him. Not meeting him, not loving him, not marrying him, not him leaving. Nothing. It had been a forbidden topic since the day he left. "What I remember," Luna said, tentatively, not sure it was the right thing, "is his arms. So big and strong and brown. Like posts."

"It was his hair that got me that first day. He came

into the coffee shop where I worked and he had the thickest, shiniest, blackest hair I'd ever seen, and those big dark eyes. Just like yours." She touched Luna's hand distractedly. "If you weren't so blond, you'd look just like him. So Spanish, not like me at all."

"How did he pick you?"

"I was the cutest one," she said, lifting a shoulder. "Long blond hair I wore in a pageboy and a good figure and I took care of myself, you know, not like some of those ranch girls. I had my nails done and my lipstick on right, and I just knew, one of those days, that some man would walk through those doors and take me away. And when your daddy walked in, I just knew he was the one."

All at once, she crumpled a little, putting her hand to her chest, rubbing hard. Luna jumped up, alarmed. "Mom!"

Kitty raised her head, tears making her eyes neon. "Sit down, Luna. I'm not having a heart attack. Not that kind, anyway." She drew on her cigarette. "It was a mistake to keep it in all those years, I can see that now. I just never knew what to say." Her fingers worried the neckline of her robe, and she tapped the ashes off the cigarette. Luna realized she'd hardly been smoking hers, and put it out.

"You broke my heart," Kitty continued, "missing him so much. You worshiped him—oh, Lord—like he was the sun and the moon, and I could understand him losing interest in a woman, but not his children. Not his baby."

A gulf opened in Luna's chest, and she saw it like the bloom of a rose, dripping blood. "I used to fantasize that he'd come for me after school. Just me. He'd drive up in his truck and whistle like he did, you know, and open the door and I'd jump in and we'd just drive away." She looked upward, to the tops of the trees. "And then I'd feel guilty for not caring if he came for you guys."

"I used to hope they'd find his body at the bottom of a ravine somewhere. Or his truck in a river, lost to time."

"So there'd be a reason."

She nodded.

"You never had the sense of anything being wrong?"

She lifted her head, a perplexed little smile on her mouth. "He was a drunk, honey."

Luna went still. Everything in her—every cell, every molecule, waiting.

"You don't remember anything about it because he was careful. Didn't start drinking until you went to bed. He—" Her voice caught and she looked away for a minute. "He stayed sober for work, but barely."

"I see," Luna said, and it said so many things. Then, "Why did you stay with him if he was an alcoholic?"

"The first time I went out with him," Kitty said, and reached for her hand, "I slept with him. I did it even though I was a good girl, even though I knew that wasn't the way to get what I wanted, because I was head over heels in love with him from the first minute I saw him. And nobody ever looked at me in my life the way he did—like I was the queen of everything."

Luna knew the look her mother was talking about. She'd seen it in her father's eyes, too, when he looked at her and said, "You're my sweetheart, you know that? Daddy's girl." She'd seen it, every night, when he came in the door for supper and Kitty came out of the kitchen in her ironed apron to kiss him hello. "I remember it," she said. "If you can't trust that look, what could you possibly trust?"

"Exactly."

They sat side by side in the lowering light, lost in their own thoughts. After a long time she said, "We need to see the land, Mom. I don't know what was in his mind, but we need to at least see it before we make a decision."

Kitty covered her mouth, as if trying to catch the pained noise that escaped through her fingers. "I can't," she said, and real tears appeared in her eyes, ran down her cheeks. Her fingers tightened on Luna's. "I have to go away for a little while, baby. Frank's made arrangements for a cruise, and we're leaving Friday."

"But—" *You can't!* she wanted to say. *I need you. Joy needs you, I don't know what's happening with Thomas or my life and I feel lost, too.*

However, her mother had earned this respite, this right to retreat after so many years of being brave. Luna really loved Frank in that moment, for seeing that Kitty was so wounded, for being there to take care of her. "That's a great idea, Mom," she said. "I'll take care of the house, like always. How long will you be gone?"

"Two weeks. Greek islands." She said it like they were going to drive to Denver for a couple of days.

Luna laughed, squeezing her hand. "You're getting to be such a jaded traveler that Greece doesn't excite you?"

Kitty smiled wanly.

"Mom," she said quietly. "I need to see that land. I need to see what he left us, see if it helps me make sense of things. Before we sell it, I need to see what he saw."

"I was hoping you would," Kitty said. "You loved him even more than I did, Luna, and you were, right or wrong, the apple of his eye. I don't know what demons drove him away, but maybe you understand him better than Elaine or I."

"Because of the alcoholism?"

"No. Well, maybe, partly, I suppose, but I meant be-cause you're most like him. Driven and joyful and sad and so alive. You're as alive as he was, or at least you were. Maybe if you connect with him on some level, you'll finally get past all the betrayals in your life."

Luna took a breath. "I didn't know you saw me that way," she said in a small voice.

"Oh, baby, you're so great. I've never been able to get it through your head how marvelous you are."

"Thank you." They sat quietly together, united in that invisible longing. "It's okay to say you loved him, Mom. That this hurts you. That it hurt you then and it's never really healed."

Kitty lifted her chin. "Oh, I loved him. A part of me always will. But I can't go back there, not if I'm going to survive. Frank is a good, honest man who loves me for real. He'll never hurt me. Not ever."

"I know," she said. But how did you really ever know something like that?

And because it was getting too heavy, too deep, she said, "Hey, how about you let me fix your hair?"

Kitty smiled. "I guess I could do that. Let me get a shower and wash these cigarettes off, first."

"All right. I'm going to call Joy." Luna stood up, brushing off her rear. "And Mom, maybe before I go I could just sit in the Toyota again. Joy's not happy with me not driving."

"Sure. Get the keys now and you can try it while I'm in the shower, so nobody is watching."

Luna hugged her. "You know I love you, right? That I feel like the luckiest woman in the world, to have you as a mother?"

Kitty hugged her back. "Thank you, baby. I love you, too."

"I know."

• • •

While Kitty was in the shower, Luna took the car keys from the hook by the door and slipped downstairs to the garage. The car, clean as dawn, sat waiting for her, dark blue and somehow affluent-looking. She opened the door and got in.

For a little while, she just sat there with the door open, enjoying the luxurious smell of it, the comfort of the seat, the high-tech look of the dash. She hadn't had a car in a long time, and the ones she'd owned after leaving Marc had not been new. Good thing, too, since she'd wrecked all of them.

Wrecked cars. A gurgle of unease went through her. Sitting inside the dazzling machine, Luna rubbed her hand over the steering wheel and remembered each one. The first had not been terrible—early in her days in Albuquerque, she'd hit the gas instead of the brake when she pulled into a parking lot and totaled a 1983 Volvo on a light post. Minor scrapes and bruises, but the car was a loss. And because it had taken place in her apartment complex and there was no property damage but her own, she'd skated out of anything more than a slap on the wrist.

The second had been more serious. Maybe six months later. She only vaguely remembered it—she'd been very drunk indeed and had gone through a stop sign without even a glance. A pickup truck broadsided her, luckily hitting the back half of the car instead of the front, which would likely have killed her. She'd spent a couple of days in the hospital for broken ribs and bruised internal organs, but luckily, the truck driver wasn't hurt, and even his truck had sustained only minor damages.

That one had lead to some community service and supposedly drug tests to check her sobriety, but she slid through the system pretty easily, simply changing addresses and taking to walking everywhere. No one came after her.

The third one had been the bad one. She rolled a borrowed car into a ditch, and she couldn't remember a single thing about it. That accident had marked hitting bottom, at least. Which led to coming home, which led to getting sober, which led to this moment in a Toyota in her mother's garage, just waiting for Luna to be ready to drive. Frank and Kitty had chosen the safest model on the market, not because they doubted her intentions, but because they wanted her to feel protected behind the wheel.

Safe. Luxurious, or semi-so. Taking a deep breath, she closed the door, adjusted the seat and mirror and felt okay. She opened the garage door, then fit the key into the ignition. Her heart didn't go skittering into anxiety, so she turned the key. The engine caught, a smooth, low rumble, and she sat there with her hands on the wheel, thinking about putting it into gear. Still no freak-out.

Very cautiously, she put the car into reverse and started to ease it out of the garage.

And that's when it hit. Pure panic. She slammed on the brakes too hard as her body seized itself, her throat closing, heart stuttering, sweat breaking from every pore. Even the edges of her vision started to go black. Very slowly, very easily, she put the car back into place, turned it off, and returned the keys to the hook.

Not yet.

But maybe it wouldn't be long.

Neck
Right Side—the name Makaveli
Back Side—There is a (Makaveli type) Crown and then under
that picture is the word "Playaz." Under "Playaz" are the words
"Fuck the World."

A big cross is on his back with the words "Exodus 18:11,"
meaning, "Now I know that the lord is greater than all gods: for in
the things wherein they dealt proudly he was above them" in the
middle of the cross. On each side of the cross is a clown mask.
The mask on his right is crying and under it, it says "Cry Later."
The other mask on his left side is smiling and it says "Smile Now."

Seventeen

Maggie's diary

23 Septiembre 2001,
San Jeronimo

Dear Whoever Is Listening,

Tonight I went to see the *bruja.* I was very scared,
walking home from school, thinking about it, but my
mom is not getting better. She's getting worse. I don't
think she's been awake more than two hours since last
Sunday. That's scary, you know? And I'm so lonely. The
doctors keep giving her more and more drugs, but
they're making her more fuzzy, not more clear. I want
my mom back.

So I went home after school, checked on her and
found her asleep. I kissed her head and she hardly

woke up at all, just said there was some stuff in the freezer. I ate an apple I bought at the Kwikway on the way home, then went upstairs and changed into a skirt, which I thought the old lady would like better than my jeans, and I put a rosary around my neck for protection—the special one made of amber beads with little things caught inside them that my dad brought me back from a trip to Mexico he had to make for work once—and then I looked around for something I could take to her. I don't have any money, and anyway, I think you're not supposed to use real money, only trade. There wasn't much in my room that would be any good to an old woman. I wished for some of my mom's chokecherry jelly to take, the pretty little jars with orange fruit on the lids that my mom makes every year but not this year, but it was all gone. I had my candles and clothes and stuff, but nothing *good*.

Then I remembered this barrette I have. It's abalone and silver, shaped like a butterfly. I bought it at a flea market once, from an Indian, and it's pretty. I thought the *bruja* might like it—she has pretty hair. I put it in the pocket of my skirt, then I set out walking, staying on the sidewalks till they gave out, then keeping to the edge of the road by the acequia. Dragonflies, all bright blue and black, zoomed by and they made me feel happier. The mosquitoes were sleeping, thank heaven, because they eat me like I'm a cheesecake, bringing all their friends to munch me up from head to toe.

At the old lady's house, I got scared again, and stopped because I was out of breath from climbing the hill. It didn't look like anybody was home. The truck the grandson drives was gone, along with a Lowrider that was there last time, a pretty one with sparkly purple paint. The whole house looked totally quiet, and I was disappointed, because I was pretty sure it would be days before I could get my courage up to do it again.

But I was there, so I went to the door, my heart pounding like crazy, and knocked. A dog barked inside, and I remembered the big tan dog that was there last time. He sounded mean now, though, like he could attack, and I felt sweat break out on my neck. I jumped when the door opened.

Mrs. Ramirez was standing there, looking not like a witch at all this time, but just a really, really old lady. Her hair, white and black, hung down around her shoulders and I took out the barrette and shoved it at her. "It's all I have," I told her. "Please help me."

She looked at the barrette for a long, long minute, then she turned around, saying over her shoulder "*Vamos*," which means come on in Spanish. So I followed her.

In the daytime, the house looked totally different. Sun buttered the floors and showed how clean and easy things were. In the kitchen, I smelled meat cooking, and the old lady pointed to the table, where there was already a bowl of beans and meat and a tortilla holder with a lid, dark blue painted with yellow flowers. "Sit," she said to me in English and went to the stove. She put something in another bowl, and I started to tell her I was sorry for interrupting her meal, and to get up and go, but she came back to the table and put her hand on my shoulder, not mean, but kinda nice, and said, "Eat." She put the bowl in front of me. Pintos and meat, in this gravy that smelled so good, like everything my mom used to cook and doesn't anymore. I could see onions and little pieces of green chile floating around, and my stomach growled all loud.

But I didn't want to eat here. "I'm not hungry," I told her. "I just need your help."

She sat down in the other chair, so tiny her feet almost didn't touch the floor. *"Coma primero,"* she said in Spanish. Then, like I might not understand, she said it in English, in a whisper. "Eat first, eh?"

I didn't know what to do. She tapped my hand, the one holding the barrette, and I turned it over, opening it up to show the abalone wings. She didn't take it, though, just went back to eating and told me again that I should eat.

And here's the thing—I was scared to. If I ate, maybe I'd get sick, or be under her spell forever, or something. But if I didn't, I was pretty sure she wasn't going to listen to me. And then I thought she must cook for her grandson, and he seemed okay, so maybe it would be all right.

But I gotta tell you, it was the smell of that soup that was making me crazy. I picked up my spoon and I wanted to cry for wanting to eat it so much and not wanting to eat it so much. I put one hand on my rosary beneath my shirt, and said a quick prayer to the Blessed Mother to protect me and put some food in my mouth.

And it was so, so, so, so, so good. Hot, but kind of sweet-hot that makes you know it was jalapeños, not serranos, that she used to spice it up. I felt like I hadn't eaten for a million years, and after that first bite, I just ate like crazy. Mrs. Ramirez opened the tortilla cover and I took some of those out, too, homemade, but perfectly even because she's been making them of course for a hundred years.

You just don't know how good that can be, homemade bean soup with homemade tortillas. It made me think of my dad and mom and the way things used to be, and it filled this empty place inside of me and it wasn't till I was all the way to the bottom of the empty bowl, wiping it out with one more piece of tortilla that I realized that if the *bruja* was going to bewitch me, I was done for. I wiped my hands on a paper napkin.

"Will you help my mother? Please." I put the barrette down and pushed it across the table to her.

She asked in English if I spoke Spanish. I told her I did and she said everything else in Spanish, but I'll write it in English for you, especially because I don't spell Spanish so good. She said, "Your mama is heart-sick. Her heart is so sad without your papa. I can't do nothing for her, *h'ita*."

"No spell, a tea, something like that?"

She crossed herself, shuddering. "No, no, nothing like that."

"But you're a witch! Everybody says so, and they say you can do anything. You made that charm for my mom, and all those teas."

She looked at me for a long minute, and I thought she didn't understand, so I started to say it again, in English to make it better, but thunder was gathering on her forehead, and I got scared and shut up. Those claw hands folded tight, then she exploded. Not yelling, which is what I expected. Laughing. Her shoulders started to shake, and then her loose bosoms, and she rocked back and forth, laughing and laughing and laughing. She even slapped her hands on the table. I stared at her, half in horror, half in amazement, until she finally stopped. She gave me a big old grin. "So that's what they say, huh? I'm a witch?"

"You aren't?"

She shook her head sadly.

"What am I going to do then? She's gonna die and I'm gonna be all alone!"

"Never alone, *h'ita*. What would your papa tell you? We always have the Blessed Mother, eh?"

"I guess." I touched the rosary under my blouse. But Mary isn't exactly helping me out here, either.

Right then, the grandson banged into the kitchen, all sweaty from work, and I thought again that he was okay for an old guy. He went to the fridge and got out a pitcher of something and poured a big glassful, then drank it all at once. I didn't realize I was staring at him till he says to me, "How're you doing, kiddo? How's your mom?"

I blushed. He was so nice! And he remembered that I was there with my mom before, which is a good sign, because maybe he noticed my mom, who really is pretty when she fixes herself up. "She's okay," I told him. "Working." Which was a lie, but I didn't want him to think she was all pathetic. I remembered, right then, that she had been complaining about something. "She's been looking for somebody to do yard work for her, though. It's totally out of control over there."

He was already someplace in his mind, I could tell, but he said he had a name we could call. I was hoping he'd say he'd come over himself and help her out, and they maybe would start talking, and—well, he didn't, that's all. But you could kinda tell he was worried about something. He picked up the phone and started stabbing numbers in it.

I got up, ready to go. "Thank you for the soup," I told her, and pushed the barrette over to her side of the table. "You could keep it. I never wear it and you have lots of hair."

Then I walked to the door and nobody stopped me until I got all the way there and then *Abuela* said, "*H'ita*. Remember what I said." She picked up a rosary made of wood and rattled it in the air at me. "You're never alone." I just nodded my head. But outside, it was all I could do to keep from crying. In fact I did cry, I won't lie. Cried all the way down the road to Sleeping Beauty's castle. I didn't know why my dad had to die and why I had to deal with all this when I really wasn't old enough and I need help and nobody's around to give it to me. And I just didn't know what to do.

And then, the weirdest thing happened. This piece of paper blew on my foot. I jumped, scared, thinking at first it was a snake, but then I looked down at it, and got chills from my head to my toes, because it was a magazine cover. *Rolling Stone.* And the person on the cover was Tupac Shakur. A headline said, 1971-1996 TUPAC SHAKUR, THE STRANGE AND TERRIBLE SAGA.

My hands were shaking and my heart was pounding when I looked at that, because I'd been feeling almost as bad as when I got that dollar the day of my dad's funeral, the day I got the dollar bill, and it was like a sign. I decided right there, to find out everything I could about Tupac and whether or not he was still alive. Maybe he's communicating with me, hanging out with me. Maybe I'm not really alone and I can be tough like him, get through even though it's hard, like a rose growing in concrete, which is what his one and only book is called.

My dad used to say there was always help if you looked for it, and I think this is my help. I don't know how it'll all help saving my mom, but all I can do right now is just follow the clues wherever they go and hope something makes sense.

Now I'm gonna go read some of the stuff I just checked out.

Maggie

Y si vuelvo a nacer, yo los vuelvo a matar.
Padre no me arrepiento, ni me da miedo la eternidad,
Yo sé que allá en el cielo el ser supremo me ha de juzgar
Voy a seguir sus pasos, voy a buscarlos al más allá.

And if I'm born again, I would kill them once again.
Father, I do not repent, nor am I afraid of eternity.
I know that there in Heaven the Supreme Being will judge me.
I will follow their steps, I will follow them as far as they go.

Eighteen

Friday morning, Thomas stood in the hot September sun, smelling the wind, feeling a thickness gathering in the still air. The crew was building an adobe wall for a movie star's estate, incorporating natural flaws and bits of tin and rusted old western nostalgia. It was turning out very well, he thought, pleased especially by some of the blue pottery one of his men had tossed in, here and there. The shards gleamed like hidden treasure in the finished bricks.

There was nothing that should have caused his sudden distraction; the same rhythm of every workday flowed around him, some of the crew carrying the heavy rectangular bricks to the wall, where others placed them. Still others formed new bricks on-site, packing reddish mud and straw into wooden forms. Thomas squatted in the sun, putting his hands in the heavy mud, trying to sense what was awry all of a sudden.

He could see nothing wrong, nothing to indicate the

weather was changing. The sky stretched toward the mountains, arching over the valley in a deep blue bowl, steady and endless. No wind tossed the trees.

Running alongside the road, irrigation water flowed with little chuckles through a ditch, and the silence was so deep he even heard the soft chittering of a squirrel far above. Restively, he gathered mud into his hands and patted it smooth. The weight and suppleness pleased him, and he curved his palm over it distractedly, thinking of Luna's body against his hands last night and the night before. Little shocks of memory traveled down his spine, popping in the small of his back, shivering over the inside of his thighs. Her colors were like the day around him, hair like the light gilding leaves suddenly gone yellow overnight, her eyes as dark as the fur of a bear, her skin—his palm curved around mud, weighed it, smoothed it—the same smooth light brown of adobe. His fingers pinched out the shape of a nipple, and he held a replica of her breast in his hand, wondering if now he'd think of her when he saw adobe, forever.

"Cabrón!" The shout was sudden and startled Thomas. He looked up from his reverie to see Tiny leaping toward John Young, a gangly boy with more back than sense who baited Tiny with no sense of consequences. A fight had been brewing between them for a long time, and Thomas leapt up, shame making him smash the breast between his hands. He buried the mud, his ears hot at what he'd shaped, and whistled loudly. Neither man heeded him. They were flying at each other, Tiny's sharpness no match for the brute fist of the younger man . . .

Until the rage kicked in.

Like Thomas, other members of the crew had seen Tiny's volcanic temper and they dropped what they were doing to race toward the pair, yelling his name. "Tiny!" Thomas yelled. "Let it go. John, back off!"

Neither of them listened. John was too stupid and Tiny too stubborn. Thomas was too far away to break it up, but one of the other men, an older man called Lorenzo, attempted intervention, grabbing Tiny's arm, pulling him away, telling him, "You don't need this, come on, you'll be in trouble and you already got enough."

But John wasn't having it. "Yeah, go ahead, quit. I'll be sucking her titties all night long."

Shit.

Thomas bolted into a full run, but it was too late. Tiny's rage, a living being, a demon, gathered itself up and roared out of him, shooting out of his fists, his arms, his legs and feet and head, a whirl-like funnel cloud that left John dazed on the ground, bleeding from nose and mouth and a cut on his cheekbone, when Lorenzo and Thomas managed to pull Tiny away and restrain him.

Thomas knelt and pulled the younger man to his feet. Blood gushed out of his nose, and Thomas wanted to slap the kid again for bringing this trouble. "Put your head back," he said, "let's get you to the doctor."

Wobbling, the boy leaned into Thomas. "Jesus, he hits hard."

Thomas lifted his chin toward Lorenzo, giving him charge. "Either of you do that again, and you're both fired," he said. Once the boy was in the car he said, "And if you say who did it, you're fired on the spot. I can't afford to lose Tiny, and you're an idiot for baiting him. Got it?"

"Got it."

As he rounded the truck, three ravens flew overhead, cawing out. He glanced at them darkly and shuddered.

Damn. He was going to have to stop listening to his *abuelita*. She was making him superstitious.

The Pay and Pack was swamped, especially the floral department. An art festival of some sort had come to town for the weekend. There were lots of them, all the time through the year. The attendees started showing up Thursday, filling the motel and hotel parking lots with their SUVs and Volvos and ever-so-retro Volkswagen buses. The coffee shops perked with their longhaired, hiking-boot clad number, and boutiques happily sold their better items. Luna tried not to get exasperated with the requests for exotic cheeses and organic Japanese vegetables all day long, telling herself this was a crowd that had serious money to spend and most of them had come a long way to do it, but it wasn't easy. For one thing, they were so young to be so wealthy. So self-consciously unselfconscious, so perfectly exercised and tanned and dressed, so very graciously aware that their tastes shaped the world and they took it seriously and put Mother Earth first.

But it did mean all the restaurants in town would be crowded all weekend, and if she had harbored any hopes of sneaking away with Thomas somewhere, their chances of finding a room were slim to none, and that was very disappointing. It also meant that the floral department was too busy—these people sent one another flowers like air kisses—for Luna to take her customary early day.

Sometime after lunch, Allie called. "How's it going, stranger?"

A thread of guilt wound through her. Aside from that one afternoon at the shop, she had barely seen or spoken to Allie at all. And there was so much going on that it struck Luna as odd. "Allie! Hi! Are you swamped today?"

"Have been—twelve readings. If I were charging money, I'd be making a fortune. And these folks think a trinket is a good trade." She made a noise. "Anyway, I just wanted to catch you before you made big plans. Can you go out tonight? Maybe go over to the casino and play the slots for a bit?"

"Is there something wrong?"

"No, not really. I'm just restless. Feeling the baby blues again." Allie was single, by choice, and had no desire to get married to anyone, ever, the legacy of a childhood spent with an abusive father. She didn't regret her choice to go it alone, taking lovers when she wanted, but the baby blues had been biting her quite a bit lately.

"You know, I wouldn't mind that at all, actually. There's been so much going on in my life and I haven't had a chance to tell you about it."

"Oooh. Are you having good sex often?"

Luna laughed. "I'll tell you more later."

"C'mon! Just a hint. Have you had sex at all?"

Over her skin moved a tactile memory of Thomas's thick, cool hair falling over her, but there also came a strange resistance to discussing it. "I'll tell you later," she said.

"That means yes, doesn't it? Oh, I can't wait to hear." A short pause. "Jeez, I think I'm jealous, Lu. That is one delectable drink of water."

"Hmm. Well, let me check bases with Joy and make sure she doesn't mind, and I'll get back to you later, okay?"

"Okay. Maybe we can sneak over to Rita's. I'm dying for a good margarita. Surely she won't have too many people."

It was a tiny restaurant in Angel Fire, a family-run

Mexican with the best *menudo* in the county. Not that Luna ever touched the stuff, but that was what everyone said. "I'll call you around three, let you know."

"All righty. Looking forward to it, kiddo."

Luna hung up and rubbed the tenseness in the back of her neck. She used to go outside for a cigarette when she felt this way. Lately, she'd been hanging out in the break room inside, but it was a grim place, with bad fluorescent lighting and indifferent furnishings all in shades of industrial blah to match the rows of green lockers along the wall. Not exactly relaxing. She also really missed her smoking buddies.

What the heck. She'd risk it today, just sit out in the fresh air and breathe secondhand smoke for a little while. If it was too hard, she could do something different tomorrow. "I'll be outside for twenty minutes," she said to Jean.

She scowled beneath her plastic hair. "You aren't smoking, are you?"

Luna gave her a mother look. The one that says, *Child, who do you think you are, presuming to speak to your elders that way?* It worked. Jean said, "Well, I'm just concerned about you, that's all."

Luna didn't bother to answer, and it was an oddly freeing feeling. She slipped out the side door and wandered into smoker's corner, a picnic table on a grimy patch of pavement. It was to the north of the building, so it was always shaded, and a pair of tattered scrub oaks offered a little privacy. They could see through holes in the branches to the parking lot, but no one much ever saw them.

There were three people sitting there this morning. Diane, Ernie, and—Luna started a little—Angelica, the estranged wife of Tiny Abeyta.

"Hey, hey, look who's here!" Diane, one of the check-

ers, said as she came around the corner. Diane wore
Egyptian eyeliner, thick and black, angling out and up
at the corners, and some glitter lotion over her cheekbones. Her smock was opened to show her low-cut T-
shirt and lots of creamy cleavage. She was as beautiful
and flamboyant as a Jacob's Coat rose—once upon a
time, Luna had ached to look like this. "You falling off
the wagon, girl?" Diane said.

She had to smile softly over the "girl." "No, I just
came to visit."

"Cool!"

"How you been?" Ernie asked. An ex-military man
whose plain white shirts and blue work pants were as
crisply pressed as folded paper, he was one of Luna's favorite people. A native *Taoseño*, he'd escaped at seventeen to go to the Army, then to war, and afterward
wandered the world with his wife until he retired at
thirty years and came home. He worked part-time in the
bakery department, and studied for a bachelor's degree
in Spanish in his spare time. Sometimes he brought
Luna Spanish poets to read.

She touched his hand lightly, briefly. "Miss you,
Ernesto. Whatcha been reading?"

"Not so much lately. School started, you know. I'm
taking three classes this time." He tucked the cigarette
into the corner of his mouth, and it fit like a cartoon
drawing, the smoke politely blowing away from his angled cheekbones. "You?"

"No, me either. My daughter is living with me!"

"Oh, that's right! How's it going?"

Luna launched into the tale both Ernie and Diane
wanted to hear, the wonders of her beautiful daughter,
who was getting along just fine in Taos. Angelica, a little apart, kept her attention focused away, smoking in

private silence, but her presence tugged at Luna in some way she couldn't name.

Angelica stood up to put her cigarette in the big, sand-filled concrete container meant for that purpose, and then ducked down abruptly. "That's my husband out there!" she said, and scrambled beneath the table. "Shit!"

Luna's heart sunk as she peeked through a hole in the bushes and saw Tiny climb out of a very beautiful purple Lowrider. He wore work clothes, adobe smeared on him from head to toe, even in his hair, and she thought it looked like he had blood on his mouth.

"You want me to call the police, *h'ita*?" Ernie said.

"No," she said urgently, holding up a hand in protest. "He'll go to jail and then we won't have no money at all. It's already hard. No." She curled herself even more tightly together. "I'll just stay here and he'll get tired and go home."

"I'll call Thomas," Luna said. "If you want me to."

Angelica looked at her, not comprehending for a moment, and Luna realized that while she'd seen Angelica at the VFW, and knew the whole story, to her, Luna was just the woman who ran the floral department. "His boss, Thomas?"

Luna nodded. "He's a friend of mine."

"Okay. Yeah. That would be good."

Luna looked through the hole in the bushes and said, "He's coming this way. He knows the smoking area is here?"

"Yeah. He knows it's my break time."

"Come with me," Luna said, standing, and glanced at Ernie, who stood up and went to the opening in the bushes, standing with his hands in his pockets, his cigarette tucked right at the corner of his mouth. Blocking the view. Luna gestured for Angelica to follow her and they dashed into the door that led to the long dark room behind the floral counter. "Sit over there until he leaves."

Angelica did as she was told, but she was worried. "I'm gonna get in trouble for being late back, it's so busy today."

"I'll take care of that." She rounded the counter quickly, found Jean and told her to go to the checkout and cover for Angelica. She started to murmur and protest and Luna gave her the mother look again.

Jean narrowed her eyes. "Gee, you're so mean today, what's wrong with you?"

"Go." She didn't wait to see if she would listen, but went back outside like she was coming out for a break. Tiny was talking to Ernie, appearing to be normal, and Luna raised her eyebrows in surprise. "Hey, guy, what're you up to?" Slumping down on the picnic bench, she said, "Diane, I need a cigarette. Can I bum one?" Then she widened her eyes in mock worry in Tiny's direction and said, "Don't tell anybody."

It served the purpose of putting him on her side. "Nah, I know how hard it is." Using only his left hand, he pulled out a cigarette of his own. "Mind if I sit with you guys? Need to see my wife for a minute and she's usually on break at this time."

"No, go ahead." Luna scooted over, casually, and patted the spot next to her.

Diane, wide-eyed, gave Luna her lighter. "I gotta get back inside. Bring it to me later."

As she left, her unfashionably round figure swaying, Tiny watched her. Ernie turned, winking. "Don't make girls like that every day, eh?"

Tiny whistled his agreement, and blew out some smoke.

Luna wasn't quite sure what to do next. She needed

to call Thomas, but it seemed more important to sit with Tiny, keep him from going inside to find Angelica. Tiny was flushed and had obviously been fighting. A smell of sweat and agitation came off him and his knee jiggled as he smoked. Coiled tight. Luna had an idea. "Ernie, do you know Tiny Abeyta? Tiny, this is Ernie Medina."

They lifted chins at each other. "How you doing?"

Luna met Ernie's eyes. Held them. "I met him because he's living with a new friend of mine, Thomas *Coyote*. They work together, too, at Coyote Adobe."

He got it, what she needed for him to do. He winked, teasing lightly, "Coyote and Luna, eh?"

Luna smiled, nodding a little. Her heart was racing too fast, whether from the cigarette or the excitement, who knew?

Ernie casually put down his cigarette and waved. "Time for me to get back."

"See ya."

Which left Luna and Tiny sitting in the smoking area by themselves. "What's up, Tiny?" she asked gently. "You have a fight?"

He bent his head. Nodded.

"You left work?"

A shrug. "It was break time. I got a right."

"Thomas let you go?"

He took a quick, sharp drag on his cigarette. His knuckles were bloody. "He had to take the guy to the emergency room." He shot a mutinous glance at Luna. "I broke his nose, I think. But it wasn't my fault, I swear to God. Dickhead just kept trying to get to me, telling me all this shit about my wife—"

"Tiny," she said quietly, and risked putting a hand on his shoulder. He flinched, but let it settle. "You want to go somewhere, get something to drink, a soda or something? My treat."

A quick, sharp shake of his head. "Nah, I need to see her."

"You're already in violation. Right now, sitting here, leaving the job without permission. Fighting."

The muscles beneath Luna's hand were whipcord tight, and he made a face like he'd cry if he weren't such a badass. He wasn't as old as she first thought—not more than twenty-seven or twenty-eight. In love, burning to make something right that wasn't ever going to be. "Can I tell you something?" she asked.

He didn't protest, so she rubbed his shoulder a little. "When I was seven, my dad left home. It was terrible, Tiny, I missed him so badly it was like somebody cut off one of my arms. I still miss him and I just found out he died and I'll never see him ever again."

Tiny raised his head. "That's sad."

"Your kids love you. Don't do anything that's gonna take you away from them. It's too much. They need you."

He ducked his head abruptly. Nodded.

"You want to go somewhere? Really, my treat."

His mouth worked as he stared hard at a place on the table. "Nah. I'll go home. To Thomas's house, that home. Talk to *Abuela* for a while."

"That's a great idea." She let her hand drift down, and realized the cigarette had burned away, unnoticed. She stubbed it out. "Let me have another cigarette, will you?"

He made a soft sound of amusement. "Sure." Standing, he looked around, suddenly unsure again, and handed the cigarette to her. Offered to light it, and she showed him that she still had Diane's lighter. He stood

A Piece of Heaven   273

there a moment more, then said, "I guess, uh, I'll go. If you see Angelica, tell her I was thinking about her, eh?"

Luna nodded. Lit the cigarette, and this time smoked it, her heart squeezing with terror and relief and worry. "You know, Tiny," she said. "If you ever want to talk it through, any of it, feel free to call me. Anytime, day or night. I used to be pretty good at this kind of stuff."

"Why would you help me?" he said cynically.

She raised a hand. "For keeping my secret."

A half smile. "Thanks."

Luna watched him wander to his car, his head down as he smoked the last of his cigarette. Best Friend Barbie, her hair hidden beneath a scarf, poked her head from between the curtains and watched him drive away, pulling his car gently into the street. Driving like a little old man. *He'll kill her eventually.*

"Yep," Luna said aloud. Unless something happened, he definitely would. It broke her heart for all of them. Jail might not be the answer, but she wasn't sure there was anything else that would counter hundreds of years of social conditioning and the brittle temper of a man who was lost. She finished the cigarette, put it out, and went in to let Angelica know the coast was clear.

She was gone.

Even after leaving the store, Tiny couldn't come down from the mad. He kept thinking it was going away, but then it would shoot through his veins like straight pins, pricking his inner elbow, the base of his skull, the corners of his eyes, making him see a red smear at the edges of everything. Lorenzo, an old man on the job, had talked to him low, in Spanish, the words pouring over him like something cool, *Let it go, let it be, you don't need no trouble, he's a boy, a fool, a crazy Anglo boy. Nothing.*

But every time he started to feel it slipping away, Tiny saw John's big white hands on Angelica's breasts, those big ugly hands over the white skin and freckles. She had beautiful breasts, big and round and heavy, with dark, dark nipples like crowns and just thinking of them, thinking of her around him, made him ache with a sharp, shooting desire. *I'll be sucking on her titties all night long.*

From seven in the morning until five in the evening, the ankle monitor was inactive, more or less, because he was at work, miles away from the machine that went off if he strayed the rest of the time. It basically came down to house arrest combined with work release. Usually Thomas was there to see that Tiny didn't break the terms of the arrangement, but he'd be at the hospital with John for a while.

Tiny had an hour, maybe two.

After he left the grocery store, he just drove around for a while, not going anywhere, just thinking. He thought about what that woman, Luna, said to him. And he thought of putting his face in Angelica's neck, smelling her, and how that would fill him back up, take away this empty feeling. He needed to see her. It was like an addiction.

He could go to her house and wait there till she came home. He thought about that for twenty minutes or more driving up to Rancho de Taos and through the back roads, then over to Peñasco, and back to Taos again. If his car was on the street, someone might see it and they might all get in trouble. Instead, he parked three blocks away, the car hidden behind some trees by a vacant lot. He walked away from it and took a short cut through the fields, beneath a big willow brushing the ground softly, and came to his house from the alley. The back door was open.

And standing there in the sun, his hair so hot from it that it burned and he put a hand over it, he wondered why it had never occurred to him to come here during the day before, when the kids were at school and they could be alone. All alone. Anticipation made him feel faint.

Thinking of her skin, of her heavy hair, he opened the back gate and went up the ancient walkway, broken a little with time and too much weather, the top layer grating away to show the pebbles and dirt that made concrete. Late pink roses dripped over the fence, filling the air with a thick sweetness and he paused, feeling dizzy, to pluck one.

Through the open door came the sound of the radio playing the pop she liked, and he opened the screen door quietly, moving on soft feet into his house, seeing with a kind of weakness all the things he had been missing—his chair at the table, the salt and pepper shakers with silver tops he'd bought at the flea market one day because they were crystal and she liked nice things. It was all spic and span, no dishes on the counter, the floor so clean you could lick it. A crisp white curtain lifted on the breeze, and he smelled ironing.

A swell of agonized love came up in his chest. She liked things to be nice. She worked so hard to keep them like that for all of them. Little things—the blue bowls of stuff that smelled good, the way she kept gloves in the bathroom and special rags by everything that could get dirty, and her three mops for different jobs. It mattered to her, things being clean.

And the kids looked like that, too, their clothes all perfect all the time, their hair never too long, their socks never sprung. She would do without meat to get new shoes for one of the kids.

He stood in the kitchen, absorbing his wilderness of

love for this house and family and wondered how it could be that they lived apart now, even for a little while. He turned the rose between his thumb and forefinger and then turned toward the living room, going down the hall with the flower in his hand.

She stood before the ironing board, pressing a skirt, singing along with the music. Her hair was caught in a clip at the back of her head, and pieces of it fell down against her jaw. She'd washed off her makeup from work, so he could see the brownish mask around her eyes, and she wore only a pair of baggy shorts and a sweatshirt and thongs, but he almost couldn't breathe for loving her, wanting her.

"Angelica," he said, quietly.

She jerked violently, startled, and for a single, painful moment, he saw true fear, even though she recognized him. It turned to happiness when she saw the flower. Her eyes widened, and she rushed to the front door to close and lock it before anyone saw inside. "Tiny!" she cried, pressing her back against the door. "What are you doing here?" She whispered, like someone might hear. "You'll get in trouble and we won't be able to live together at all anymore. You have to go."

"I will," he said, nodding, coming toward her. "I just wanted to see you so much." He gave her the flower, pressed close to her, put his hands on her hips—sturdy hips like a woman, not a girl. "Touch you."

Her breath came out of her on a quiet sigh. "Oh, it's beautiful," she said of the rose, and put her arms around his neck. "I miss you so much," she said, and he kissed her, and it was like lightning, like a storm boiling up out of the south, a thick, wild honey pouring off her tongue. He groaned and pulled off her sweatshirt, baring her breasts, kneeling down to kiss them, pushing off her shorts and panties and sinking into her right there.

Her cries were guttural and too loud, she covered her mouth, but then he covered it for her, liking it when she bit his hand almost to bloody, their bodies banging hard against the floor as they fell, as they roared together into the need, the release they'd been wanting, an agony, a relief, a sorrow, a joy.

There was no one else, ever, in his heart, in his mind, than this woman, his Angelica, his angel, his woman, his wife. "You're mine," he said fiercely. "Mine."

"Yes," she cried. "Yes."

1. *We admitted we were powerless over alcohol—that our lives had become unmanageable.*

2. *Came to believe that a Power greater than ourselves could restore us to sanity.*

3. *Made a decision to turn our will and our lives over to the care of God as we understood him.*

Nineteen

For the first time, Joy wasn't there when Luna arrived home. Luna had bummed a ride from a coworker, too tired to walk two and a half miles. When she came in, the message light on the phone was flashing, and she distractedly sorted the mail while she listened. There were four messages: the first from the high school registrar, asking for some paperwork Luna had asked April to get for her.

The second was from Thomas, telling Luna he appreciated her help this afternoon more than he could say, and promising he would call later when things were stabilized.

The third was from Marc. And it was such a Marc kind of message Luna was gritting her teeth within three seconds. "Lu, look, we need to talk about this situation. I thought I'd be all right with Joy living with you, but I'm not comfortable with it after all and I think we should talk seriously about what's best for her. I've been reading about the gang activity there and it can't be good for Joy to be in that environment, and I know you have recently purchased a home, but she also tells me you still don't drive, and she just has so much more of everything here."

A pause, one he used to take a breath. "Lu, you love her. Do the right thing, huh?"

"Right," she said, and punched the number seven to erase the message. "That I will do, sir."

The fourth message was from April. Her voice was high and brittle. "Hi, sweetie. Just calling to let you know we got your letters. Thank you so much. You're a peach. Give us a call when you have time. Your dad will be out of town all weekend, so we're doing movie days and things like that. Anytime, honey."

As she stood there, Allie called. "So, are we on or what?"

A stab of guilt touched her. She'd forgotten again. "You know, Allie, I'm tired. I don't think I really want to go out. How about tomorrow? I might enjoy myself a lot more then."

"You don't have the thing with your mom?"

"She's going to Greece, poor baby. We're going to have it here tomorrow night. Can you come over?"

"That sounds good. Maybe I'll go over to the art festival tonight, check out the boys in their Wranglers."

Luna chuckled. "Good idea."

As she hung up, she did take a second to wonder why she still hadn't said much about Thomas. Come to that, she hadn't shared it with anyone. Not Allie or her mother or Elaine. Interesting. She'd have to think about why. When she had a second.

Right this minute, she had to return Marc's call no matter how much she loathed the chore. Especially if he was going out of town for the weekend. His secretary put her through right away, and he said, "Lu!" in a hearty voice. "Thanks for getting back to me so quickly."

"I'm not sending her back, Marc."

"Lu, that's not reasonable. You're being—"

"You need to listen to me," she said. "If Joy chooses to go back to Atlanta, I'm perfectly willing to let her go—but this isn't about me or you. It's about her. She's old enough to make these decisions herself, and you can bully her as much as you like, but she's even more stubborn than you are, and all you'll do is push her away even further."

"Lu, what can she get in Taos? Really."

There was a lot, but that wasn't what this was about. Not Taos, not Luna, not even Joy. "Why did you change your mind, Marc? Why send her away then yank her back? Did the newspapers get wind of it? Did your campaign manager tell you that Joy would be an asset to you?"

A slight pause told her it was one of those things. A red-hot blister of anger burst in her. "Are you ever going to stop using people?" she asked bitterly.

"I'm not using her. She's my daughter and I love her."

"Especially when she can advance your agenda."

"I'm also not bullying her, Lu. That's an exaggeration."

"Is it? You promise to send her an allowance, then you withdraw it a week after she arrives? What would you call that?" Luna flung her hair out of her face. "Maybe it's not bullying. Let's just call it manipulation."

"There's no need to raise your voice."

Luna closed her eyes, putting a finger against the place between her eyebrows that had suddenly started to throb. "I am not raising my voice, but there's a good reason if I so choose—I'm furious with you for using your daughter as a pawn, and I won't let you do it. Not now. Not ever again. The custody agreement has been changed and whether you want to do it or not, you owe us both just a little time together."

"I can go back to court, you know."

It felt like all the air was suddenly sucked out of her lungs. *Old memory,* said Therapist Barbie. *Take a deep breath.* "Yes, you can," she managed evenly. "And you'll have everything on your side, just like you always do." She thought with terror of the night in the motel with Thomas, of her developing relationship with him, thought of sitting outside today with a known wife-abuser, thought of Marc's connections and money and knew if he really tried to fight her on this, he'd likely win. "I keep hoping, day after day, that you'll one day recognize how much you hurt her. Then and now. Try, for once in your life, to do the right thing, huh?"

She hung up, tears of anger threatening to spill into her throat. How could she *ever* have loved this man? Had there been even an ounce of goodness in him? Anything but his own blindly selfish ambitions?

Once, there had been a good man in there. He'd come from nothing, clad only in his ambition and a fierce will to succeed. Once, it had been a noble kind of fight and Luna had admired him. But as so often happened, his gift had also proved to be his fatal flaw.

Staring out the window at the mountains, immovable and somehow wise-looking, another wave of anger swept her. Hadn't she paid enough? Did she have to keep giving up everything that mattered to make the gods get off her case?

She didn't want Joy to go back home. Didn't want to give up the richening bond between them, the sweet pleasure of just seeing her every morning, dragging into the kitchen rumpled and swollen-eyed with sleep. Luna loved the sound of Joy's laughter, the way she gripped her pencil as she did her homework, loved seeing the emerging ghost of the woman that would one day take her body.

Luna loved her more than anyone or anything else in the world.

She crossed her arms. This time, she wouldn't crawl away, wouldn't crawl in a hole and hide, lying low so the forces of evil just wouldn't see her.

She would fight him. She would find a way—whatever it took—to stand up for Joy and herself, for the right to raise her daughter, even if she wasn't rich or successful, even if she'd had some bad years in her life and made some mistakes. Lots of great parents had made mistakes.

More than that, her gut just said Joy needed Luna now. She needed her mother as she made her way through these difficult years. She needed the influence of Kitty in her life, and the gentler world of Taos and all those other things. Luna wouldn't let Marc's egotistical charge take that away from her.

Joy came in just then, red-faced from the heat. "Hi," she said, and went to the cupboard for a glass she filled with water and drank down, then filled up again. "It's hot out there today. Wonder when the weather will break?"

Luna felt guilty all over again about the car. "Not long now," she said, then gave her a rueful smile. "But then it's going to get cold."

"I can live with cold." She plucked a handful of grapes out of the bowl. "What's going on?"

Truth was always best. "I just talked to your dad. He wants you to come back to Atlanta."

She lifted a shoulder, tossed a grape in the air, caught it in her mouth. "Yeah, so?"

"I'm willing to fight to let you stay here, Joy, but if

you feel ambivalent at all, maybe you'd be happier living there. More money, more room, better schools."

"More hassles, more fights, guns in every locker, people who call me names when I date somebody who isn't who they think it should be—" She paused. "And no you."

Luna didn't want to show how much that meant to her, and turned away, scrambling for a glass out of the cupboard. "Okay, then," she said. "I'll just keep telling him no every time he asks."

Joy ducked into the fridge, pulled out a wedge of cheese, chewed on her mouth in that funny way. "Mom, I really want you to know that I like being here because of you, okay? Not because of the town or just to get away from my dad, but because I just think I'm more like you than like anybody there. And I want to be with somebody who understands that being different is just how you are sometimes."

Luna hugged her, fiercely. "I'm so lucky to have you for a daughter."

Joy hugged her back and into her ear said, "So, how much do you love me?"

Luna laughed. "What do you want?"

"Do you think I can get my hair back to blond? Ricardo keeps teasing me and calling me girl with wrong hair. I think he'd like to see it blond."

Luna gave her a look.

"Oh, I know, I know. I'm not changing myself for a guy." She lifted a shoulder, lowered her eyes, concentrated on a crumb of cheese she put in her mouth. "Nobody wears this here and I'm starting to feel kinda dumb about it. *And* we're taking pictures next week."

"In that case, I'll be glad to do it for you. It shouldn't even be hard. What do you say we call Grandma for a ride and go get the stuff now?"

"Cool." She smiled shyly. "I think we're going out later. Me and Ricardo, that is. Is that okay?"

"Hmm. Let's talk about that in a minute, after I call Grandma."

Thomas couldn't stem his agitation, and he wanted to take off looking for Tiny or his car—which wasn't, after all, a hard thing to spot. Instead, he paced the porch, up and down, and peered down the road every time he saw a dirt trail out beyond the cottonwoods. He told himself Tiny would be home on time, by 5:30, or the alarm on the ankle bracelet machine would go off at headquarters.

But it was getting close now. Five minutes past five.

The phone rang and Thomas snatched it off the porch railing. "Hello?" he said gruffly.

"Thomas?" Nadine said in a thin voice. "Can you talk now?"

Guilt—he'd been ducking her—slugged him. "Sure, kiddo, what's up? Sorry I've been so hard to get hold of, but there's a lot going on here right now. Work and *Abuela* and—ah, hell, lots of things."

"It's okay. I understand." She sounded airless, her voice dull.

"Is the baby okay?"

"Fine," she said with a fragile laugh. "I'm huge."

Maybe it was that thin, brave laugh, but suddenly Thomas was slammed with a sense of loss again. It came in powerful images—her long thick hair, her rich mouth. Her body, so lush and sexual, spread naked on his bed. "I'm sure you look as good as you always do."

"Well, I don't." There was a maturity in her sigh, a womanliness. "I guess that's kind of what I wanted to talk to you about."

"Lookin' good?" he joked.

"No, silly."

At least she wasn't crying. She just sounded so tired, so worn. Maybe it was being pregnant. A sudden swell of sympathy made him kind. He leaned a foot on the rail. In a juniper tree nearby, a pair of wrens started warbling. "What's up?"

"First I wanted to tell you that I'm sorry for being so emotional on the phone the other day. I was just so freaked and I didn't know where to turn."

"It's all right."

She sighed. "There's no easy way to say this, Thomas," she said, and he felt a swoop of dread move through his belly, a nameless warning that made him want to keep her from saying it, but he only grunted.

"It's ironic," she said, "but I'm pretty sure your brother is cheating on me." She said it calmly, like it was no big deal.

But Thomas's body said otherwise. Every muscle in his body contracted, winced away from it. "It would be ironic," he agreed mildly. "But I'm not sure what I have to do with it."

"I don't know either," she said, and her voice cracked a little. "I told myself so many things, Thomas, when we were . . . when he and I—"

"I get what you mean."

"When I cheated on you with him," she said, more firmly, and he had a sudden visual of her tossing her long dark hair away from her face resolutely. "I told myself it was beyond my control, that passion swept me away, that we were soul mates and that made everything worth it." Her voice went a little ragged. "Soul mates."

He gripped the phone more tightly, feeling sweat make his palm slippery. Dread moved through his limbs like a swarm of flies, black and buzzing. A soft protest built in him: *Don't take me there, not again, I can't breathe*.

"The thing is, Thomas," she continued, "is that was so much bullshit, and I can't believe how selfish I was, we both were, to hurt you like that. You were my husband and he was your brother, and it was so ugly of us. I should never have—"

"Stop," he said, harshly. "I don't know what you want from me. Sympathy? Forgiveness? What?"

"Nothing," she said, and there were soft tears in her voice now. "I don't want anything. I just wanted to tell you that I understand now, and it was so wrong of me, and you are a good man and you didn't deserve it."

She understood now, Thomas realized with a distant ping of sorrow, because she truly loved his brother. He looked down the road toward Luna's house, invisible just beyond that line of scrub oak. He thought of her throat, her hair, her mouth, and the dread in him eased. He drew a breath and said, "Maybe you should get some counseling, Nadine." He avoided the obvious, that a man who could sleep with his brother's wife was probably not the wisest choice as a husband, and with some weariness, he realized that Nadine was about to learn the same lessons his mother had learned. "It's not just you now. You have to think of what's going to be best for the baby."

"So I'm supposed to just look the other way?"

"I can't tell you what to do, Nadine. It's none of my business."

A thick beat of silence. "I guess it would be foolish of me to ask if I could come stay with you for a few days, just to sort things out."

He thought of Luna, her wary dark eyes, her tentative smile. "Sorry. That's not something I can do."

"Because of the white girl?"

Her bitterness somehow didn't touch him. Calmly he said, "Yes. It would hurt her."

Nadine was silent. "I'm sorry. That was wrong of me. I apologize."

She hung up, and for a long moment, Thomas wondered if he ought to call her back. If she were swearing, wild, even weeping hysterically, it would be a lot more in character. It was one of the things that had most attracted and most repelled him—dramatic intensity.

And he realized that one thing he very much liked about Luna was that lack of drama. She was steady, calm. She saw, as he did, that life held enough drama without manufacturing it. With a sharp longing, he wanted to see her, be with her. Not for sex. Just to look at her calm brown eyes.

He punched the button on the phone and dialed her number. Joy answered with a breathless hello.

"Hi, Joy. This is Thomas Coyote. Is your mother there?"

"Yeah," she said with obvious disappointment. "She's in the garden. Let me get her."

Thomas smiled. "Expecting a call?"

"Maybe."

"Want me to call back in a little while?"

"No, that's okay. She'll kill me."

"I have an idea, then. Hang up. I need a little walk anyway."

"Really, Thomas, it's okay. I was just cranky. I'll go get her. Really."

"I insist. I want to see her more than talk to her anyway." And before she could waver anymore, he hung up and went to find his grandmother. It wasn't until he came into the kitchen that he realized he was whistling. Placida was in her rocking chair, her mouth open as she snored, and instead of saying anything, he just kissed her head. "You okay?" he said when she snorted awake.

"Fine, fine."

Thomas suddenly remembered Tiny and blew out a heavy gust of air. "I'm going down to see my friend. If Tiny comes, tell him to stay put. If the monitor goes off, page me."

But right then, the sound of a heavy engine rumbled in front of the house, and Thomas strode out on the porch to meet Tiny, who had the beginnings of a black eye but otherwise looked calm and cheerful. Thomas narrowed his eyes. "Where you been?"

"I went to see Angelica, okay? I won't lie. I just needed to be with her, calm down a little. And we're fine, okay?" He touched his heart. "I swear, brother."

Thomas said, "Two weeks, man. That's all you got left. Don't blow it."

"I know."

He did look fine. Calm. And Thomas wanted, even more, to see Luna. "Look out for *Abuela*, man. She looks tired." He pulled his keys out of his pocket. "I'm going out."

Tiny grinned, slapped his arm. "See? A woman makes life better."

"Yeah," Thomas said. "Some of them do."

One of the things that had snared Luna about her house when she was looking (and looking and looking and looking—it took a long time to find a house she liked that was also within her budget) was the patio. The house was an L, the living and dining rooms and kitchen in one wing, the sunporch, the bedrooms, and the bath in the other. Nestled between them, sheltered by an ancient cottonwood, was a patio laid with old, old brick. It was uneven after so many years, and things sprouted up in the cracks all the time—grass and weeds and a stand of cosmos in one corner that she let grow. A bench formed of the same adobe that made the house ran along side it, all the way around the L, and she put a table and chairs out there, planted roses and petunias in tubs, and nestled pots of lavender and rosemary at intervals for the good smells. She didn't have a fireplace, but hoped to one day add one.

She stripped the red and black out of Joy's hair and they found a tint, Pale Wheat, that was very close to her natural color. The actual process didn't take long—they ate a supper of fast-food hamburgers before they started, and munched on pistachios in the shell while they waited for the dye to take, sitting outside on the patio, enjoying the soft pinkish light and the cool breeze. Joy took off the black nail polish she'd been wearing and tried a coppery color. "Why do you think it's so comforting to paint your nails?" she asked.

Luna grinned. "I don't know. Same with getting your hair done, or getting a facial. Even shaving my legs makes me feel better sometimes."

"I know why it feels good to get your hair done," she said. "Somebody's hands on your head feels good."

"That's true." Luna rubbed the old polish off her own nails. She had to keep them fairly short because of the work she did, but at times in her life, they'd been very long indeed. They grew with no help from her whatsoever. Now she picked through the tray of bottles, chose a dark purply-plum and shook the bottle. She liked the ones with little beads inside. High quality product.

"Not purple, Mom. Be wild for once."

"Wild? Why?"

"Just for fun." She pulled out a turquoise shade. "This one. Trust me. It'll make you happy all week."

Best Friend Barbie, taking the color off her toenails, gave her a look. *Listen to your daughter.*

What the heck. She could be a blue jay for a week. "How's your friend Maggie doing?"

"Okay, I guess. Her mom is not going to work, though, she said. That's a pretty bad depression, isn't it?"

Luna frowned. "Can be." Stop procrastinating, she told herself. Picking up the remote phone sitting beside them on the table, she asked, "Do you want to invite them over tomorrow? We'll have Grandma come here instead of going there. Allie's going to come, too."

"Sure! That's a great idea. Maybe we can play a game or something."

"What's the number?" Luna punched them in as she said them. A girl answered on the second ring, breathless. "Hello?"

"Hi, Maggie," she said. "My name is Lu McGraw, your friend Joy's mother. Is your mom home?"

"Um, she's in the shower right now. Do you want me to have her call you? I think she's got something to do tonight, but maybe in the morning?"

"That's fine. In the meantime, we wanted to invite you both to come over tomorrow night for supper. Just a quiet thing, me and Joy and a couple of others. We'll watch videos or play games or something."

"Oh!" She sounded so startled it pained Luna. "I'd love to. I'll ask my mom if she wants to come, too. I mean, if it would be okay if I came by myself if she . . . uh . . . has something else to do?"

"Of course! Both of you or you by yourself, however it works out."

"Thanks. Can I talk to Joy?"

Joy shook her head, but it was too late. Luna held the phone to her ear so she wouldn't mess up her fingernails.

"Hi, Maggie, my nails are wet. Can I call you in a few minutes?" She listened. "Promise. Just a few minutes."

Clicking the button to hang up, Joy sighed. "She's really got this weird Tupac thing going, trying to prove he's still alive. Why do people do that? Pretend dead people are still alive?" Then she raised her head. "Oh! She's doing it because of her dad, huh?"

"Probably. And really, unless she takes it too far, it's not a problem. It gives her something to believe in when it's really hard to believe in anything else."

Joy nodded. "I can't help it, though, it drives me a little crazy. I don't want to talk about it all day every day." She held out her hands, admiring the copper. "This looks good, doesn't it?"

"It does."

When it was time for the tint to come out, Joy went inside to shower, taking the phone with her. Luna told her not to use it in the shower itself. "Duh."

Luna shrugged. "Better safe than sorry."

Her nails were dry, so she pulled on a pair of gloves and found her shears, and started puttering around the patio, deadheading the Jacob's Coat rose and the bright yellow stands of coreopsis and the wild, thick corner of pink and white cosmos. Some of them were nearly as tall as she was and their cheerful prettiness gave her loads of pleasure. They grew all over town, ferny and simple, adapted perfectly to the bright, hot, high altitude sun and cool nights. Nothing like a stand of cosmos to make her homesick when she was away.

The tasks eased her. Aside from the stressful day at work, she'd had a restless night, filled with bad dreams of leaving Joy in a car and not being able to get back to her before she suffocated in the sun, and of running and running and running to accomplish some unnamed task upon which the fate of the world depended. Twice, she'd awakened, haunted by tattered memories she would rather have not seen again.

She was sure the dreams had come out of going down to her mother's garage to start up the little blue Toyota.

Once she heard the water go off in the shower, she turned on the garden hose and started watering by hand. The silvery scented water, the angling of pink light over the old bricks and the plants and the adobe walls, the quiet of birds chirping and crickets singing, all of it eased her. Soaking a pot of lavender, she breathed in the scent of the leaves and called out the demons of memory, dared them to face the light.

Sometimes, she thought it was a miracle that she'd never been hurt more seriously during her drinking days—raped or killed. A lot of that time was mercifully blurry—waking up late to the musty smell of her one-bedroom apartment in Albuquerque, working as a waitress in a diner on the highway, then getting down to the serious business of the day: stopping the pain with as much alcohol as it took.

Sometimes, it took a lot.

There were plenty of companions. Men and women, young and old, all seeking the same thing she did: to drown their pain or hide from some awful thing or simply falling in love with the spell of the bottle, with the softer colors there, the easier way of being.

Because it *was* easier in ways to be a drunk. She clipped a rose and thought of the ocean-green that tinged the world when she started drinking. In that cool, soft world, she found she could take a breath without agony, forget all the things she wasn't and be happy with the things she was, happy with other drunks, happy letting go of all that couldn't be fixed.

Of course, there was that nasty little problem of side effects. Hangovers, blackouts, the pesky problem of needing to be together enough for part of the day so that she could earn enough money to drink.

Hitting bottom took a while. And it was a pretty dark place. She woke up in a service station restroom, with absolutely no memory of how she had arrived there—woke up all at once, banging her head on the stall door. The floor was dirty, and the first thing she noticed was the torn bit of paper towel under her foot. There was a little smear of blood on it. Luna got to her feet slowly, body and head a single dully aching pain, with brighter spots of sharpness here and there—her palms, dotted with ground-in gravel, the nails broken and bloody; skinned knees and elbows. The left elbow was swollen badly enough she thought there might be something really wrong with it, and in seconds, she discovered she couldn't move it without tremendous agony. In fact, the discovery of this particular pain sent her to the sink to throw up. Mental note: *don't move left arm.*

She looked in the mirror and saw herself—really saw herself—for the first time in a year. She was haggardly thin, and there was a good reason. She couldn't even remember the last time she'd eaten. Her hair was tangled and dirty, her cheekbones sharp as blades, her collarbone sticking up out of her dress like a hanger. There was a mark on her forehead that had some blood on it, and judging by the red around her left eye, it would be a mess in a few hours.

And Best Friend Barbie, omnipresent companion, put her hand on Luna's back, leaning in close to look at the reflection with her and said simply, *What if Joy saw you like this?*

Luna bent over the sink and wept. Turned on the water, kept her left elbow close to her to avoid jolting it, and just let it all go, sobbing giant, gulping tears of shame into a grimy little sink. She cried until there was nothing left, then washed up as well as she could and used the hand dryer to dry her hair and face.

When she stepped outside into the bright light of day, she saw that she wasn't that far from home, but there was no sign of the car she'd been driving. Or rather the car she'd borrowed. She didn't even have the energy to wonder where it was. Instead, she walked around the corner to a pay phone, put in the three dollars she found in her pocket, and called her mother, who simply said, "Go home. I'll come get you."

It took twenty minutes to walk four blocks, but Luna made it, showered the worst of it off and sat in the living room without any music or the television, waiting.

Kitty showed up in three hours flat, and insisted on taking Luna to a doctor. Who found a broken finger, a cracked toe, the various bruises, and a shattered left elbow. She was in the hospital for two days, during which time they found the car she'd totaled, then Kitty took her home to Taos and put her to bed. Luna slept for two more days, then woke up to cry for three more. Wept and wept and wept and wept, like there was no bottom to the depth of her sorrow. Wept out losses, wept out shame, wept over Joy—not that Joy didn't have her mother, but that Luna was so lost without her as an anchor. She missed her every single minute of every single day, but it was a pain she was going to have to learn to live with.

She hadn't had a drink since. Most of her memories were fairly blurry and ignorable, but every so often, she thought about that last blackout and wondered what had happened. The one disconnected, strange thing she remembered was a giant, exaggerated pink rose, as overblown and sensual as an O'Keeffe. It filled the air with its scent and the petals arched over her protectively so that she could sleep.

In the sanity and calm of a Taos evening years later, Luna could smile over that. Funny how the mind worked. Something had certainly protected her. She supposed she would never know what.

Out of the corner of her eye, she caught sight of a figure and whirled. "Oh!" she said, finding Thomas standing at the edge of the garden. "You startled me!"

He stood there for a moment, backlit by that pinkish sunlight, so big and protective and fierce, and she wanted to pull him to her, rest her head on his shoulder. But there was something burning in his eyes tonight that she hadn't seen before—something she didn't quite understand until he came forward and put his hands on either side of her face and bent in to kiss her. "You are so peaceful, Luna. You're like music."

Luna rested her head in the spot she wanted, and let the day and the memories flow out of her. "You're the peaceful one."

"Maybe we're both just worn out." His hands moved on her back lightly.

"Maybe so." Mindful of Joy, Luna lifted her head and moved away. She peeled off her gloves. "How's everything at your house?"

He settled on the bench, folding his hands loosely between his knees. "Okay, I guess. Tiny's sleeping. He promised to see a psychologist tomorrow. I give them good health insurance. It'll pay."

"You want to talk about all this?"

Slowly, he shook his head. "No. I want to take you someplace and eat with you. Someplace quiet. Can you go?"

"I already ate. Sorry."

"Will you come with me? Just sit with me?"

Luna thought of Joy, of breaking her date with Allie.

"I wouldn't mind, usually, but it's . . . complicated tonight."

He lowered his eyes. "I see."

Joy popped out of the back door just then. "Ta da!"

Her hair, long and silky, restored to its normal color, flowed down around her neck and shoulders. "It looks fabulous, Joy."

"Hi, Thomas," she said easily. "What do you think?"

"I like it a lot."

She had makeup on, and a nicer T-shirt than she usually wore, one that showed the ring in her navel. "I'm going to go, then, okay? Ricardo is picking me up in five minutes."

"Home by ten, right?"

"Right." She floated over to give Luna a kiss. "Thanks, Mom. Why don't you go do something, too?"

She smiled. "I'll think about it."

"Bye, then!" She dashed back into the house and Luna could hear the front door slam as she waited out on the porch.

Thomas looked at Luna. "Any other complications?"

"I broke a date with a friend of mine. I don't want her to think I broke it to be with a guy."

His face cleared. "Ah! Okay, I get that. Just come out for a while and if we see her, I'll do the explaining. Okay?"

And really, he looked so good, and Luna had such a crush on him, and in truth, she wanted the escape into the bubble he seemed to cast. "Okay. Am I dressed right or shall I put on something else?"

"You're fine, just as you are." He held out a hand and she took it, feeling grateful all of a sudden to have this chance. His touch lightened something in her. As they walked toward his truck, parked on the street, she smiled to herself.

"What?"

Luna shook her head with a rueful grin. "You just have no idea how long I had a crush on you. Every time you came into the store, my heart raced and my hands got sweaty. It's so strange that now—" She stopped, embarrassed by the sudden outpouring.

He rubbed his thumb over the center of her palm. "How did I miss seeing you?"

"You were in love with someone else."

A flicker of something crossed his face, something strong. "Yeah, I guess."

Best Friend Barbie said, *uh-oh, girlfriend, trouble there.*

No question. "Is there something bothering you, Thomas, something other than Tiny and all that mess?" She stopped, looking up at him. "Something to do with your ex?"

He nodded soberly. "She called me tonight. I'll tell you about it at dinner."

Shit. She should never have started this, a relationship with a man who was still damaged from the last one. She didn't want to be his transition person. But he rounded the truck as evening colored the air, looking toward the south and maybe the woman who had hurt him, and Luna looked at his big, gentle hands, and all she wanted to do was smooth the gravity from his cheeks, touch his hair, make him smile. "You can buy me something decadent to make up for never seeing me drool over you."

One side of his mouth lifted.

Victory.

Major Arcana. A choice between allurements, the struggle between sacred and profane love. Attraction, beauty, harmony of the inner and outer life. The power of choice means responsibility. If reversed: Parental interference, danger of marriage breaking up, quarrels over children. The possibility of wrong choices.

Twenty

Thomas took Luna to a hidden little restaurant off the plaza. It was agreeably busy, mainly local types with a few tourists mixed in. A man with a guitar and a gravelly voice sang acoustic rock 'n' roll—a little Jackson Browne, Dan Fogelberg, even Cat Stevens. Perfect, Thomas thought, feeling the tension ease in his neck.

They settled at a table beneath a skylight hung heavily with plants, and when the bartender came around with menus, Thomas ordered a Negro Modelo instead of a touristy Corona. For years, stories about the pissy quality of the beer had circulated around the area, but Thomas just didn't like it. Too thin. Luna ordered iced tea.

"You know," he said, "I almost never drink anymore, and now twice, I'm drinking in front of you."

"It honestly doesn't bother me."

"Just don't want you to get the wrong impression. I drink maybe three times a year."

"Okay." She smiled at him.

"It was a lousy damned day," he said, rubbing his chin, a tumble of images flashing through his memory—

the fight, the emergency room, the worry over Tiny, then Nadine's call.

The bartender was back in sixty seconds, carrying a beer so cold it had made her fingers red to fish it out from wherever it was kept. Luna's tea was served in a giant glass, with a very long spoon and three lemon wedges. Thomas ordered a cheeseburger, insisted Luna order some dessert. She chose a hot brownie with ice cream.

"Good girl," Thomas said with a grin.

"Yeah, that's what you say now. Wait until I weigh three hundred pounds. You'll tell all your friends, 'See that woman over there? I used to date her and look at her now. Amazing.' "

Thomas chuckled.

"My ex called today, too," Luna said, stirring sugar into her tea. "He wants my daughter to come back to Atlanta and he threatened to put his big dog lawyers on me."

"Are you worried?"

She pursed her lips. "A little. He has a lot of power and very little conscience."

Thomas touched her hand. "Sorry."

"My mother will help this time. Before, none of us had any money to battle him. Now she's married to a millionaire." She raised her eyebrows. "Not such a bad thing."

He laughed.

"You want to borrow him? Maybe it'll help with your ex, too."

He shook his head, lowering his eyes so he wouldn't have to see that faint worry in her eyes. "Not gonna help."

"What's going on, Thomas? Did you bring me here to

tell me you can't see me anymore because you're getting back together?"

Astonished, he said, "No! Good God."

She nodded, her eyes steady and disbelieving.

"But she did ask in a roundabout way, if she could stay with me."

"I see."

"How did you know?"

Luna lifted a shoulder. "Good guess."

"I told her no, Luna," he said.

She looked away, toward the band, and the sight of her profile, guarded and careful, made his chest ache. He put his hand over hers. "I told her no because of you." When she still didn't say anything, he said, "Was that the wrong thing to do?"

"You know," she said, taking her hand away, "this is really awkward and I don't know what you want me to do or say. We hardly know each other. We've had sex a couple of times. Big deal." She pushed her chair back. "If you want to let her come stay with you, I can really understand that. You wanted a baby. She's got one."

He took her wrist in a firm, insistent grip. "Luna," he said quietly. "Please don't go."

She took a breath. Looked at him. He met her gaze, trying to show her he didn't have anything to hide. "Please," he said.

All at once, she relented, sat back down. "How could I leave a hot brownie?"

Relief made him dive over the table and kiss her. Hard. "Thank you."

She scooted her chair back, lifted her tea and took a long sip. "You know, that made me want a cigarette so badly that I nearly went over and bummed one from that woman over there. I broke down and had one earlier today, too."

"I know. Tiny told me."

"He did? That rat. He promised not to."

"I'm not judging you, Luna."

"I'm judging myself. I really want to get off them this time. It's just hard."

The waitress brought their plates. "You don't really seem like a smoker," Thomas said.

"What's a smoker like?" She bent her head over the brownie, inhaling deeply, her eyes half-mast as she made a noise of pleasure. It was unconsciously sensual, and made him think of the way she looked that morning he saw her at dawn, as if she were inhaling all the light in the world, filling herself up on it. A pang of desire struck him deep, a hunger to taste that light again. He picked up the ketchup.

"I don't know," he said in answer to her question. "More blue-collar, maybe."

She laughed. "My mother was a cocktail waitress my whole life. I work in a grocery store."

He shook his head. "That's not your real work and you know it."

"What do you mean?"

"It's just not who you are. Too easy." He picked up his burger, aware suddenly that his stomach was growling. He tore into it. Hot, salty beef juices filled his mouth.

Luna swirled her spoon through chocolate syrup and vanilla ice cream and took a bite, closing her eyes. "Oh, that's why I'll never be a waif. This is so good."

He chuckled. "Waifdom is overrated."

In silence, they ate, both engrossed in the pleasure of food. After a minute, Thomas paused to take a sip of his beer. "I think," he said, "that you're still a counselor. You think about it a lot."

She hesitated. "Sure. I think about it all the time. I

loved it. I was pretty good at it." Taking exact fifty-fifty proportions of ice cream and brownie on to her spoon. "You used to smoke, right?"

"Yep."

"Why'd you quit?"

He carefully pulled onion off the burger. He would want to kiss her some more. Later. "My ex hated it," he said, and winked, patting his belly. He'd been working on it the past few weeks, doing sit-ups in the mornings, and maybe it was getting a little better. "That's where most of this came from."

"Don't tell me that," she snapped. "I don't need to gain any weight."

"Ah, it's worth it. Think of your daughter."

She took a breath. Nodded. "Thank you."

"No problem." He looked at her as he ate, feeling such a sense of connection that it was almost visible. He'd wanted, tonight, to prove to her that it wasn't all about sex, but her eyes glittered a little, and one side of her mouth turned up, and just like that—he wanted to go some place quiet, kiss her and touch her and lie close, side by side.

They ate for a while. It was a companionable quiet, and something in him ached at that. It was all he'd wanted with Nadine, a peaceful union where they helped each other. Was something like that possible with Luna?

Or would it end the same way it always did—with broken hearts and broken visions all around, having to face the lonely rooms again, rooms that were fine before a lover filled them with laughter, and were hollow afterward.

It was hard to hope, having gone through so many dark valleys, but somehow, he hadn't lost the knack.

Would it be worth it, loving Luna, if they ended in sorrow somewhere down the line?

He eyed her, digging a spoon into the pool of chocolate before her. She only swirled the bowl around, then licked it off, making her look young.

But even in the shadows, he could see the wear on her. She wasn't a kid. There were faint lines at the corners of her eyes and a certain set of the jaw that spoke of many words uttered, many things seen. As he watched, something the singer said between sets caught her attention and she flashed a quick, one-sided smile before returning her attention to her chocolate. A tiny half circle of scar cut into the right side of her lower lip.

He liked her wrists, flat and brown beneath silver bracelets, and her forehead, and the edge of a breast showing between the buttons of her blouse. He liked the angles of her—a tilt to her eyes, the arch of cheekbone, the downturn of her mouth when she had no expression. "Are you Indian, Luna?"

She looked up. "Not much." She gave a little shrug. "My dad was a quarter Apache. Why?"

"I just saw it," he said, admiring the depth of her dark eyes. "The blond hair his, too?"

"Not at all. That's a McGraw trait."

"So McGraw is your mother's name?"

"Yeah." She bent her head suddenly. "Her maiden name. She took it back when she was divorced, and so did I."

"What was your father's name?"

"Esquivel," she said. "Jesse Esquivel."

"Spanish?"

Luna nodded. "I know. Neither my sister nor I look it."

And with a searing sense of longing, Thomas suddenly saw what their babies might have been like, if they'd met sooner, soon enough, so they weren't both so old, so worn. He saw them, the babies, with wild curls and laughing dark eyes. Saw his father and hers, her mother and his grandmother, all blended into some perfection of southwestern union. The idea of it almost made him want to howl, and he reached for her hand. "I wish I'd met you a long time ago, Luna McGraw. Maybe when I was about seventeen."

"I was too young for you then," she said, turning her hand over so their palms touched.

He nodded sadly. Wasn't like he could have given her babies then, either.

"What's bothering you tonight, Thomas?" she asked softly.

He pressed his index finger to hers. "I'm not sure. Lotta things. I'm worried about Tiny and I think my grandma's wearing out and my brother is cheating on his pregnant wife, a woman he supposedly wanted so bad he had to steal her from me." He took a breath, said the truth. "It kills me so much sometimes, still. He lived with me for six months, and I had no idea, the whole time."

"I'm so sorry."

"Yeah. Well, what're you gonna do, right?"

"It does get easier, Thomas."

"No, it won't. What I can do is make peace with the fact that it sucked, what they did to me. I always want to change it, and that won't happen."

"I know that feeling. If you see it in time, maybe you could stop it?"

"No." He shook his head grimly. "I keep wanting to go back in time and catch them in the act so I can kick the shit out of them."

Her eyes lit up. "Hey! A revenge fantasy. Sort of. That's good."

"I have some other fantasies, too," he said. "But I'm trying to prove this isn't just about sex."

"It's not?"

"Not just that." He stroked her inner arm. "Want to go up to the casino for a while, play the slot machines? My treat."

"Sure. I'd love it."

Casinos were casinos, wherever you went, Luna thought. The noise, the lights, the chaotic feeling, that scent of nervous sweat. The Indian casinos she'd been to were no different aside from the fact that there was no drinking—not such a bad thing, if you thought about it—and at Taos, there was no smoking, either. It was a relief.

"What's your pleasure?" Thomas asked as they wandered the rows.

"Slots, I guess. Are you a poker man?"

"Not like this." He stopped to put a dollar in a machine. "I'm not that good."

"Me, either." They watched the symbols spin wildly and land on two cherries and a bar. Quarters clanked out into the tray. "Fairly auspicious beginning," she said with a smile.

He winked at her. "I guess you're a lucky charm." He scooped the quarters out and grabbed one of the plastic cups stationed between the machines. "What do you like to play? Quarters, dollars?"

"Electronic poker," she said. "Nickels only."

"Dangerous."

"Well, I'm just a danger-loving gal."

They found a bank of nickel poker machines and Luna took out a five dollar bill. Thomas put his hand over hers. "Allow me. I talked you into it, after all."

"All right. But the next round is mine."

Next to her was an old woman, probably seventy-five, with her purse nestled in her lap. She wore comfy polyester pants and a flowered blouse and the kind of tennis shoes you buy on special at Wal-Mart for five bucks. "I played that one for a while," she said of Luna's machine. "Didn't win a blasted thing. I'm doing pretty good on this one, though." She shook her cup. It was full of coins.

"Thanks for the warning," Luna said, but her money was already in, the lights flashing at her to come on and play, so she pushed the buttons. What the heck, go for broke—ten hands, full bet.

There was something hypnotic about gambling on slot machines. The noise, the lights, the way it took you completely away from everything on your mind. Luna never thought about anything while under the spell of a slot, and it said something that she could still lose herself like that when Thomas was sitting next to her in all his splendidness. She only came out of her hypnotic state briefly when the waitress brought around drinks—coffee for Luna, and it wasn't bad, she had to say, and Coke for Thomas. The waitress was too professional to risk losing a tip, but Luna did notice that her smile was all for Thomas. She didn't like him sitting there with an Anglo.

Luna played his five dollars, and then took out five of her own. Thomas, annoyed by the low stakes, stood up. "Mind if I go over there to the quarter machines? I never have liked the nickels."

"Not at all."

In ten minutes—just as she was about to lose her own five, and thought about quitting—he ambled over with a boyishly pleased grin. "Hey little girl. I'll give you a quarter for a kiss." He held it up between his dark fingers, wiggling his eyebrows at her impishly, and a pain went through her. God, she liked him. Not just lusted, not just wanted to be madly in love with him. She *liked* him.

She held out her hand, and he poured a bunch of quarters into it. "How much did you win?" she asked.

"Fifty dollars." He bent in and pressed a warm kiss to her mouth, his hand brushing her hair. In a low voice, he said, "I'll collect the rest later."

"Sounds good to me." She fed the new quarters into the slot, loving the little electronic beep that went along with each gulp, and wondered idly if anyone had done studies on the sounds that were most appealing to human ears—this one made her think of a Nintendo game Joy used to play. Nintendo was addictive, too. "Hey," Luna said before Thomas could get away. "Tell your adoring waitress that your love slave needs more coffee."

He gave her that great, slow grin. "Will do."

The woman next to Luna said, "Is he your husband?"

She laughed. "Not at all."

"Humph. I can usually tell. You must have been together a long time, though, huh?"

"Nope, not that either."

She snapped a bill between her fingers to straighten it. "Well, you're gonna be, then." She fed the machine and immersed, and Luna went back to hers, smiling softly to herself.

It couldn't have been more than three hands later that the dealer gave her four aces. Ten hands, four aces in each one. Luna laughed softly, and bet everything it would let her, then took a breath and punched the button. The light went off and the noise of coins adding to the total beeped wildly. Such a satisfying sound.

But it was a bigger payoff than the machine could

give, more than Luna had calculated in her light-and-sound dazed state. It filled the tray, then the light on top started blinking madly and a little whir of an alarm sounded. The lady next to her said, "Oh, fiddlesticks! That should have been mine!"

Luna shrugged, waiting for the attendant to come check it out. "Just works out like that sometimes."

"I reckon." She punched her button and kept talking. "Once, in Las Vegas, I got behind this Oriental lady about my age with three giant cups of silver dollar tokens." She paused to punch the buttons for the cards she wanted to keep. "I said, 'Whooeee! You won big.' She looked at me and said, 'I still lose.' "

Luna laughed.

"That's the way of it, huh?" the old woman said.

"'Fraid so." But tonight, she'd won. Won big. Two hundred and seventy-six dollars, to be exact. Taking the bills the attendant gave her, Luna went to find Thomas.

She spied him in a bank of quarter machines and headed toward him when a voice said, "Well, as I live and breathe, I've been stood up for a man."

Allie stood right in front of her. Luna blinked and said, "It's not how it looks. Come on." She tugged Allie's sleeve, and pulled her along. "Look! I won a bunch!"

"Oh, my God, Luna! That's so cool. The most I've ever won is a hundred bucks."

Luna, exhilarated by her win, slipped up behind Thomas and threw her arms around him from behind, spreading her palms to show him her bounty. "I guess you're my lucky piece."

And for one blinding second, it was only the two of them. His body was warm against her breasts and belly, and his hair smelled of shampoo, and there was something both comfortable and exotic about the way he felt. He took her wrists, cupped her hands, and bent to kiss her elbow before turning around to grasp her all the way, arms and legs and lips. "Congratulations!"

She allowed one moment, just one, of that blistering blue-white light to flare between them, then pulled back. "You said you'd explain to Allie," she said, waving toward her. "Explain."

"This is your friend?"

"Allie, this is Thomas Coyote. Thomas, Allie."

He stood up, holding out his hand, and Luna saw by the way Allie's face blanked, then shone, that she was off the hook. "How you doing?" he said.

"Well, my heart is broken, but other than that, I'm okay. I'm up twenty bucks, which is pretty good for me."

"Luna wasn't going to go out with me. I just showed up at her house when her daughter was leaving and made her come out to dinner with me."

"It's okay. I understand. We have a date for tomorrow."

"Good."

Luna widened her eyes at Allie behind Thomas's back, and Allie smiled. "I guess I'll let you two get back to your evening. I spied a cowboy over there with my name written over his Wranglers."

Luna hugged her impulsively. "Seven tomorrow, right?"

"I'll be there at six," she said, and in a low voice added, "Sex often and wildly."

Luna laughed. "Absolutely."

"God, I'm jealous!"

Light the color of burnt umber, probably a streetlight, came through a crack in the curtains of the theme motel where Thomas and Luna finally found a room. The

light arrowed through clouds of dust motes roused by
their energetic joining to splash on Thomas's knee, upraised beside her. Luna lazily waved a hand through it,
watching the shadows before settling her palm on the
big, solid joint. Her body felt like light itself, at once hot
and soft and weightless. The air was full of their combined scent—his hair and her soap, a touch of his
foresty cologne and the earthiness of their fluids.

They didn't talk, only lay together in the stillness,
contented. Luna curled into his side, her breast molding
itself to his lower ribs, her head on his broad shoulder.
His hand drifted lazily, lightly, over her back. Sometimes, she moved her cheek against his skin. Sometimes
he kissed her head. She dozed a little, amazed that it was
possible to let her guard down so much with him, that
they could find such an oasis in this dark little room.

After a long time, Thomas asked, "What are you
thinking?"

She stirred. "Not much of anything really. That I like
being with you. It's so easy." She moved a hand on his
stomach, admiring the pine-colored flesh. "You?"

He shifted to his side, rising up on one elbow. His
hair, which he'd taken down just for her, cascaded over
them, extravagant and wild. The sight made her ache,
somewhere deep. "I was thinking that there's love in me
still after all." He didn't quite meet her eyes, his gaze
going down her body, touching her elbow, tummy, sex.

Something very like terror squeezed her lungs, and
she put her fingers on his mouth, unable to even speak.

Then he did look at Luna. He kissed the fingers on his
mouth, and took them in his hand. "I'm in love with
you, Moongirl," he said. "That's what this feeling is,
and it doesn't matter that I haven't known you long. It
just matters that it's good."

She shook her head urgently. "Don't say that, Thomas."

"Love is a good thing, Luna. Not a bad one."

"It's not that easy."

"Isn't it?" He kissed her, smiling a little. "Is it that hard?" His hair swirled over her breast.

"No." Her throat was too tight to speak much. She thought of how many times she had admired him at the grocery store, his strength and his genial attitude toward everyone, the kindness he displayed when an old person had trouble opening a bag or a tumble of oranges had scattered over the floor. How many times had she watched him, thinking he couldn't possibly be as kind and good and honest as he appeared to be? Nobody was.

And yet, he seemed to be just that.

Tears came into her eyes, and feeling foolish, she turned away, pulling out of his embrace. "You know that's not it." She wiped the tears away, but absurdly, they sprang fresh and easy from some underground well and spilled over her face, and she found a soft, breathy sound in her mouth.

"Oh, Luna," he said, and tenderly, so tenderly, he fitted his arms around her body, his chest to her back. His nose touched her nape. "Let me love you. I'm really good at it."

Yes, he would be. She had seen that, too.

And suddenly, she saw her father, laughing as he came up the sidewalk to the house. He saw Luna's Barbie doll lying in the rain and picked her up and smoothed her hair down and carried her inside. It was a quick little flash of memory, slicing like an instant razor through her mind.

She turned, the tears going away. "I'm trying, but—" She frowned. "It's almost impossible to just . . . trust someone." She looked into his dark eyes, touched his scarred cheek. "You remind me of my father. I didn't realize that until just now."

"That's not so unusual, is it? Girls look for dad, boys for mom."

"Am I like your mother?"

He considered, raising a brow. "In ways. Maybe quite a few if I think about it. She works for the state in Colorado, with child welfare." He grinned suddenly. "You're more like *Abuelita*."

"Oh, thanks ever so! Mean and mysterious."

"She's not, though. She's strong and scrappy and full of love and worry and she's always trying to take care of everybody. Where do you think I learned to take in strays?"

Relieved that the conversation had taken a lighter turn, she laughed.

Suddenly the last of the light blinked out behind the curtains and the room was plunged into deep gloom. "Uh-oh," Thomas said. "I have to feel my way now." His big hands moved. "Ah, this must be breast. Maybe I should taste to be sure." His lips covered Luna's, suckling lightly. She laughed throatily. And that was easy, the giving and taking of this new delight in each other's bodies.

But when he was in her, moving slowly, making it last so they didn't have to go just yet, Thomas lifted his head and put his hands on her face. He kissed her gently. "Too late," he said quietly. "It's love, Luna-Lu."

And she wanted to say *It was love for me the first minute you showed up,* but she only pulled his head to her, wrapped her hands in his hair and absorbed him, every molecule of him, into her.

The Memorare

Remember, O most gracious Virgin Mary, that never was it known that anyone who fled to thy protection, implored thy help, or sought thy intercession, was left unaided. Inspired by this confidence, I fly unto thee, O Virgin of virgins, my mother: to thee I come, before thee I stand, sinful and sorrowful. O Mother of the Word Incarnate, despise not my petitions, but in thy mercy hear and answer me. Amen.

Twenty-one

Maggie's Diary

24 Septiembre 2001,
Sra de la Merced (never heard of her)

Dear Tupac,
  Oh, this was a bad day. It started out bad and then got good for a while, and then turned really, really bad.
  The way it started out bad was that my mom's boss called, early, and told me to get her out of bed. I wouldn't do it for a while, then I finally did because he wouldn't give up and called back, even, so I took the phone into her room and woke her up and gave it to her. She woke up enough to talk, and I went back out into the kitchen to make her some coffee, which she totally loves, so maybe the smell would get her out of her room for a change. I could hear her, though, saying she was sorry, that she'd be in on Monday, no matter what.
  Which was good. She went to the bathroom and I

heard her brushing her teeth, all that, and she came out into the kitchen wearing her robe, her hair brushed, and said, "Hey, that smells good!" And she drank a big cup and then we fixed scrambled eggs.

I mean, I can't even tell you how happy that made me. She was almost like her old self, skinny, but not so tired, tired, tired. She said she was sick of lying around, and maybe we should go get some new school clothes at the Wal-Mart today. I said that would be good and could I get some other stuff, too, like more notebooks (I've been using one I got at Safeway, but that was all the money I had) and maybe some markers and pencils and she said sure.

I was thinking that the charm might be working, finally, the one Mrs. Ramirez gave her. I don't know what happened right after, but maybe it just took some time to work. I also have been saying the rosary five times a day, the whole thing, plus *memorares* and St. Francis's prayer. It's gotta help sooner or later. I mean, my dad really believed and he'd be so sad with me if he knew how mad I've been at God and the Blessed Mother for letting him get killed. I know just what he'd say, that it's wrong to question God. But he didn't have to give up his dad so soon, either.

Anyway, my grandma came over when my mom was up, eating in the kitchen, and she was so happy, too, and we ate doughnuts my grandma bought, and I saw mom eat a whole glazed one, not even tearing it all apart like she usually does. So, now Grandma can stop worrying that I need to come live with her, too, because my mom was doing okay.

We went shopping and I got two new shirts and a pair of jeans. She wouldn't let me get hip-huggers, but I got some really long ones with silver studs down the side, and a cute top with laces at the neck. Also some new underwear, a pack of pencils, three spirals, and she even let me get this cool pen, that I'm writing with right now, called a Rolling Writer. It's purple, as you can see. It makes my handwriting look good.

At the end of the day, she was really worn out, so she took one of her pills—which is the right time to take one—and told me I could order a movie on Pay-Per-View if I wanted. I guess she doesn't know the cable is off, and so is the Internet, which is why I have to keep going to the library to use it. But I didn't say nothing. She was so happy and it was a real good day, so I just decided I could read stuff I brought home.

But then, Joy calls me and says her and Ricardo had gone out, but then somebody called him on his pager and he had to go to work (he's a cook, a really good one, at this good restaurant) so he had to bring her home early and she was all sad. Her mom went out and she's alone and could I come spend the night? She had all kinds of popcorn and stuff. We could watch movies. So I asked my mom and she said okay, so I walked over there at like eight o'clock.

It was so fun! Her house is this funny place, all bright colors and things painted on the furniture, like birds and jungles and stuff. Almost like my mom's plates from Pier One, but all over everything. And the couch has all these bright pillows so we could sprawl all over it, eating the piles of stuff Joy brought out on a tray, all nice, like a fancy party. There were grapes and popcorn and cheese, and this really good turkey. At first, I was shy, but it was all so good I just ate and ate like a pig, and Joy ate just as much. Then we made root beer floats, only with this vanilla pop that was so delicious I felt like a rich girl.

We watched videos for a while, and one of your

videos came on, and Joy said, "Tupac really is hot. Too bad he died."

"Maybe he didn't, you know? There's a lot of people who don't think so."

I could tell she didn't want to talk about it. She made this face and pulled her hair back (which she dyed blond again, and boy, Yvonne is gonna hate her guts on Monday for sure, because she is a really cute girl and all the guys will notice). So, maybe to just get me thinking about something else (which I admit I've been talking about you a lot) she says, "I went out with this black guy back in Atlanta."

"Is he the one who likes rap? Did you fall in love madly?"

She shrugged. "Yeah. But it was kind of stupid—he wasn't a very nice guy, really. My stepmom was the one who said she didn't think he was, and I thought she was being like a southern belle, you know, no race-mixing, but she just saw that he was a jerk." She rolled her eyes and popped some grapes in her mouth. "Then I found out he *was* a jerk, just like ninety-nine percent of all the other guys in the world."

I told her I didn't think they were all jerks, but she says, oh, really? And starts counting up the guys in her life, and it's not great. Her dad cheated on her mom, then now he's cheating on her stepmom, her grandpa left her grandma when she had little kids, and then her first boyfriend turns out to be a jerk. So I guess I can understand how she might get the wrong idea about guys.

So, for once I had something good to tell somebody. I told her about my grandpas and grandmas, who were both married for like a million years, and all my uncles. I only have one uncle who ever cheated, and it was a really big deal. Like nobody talked to him for ages, and they gave him lectures all the time, and it was a drag for him. I don't get why it's no big deal in the movies. Like everyone just says, "Oh, he fell in love with somebody else," like it's normal to break up families and leave the kids all sad and the moms without anybody in their corner after they worked hard to make a good life.

My dad loved my mom totally. I know it in my heart. That's why she's so sad.

Joy gave me this look. "I bet they're just careful, those guys, not to get caught."

"Joy, no. That's so sad you think that way!"

She looked all miserable, and even got tears in her eyes. "That guy? He talked me into having sex with him." She wiped her nose, real quick. "And I was so crazy about him. He had this beautiful face, these beautiful hands, and a great voice." She kinda shivered. "And I was so humiliated when I found out he was just using me."

I hugged her. "It's not your fault. I'm sorry he hurt you, Joy, but it's because *he* was bad, not you, okay?"

She hugged me back, really tight, and kind of sighed in my hair. Like she needed, really bad, to tell somebody, and she figured she got the right one. So then we got embarrassed and scooted away from each other, and I told her about my dad and how old-fashioned he was. "Everybody always said that it was bad luck that he was overprotective and all that, but I didn't mind it. He wanted to keep me safe, you know?"

"Yeah. My dad's never home. He'd never know if I was safe or not. That's what I like about my mom. She's here so much it almost drives me crazy." She laughed to show she didn't mean it. "I just wish I hadn't done it now, you know? Like it took some of the specialness out of it, to do it with him and have it go bad."

I had a good idea, then, but everybody always thinks I'm so boring that I was afraid to say it, but then I did anyway. "Maybe you could just be a new virgin."

"What do you mean?"

"I don't know, just do whatever, you know, like tell the Virgin you're sad about it and ask her to make you a new virgin, and you could start over."

"I'm not Catholic," she said, and I was about to feel really stupid, but then I heard the echo of her words, like she wished she was, so she could do that, and I said, "I don't think she'd care. It's not like she's only the Holy Mother to Catholics, even if we're the only ones who call her that. She can be anybody's Holy Mother, right?"

Joy blinked hard, like she was going to cry. "Would you help me?"

"Yeah! My dad, he was like totally crazy for her, so I know a lot." And then I remembered something. "Maybe, if I get to have a *quinceañera*, you could come, and you could do what I do. I don't know if I can do it, now, because I was supposed to have it and then my dad died and everybody forgot."

She didn't know what that was, and I told her. "You go through these classes at the church to learn all about the Virgin, and then, on your fifteenth birthday, you get to have a big Mass just for you, and dedicate yourself to staying a virgin till you get married, then you have a big party and everybody comes. I had all the favors and my colors picked out. And you should see my dress. It's just like a wedding dress, with silver stuff on it, the skirt and the sleeves. I even had silver nail polish to wear, and my mom was gonna let me have fake nails, just for the day."

"And then your dad died and you didn't get to have it?"

It was too soon, I told her. Only two months after he got killed.

Joy got all quiet, then says, "Do you hate talking about it? Your dad, I mean. What happened."

I told her no. "I hate it more that everybody wants to act like he was never alive. He was in a car wreck—driving in the rain and a truck hit him. I couldn't believe it when they told me. Like it was some bad joke and somebody was going to say, any minute, 'Not really!' Or that they were wrong, that he'd come home and it would be some other guy."

But it was him.

"I miss him," I told her. "He was fun, and he made everything good. He would hate it that my mom's acting like this."

Then she told me her mom used to be a psychiatrist or something, and maybe it would be good if my mom came over.

And then this is where the day goes really bad again. Because we heard this car door outside, and Joy gave me a weird look, like guilty, and she said, "Maggie, I been meaning to tell you something about my mom's new boyfriend, but I couldn't figure out how."

"What?"

Joy looks over her shoulder, all worried, and we heard two voices, man and woman, coming up to the door. "He's the one you wanted for your mom."

"I don't know what you mean."

But then in walks Joy's mom and behind her is her new boyfriend, and they're liking each other a lot and it was the *bruja*'s grandson. He smiled at me all nice, and says, "Hi, Maggie. How's it going?"

I gave Joy a look and I could tell she got it, because she looked sad. "I was just about to go home," I said.

And here's the bad part, Joy's mom was so pretty,

with all this pretty hair, so blond, like Joy's, it was almost white, and it fell down in curls around her face, and she has these beautiful dark eyes that took up half her face, and she had rosy cheeks like she was crazy in love. When she saw me she smiled and said in a voice that was all warm, "You have to be Maggie. I've heard so much about you." She held out her hand, but I pretended I didn't see it.

"I gotta go," I told them.

But that's why the grandson came in, because they saw us and he thought I'd need a ride home, so late. "I just want to walk, okay? I do it all the time."

"Hey, it's right on my way," said the grandson. *Tomás.*

I shook my head, but I could see I'd lose. No way two grown-ups were gonna let a girl walk home alone at night, even if it was Taos. So I just pretended to be glad. "Okay." And I let him take me home, but I didn't talk.

So now I don't know what to do. If there's no guy out there for her, my mom's gonna die.

Maggie

Five Stages of Grief

1. *Denial and Isolation*
   At first, we tend to deny the loss has taken place, and may withdraw from the usual social contacts. This stage may last a few moments, or longer.

2. *Anger*
   The grieving person may then be furious: at the person who inflicted the hurt (even if she's dead), or at the world, for letting it happen. He may be angry with himself for letting the event take place, even if, realistically, nothing could have stopped it.

3. *Bargaining*
   Now the grieving person may make bargains with God, asking, "If I do this, will you take away the loss?"

4. *Depression*
   The person feels numb, although anger and sadness may remain underneath.

5. *Acceptance*
   This is when the anger, sadness, and mourning have tapered off. The person simply accepts the reality of the loss.

Twenty-two

Saturday morning, Luna went to her mother's house to pick up the list of chores and the keys. To Luna's relief, Kitty flung open the door even before she got there, and she was herself again in a gold-and-white pantsuit with gold sandals. A trio of very thin gold chains adorned her tanned cleavage and gold hoops swung in her ears. "Hello, darlin'," Kitty said. "Come on in."

The thing they'd always done after a breach was just go on as if it never happened. But today, seeing Kitty so much her old self again, Luna couldn't help herself. She followed her into the kitchen and threw her arms around her. Tightly. "I was so worried about you," Luna breathed, smelling watermelon hair gel and Jean Naté cologne.

Kitty didn't even resist. She hugged Luna right back. "I'm tough, honey, you know that."

Luna thought of Thomas, describing Placida, and let her mother go with a smile. "I hope I'm just like you some day."

"Oh, phooey. You've been tougher than me since the day you were born." She clattered over to the sink, her little tush twitching in response to the high heels. "Like rawhide, your daddy used to say."

Best Friend Barbie huffed. *So, just like that we're gonna talk about him? Memories and all that bullshit you wanted forever and couldn't get from her? I don't think so!*

But Frank came into the kitchen, and Luna didn't pursue it. He gave her one of his hearty embraces, half hug, half shake. "How's my girl?"

"I'm good, Frank," she said, kissing his cheek. She couldn't help wondering for the hundredth time how her life would have been different if Frank had arrived a little sooner. Kitty would have been free to shop and keep the house sparkling and cook beautiful suppers for all of them. Maybe Elaine wouldn't have needed to insulate herself beneath all those layers of protection and beneath the umbrella of her religion. Maybe Luna wouldn't have been so driven and wouldn't have gone to college so soon and would never have met Marc.

But that would have meant no Joy, and she wouldn't trade her daughter for any reason.

"Are you guys on time?" Luna asked, picking up a neatly printed list of instructions about the house and yard, including various numbers for the handyman, gardener, and housekeeper, who would still come once a week. The cruise details were there, too, with the list of stops sounding exotic and refreshing. "Greece," she said with a sigh, pictures in her head of stark white houses tumbling down a hill to a vast, deep blue ocean. Taking a breath, she could almost smell the air, see the sunlight glittering off the waves. "You're going to have a marvelous time."

Kitty, bent over a cosmetics bag on the counter, murmured something and clicked into the bedroom. Luna looked up and caught Frank staring soberly after her, a very real pain on his face. She touched his hand. "This was a very good idea. And in case I've never said, thank you for taking such good care of my mother."

He squeezed her fingers. "Darlin', she's the one who takes care of me."

The sound of her shoes came back toward them. Kitty reappeared with a new sheaf of papers in her hands. "I almost forgot this," she said. "It's what the lawyer sent me—contact information, where the land is, everything. It's all yours, sweetie."

Luna nodded slowly, looking over the paper. "Do you want to know what I find?"

Kitty raised her bright blue eyes. "No, I don't believe I do."

"No problem." She tucked the sheaf of papers into her purse. "Um, listen, will you leave the keys to the Toyota, too? No promises, but I'm going to keep trying." She took a breath and confessed her secret. "I got my license back this week. Took the test, everything."

Kitty squealed and hugged her. "I'm so proud of you, honey!" She took a ring of keys off the hook on the wall. "I'll bring you a super-duper Greek key ring and you can have it when you start to drive, how's that?"

Luna laughed. "Great idea. Thanks."

And really, there was no reason not to go then. Her mother would be back in a couple of weeks. It wasn't as if they needed her help, either. So why was she standing here with her hands in her back pockets?

Thomas.

"Frank," she said. "Can you give me ten minutes with my mom?"

"Sure thing, honey. I wanted to have the service station fill up the car and check the oil anyway." He pressed a kiss to the part in Kitty's hair. "I'll be back in half an hour."

She brushed a hand over his. "I'll be ready."

When the door closed behind him, Luna said, "I met someone."

"The someone you had to rush to meet a couple weeks ago?"

Had it only been that long? It felt, in terms of depth, much longer than that. As if she couldn't imagine how her life had flowed without him in it. "Yeah," she said airlessly, wanting a cigarette. It would give her time to think, to breathe, if she could take one out, tap it on the counter, play with the lighter. Of course, she wouldn't be smoking in her mother's kitchen even if she still smoked. "He's scaring me," she said quietly.

"Scaring you how?"

She thought of their long, long conversations by phone late at night, the way it felt, lying in bed and talking to him. Thought of the note he sent to work, "Please make the florist a bouquet of blue flowers." Thought of wanting to see him so badly this week that it was like a physical pain—and not being able, for one reason or another, to work it out. But that didn't seem all that coherent, and instead, she said, "I've wanted to meet him for two years."

"I don't follow you."

"I know. I don't know either. I don't even know what I wanted to say except that I met him. He seems too good to be true, so it probably won't work out."

"Sometimes," Kitty said, "men really are what they seem to be, baby. Not all of them desert you or betray you."

"How can you even say that? Our lives were really hard because my dad just walked away, and then I found somebody else who also betrayed me. It's not that easy, Mom, to just say, 'Hey, maybe I'll give it a chance.' "

Kitty paused. "I know. But you need to remember your daughter."

A wave of guilt hit her. "It's not like I'm making him a part of her life yet or anything. I—"

"That's not what I mean." She touched Luna's hand. "What you need to remember about Joy is that she hasn't seen many good examples. Her father has betrayed two women, your daddy left you, and you don't want her waiting until she's forty to trust somebody. You don't want her shutting herself off because it's dangerous and sometimes you get hurt."

"Like I have?"

She gave her a sad smile. "Yes. And where do you think you learned it?"

Luna took a breath.

"Trust yourself, Luna, and let her trust you. Let her see you taking chances, falling in love, feeling things, living. It's better like that, than living behind some wall forever."

"I don't know if I can," she said, and that was more terrifying than doing it. "How could you stand it?"

Kitty lifted a shoulder. "One day at a time. That's all it takes."

"I'll think about it."

Luna started home, keys in her pocket. All the keys. As she walked, she jingled the Toyota's pair against her fingers. It was a hot afternoon, belying the gold on the leaves, the whisper of winter settling in the arroyos and breathing across the evenings. It made her oddly melancholy, and glancing at her watch, she stopped in the coffee shop for a latte, then took it around the corner to the plaza, where she found an empty seat right away. That would have been impossible two weeks ago, or even last week.

Now, for the first time, she noticed the summer crowd had thinned and the few tourist clusters wandering around the shops were child-free. One very young pair, both with long blond hair and loose clothing that barely covered their perfect bodies, strolled hand in hand, obviously in love. In love with themselves, each other, with Taos—everything. She wanted to be them. Either one of them, with everything ahead and nothing behind her to regret.

Barbie, using an emery board, said, *Get over yourself, babe. Please.*

Good point. Those two had a lot of shocks ahead. Everybody did—that was the bitch of it, wasn't it? Nothing ever stayed smooth and beautiful and good, not skin, not faces, not the road of life. What mattered was the way you lived with what happened to you.

Wishing for a cigarette, she thought about that. What was ahead of her when she was that age that she wished she hadn't lived through? What would she change?

Taking a little notebook out of her bag, she opened it and, pen poised above the page, gazed toward the horizon, admiring the blue mountains, the bluer sky, the softness of adobe buildings.

Number One, she wrote, and paused again. Then she drew a circle around the words and wondered why she hadn't just written 1.

The obvious one was drinking. Going insane with drink in Albuquerque until she had an accident she couldn't remember.

Doing it again. Barbie flipped her shoe off her toe, popped a bubble.

"Shut up." She raised her head. On a balcony over the square, a woman leaned on the wall and gazed down at everything. She wore a gold blouse and her hair was a soft red and she looked happy to be where she was. Luna reached into her bag and pulled out the sheaf of papers. What would she change?

Betrayals.

Suddenly, she stood up. She didn't want to brood anymore. She didn't want to whine. She was sick to death of being afraid all the time—afraid of the past, afraid of Marc, afraid of driving, afraid of herself. She was sick to death of second-guessing every thought, every move, every decision. With firm strides, she marched to the pay phone and called a cab.

There was one thing she could change today. Right now.

Once again, she went to the garage of her mother's house and opened the door of her car. It was still adjusted to her specifications from the last time she'd tried, but she touched the mirror anyway.

She felt fierce. Scared, but ready, as she put the key in the ignition and started the car, then took a breath and eased out of the garage. The first flutters of panic started, and she forced herself to just breathe. In. Out.

She made it to the little flat spread of driveway and took a break. She even turned off the car for a minute and got out, walked around, remembering to breathe. In. Out. Just breathe.

Barbie climbed into the passenger seat and put on her sunglasses like she had all the confidence in the world. *Come on. We can do this. I'm right here with you.*

For a minute, Luna wanted to put her head down and cry. But somehow, Barbie gave her courage. She knew she was imaginary, knew it was a silly game she played with herself, but it was enough. Enough courage to climb back in, put the car in drive, and ease out on to the road.

Luckily, there was little traffic. Trying to get used to the feeling of the enormous, deadly machine around her, she drove about five miles an hour down the narrow lanes around her mother's house. It had worried her, ahead of time, thinking about driving those lanes, but the car was neat and somehow fit Luna's sense of space in a good way, so it wasn't as creepy as she had anticipated, even when an SUV came up on the other side, pretty fast, and just passed her. Luna was holding her breath, her hands gripped hard on the wheel, and made a few of those stop-start moves with the gas, which was kind of embarrassing.

And then, she got to the main drag and a stop light. Which was red. The panic started coming back and she had a flash of—something—before she remembered to breathe. In. Out. She was sweating so much she took a second to press the button to roll the window down, and a wind freshened by chamiso blew into the car, rustling her hair.

Doing great, girlfriend.

The light turned green and she eased forward, knowing she now had to go at least twenty or get honked at, which would be highly alarming and she didn't need the aggravation. So she pushed the pedal down and sailed around a corner, down into the warren of streets that led to her house. Here she could go more slowly, since the streets were tiny and covered with gravel and only idiots drove fast.

The sense of explosive accomplishment she felt when she pulled into her own driveway was like a cannon going off. Two and a half miles. She'd driven two and half miles!

Slamming out of the car, she went inside to call Joy, but she wasn't there. Luna was crushed. Maybe she'd gone to Maggie's house. Luna could drive another half mile, surely.

Joy had been worried about Maggie all day. She'd called, but Maggie never answered, and Joy had finally gone to all their hangouts—to the Loaf and Jug and down to the park, and even to the deserted school. She saw Mr. Romero there, and asked if he'd seen her, but he hadn't. So Joy walked back to Maggie's. She knocked for about five minutes, waiting politely in between, but no one was there, and that made Joy's stomach hurt.

Taking out a piece of paper, she wrote a note.

Dear Maggie,
I'm really, really sorry I hurt your feelings. I didn't mean
to! I kept meaning to tell you that my mom's new
boyfriend was the same one you'd been thinking about for
your mom, and I just forgot (you know already that I'm a
space case!). Please call me and tell me you're all right. I'm
gonna be totally freaking out!!!
PS. I really want to see your ~~kw qunnsyera~~ quinsinyera
dress. I think that's so cool!

Your friend Joy (for real!!)

• • •

She folded it into an envelope and put it in the mail-box, with Maggie's name on the outside, then headed down the street toward her own block, her heart kind of heavy. She missed Maggie. She was her only friend here, and if she couldn't patch things up with her, who would she talk to? She wished for her little brothers. They'd be getting home from soccer practice, their hair and clothes wild and dirty, their freckles beautiful across their little noses, and they'd have stuff to tell her about, their big moves and how they got yelled at by the coach. She really missed them a lot.

Enough to go home?

No. The feeling was surprisingly solid. She really liked being here. She liked her teachers, especially the art teacher. She loved living with her mom—it was spe-cial, somehow. She loved the house and the town and everything else. She just wished she could have her brothers with her, too.

Car tires spitting out gravel at a low rate sounded be-hind her, and Joy glanced over her shoulder, half hoping it was Ricardo. It was just a plain blue car, and Joy moved to the far right, hoping it wasn't going to be some gooney man. Once, in Atlanta, a man had driven very slowly beside her all the way down to a park, and when she finally realized maybe he needed directions, she'd bent down to ask and saw that he had his thing in his hand.

Disgusting.

The car did slow down, and Joy kept her face stub-bornly forward, even when the car window rolled down on her side. It kept pace with her for a few seconds, then somebody said, "Hey, you silly girl. Look at my ride. Get in!"

Joy turned around, her mouth dropping. "Mom?"

Luna was behind the wheel, her hair windblown like she'd been joyriding all over town with the windows down. "Whoo-hoo! I got my license!"

Finally realizing it was *really* her mother behind that wheel, Joy opened the door. It was a pretty nice car, really, electric blue with power windows and nice leather seats. "Where'd you get the car?"

"Told you I had one. My mom bought it for me two years ago." She pulled sunglasses down over her eyes and looked in the rearview mirror before taking off, very gently. "You aren't the only one who's been nagging me to get back in the driver's seat."

Joy wiggled into the seat. "It's beautiful!"

"Wanna go to DQ and get a sundae to celebrate?"

"Sure!" Impulsively, she leaned over and kissed her mom's cheek. Luna patted her hand.

At the Dairy Queen, they ordered their sundaes, hot fudge for Luna, strawberry for Joy, and carried them outside. Joy's mom was cheerful, almost giddy, and Joy loved her like crazy. All of a sudden, she was tired of carrying around her big secrets, and she said, "Mom? Can I tell you about some things?"

"Of course."

So Joy took a breath and told her all about the boy in Atlanta, and how ashamed she was of herself for the whole thing, and her mom just listened, didn't try to make it less than it was, or freak out. In the end, Luna said, "It's a tough lesson you had to learn, but it's not such a bad one, in the long run, you know?"

"What d'you mean?"

"Well, now you know that people just use each other for sex sometimes, and that you don't feel good about having sex under those conditions. You need more, and that's smart."

A giant, giant weight just fell off of her then. "Oh!" She blinked. "I never thought of it like that."

"Nothing wrong with making mistakes as long as you learn from them."

Joy nodded, gathered her courage and said, "There's something else."

"Okay."

"It's about Dad."

Luna gave Joy her poker face. Patient, listening, non-judgmental, but Joy felt the tension in her mother's body. "I'm listening," Luna said.

"He's having another affair. He has been for a really long time. I don't think April knows, or at least she doesn't know *know* and it was making me so mad that I couldn't hardly talk to him."

The therapist's face cracked open and Joy saw real sorrow dawn. "Oh, honey, I'm sorry. That had to be a terrible situation to be in."

"I never knew if I should tell her or not."

Luna shook her head. "Not your responsibility."

"Would you tell her?"

She said nothing for a moment. "No. It's not mine, either. It's entirely possible she knows and is only able to keep her dignity by not saying anything about it."

"But how could you stand to live with that?"

"People live with all kinds of things, sweetie. I'm glad you told me."

Joy let go of a heavy breath. "Me, too."

Winter blew in at suppertime, whirling down from the mountains to slam hard into the city. It came like a giant broom, sweeping summer out of town. Thomas lit a fire in the fireplace in his living room for the first time this season, taking pleasure in the ritual of cleaning, laying, lighting. Tiny had gone to his domestic violence class, leaving Thomas and Placida, Tonto and Ranger, to eat supper in the cozy kitchen. Thomas ate two big bowls of beef stew with sliced bread, following it with giant cups of red Kool-Aid.

It was only as he finished that he realized Placida wasn't speaking, or even eating, come to that. "You feeling okay, *Abuelita*?" he asked her, his hands on her tiny fingers.

"Just tired." She looked toward the windows, her lips turned down. She rubbed her hands over her upper arms. "Maybe I'm going to church tonight."

"I'll come with you."

She nodded. "It starts at seven."

"Maybe you should go take a little rest until then."

"You won't forget?"

"Promise," he said earnestly, putting his palm on his heart.

She pushed herself to her feet, and with a pang, Thomas saw that she was frail. Old. Very, very old. It was easy to forget because she was so busy, and such a busy*body*, but once in a while, it showed. Tonight it was in the hunching of her shoulders, and the shuffling of her feet as she moved toward the door. Thomas put his napkin down, wishing he could pick her up and carry her—she was so small and he was so big—but she would never allow it.

The phone rang as she came close to the door, and her hand whipped out, fast as the tongue of a snake, to capture the receiver before anybody else. Thomas allowed himself a small, hidden grin. "*Hola?*" she said too loudly.

He collected his dishes and carried them to the sink, pretending not to be interested in the conversation. From the other end of the line, he could hear a female voice, upset, and he thought it might be Angelica.

"No," Placida said, her mouth hard. "Don't call here no more. No more." She hung up.

"Who was it?"

Placida lifted her chin. "Nobody. You never mind." She shuffled away, and Thomas let her go, then picked up the caller ID and pressed the button. "James Coyote, 505-555-2122."

Nadine, not Angelica. What was going on? Outside, the wind whipped hard around the windows, sending sprays of light pebbles into the glass. He decided to let it go. If it was important, she would call back.

Placida could not fall into a deep sleep, only lay on the bed, thinking, her head full of pictures like always lately. She had not slept well for many weeks, not since her house burned down. Every night, she dreamed of beasts with big teeth and panting tongues. She dreamed of snakes crawling out of the heart of a rose, and of a pregnant black dog with a torn ear, coming to bring danger.

It was fitting Tomás should come with her, to church tonight. Tomás, her last one. He was gentle with her, holding her elbow to help her into the high seat of his truck, then making sure she secured her seat belt. Her sweater was buttoned all the way to her neck and she put the scarf she brought over her head, because the wind was bringing winter.

She stared out the window as they drove to the church, seeing now that the trees were getting ragged. Soon the snows would come. She would ache, all day and all night. Mornings it would take a long time to crawl out of her bed, and nights would mean putting her body in just such a way to make it not hurt. She didn't want no more winter. Enough.

At the church, she waited while Tomás came around.

She looked up at the church, seeing the light spill out into the night, a yellow that made her think of her girlhood and the candles they had used. Hard days, those, not like now, but she missed them anyway sometimes. Missed her sisters and her mama, mainly, and the smell of cinnamon in *empeñadas* cooking for Christmas.

The passenger door opened, startling her, and she blinked at Tomás, forgetting for a minute why he was there. What a handsome man he had always been! Not pretty like so many of the boys in her line. Pretty faces caused trouble. No, Tomás had steadiness in his broad shoulders, kindness in his big hands, gentleness in his heart. And he was so lonely, this one. "All I was doing was bringin' you a wife," Placida said in Spanish. He smiled, and she remembered that he didn't speak Spanish too good.

Never mind. *La Señora* spoke all languages, and it was to her that Placida prayed tonight. She knelt in the cool quiet of the church, focusing on the statue of *La Señora* at the back. "*Señora,*" Placida said in her mind, her forehead pressed against her thumbs which held the rosary of rosewood she saved for special times like this one. "I am an old woman and asked for the wrong things. Forgive me for thinking I know more than *Nuestro Padre*, and help me now to fix this mess I have made."

Her mistake had not been in asking for a wife for Tomás, because a wife he needed, and it was the way of men and women to travel in pairs. She could not go until he had a wife that would stick.

But her error had been in thinking she knew which woman would be that wife. Placida had thought to help the little girl's mama—the sad widow who wanted to crawl into the grave behind her husband. Help Tomás, help the widow, help the girl. All would be well.

Instead, the Madonna had brought that sturdy strapping white girl. Placida didn't even know her family. Sally, the widow, was a good woman, who had been in church every week and did not carry on or go to the bars looking for men even though her heart was breaking. She was a good Spanish woman, who would make Tomás a good wife and had already a daughter Tomás could raise.

But that was the wrong thing to ask. "Forgive me, *Madre*," Placida whispered. "Bring him the one who will stick. That's all." She bent her head, her neck so weary from praying so many, many years, and said, "The one who will stick."

From the *Taos Three Penny Press*:

Rules to Live By

For a bowl of water give a goodly meal;
For a kindly greeting bow thou down with zeal;
For a simple penny pay thou back with gold;
If thy life be rescued, life do not withhold.
Thus the words and actions of the wise regard;
Every little service tenfold they reward.
But the truly noble know all men as one,
And return with gladness good for evil done.

— SHAMAL BHATT
GUJARATI DIDACTIC STANZA

Twenty-three

Just after Luna and Joy got home after their trip to Dairy Queen, a cold front blustered into town on a hard wind, dropping the temperature in town thirty degrees over an hour's time. By nightfall, Luna had to turn the heat on in her house for the first time this season, and it sent a smell of old dust through the rooms as she chopped veggies for their Saturday night supper. Kitty wouldn't be there, of course, but Allie would be, and Elaine was driving down from Raton as always. Luna had tried calling Sally and Maggie, but there had been no answer. Still, you never knew. She'd try again in a little while.

Joy camped in her bedroom with the phone, her music finally low enough that Luna could play something a little less . . . agonizing . . . on the small CD player in the kitchen. She put on "White Bird" again, thinking of Thomas, wondering if she'd always listen to this and think of him kissing her, and if it would always be a good memory. Last night had been—well, equal parts alarming and thrilling.

Allie showed up at six, her hair a wild tangle, her cheeks ruddy from the short dash from the car. Her dog tripped on himself trying to get in, and nearly knocked both Allie and Luna down. "Jack!" Allie cried, scolding, but he was already on his way to Joy's room, where he sat down and scratched hard. Joy opened the door, let him in with a wave at Allie, and closed the door again, the phone firmly stuck to her ear through the whole process. Allie grinned. "Must be a boy."

"He's really cute, too," Luna said. She took the fondue pot Allie was carrying into the kitchen. "Come on in here for now."

"I haven't made a fondue in ten years," she said. "That thing was so dusty you wouldn't believe it."

"It's one of Joy's favorite things," Luna said. "I got my mother's pot, but I wanted to do two—one cheese, one chocolate." She gestured to the counter, covered with bananas and cherries and strawberries, and angel food cake for the chocolate; broccoli, bread, and an assortment of other veggies for the cheese.

"Yum." Allie lifted a lid on a saucepan over the stove. "You're cooking? Like, from scratch?"

Luna grinned. "Yes. My mother assured me that even I could manage fondue without much trouble, and if you'll taste it, smarty-pants, you'll see that she was right."

"Smells great." She plucked a square of sourdough bread off the counter and dipped it into the pot of cheese. Popping it in her mouth, she said, "Mmm! That's not just good—it's fantastic! What's the secret?"

"I am not at liberty to say." It was a half can of beer, but Kitty didn't give out her recipes. "She would only write it down for me because I'm blood."

Allie laughed. "God, I love your mother."

"Me, too." Luna picked up a knife and started trimming broccoli stalks. She gestured to the strawberries. "You can help."

"Let's at least sit down." She picked up the quart of strawberries and carried it to the table in the corner. "I want to hear about TC."

Luna joined her. "What do you want to know?"

She made a huffing noise. "Everything."

Again that strange resistance rose in Luna. A wish to keep it private, secret. Sacred. A vision of him, smoothing his big, heavy hand down her body, flashed in her imagination. "I don't know what to say." She kept her attention on the tiny trees beneath her knife, taking care to leave enough stalk to dip the top into the cheese. "He's . . . amazing, Allie."

"Yeah? Amazing how?"

A jumble of things came up—so many she had trouble choosing among them. "His hair makes me crazy," she said, finally, smiling. "And he kisses me like I'm something very precious." She thought of his comfort in washing her the first night they had sex and a ripple of something that was almost painful moved over her belly. "And he's really earthy and really kind and he seems to really like me. Warts and all."

Allie's attention was focused on the top of the strawberry in her hand. "Sounds pretty serious."

"I don't know if that's the right word."

"Let me rephrase. It sounds like you're falling in love, Luna."

Luna lowered her gaze. Nodded. " 'Fraid so."

"Oh, babe! You're not supposed to fall in love with every guy that comes along!"

"I don't," Luna said, realizing this was why she'd resisted talking about Thomas to Allie or her mother or anyone else. "I don't know how to tell you that it's right, Allie. All the sensible things say I need to watch my back, guard my heart, take it easy. He's on the rebound. He's too gorgeous for words and there will always be women who want him and try to seduce him. He's . . ." She paused, looking over Allie's shoulder, seeing him in her mind's eye, worried about his grandmother and Tiny and showing Joy how to fish. "He's so much, he's dangerous."

"Exactly," Allie said, and she leaned forward. "He's the kind of man you have a lot of good sex with, somebody you keep a little at a distance because he'll break your heart into a billion pieces."

Luna was quiet for a moment. Neither of the Barbies popped up to give her any direction here, so she went with her gut and told the truth. "When I put my head on his shoulder, when he touches me, when we're laughing together"—she paused, trying to think how to say it—"it's like everything feels right. Like a circle is completed. It's just *right*, that's all."

"Luna!" Allie inclined her head, "How long have you even been dating him? A few weeks? A month? How can you give your heart so easily?"

And to her own surprise, Luna laughed. "I don't! Not to men. I don't give it out at all. I gave it to my father, and he broke it. I gave it to Marc and he—"

"Fucked you over, big-time."

"Who's telling this story?"

"Sorry."

"I haven't given my heart to any man since Marc. I've dated. I've had sex. I've even had some relationships, but there was always this big piece of myself that I kept apart from them. And maybe I'm just tired of living that way. Maybe there's more to life than trying to be safe all the time. What if he really is the man I can love for the rest of my life and I don't take that chance because I'm afraid? What kind of life is that?"

"Wow." Allie slumped against the back of the seat, her pentagram glittering wildly in the light. For a long moment, she said nothing, only looking at Luna with speculation and surprise. Finally she said, "You're right. I'm not there yet, but that doesn't mean you aren't." She reached over the table and squeezed Luna's hand. She shook her head, smiling ruefully, her eyes closed for a second. "I am *so* jealous."

Luna laughed.

"He's so gorgeous and he has that light all around him, you know?" Allie sobered, her eyes sad in spite of her smile. "The way he touched you last night, I could see it. That he's going to take you away from me, and then I'll have to go prowling all by myself."

"You'll never lose me, Allie."

"Not true. Women always lose women when men come along."

Pierced, Luna gripped her hand. "Not me, you silly goose. In case you haven't noticed, I do give my heart, my whole heart and soul, to women. And you're one of them." She said it again. "You will never lose me. I promise."

Allie almost teared up, but then she yanked her hand away, waved them both in the air. "Okay, enough of that corny shit." She let go of a breath, and got a wicked smile. "Let me tell you about the wranglers I met last night, since you're obviously not going to give me any juicy details yourself."

"Oooh. You met someone?"

"Not met someone, met someone. I did have great sex, though. And he was only twenty-six!"

Luna laughed, as she was meant to. "You go, girl!"

"Oh, no! He went. And went. And went."

"Are you going to see him again?"

She shrugged. "Guess we'll find out. He took my number."

The door to Joy's room opened, and Luna touched a finger of shushing to her lips. Allie nodded. "Hey, Joy," she said, as the teenager hung up the phone and rubbed her ear.

"Hey, Auntie."

"New boyfriend, huh?"

Joy's whole face lit up. "Yeah. His name's Ricardo. He's really nice."

"Now that you're off the phone," Luna said. "Why don't you try calling Maggie again?"

"I tried a little while ago. No answer." She rubbed her tummy, frowning. "I'm worried. Do you think we ought to go over there?"

"Well, it might be kind of rude to go haul them out of their house to come over and have supper with us if they are not coming for some reason. You know? Maybe they've gone to a relative's house or something."

Joy sighed. "Well, there's more to it than that. Maggie's mad at me."

"Oh. Why?"

"She kept telling me that there was a man she thought her mom might kinda like, you know that her mom kinda perked up when he was around, and she was trying to matchmake them, or at least figure out some way to match them up."

Luna guessed. "Thomas?"

"Yeah." Joy twisted her hair into a knot, showing all of her earrings. "I didn't realize it was the same guy for a while, and then I couldn't figure out how to tell her, and it just got all tangled up."

"I'm so sorry," Luna said.

"No, no! I don't mean that you shouldn't like him. 'Cause he's cool, you know, and he likes you and you like him, and that's good. But I feel bad that Maggie had this big plan, and I didn't realize until too late that it wasn't a good plan."

"Okay. I understand. So, maybe she's just taking a day or two to lick her wounds and you can make things up with her on Monday."

Joy nodded without much hope, and Luna's heart broke for her. The doorbell rang and Allie said, "I'll get it."

Luna smiled gratefully, and took a moment to hug her daughter. "You didn't do anything wrong, sweetie. The path of love never does run smooth."

"I know."

Elaine came in, wrapped in an unbelievably ugly orange coat with dancing bears all over it. Luna tried not to wince, but she didn't understand why her sister always picked the most unflattering clothes. It wasn't the bears or the bright color—lots of people loved that kind of thing—it was the orange, which was just about the worst color Elaine could wear. And it was a pattern—the glasses were the least flattering frames she could pick. Her hair was fried to a crisp with a perm. Her face was bare of makeup and she was wearing pink stretch pants with green paisleys. With an orange coat.

This could not possibly be Kitty's daughter.

Best Friend Barbie spoke up. *Maybe you could stop judging her all the time and give her a hand, huh? Maybe she just doesn't know how to pick things out. It's not that easy for large women to find flattering*

clothes, you know. The designers think fat women are
stupid and dowdy, so that's what they make for them.

Good point. A ripple of shame touched her cheeks,
and to make up for her nasty thoughts, she gave Elaine
a hug. A big hug, one Kitty would have given her. "I was
kind of worried that you might not be able to come,
with the weather kicking up."

"I'm going to stay at Mom's house."

Luna nodded. "Are you free tomorrow? There's
something I want to do, and I'm hoping you'll do it with
me."

"I can be. What's up?" It hurt Luna to see how much
her sister wanted to be included. How could she never
have realized how lonely she was?

"We'll talk about it after a while. For right now, give
me whatever luscious dessert you've cooked up and let's
get this show on the road."

The phone rang and Joy made a truly impressive leap
for it, a football receiver leaping over all hurdles to land
the catch. Luna chuckled at her breathless "Hello?"

They milled into the kitchen, Luna not paying much
attention until Joy snagged the back of her shirt, hard.
"What?" she said into the phone. "Maggie, I can't understand you. Try to take a breath and then say it
again." Joy's eyes widened urgently at her mother.

Luna took the phone without ceremony. "Maggie?
What's wrong, hon?"

"It's my mother . . . she's . . ." a huge, gulping sob. "I
don't know. There's something wrong. My grandma's
not home and I didn't know who else to call!"

"I'll be right there. Don't move honey. I'll be there in
one minute, okay?" She plucked her keys off the table
and said to Joy, "Come on. You need to come with me."

"You want me to drive?" Elaine said.

Luna gave her a smile. "I got it."

• • •

Joy had a sick feeling all the way over there, and bit down on her thumbs so hard they hurt when she took them out from between her teeth at Maggie's house. Every light was blazing, and the porch light was on, and Maggie, without a sweater or even any shoes, was standing there waiting for them on the porch. Her hair was in a ponytail and blew up like something out of the comics. Joy hardly waited until the car was stopped before she leapt out and ran up to her, putting her arms around her. "Are you okay?"

Maggie could only take a giant gulp of air, and point toward the house. "I can't wake her up!"

But this was when it was good to have a mom who knew things. Luna took the steps two at a time. "Show me where she is, sweetie." She pushed on Maggie's shoulder, not unkindly.

The house smelled like dead fish, and it made Joy's stomach hurt. Feeling ghoulish and curious and scared, she followed them down the hall, afraid to look, suddenly remembering things like slit wrists and gory stuff like that. But Maggie's mom was just lying in the bed. Luna went over and spoke to her, "Sally? Sally can you hear me?"

Nothing. Luna said, "Maggie, get me the phone," and while Maggie went to get it, Luna put her hand on Sally's chest, maybe to check her breathing. She swore under her breath, and then looked around the night table picking up a couple of prescription bottles, one after the other. Her shoulders were tight and hard. She picked up the last one. "Shit!" she said aloud, and bent down to put her arm under Sally's shoulders, dragging her limp body into a sitting position. She yelled "Sally! Sally!" and moved her around. "Come on, Sally, you gotta wake up."

Maggie rushed into the room and Luna barked, "Dial 911 and tell them we have an overdose. Joy, go get a wet washcloth with some ice cubes inside and bring it back to me. Hurry, sweetie."

Joy ran down the hall to the kitchen and pulled open drawers at random until she found the one with towels. She turned on the water in the sink, cold, and threw the towel under it, and while it was getting wet, she opened the freezer and found some ice cubes. There was nothing in there but the ice, so it wasn't hard. She wrapped the ice cubes in the squeezed out towel, and was proud that her hands weren't shaking.

When she ran back to the room, her mom was moving Sally, whose head bobbed just like a dead person's, like she had no bone in her neck. Joy rushed over and put the towel in her mom's hand, then went to stand with Maggie, who had her arms crossed over her chest. Her eyes were all red from crying, and Joy didn't know if she ought to take her hand or not, so she did, just in case it would help. Maggie took it and squeezed it hard. "Is she gonna die?"

"No!" Luna said from the bed, rubbing the cold cloth on Sally's face. "Sally!" she yelled. "Your daughter is here. She needs you. Stay with me!"

And then there was the sound of sirens and Maggie ran to let in the ambulance attendants, who rushed in with squawking radios and their neat uniforms. Luna said, "Thank God. Acute overdose, possible accident, possible suicide attempt. She needs to be admitted for evaluation."

"Are you her counselor?"

Joy was looking at her mother's face, and it went hard. "No. But I'm a therapist, and I'm familiar with her case. She's extremely depressed after the death of her husband."

Then the men were hustling around, getting Sally on the stretcher and rolling her out, calling in details on their radios. Luna came right over to Maggie and took her into a giant bear hug, and Maggie burst into tears and cried like she was going to die. "It's okay, sweetie," Luna said, over and over. She rocked Maggie back and forth. "You did the right thing. You saved her life. She's going to be okay. She's going to get some help. You did the right thing."

And it was only then that Joy realized everything that happened. "Can she come to our house, Mom?"

"In a little while. Let's go to the hospital now, huh? And Maggie, you can see for yourself that she's okay." She picked up the cold, wet towel. The ice cubes tumbled out of it and Joy picked them up off the bed as her mother bathed Maggie's face.

"Come on," Luna said gently. "Go get a coat and some shoes and we'll go to the hospital."

Maggie looked blank.

"Joy," said Luna. "Why don't you help her?"

"Okay. Come on, Maggie. Let's get you some stuff."

Placida hurt in every bone, even when she sat in the warm kitchen, wrapped up in an afghan one of her daughters had knitted for her a long time ago. She rocked in her chair, saying the rosary against the pressing darkness she felt rolling toward them, a darkness she couldn't name, one that filled her chest, reached out all around and pressed down on everybody. Everybody.

She told herself it wasn't anything, that she was just tired and grumpy from the weather change. But her heart stayed heavy. She heard Tiny fighting with someone on the phone, and said an extra prayer for him to be peaceful, to learn grace. For a minute, when she heard him hang up, mad, she thought she could call him into the kitchen for hot chocolate, the kind that came from Mexico in hard cubes and had cinnamon in it. But the thought of grinding up that hard chocolate was too much for her.

Tomás, good man that he was, sat with her in the kitchen, going over accounts. He, too, was worried about Tiny. Once he went into the other room and spoke to him in a firm voice, then came back and went back to his columns and figures. A good man, her Tomás. They didn't make too many like him anymore.

She heard sirens on the road and felt even colder, but though they seemed to stop somewhere close, she couldn't see which of their neighbors might be struck by bad luck tonight. Or maybe it wasn't no big thing—a kid with a bad cut or something. Not everything was always death coming on big feet.

But when the doorbell rang, Placida cried out her fear. And when in walked *La Diabla*, pregnant as an old sow, her eyes all red from crying, and threw herself into Tomás's arms, she knew what she'd been dreading. Oh, not this one! Not this one, *Madre*!

But then she remembered her prayer tonight. She was a vain old woman. What did she know? Maybe this one would stick finally. And at least she was bringing a son with her.

Nonetheless, she was glad when Tomás pushed *La Diabla* away, as if she had a disease. Which she did. The unhappiness disease. No matter what happened to her, forever, she would be unhappy. She drew it to her like a cloud because she liked the thunder and lightning, got bored when she had simple good fortune in her hands.

In disgust, Placida rose. "I'm going to bed," she spat, in Spanish because the foolish girl never understood it and she didn't deserve to.

• • •

Luna called Elaine and Allie from the hospital and told them what was going on. They opted to stay and wait for Luna's return, and Allie volunteered to track down relatives via the telephone numbers Maggie supplied. Two hours later, Allie reported that everyone had gone to a wedding in a little town south of Santa Fe. "Maybe that was what set her off, huh?"

"It's possible," Luna agreed. She hung up and found the girls sitting quietly in the waiting room. Maggie had just come back from seeing her mother, and there was about her mouth the sudden giving away of someone who has just about reached the end of her rope. "Come on, sweetie," Luna said. "You come home with us tonight, all right? We'll come back first thing in the morning if you want to."

She moved like an automaton, but she went. Back at the house, Luna reheated the fondue and they all sat around the table in the dining room with quiet music in the background, and Maggie ate like a starving child. Which she probably was. Luna got her settled in Joy's bedroom, and gave Joy her own bed for the night, and brought out pillows and blankets to the couch for herself. Elaine helped—cleaning up the dishes, getting the coffeemaker ready for morning (Luna didn't have the heart to tell her that she hated the automatic feature because the water wasn't cold enough to start, and so it wasn't hot enough once it brewed). Allie packed the leftover fruits and veggies into plastic bags. They didn't talk much. Allie left first, kissing Luna's cheek. "Call me if you need anything."

Then Elaine put on her coat and took out her car keys. "Was there something you wanted to ask me, Luna?"

Luna took a breath. "Yeah," she said, and nodded for emphasis. "Yeah." She chewed on the inside of her cheek for a minute. "I wanted to ask you if you would go with me to the land tomorrow. I need to see it, and I'm scared to go alone, without you."

"You just want me to drive, don't you?"

Luna met her sister's eyes. "No, not at all. I need *you*. Mom can't do it, and I want somebody with me who will understand . . . everything."

Elaine looked at her keys, flipped through them. "I don't really remember him, Luna. I was only five."

"I know. But it hurt you as much as it did me and Mom. Maybe more."

"What do you think you're going to find, Luna?" Her tone was angry. "Some letter saying, 'Dear family, this is why I was such a jerk and left you'?"

"I have no idea, Elaine. I just know that I have to go. And I really don't want to go alone." She took her sister's hand. It was cold. "Please, Sissie? We can take the girls with us, and maybe we can find some really great place to have lunch, and then we can go ahead with the sale and we'll have plenty of money."

A long pause. Then her glasses flashed reflected light as she raised her head. "Okay."

Luna hugged her. "Thank you. Come over whenever you get up and we'll get going after I take Maggie over to the hospital to see her mother."

"What if she wants to stay?"

"She won't be able to. Her mother needs inpatient psychiatric care for a little while. It'll be better for Maggie to be moving, to be with other people."

"Right." She said it like it was a surprise. "Luna, why don't you go back to counseling? You're good at it, and like Joy told me, it's a sin to waste a talent."

Sudden tears, probably a response to everything that had gone on tonight, sprung to Luna's eyes. "I'll make you a deal. Find a blues band to sing with and I'll update my certification."

Elaine laughed. "See you in the morning."

Luna washed her face and put on a long-sleeved nightshirt with some sweats and her moon-and-stars slippers. No way she was going to sleep anytime soon, even if it was nearly midnight. She put the kettle on the stove to boil water for a cup of tea. The house hummed quietly around her, the heater blowing soft air efficiently through the rooms, and it gave her a sense of security to think of the shiny new furnace doing its muscle work. Gave her a lot of pride to have this home of her own, a place that could be an oasis for a lost girl, a place where her friends and family could gather.

And suddenly, she realized she hadn't once thought of having a cigarette tonight. She didn't even want one now.

Getting there, Barbie said.

Yes. She supposed she was. Standing there in her long, cheery kitchen, surrounded by silence and herself, she realized she wouldn't be anyone else in the world right now. And by extension, that meant she wouldn't be able to change her past and still be herself, standing here in this room, flush with the knowledge that she'd helped Sally tonight, that there was a man in the world who made her feel good, that she was a good mother and maybe even a good person most days.

In some wonder, she touched her elbow, that scar that had always been a reminder of all she didn't want to be. Now she wondered if it might just be a battle wound, a mark of life. She didn't have to be proud of it, but she could embrace the fact that it had taught her something, carried her forward.

The kettle started to whistle and she picked it up

before it woke Joy or Maggie, pouring water over the tea bag and stirring in sugar.

The phone rang, startling her, and she grabbed it with a sense of dread, praying it wouldn't be bad news about Sally.

"Hello?"

"It's not bad news," Thomas said.

"Thomas!"

"Were you sleeping?"

"No." She took a breath. "I'm so glad to hear your voice. It's been a long, long night."

"Here, too. Tell me about yours first."

Luna launched into the tale of Maggie's mother, the trip to the hospital, all of it. "What's yours?"

"You know, I'm listening to your voice and wishing I was seeing your lips move. Can I come over? We could sit on the porch."

Luna smiled, her heart lightening. "If you promise to be very, very quiet, we can go to my workroom."

"It's a deal. Be there in three minutes."

She laughed, and the sound was low and sexy. "I'll meet you at the back door."

"Luna!"

"I'm here."

"What are you wearing?"

Her laugh this time was self-mocking. "A very old nightshirt and my sweats."

"Don't change. Promise?"

"Sure. What the heck."

But she did check her face to make sure there was no mascara smeared under her eyes. Her face was devoid of makeup and she looked tired, faint dark circles adding age, her cheeks completely pale, as they always were without the assistance of blush. Not beautiful. Kitty would have touched a smear of lipstick to her mouth, spritzed cologne over her hair, maybe put a little Vaseline on her lids and lashes to look dewy. Luna decided she'd rather just be herself for right now.

She heard his truck and hurried to let him in, shivering a little at the open back door waiting for him to cross the yard. His hair was down.

He leapt up the stairs, his body cold when he took her into his arms and kissed her. Luna pressed into him, loving the fresh smell of him, that distinctive scent that was his alone, fire and sage and a New Mexico wind. "Hi," she said quietly. "Come in before I freeze."

He closed the door behind him, holding on to her hand, and looked her over, head to toe. "Elegant."

"You told me not to change."

"I wanted to see you as you."

She led him into the workroom and settled on the couch. "The bedrooms are right there, so we have to be quiet." She sat cross-legged. "You want some tea or something?"

"No, thanks." He laced his fingers through hers. "I wanted to talk to you in person because I need to tell you something."

Uh-oh.

"I'm listening."

He took a breath, raised his eyes. "Nadine showed up at my door tonight. She was hysterical and exhausted and looked like hell, so I—took her in, Luna. I gave her a bed to sleep in. Not mine."

"Okay."

"That's it? Just 'okay'?"

"What did you want me to say?"

He bent his head, lifted a shoulder. "I don't know."

Luna let the silence stretch, wondering what he wanted, what this was about.

"Does it make you uncomfortable?"

She shook her head. "You have to do what you have to do."

"If it bothers you, she can go somewhere else."

"No," she said quietly. "I think you have to be who you are."

He rubbed his face. "She's due in two weeks. I thought I could put her up until then if she can't work things out with my brother. But only if you're okay with it."

"I haven't known you long enough to be a voice in your life, Thomas. You have to follow this through, see where it goes." Her hand felt cold and she took it away to tuck beneath her armpit. She sighed and shook her head. "And I have to tell you that I sort of knew this would happen. I started out knowing I'd be a transition person for you, and I took the chance."

"Luna, you're not."

She ducked her head, weighing the options open to her. She could ask him to leave so she could think about it, but he'd go home and put Nadine out and feel guilty. *Just tell the truth,* said Barbie.

"This is a good chance for you to figure out where you really stand in your feelings about her."

"Maybe I'm more interested in where I stand with you."

"I think this has moved too fast," Luna said honestly. "I've told you—I don't know if I can really make a commitment. I just don't know."

His long dark eyes showed disappointment. Sharp disappointment, actually, which she avoided by ducking her head. "I'm sorry," she said.

For a long time, he didn't say anything. "Luna, we're both old enough to know that happily ever after is a fairy tale. Life is long and things happen." He took her hand. "It is fast and we've fallen in love and that's a good thing. The only promise I can give you is that I will always tell the truth. Always, okay?"

She didn't know what to say.

He stood, touched her head. "You know where to find me."

She nodded.

"Sometimes, Luna, a man needs to know how a woman feels."

He left.

Tiny could not sleep. He lay in his bed, tossing and turning and sweating, his blood too hot for his veins. He could feel it running in him, like lava, burning through his arms and belly and groin.

Angelica didn't want him anymore. She told him on the phone. No more.

But this time, instead of going totally insane, some quiet thing came to him and whispered to be calm. Oh, not all calm—he cried on the phone with her, begged her to change her mind, told her he'd quit drinking and he would never hurt her again. Ever. Even if she hit him with a frying pan, which she had done once. Cracked his skull.

But she didn't listen to him. Didn't listen.

Something in him went quiet, then, like he was one of his Comanche ancestors—still and quiet and burning. A plan. He went to bed, conscious of the heavy bracelet on his ankle. He tried to sleep, but that river of heat in him kept jerking him awake. He dreamed of big hands on his wife's breasts. He dreamed of *La Llorona*, screaming down the river at him. He dreamed of roses, pink ones, falling down on his head. Only the last one cooled him at all and he even slept a while in their perfumed snow.

The children would be sleeping at their grandmother's

house, so they could go to Mass this morning. Angelica
would be alone. Before she got up for church, he would
go see her. He would talk, face-to-face. He would kiss
her, because that melted her heart when it turned hard.
He would touch her. Gently. Only gently.

He would pour out this passion and love on her and
she would see the truth.

And he could do it because it was Sunday. Because
there was time for him to run errands on Sundays, and
he had learned by accident that sometimes the monitoring center didn't get to calls as fast on Sundays. There
was room. There was time.

He would convince her. He had to.

Rose History

For Catholic Christians, the Rosary of course comes from the flower. Early rosaries were made of rose petals. Some folks make beads in this manner and claim that as body heat warms up a necklace made of petals, you can smell their fragrance.

Twenty-four

As Luna had predicted, Sally was admitted to inpatient treatment and was not allowed visitors until a thorough assessment of her condition had been completed. Luna had prepared Maggie for the possibility, so she didn't appear to be devastated by it. "This means she's gonna get help, right?"

They were sitting alone at the kitchen table. The weather bluster of the night before had died down completely. "Yes. She definitely will get help now." She touched the girl's hand. "I'm so sorry this is happening to you, Maggie. You've been really brave and together, and you should never have had to do all that by yourself."

She nodded sadly. Her big topaz eyes were wise beyond their years. "I was startin' to lose it, though. I just didn't know what to do."

"Joy told me you made a shrine to Tupac. Did that help?"

Maggie lowered her eyes. "It sounds crazy, huh?"

"Not necessarily. You must have picked him for a reason, right?"

"Yeah. I got a sign the day of my dad's funeral. And

then I started reading about him, and he had this bad life, really hard, but he ended up being okay. He wrote this book called *A Rose That Grew from Concrete*, and it's so beautiful. Like, full of faith, you know? It made me feel stronger to just . . . talk to him or something."

"You felt pretty lonely."

"Totally." She raised her eyes. "I really, really miss my dad."

"I bet. That has to hurt a lot."

Maggie nodded. "Sometimes, I want to do anything I can to get away from it. Sometimes it hurts so bad I want to take a knife and cut my arm, you know, like the Indians used to do? I wanted to have a scar that showed the world I lost something big." She pressed her thumb hard into a glazed doughnut. "Then I realized that the only way to get through hurting was just to go ahead and hurt sometimes. Not break stuff trying to get away from it, not cut myself. Not take pills like my mom. That's what she did, you know, kept hiding from it, but it can't go away unless you face it."

Luna blinked, and then she went ahead and let go of the laugh of startlement. "You know, Maggie, I was a therapist for years, and sometimes I worked with people who were in their sixties who still didn't know what you just said. You're so wise."

"Wise?"

"Yeah. Even the way you wanted to cut yourself makes a lot of sense in a way. People do all kinds of things to mark their grief. They cut their hair, they cut themselves to make a scar, like you said. It hurts, so much, to lose somebody you love, but you figured out the truth—that you have to just go ahead and hurt."

"You know, it's not so bad for me anymore. I still miss him. I still think about things I want to tell him, but sometimes, I go all day and forget that he's dead. Or not exactly forget, but it's okay not to think about it every minute."

"Right. That's how you heal."

"Maybe my mom will learn how, too."

"She will. And you know she loves you with all her heart, don't you?"

"Yeah. The *bruja* said she was heartsick. You can't help that, really."

"She's going to get well, you'll see."

Joy came out of the bathroom then, her hair wrapped up in a towel. "I'm starving. Mom, will you make French toast?"

"Sure. Do you like it, too, Maggie?"

"I *love* it."

Thomas awakened long before dawn, even though he'd been out so late at Luna's house. He was so early he beat Placida to the kitchen, and it worried him enough that he peeked in on her. She was snoring, loudly, so she was still alive. He smiled to himself and closed the door.

A little ache was in his chest this morning. Luna, Luna, Luna. He wanted her. Wanted her here.

And instead, Nadine, who'd made his life hell, was back, sleeping upstairs with her big belly. He picked up the phone and dialed his brother's number. James answered on the first ring. "Nadine?" The word was rife with worry and urgency, and Thomas frowned.

"It's me, bro. She's here."

"With you?"

"No, not like that, just here. What's going on?"

"I tell you the truth, Thomas, she's fuckin' wacko. She just is. I mean, I don't know what she's thinkin', like her brain went into her belly."

"She thinks you're cheating on her, James."

"Yeah, I know. But, I'm not, Thomas. I love her. How do you prove to somebody that you're not cheating?"

"You're not?"

"You thought I was?"

"Well, it crossed my mind." Thomas pursed his lips. "Done it once or twice before."

"I know." He paused, and then said, "Thomas, I would never have done that to you if I didn't love her so crazy like she's in my blood. She drove you crazy, but all the stuff you hated, I liked. I still like it. Even when she's wacko."

"Maybe you need to come up here. Convince her."

"Okay. I'm leaving in just a few minutes. Just gotta put on my shoes."

Thomas hung up the phone and stared at it. Not cheating. Well, at least that was something good.

He picked up the phone and dialed Luna's number, but before it could ring, he hung up, scowling. Not this time. This time, he wasn't going to be a fool for a woman. If she wanted him, she had to come to him.

It was surprising how little time it took to drive to Trinidad. Less than two hours. All this time, Luna thought, he'd been close enough to . . .

The land was a ranch, a working ranch judging by the herds of sleek cattle grazing on the pale yellow grass. A scattering of outbuildings looked deserted, but they kept driving until they came to a plain house, a manufactured home painted red. Nothing fancy, but there were some marigolds planted around the base. A sharp swell of recognition went through Luna—a memory of her father telling her that marigolds were a way to remember the dead.

"My hands are shaking," she said to Elaine.

Elaine stared through the windshield. "Now what do we do?"

"Maybe," Joy said from the backseat, "we should just get out of the car."

"It's a good start anyway." Luna took a breath and stepped out. A smooth breeze came across the high plain and rustled her hair as she stretched, then shook her sleeves down.

A man came out on the small wooden stoop that led to the door. He was in his sixties, his hair thick over a rancher's face. He wore a flannel shirt and jeans and his legs were bowed in the distinctive way that marked a man who'd worked with horses his entire life. "How you doing? Can I help you?"

"Hi," Luna said, and came forward, her hair in her face. She tossed it away and extended her hand. "My name is—"

"You're Jesse's girl. Damn, you look like him." He lowered his chin a hair, swallowed away some strong emotion. "'Scuse me. It ain't been that long and I'm heartsore over it."

"I'm sorry," Luna said.

"Y'all come to see about the land?"

"Yes. This is my sister, Elaine, and my daughter, Joy, and her friend Maggie, who just rode along. We just wanted to see it, really, before we made any decisions."

"I'm Ralph." He looked at them all for a moment. Then, "Well, whyn't you come on in for a minute. There's some of his things here still. I reckon you might like seeing them."

Luna's heart squeezed, very hard, one time. Then she moved toward the house.

Elaine said, "I'm going to stay outside."

Luna paused. Then she nodded and went in alone. She was the one who wanted answers, after all.

The inside of the house was no more upscale than the out. It was serviceable, furnished with a sturdy tweedy carpet in browns and golds. A functional couch and chair faced a big-screen television, and there were no adornments on the wall. The kitchen opened to a small dining area, and a hall led to what Luna assumed would be bedrooms. "Did you live together?"

"Yep. Couple of old bastards, just seemed a way to have a little company, anyways. I moved out here in '87, I guess. He took me in, Jesse did, when I didn't have a pot to piss in." His mouth moved. "Drank away every goddamn dime I made. till then, went through three wives and two families before I landed here in jail and got myself to AA."

Luna smiled. "I've been sober four years."

"That right?"

"Yeah." She rubbed her hands on her thighs. "So he was sober, too, my dad?"

"That he was, darlin'. He didn't talk too much about his lost days, but I gathered they were pretty bad, but he'd earned a twenty-year strip by the time he died."

"That's great." Luna suddenly sat down, winded and overwhelmed.

The old man gave her a respectful moment, then said, "Why don't I go get that box of stuff for you?"

"I would like that."

He disappeared down the hall. It was so quiet that she heard the sound of a ticking clock somewhere, an old one, *tick-tock, tick-tock, tick-tock*. The old man had been doing a book of crossword puzzles, and had almost made it through the book by the look of it. A *TV Guide* and an *Outdoors Man* were the only other things she saw out.

"Here we go," he said, returning with a box about

two feet square. "He didn't have a lot—put it all in the land, but this is what he left."

Luna felt unexpectedly shaky as she reached for it, and it nearly slipped out of her grip before she caught it tight and settled it at her feet. "He left home when I was seven," she said. "We never saw him again."

He nodded, but it was the patient nod of a person ready to listen, not one of knowledge, particularly.

"I never stopped waiting for him to come home." She opened the flaps and looked inside. It wasn't as hard as she'd expected. There was a jumble of odds and ends—a watch, an AA marker, a jar full of matches collected from various places. "He liked Las Vegas, I guess, huh?"

"Went once a year, rain or shine. Loved those slot machines. And probably a few wild women." He winked.

She put the matches aside and looked deeper into the box. And froze.

Blue curtains, dusty with desert air. The couch, a nubby brown beneath her elbows. Something sticking her knee—a broken spring, probably—as she stared out the picture window. A forgotten Barbie lay beside the sidewalk to the house and somebody should go get her before she got messed up, even though it was one of the ugly ones with short hair and straight knees. Ancient.

Smell of supper in the air. Onions and meat and something sweet baking in the oven, a little extra.

Concentrate. See him coming up the walk. A tank top showing his big brown arms, tanned so dark, dark, dark. Jeans dusty with concrete. Black boots. A black metal lunch bucket in one hand, his hard hat in the other. Black curls stuck to his head with sweat.

In the bottom of the box was a Barbie doll. Luna pulled her out and saw the hat-pin earrings she'd stuck into the lobes of her ears. It was an old one, with short dark hair in a bob, and straight legs. Most of the paint was worn off her face now, and her knees and ankles were grimy, as if she'd been handled over and over again. She didn't have any shoes, but she wore the blue gingham dress Kitty had sewn for her.

"He loved us," Luna said. "I always knew that. This was my doll. He must have picked her up on his way to work. Or maybe he knew, that day, that he was going."

The old man nodded.

"Did he ever say? Why he left, I mean?"

"That I don't know. He didn't go back after he was sober because of the ninth step. I do know that. He didn't want to do your mama any more harm."

The ninth step in AA was making amends to people you'd injured, except when to do so would cause further injury. And Luna thought of Kitty, sailing in Greece with a man who adored her. She thought of her, chin up all those years, never showing for one minute how much she hurt except when she had to put on the Beatles and think about it now and then.

"He did the right thing," Luna said. "But I would have loved to have seen him." Then she bent her head and cried. Ralph didn't do anything but just let her.

They walked around afterward, through pastures and spotty forest, along a small, deeply prized creek. The mountains here had an odd feature—they were very high mesas, their blue tops chopped off as clean as if an ax had done it. Luna imagined the vast sea that once flowed here, thought about the prehistoric creatures who'd died to make the sand beneath her feet.

And she thought of her father, seeing this land. Knowing he would leave it to Kitty and his girls. It made her ache, but finally, it was a sweet ache, not a sad or yearn-

ing one. There was a lot of comfort in closure, somehow.

Ralph complained about the "New Age groupies"
who wanted the land because it was on a ley line—
"whatever the hell that is"—but he had a greater horror
of the upscale developers drifting northward from the
Santa Fe/Taos block.

"What happens if we sell?" Luna asked when they'd
circled back to the car.

Ralph's mouth worked. "Not much, I reckon. They'll
bring in a temple or some foolishness, but they want to
buy it to keep it from developers, so the cattle can stay.
I'll still be caretaker."

Luna nodded. "Thanks, Ralph." She stuck out her
hand and he took it in both of his.

"I want you girls to know he was a good man. He
was a sinner, no question, but he spent a lot of years trying to make up for that. It'll do him some good if you
forgive him, even now."

"Thank you for your time," Elaine said briskly. "We
have to go now."

They stopped at a Trinidad café for lunch. It was a
plain, homespun place with biscuits and gravy and pot
roast on the menu, and a pie keeper on the counter.
"Oooh," said Joy. "They have pecan. I love pecan pie."

"You can have some for dessert."

Elaine had been quiet the whole way into town, her
jaw set in that grim way, and after they ordered, Luna
said, "What are you thinking, Sissie?"

"You know what I'm thinking." She stirred artificial
sweetener into her tea. "I'm thinking I want the money.
I don't care about the land, and I can see you getting all
soft and misty-eyed and I know you aren't going to sell
it, so just tell me straight out, okay?" She crossed her
arms on the table, hard.

Luna lifted her eyebrows. "Got me all figured out, huh?"

"I know how you are, Lu. Miss Sentimental."

"Well, you're wrong." She pulled the Barbie doll out of the box she carried in from the car. "I got what I wanted."

"Oh, my God!" Elaine said. "I mean, gosh." Her hand went for the doll. "He kept it, all this time?"

"Yeah."

Elaine stroked the doll's hair with a thumb. In a voice devoid of air, she said, "I cried every night."

Maggie, who was sitting next to her, put her small hand on Elaine's arm. "You can cry, you know. We won't care."

And Elaine did exactly that.

Sins cannot be undone, only forgiven.

— IGOR STRAVINSKY

Twenty-five

Placida was restless. There was something wrong.
Something really wrong. She listened for the ravens but
did not hear them. She looked for that ragged black dog
and did not see her. She went out to the porch, listening
for the whispers of Santo Niño who might tell her what
to do, but the air stayed still and hushed as death.

But still she felt the press of danger in her chest, pressing down hard. She couldn't sit still for it, and carried
her rosary clenched in her hand, rubbing that place
below her breast that was hurting.

Tomás came to find her after James and *La Diabla*
were curled and crying in the living room, making like
lovebirds in the house of the man they had wronged.
Evil. There was no respect in the world nowadays.
None. Once, a man could have killed his wife if she did
that, and he would have killed his brother for certain.
She didn't understand a world that overlooked it, left so
many hurting when men didn't take care of their families, when women didn't care for their children. So
much pain it caused, those broken vows, couldn't they
see it?

"You okay?" Tomás said, bringing her some tea in a
big metal glass.

She looked out to the horizon. Shook her head.
"Something's wrong. Something wicked, somewhere."

"Oh," Tomás said, "you mean *La Diabla?*"

He used the name to please her, and Placida should have smiled, but she couldn't. Again she pressed her hand to her breastbone, feeling that hard hand against her heart. And suddenly, she had a sharp vision of roses, pink roses, snowing down on Tiny Abeyta's head. There were drops of blood on the petals, and she stood up, fast. "Find Manuel. Find him at his wife's house. He's going to kill her."

Tomás didn't jump to his feet, and she turned around, raising her arms and shouting. "Go! Go now! Go find him at her house."

Something in her face or voice must have frightened him, because he listened. "I'll be right back, *Abuela*, and you'll see he's fine."

"Go," she commanded, and he went. She sat in her chair and pulled the rosary into her gnarled fingers, the pressure growing on her chest. "Hail Mary, full of grace," she said aloud, holding Tiny in her head, in the Virgin's arms, cradled and protected. "The Lord is with thee."

She put all she was into her prayer. Into this last thing. This one last thing.

Thomas found his heart pounding as he started his truck and drove to Tiny's old house. It was a distance of several miles, and not a straight course. He kept hearing his grandmother's voice. *Go. Go now!* The sound was mightier than any voice he'd ever heard from her, as if her body had been overtaken by some being greater than she, a young and mighty goddess. It had scared the hell out of him.

So even though it was foolish, even though his head told him Tiny was upstairs asleep, he drove to Angelica's house. And a huge sense of relief went over him when he pulled up in front of the house, a small stucco model with pink roses growing on trellises all around it. Their petals lay in scatters on the grass, blown in great handfuls from last night's wind. They made him think of a wedding. There was no sound of fighting as he stepped out of his truck. Angelica's car was parked neatly under the carport, and her hoses were rolled up on a special gizmo designed to keep them out of the way.

He felt downright silly going to her door. Hesitated at the gate, thinking it was Sunday morning—maybe she'd want to sleep in and his knock would bring her out of bed. A curtain fluttered out of a window. He turned in a circle, listening for anything amiss.

Go. Go now.

Taking a breath, he opened the gate and let himself into the rose-scattered yard and went up to the door, and knocked.

Nothing.

Maybe she wasn't home. He'd never known her to be here without playing the radio, and that was kind of weird. Or maybe he was being infected by his grand-mother's paranoia and he ought to just go back home and check on Tiny there. He'd probably find him asleep in the big pile of comforters he liked, his head buried, a pillow tucked to his chest in place of the woman he missed so much.

He tried knocking a second time. And this time, there was the faintest whisper of sound. Something not quite . . . right. "Angelica?" he called. "It's Thomas. Are you okay?"

"Go away, Thomas," Tiny called. "We're fine."

Shit. Shit, shit, shit. "Angelica, I'll only leave if you answer me. Are you okay?"

A mumble of sound, then a scream. "Help me!"

Thomas tried the door, found it locked. "Tiny! Listen

to me, man. You don't want this. You've got a good life. You can't do this."

"Go away!" Tiny cried, and there was a sob in his voice. "We'll work it out in private."

Thomas stood back and gauged the door, then lifted his booted foot and aimed for the hinged side. The door cracked, but didn't give way, and he kicked again. Another crack, and he heard Angelica scream. Thomas kicked one more time and the door fell open. He rushed in.

The first thing he saw in the gloom was more rose petals. More roses. They were everywhere. Enormous piles of them, chopped in a fury from some butchered shrub. They were all over the floor, petals and flowers and leaves and stems.

"Get out of here, Thomas!" Tiny had Angelica on her knees, her long hair twisted around his wrist, and he had a knife in his hand that didn't quite qualify as a machete but came damned close. He held it in the air.

Thomas halted. "Tiny. Don't do this." He raised his hands to show he had nothing with him.

Both of them had tear streaks down their faces, rose petals stuck to their clothes. Scratches covered Tiny's face, and Angelica's arms and neck. From thorns, Thomas realized. Angelica wore only a plain sleeveless cotton nightdress. Tiny was disheveled, his hair mussed. Fighting or sex? Probably both. Tiny had a black eye coming on. Angelica's lower lip was swollen. She sobbed softly.

"Come on, man," Thomas said quietly. "Put down the knife. Let her go."

"Go away! Let us handle it."

Thomas took a chance on taking one step. "This doesn't solve any problems. This makes problems."

Tiny winced, as if he'd been struck. "No, it doesn't,"

he said. "This is my life. My only life. Don't you understand?"

Angelica stared at Thomas without a word, terror in her eyes. He hated himself for not taking steps sooner. Hated that love could turn to disaster, so often. Hated that this was the oldest and one of the saddest stories in the book of life. He had no idea what to do. "I don't understand," he said softly, thinking of Luna drawing Tiny out at the river. "Tell me."

"We're a family! A family is all a man is, everything he's about. If I don't have my wife and kids, man, what am I? I ain't shit but a Lowrider son of a bitch." Tears streamed down his face. "I just can't make her listen. She won't hear me. She's found some other asshole to take care of her now, probably better than me, huh?"

"Think of Ray, Tiny. Think of him. Do you want him to hurt?"

"No," he said brokenly, and at least the arm holding the knife up fell down. His shoulders sagged. Thomas edged closer. "I don't want nobody to hurt. I want us to be happy again. I'll do anything."

Angelica's eyes streamed with tears, too, and her shoulders started to shake. She bowed her head, weeping silently and in great grief.

"This ain't the way, Tiny," Thomas said quietly. "Let me have the knife." He covered the last few steps and held out his hand.

Tiny raised his hand. "I can't go to jail, man. What'll my boy think of me then?"

"It won't be long, Tiny."

"Nah," he said, shaking his head, his eyes brighter than moonlight with the tears in them. He wiped his face with the sleeve holding the knife, still shaking his head. "I ain't got a future without my family."

A jolt of horror went through Thomas as the knife

waved around. "Tiny," he said urgently. "You saw me when Nadine left me, right? Remember?"

"Yeah, I remember."

"I thought I was gonna die of the pain, that it would just shred me up inside, and there wouldn't be anything left. I was lost, man. Really lost. I know you remember it."

Tiny listened.

"And look at me. I'm in love, big-time. And her name matches mine—Luna and Coyote. I'm howling at that moon. It lights up my whole life. And maybe if you guys get some counseling, together, you know as a married couple, you'll get back to being a family, but you won't have any of it if you don't stop right now and give me that knife and come out of here." He held out his hand. "*Abuela*'s praying for you, right now, praying so hard she's gonna give herself a heart attack if you don't come back with me. Come on."

Tiny closed his eyes, swaying. In that moment, Thomas saw the exhaustion, soul-deep, that had stolen his sense. Saw the grief and the loneliness and the very real love.

He dropped the knife. Bent and kissed Angelica's head, and stumbled toward Thomas. Angelica collapsed on the floor, sobbing. "I love you, Tiny, I do. I'm sorry."

Damn. Thomas put his hand on Tiny's back. "Keep walking, man."

And maybe it was the prayers. Maybe it was just time. Maybe it was just being exhausted beyond measure, but Tiny didn't turn. He didn't look back. He put one heavy foot in front of the other, his hands loose and defeated at his side, waited while Thomas opened the truck, and didn't even turn around when Angelica came to the door and cried out in a heartbroken voice, "Tiny! Don't go! I love you. I'm sorry!"

Thomas said, "Call the police, Angelica, or I'll do it when I get home."

Tiny, all wrists and cheekbones starved into exaggeration, slumped in the seat and did not look back. "Did you rape her?" Thomas asked in a hard voice.

Tiny shook his head, plucked a rose petal from his jeans. "She wouldn't have sex with me."

It was something, anyway. No rape and no murder. Everybody still alive. Amazing how valuable that could seem at times. "You gotta get help, Tiny."

"Yeah," he said, exhausted. "Yeah, I do."

After lunch, Elaine asked to have a few minutes to herself. She walked to a small park. Luna and the girls wandered into a department store downtown and like moths to the flame, were drawn as a group to the makeup counters. Joy, with her vanity about her nails, drifted over to the nail polishes, while Luna admired lipsticks—which she never wore and always thought she should try—and Maggie stood beside her, dazzled. "What do you like?" Luna asked.

"Eye makeup. Eyeliner, mascara, eye shadow, all of it."

"Me, too. I bet your eyes are amazing when you do them all up, huh?"

Maggie shrugged, shyly. "My dad didn't let me do it too often."

"Well, it's better held for special occasions, the big stuff, anyway. My mom always says makeup is to enhance your natural beauty and hide your flaws, so it should look fairly natural." Luna grinned. "Not that she exactly follows that advice."

Joy laughed.

They drifted to the perfume counters. Joy said, "In Atlanta? There's this store called Sephora?" She shook her head in quiet awe. "You go in there, and there's all these colors and lotions and it smells right and everybody knows what's good for you." She closed her eyes in reverence. "It's a makeup store like no makeup store in the universe."

"We'll have to go there sometime, Joy." She lifted a bottle of musk and sniffed the top. "Nice." She sprayed a little on her wrist, held it out to Maggie. "What do you think?"

She nodded, eyebrows raised. A fake cheerfulness. She was probably getting tired now. "I like this," she said, and held out a small bottle. Essence of Roses—and Luna was surprised at how good it was.

"That's very good. Usually rose scents are too sweet for me." She narrowed her eyes and inhaled it again. It made her think of a summer afternoon, grass and sunlight and a tangle of roses coaxed to full breath by the heat. "Let's buy this, huh? I'll buy it for you, but you have to let me put some on."

"No, that's okay, I mean I wasn't hinting or anything."

Luna smiled. "I know. It suits you, that's all. You look like a girl who would smell of roses."

"I do?"

"Yes," said Joy. "Totally. Mom, you're so smart about this. What would I smell like?"

Luna cocked her head, narrowed her eyes—then laughed. She looked around the counter for the perfume and saw it, deep in the locked bowels of the glass case. "I know exactly the thing." Spying a girl at another counter, she said, "Miss? Can we have some help here?"

The girl, excited by the possibility of a sale, scurried over. She took out the bottle of perfume Luna pointed out and offered it to Joy, whose mouth fell open. "Oh, that's beautiful! What is it?"

Luna laughed. "It's Joy, one of the oldest and most revered perfumes in the world."

Joy tilted the bottle and widened her eyes. "And really expensive."

"Yeah, well, I have gambling winnings to blow—and we're celebrating. We'll take this, and this bottle of Essence of Roses, please."

"What about you, Mom? You deserve some good perfume for quitting smoking."

"I can never decide," she admitted, handing over her credit card. "I'll think about it, though, okay? Maybe I'll come up with a signature scent of my own."

"Like Grandma and her Jean Naté."

"Right."

Maggie said, "I think you smell good the way you are. You smell like sunshine, kinda."

Touched, Luna said, "Thank you, sweetie."

By the time the perfumes were bagged and paid for, Luna started feeling that a lot of time had passed, but on the way out, she thought of Elaine. "Wait," she said. "I want to get Elaine some perfume, too. What would a blues singer wear, Joy? What do you think?"

"Something really sexy and female."

"Musk. That musk we smelled," said Maggie.

"Perfect." They hurried back and bought the third bottle. It was an important day. They all needed something to remember it, mark it. She had her Barbie doll. The others would have perfume.

Elaine was waiting by the car, impatience in her crossed arms and scowl. "We brought you a present," Joy said and made a ceremony of handing over the wrapped box.

The impatience was erased completely. "Really? What is it?"

"Open it and see, silly."

Elaine shot a look at Luna, perplexed and pleased, and Luna's heart ached. Why had she never been able to see that all Elaine needed was a little nurturing? When she'd torn off the paper, she looked confused. "Perfume?"

"It's perfume," Joy said, "for a blues singer. Smell it. It's so sexy."

Elaine sucked in her bottom lip. "I'm not very sexy."

"You will be in that perfume," Luna said. "Put some on."

Laughing, Elaine did. "Oh, it's really nice. Thank you." She hugged Joy.

"It was Mom's idea, not mine."

"Thank you, Lu," she said, and there was a suspicious shine behind her glasses. "For the whole day."

Luna hugged her. "Thank you, Sissie. Thank you so much."

Maggie took out her perfume. "You wanted to put some of mine on, right?"

"Yes!" She anointed pulse points, smelling a hint of musk from her left wrist, and it mingled perfectly with the summer roses, and suddenly, quite urgently, she needed to see Thomas. She'd been an idiot last night. An idiot. "Come on, guys. Let's get back."

Elaine dropped them off at Luna's house, and took off for home. Luna couldn't even stand to walk the three blocks—she grabbed her keys and told the girls she'd be back in a little while. Joy grinned. "Have a good time," she said, leaning into Maggie, who laughed.

It was a brilliant day, clear and cool after the winds last night. She didn't see Thomas's truck anywhere, and her heart sunk. Maybe he'd just run an errand or something and would be right back. She'd at least go check. Even if it meant facing Placida for the first time since the night she'd dragged her out of her house. It seemed like a long time ago. As she climbed the railroad ties to the porch, she spied the old woman in a rocking chair on the porch, her shoulders wrapped in a brightly knit sweater, a rosary in her hands as always. Her feet didn't quite touch the floor. Luna's stomach flipped.

Barbie spoke up for the first time all day, laughing. *You're scared of her!*

Luna pasted a smile on her face. Yes. Yes, she was. Pausing at the foot of the porch steps, she said, *"Buenos días, Señora."* That should be respectful enough. She couldn't think how to ask in Spanish if Thomas was there, so she asked it in English. "Is Thomas here?"

Placida crooked her finger, gesturing for Luna to come to her. Feeling a little nervous, Luna went, and sat down in a chair next to the old woman. She didn't look well. Her face was pale. The eyes, beneath their spectacles, were strained in some way. "Are you all right?" Impulsively, Luna took her hand, and found her skin quite clammy.

Placida turned her hand and gripped Luna's. Hard. She closed her eyes and breathed in deeply, and a soft smile came over her mouth. *"Gracias, Madre,"* she said, then turned to Luna. "Listen," she whispered in English, and gripped Luna's hand. "He is a good man."

"Oh, he is. He is."

Placida nodded. Then she took a breath, put a hand to her chest, let go of the sigh, and closed her eyes.

Luna didn't get it for a minute. Not until the rosary in Placida's right hand dropped to her lap and her grip eased on Luna's hand. *"Abuela?"*

She fell over forward, and Luna barely managed to catch her, a tiny weight of birdlike bones. Luna cradled her, lifting her, feeling the lack of breath in the old woman. For a moment, Luna wasn't quite sure what to do. In the end, she carried her through the open door to the house, and put her down on the couch in a room that was more beautiful than Luna could have guessed, filled with things made of wood she somehow knew Thomas had carved. A phone was on the table by the couch, and even though she knew it was going to be too late, she called 911 for the second time in two days.

Then she sat down to wait in the sunstruck room. Placida's face was peaceful, calm, almost . . . cheerful. For some reason, Luna took her hand and held it, as if it would bring comfort. She heard a truck outside and saw Thomas come up the steep grade to the front door, a scowl on his face. Tiny followed behind him more slowly.

Luna just waited. The two of them came inside. Luna saw that Tiny had been fighting, and all the life was gone from him, so much so that Thomas more or less led him to a chair and pushed him into it. "Stay right there. I'm going to call the police."

It was only then that he saw Placida, stretched out on the couch, her face arranged in a peaceful smile. He fell to his knees next to her, picked up her hands and kissed them. *"Te quiero, Abuelita,"* he whispered, and took off her glasses. Kissed her brow. *"Te quiero.* God speed."

Luna blinked back tears and went to stand by Tiny as the ambulance roared up outside and the EMTs scurried in, all noise and importance. One of them recognized Luna from the night before. "Jeez. You're like a black widow, huh?"

"I guess."

"What happened?" Thomas asked.

"I came by to see you," she said, meeting his eyes, trying to telegraph her intent without words. "She was just sitting there and she talked to me for a minute, and then she just . . . took a breath and keeled over."

"I think she was having a heart attack when I left—" He made a sound, a growl, a glare at Tiny. Then he shook his head. "What did she say?"

Luna looked away. "I'd rather not say right this minute."

He inclined his head. "Okay." He frowned. "Did you understand her?"

"Sure," Luna said. "She spoke in English. Or whispered, really."

Tiny said, "She spoke English?" incredulously.

Thomas laughed.

"I don't get it," Luna said.

"I'll tell you later."

Thomas took Luna's hand, raised it to his lips. "I want to hear what she said. Don't go away. It's gonna get crazy here, but don't go. Okay?"

"I promise."

He picked up the phone.

Luna sank down next to Tiny. "Are you okay, guy?"

He shook his head. "He's calling the police to come arrest me. I went to Angelica's. We fought." He folded his hands, refolded them. "I took a knife. I was going to kill her, then me."

Ice rushed down her spine and she put her hand on his arm. "Oh, Tiny, I'm sorry. Is she okay?"

"Yeah," he said. "I didn't do it."

"That's good, Tiny. That's really good."

"I'm gonna be in jail awhile now."

"Yeah, probably." She smoothed a hand down his back. "But it won't be forever. Maybe it'll help you see things more clearly."

His throat worked, and she saw that he was folding his hands over and over again because they were trembling so badly. "I got no right to ask it, but would you come see me there? Just talk?" He lifted his eyes, filled with sorrow and pain and regret.

It was that expression, that one of hopelessness daring to cling to one pinpoint of light, that had drawn her into the work she'd done. She'd never wanted to make a ton of money. Never cared if there was prestige in her counseling work. She just wanted to hold out a hand to people who were absolutely sure there was no hand, not for them. And maybe she was even better prepared to offer that hope, having been so devoid of it herself, having hit bottom and made it up out of the pit herself. If nothing else, it had granted her compassion. As it had her father.

"Of course," she said. "I'd like that a lot." She'd have to do it in some official capacity, probably. She'd look into it right away, getting her credentials updated.

It was time, anyway.

Three hours later, Tiny had been arrested, Placida taken to the morgue, then to be delivered to the funeral home. Nadine and James left, promising to come back for the Mass in three days. Luna called the girls to tell them what was happening, to make sure they were okay. They were eating pizza, watching a comedy on the movie channel, and painting their nails. Maggie had talked to her grandmother, who was on her way home and would be back late. Maggie wanted to know if it was okay to spend one more night. "Of course," she said.

Just as dusk was falling, Thomas came out to the kitchen. Luna had made some coffee. "I hope you don't mind."

"Not at all. It smells good." He sank down at the table and rubbed his face. "Jesus, what a day. Pour me a cup, will you?"

The cat wove around her ankles, purring, as she did it. "What do you want, kitty?"

"It's Ranger," Thomas said, a smile in his voice.

Luna laughed, putting a cup before him. She picked up the cat. "Hey, Ranger. What do you want?" He tucked his head under her chin, purring. His fur was thick and soft, and she'd forgotten how great it was to have a cat cuddle up to her. "I miss cats. Maybe that's what you know, huh?" she said.

"Sit with me, Luna," Thomas said quietly.

She put the cat down and drifted into the chair next to him. He sighed and put his arm around her, his head falling into the crook of her shoulder. The weight was exactly right, fitting her just as it should. "Why did you come over?"

"Because I was an idiot last night and I wanted to tell you that."

"You were an idiot."

She laughed softly. "It's not polite to agree with a woman who is trying to apologize."

He rubbed his nose against her neck. "Are you?"

"Yes, I'm sorry I doubted you. You're right—you've never lied to me. You don't seem to lie at all."

"I don't." He tugged her closer, putting his other arm around her. "Come sit on my lap, let me hold you."

"I'm too big. I'll crush you."

"Come on." He straightened and made room for her. Luna settled gingerly, but his legs felt sturdy beneath her, solid as he was, and she relaxed as he put his arms around her. "I'm in love with you," he said. "It really did happen fast, but maybe that's just because it's right, you know?"

Her heart pinched at the husky, warm sound of his voice. "I'm in love with you, too," she whispered, and it felt so good to just say it. Just let it be. She put her arms around his shoulders and it was her turn to put her nose against his neck. It made her dizzy, it was so right.

"You smell like roses," he said.

"I bought the girls some perfume."

"How's Maggie?"

"She'll be all right. How are you?"

"I'm okay." He tightened his hold and his voice was raw with unshed tears as he added, "Man, I'm gonna miss her."

"I know."

"What did she say to you?"

Luna straightened. Put her hands on his face. "She told me you were a good man."

"I am," he said.

"Yes, you are." Luna kissed him.

"I'm so glad she burned her house down. I would never have met you otherwise."

"Me, too," she said.

"Are we on, Luna?"

"On?"

"You gonna let me love you? Even if I can't say it'll be happily ever after?"

"Yes," she whispered, and touched his face. "Sometimes, things can work out, I guess."

"I have a good feeling," he said.

"So do I, Thomas." She kissed him, very gently. "So do I."

From *Travellady Magazine*:

Día de los Muertos

By David Schultz

El Día de los Muertos, *or the Day of the Dead, is a traditional Mexican holiday that honors the dead. The tradition is celebrated just about anywhere there is a substantial Hispanic population, as there is here in New Mexico.*

The festivities include all manner of skeletons that are shown dancing and singing; detailed tissue paper cutouts called papel picado; *candles and votive lights to help the departed find their way; wreaths and crosses decorated with paper or silk flowers; and fresh seasonal flowers, particularly* cempazuchiles (marigolds) *and* barro de obispo (cockscomb). *Edible goodies offered to the dead are skulls and coffins made from sugar or chocolate and special baked goods, especially sugary sweet rolls called* pan de muerto *that come in various sizes and topped with bits of dough shaped like bones. All of these goods are destined for the buyer's* ofrenda de muertos (offering to the dead).

*The spirits of the dead are believed to come home for a visit on this holiday and the repast is laid out for them to provide sustenance for the journey.... * El Día de los Muertos *is not for sorrow and sadness but to celebrate the good times and to remember the happiness shared in the past. Take a day off and dance with the departed. You'll be glad you did.*

Twenty-six

Maggie's Diary

2 Noviembre 2001,
Día de los Muertos

Dear Tupac,
  Luna, that's my friend's mom, says it's perfectly okay to write my diary to you if I feel comfortable doing it, and I don't think you'd mind, so I'm going to keep doing it. Sorry I haven't written in so long, but there has been a lot going on.
  First, my mom is finally, finally better. She almost died of an overdose that was mainly an accident, but that got her into treatment and she spent three weeks in the hospital, then two more weeks going every day. They gave her some different medicine, but on *one*, something that's supposed to help keep her from getting so depressed. She also joined this grief support group, which seems to be helping. Anyway, she's lots, lots, lots better, and if she keeps getting better for another month, the doctors will let me go live with her again. I'm staying with my grandma, of course. It's not so bad. They were all worried about me after it first happened, and everybody was all sorry that they didn't see how awful it was, but I'm not mad at anybody. Luna said it's pretty normal for kids to think it's their responsibility to take care of their parents, so I was over my head, but I was doing normal things. It's fun to hang out with Ricky—I mean *Ricardo* (he was never

Ricardo before—he just started doing it lately, but that's okay, I guess, except it makes me think of Ricky Ricardo from *I Love Lucy*). Him and Joy are still going out, and they really like each other. Joy's kinda started looking different lately, too. She even wore a skirt to school one day and it was a hip-hugger thing that showed her belly ring. Yvonne was about to blow her stack, but she leaves Joy alone now because too many people like her. People are jealous of me being her best friend, but we've been through a lot together, you know? It's deep.

Joy almost had to go home to Atlanta, because her dad, the big jerk, wanted to get custody back. But then his wife, April, left him because he was cheating on her, and she promised she would testify for Joy, so he backed off. They came out to visit right after it happened, and Joy's little brothers were totally cute.

Second thing is, my English teacher sent one of my poems to a magazine and they are going to *publish it*!!!!!!!! She said that's really good for a kid who is only fifteen. I even get money—$25. They put the news in the school paper, and then it even went into the Taos paper!

But here's what I really wanted to tell you about—*Día de los Muertos.* That's today. Day of the Dead, in case you don't know. It's a really cool thing, and it was so great today. My mom and me and my grandma and oh, everybody, went to the graveyard to take care of my dad's grave. We brought all kinds of marigolds with us, and these little skeleton candies and we brought his favorite food—my mom's tamales, which she actually made from scratch, just for this, for everybody to share. She wore his favorite green dress and brought a little bit of beer to pour on his grave, then we shared it, all of us taking a sip. She's gained some weight and looked so pretty there that I saw a lot of men noticing her, so whenever she gets ready, there will be a new husband for her.

Lots of people go take care of their families' graves, so we saw all kinds of people and they were so nice to my mom. We saw Thomas and Luna and Joy, who went to take care of Mrs. Ramirez's grave. My mom wanted to stop there, too, so we did, and I realized I kinda miss the old lady. I told my mom about going to see her, asking for help, and how kind she was that day, and Thomas squeezed my shoulder.

Then afterward, me and my mom went to Luna and Joy's house for supper. It was a big party—all kinds of people were there, nearly every single one a woman except for Thomas and this guy named Frank who is Joy's grandma's husband. There was a Barbie doll in the middle of the table, the really old yucky one Luna brought home from the land, but that's why it was there, of course, because they don't know where Jesse is buried, or it's far away, so they were honoring him at home, with his favorite foods. They played the Beatles all night long and then Elaine announced that she was going to be singing at a café in Taos next week and she'd like it if everybody came. She was all shy and turned red when she said it, but you could tell how proud she was, too. Joy winked at me and took a big deep breath, so I did, too, and smelled the blues-lady perfume.

It was one of the best days I've ever had. And when I was sitting there, looking at everybody, with my mom sitting right beside me, all the lamplight falling down on people laughing, and feeling so much love in the room, I felt my dad beside me for a minute. Just loving me and my mom, seeing us. I could almost smell him.

And my heart filled up like you wouldn't believe, just almost burst open with happiness.

I kept some marigolds and put them on the shrine I made for you, since I don't know where your grave is. I guess you'd like being remembered since you died so young. I lit a candle for you, too, and I was sitting there, thinking about my dad and my mom and everything, and I saw that dollar bill with "Tupac Is Alive" on it, the one I got the day my dad was buried. And I finally realized what my dad was trying to tell me. That you are alive, even if you're dead, as long as there is somebody to remember you. You're alive in my heart, just like my dad is, because I remember you. I'll have to find out what your favorite food was and eat it next year.

And what I thought, sitting there, was that sometimes life is really hard. It just is. Things happen that make you want to die, but if you hang on, they do eventually get better. I think I should write a poem about that.

Love,
Maggie

Turn the page
for an exciting peek
at Barbara Samuel's
next book,

The Goddesses of
Kitchen Avenue

Coming in hardcover wherever books are sold
Published by
The Random House Publishing Group

Prologue

Trudy

The first time I see Lucille again, I am lying in my bed. Alone. My newly broken arm is propped on a pillow. It's very late, close to dawn. My face is hot from crying and loss and Vicodin, which they gave me at the emergency room. The drugs are not appreciably helping stop the pain in my right arm, which is imprisoned in a cast to my elbow. It's red. The cast, that is. Probably the arm, too, which feels like coyotes are chewing on it. And the world seems red, too, all around the edges.

When I open my eyes, Lucille is sitting in the chair where Rick always throws his clothes. She looks exactly the same, which should tip me off that something is slightly wrong, but in my current state, nothing seems real, so I just blink at her for a long minute.

It's been twenty-five years since I've seen her. She's wearing a shawl that a matador gave her, red with black silk fringes she plays with. There are heavy silver bracelets on her tanned arms, and she's drinking a cocktail. It's funny enough that I smile. Lucille always did believe in cocktails. My mother said she was a drunk, but she wasn't. I knew even then that my mother was just afraid of Lucille. Afraid of her sexuality, afraid of her courage, afraid of her version of womanhood. Afraid it would leak out of her house somehow, like bad water, to poison the whole neighborhood. My mother and her friends, all the ladies on the block, said terrible things about Lucille's clothes—gossamer blouses that showed her low-cut bras, the sleek way she wore her hair and let all of her back show, nape to waist, on summer days. She told me it was a woman's secret power, her back. It didn't age the way other parts might.

Men found reasons to stop by her yard when she was working with her flowers, the flowers she nudged like magic daughters from the hard ground in the desert. Poppies as big as sombreros, waving long, black, inviting stamens from their silky hearts, and roses in impossible colors, and cosmos by the thousands.

The men stopped to admire her back. And her strong brown arms, and the glimpse of her lacy bras.

But mostly they stopped to hear that wild, bold poppy laugh come out of her throat. Stopped to have her admire them. Stopped to be watered by her joy.

She was sixty-six years old when she moved into our neighborhood.

Now it has been twenty-five years and she's at the foot of my bed, not in some ghostly form, but as solid as the cat purring on my hip. When she doesn't say anything, I swallow the rawness in my throat and croak, "What are you doing here?"

"Time to take it back, kiddo."

"What?"

"Your life."

Mother, the moon is dancing
In the Courtyard of the Dead.
"Dance of the Moon in Santiago"
Federico García Lorca

2

Trudy

When Edgar dies, I am next door in my house,
reading Lorca with my hands over my ears so I
don't have to hear the wind. It's only because I
have to take them down to turn the page that
I hear Roberta's cry, that piercing wail that can
only be called keening.

It's been a long day, waiting for this. Because I
wanted to be here when the moment arrived, I
didn't go to the movies or out to the mall to distract myself from my own troubles. Roberta's
granddaughter, Jade, is on her way to Pueblo from
California, but she isn't here yet, and Roberta sent
everybody else away. When the moment comes,
she'll need someone. So I've waited. Trying to
keep warm—I'm wearing a T-shirt, a cotton

sweater and a wool one, two pairs of socks, and jeans—and I'm still cold. It's like Rick was my furnace, and without him, I'm turning into an icicle.

And the wind is driving me crazy.

People often tell me how much they love the wind. I've sat, with my mouth open, while friends from elsewhere—they are always from somewhere else—rhapsodize about the winds they know, and I can tell that they're thinking of an entirely different entity—a green goddess, trailing her veils over the beach or through the forest. They love a wind that comes with moisture and beauty.

In Pueblo, our winds are of the Inquisition variety, winds that know that the secret of torture is to begin and end, to be inconstant and constant at once, to bellow and to whisper. Endlessly.

This year, it's been even worse than usual. Every morning, it gathers, gusting and stopping. Blasting and quitting. All day, it bangs on the windows and blusters around the car and buffets the trees and tears at the shrubs. Boxes blown from who knows where skitter down the street. There is no surface without grit. Static electricity can knock you down. I play music, loudly, to drown it out, put a pillow over my head at night.

But not today. I have to listen for Roberta.

For lunch, I pour some condensed chicken and stars soup into a pot and put the kettle on for tea, huddling next to the burners with my hands tucked under my armpits. The tea is indifferent, the soup the last can on the shelf. I was lucky to find that much worth consuming, really, since I keep forgetting to go to the grocery store. Right now, when I'm hungry for something better than the cupboards have to offer, I look around for my list so I can write *good tea bags* on there, but it's gone missing. Again. I can't keep track of anything lately.

I used to spend at least two hours a week planning menus and shopping for my crew of five. Now it's only me and my seventeen-year-old, Annie, but more often than not she eats at school or at her restaurant job or with her boyfriend, Travis. As long as I keep milk and cereal and frozen pizzas around, she's covered.

I keep forgetting that it might be good for me to cook for myself. Nobody ever liked the same foods I do—my roasted veggie dishes and exotic soups. Time to indulge. On my list, I write, *Garlic, marinated pepper strips, lemon juice, whole pepper. Frozen quiches. Cheddar (the good one), Triscuits.*

I won't forget the single-serving cans of tuna, which have been the mainstay of my diet lately. It's easy, and at least the cats get enthusiastic when they hear me pop the lid. I always pour the water off into a bowl for them. They are immensely grateful and I can glow over it for a good five minutes, standing at the counter eating out of the can.

I know, I know. Cats, tuna—this has all the earmarks of a Bad End.

The kettle whistles and I pour water into my cup, think maybe I'm just getting old. Bones thinning along with my skin, muscles withering away to nothing. I think of my granny, wizened down to broomstick size, and pull my sweater tighter around my torso.

Not old, not old, not old. Not at forty-six.

Forty-six is young these days, or at least just beyond the cusp of middle age.

Wind blusters against the windows, and I hear the sound of the chimes my new neighbor hung on his porch. His things appeared abruptly overnight three days ago, like the plumage of some exotic bird—a trio of chimes strung across the porch, a cluster of sticks and painted canvas in the side yard that promised quiet and other things, a foreign car I thought might be an English Mini, strange and small and orange. A ristra, cheery, bright red chiles in a string, hung by the door, nothing strange by itself. But it almost seemed that there was a new scent in the air, spice and chocolate and the promise of fresh yeast. Shannelle, the young mother across the street, said she'd glimpsed him, and widened her eyes to illustrate her amazement.

I move to the window to peer out. My breath makes a thick circle of condensation on the glass. At first I can only see the car, a blurry round like a giant pumpkin, so I wipe away the fog and cover my mouth with my fingers. As if called by my curiosity, he comes out on the porch.

Oh.

Despite the cold, he wears no shoes, and only some Ecuadorean-style pajama bottoms riding low on hips the color of a sticky bun. Hair runs in a fine line up the center of his belly like a stripe of cinnamon. Heavy silver bracelets cuff his dark wrists. A necklace of claws, something made in a jungle, hangs around his neck.

He stretches, showing the tufts of hair beneath his arms. I find myself holding my breath with him, letting it out again only when he lowers his chin and, in an insouciant gesture, tosses back his hair to show his face. It looks good from this distance, a high brow and wide mouth. Hair, thick and wavy, pours down to his shoulders in a tangle of honey and butter.

I half expect him to look my way, feel my gaze like some magic being, but he only bends over to pick up a newspaper and goes back inside.

Lazy thing, I think, *sleeping until past noon.*

I carry my tea and soup into the dining room, put down a place mat on the table even though there's no strict need for it. It's not as if the table needs protecting—it's ancient and beautiful, if scarred from twenty-some years of family dinners—but I like the homey look of the floral pattern against the wood. I think it might be for show, in case anyone happens by, a way to demonstrate that I'm doing just fine, but that's okay, too. I get a matching napkin out of the drawer and center everything on the mat, look for a magazine to read, trying to recapture the sense of well-being such old rituals used to give me when Rick went off riding with his buddy Joe Zamora, and the kids were at friends' houses or skating or whatever. In those days, time alone was a luxury—I'd put on some music no one else liked and fix some soup only I would eat, like my very special corn chowder, and read in the blissful aloneness.

But the evening looms. The house thunders with emptiness. How could my old life be over so suddenly that after years and years of never having a minute to draw my breath now I have so much time that I feel myself sinking into it like quicksand, drowning in it?

A mother finished. A wife dismissed.

Cliché-city.

"God, Trudy," I say to myself aloud, since there's no one else to say it to. "You are boring me to death now. Do something."

So I find the collection of Lorca's poems, which I've been reading in an attempt to renew my acquaintance with Spanish—a passion I left behind somewhere. His work is appropriate to accompany the sound of Roberta's singing that comes to me between bursts of wind. The houses are not that far apart and she's got one of those big, black Southern gospel kinds of voices, like Aretha Franklin, though she pooh-poohs that comparison. I knew when I heard her that she was singing her husband Edgar's favorites for him.

One last time.

Letting him go at last. He's been in a diabetic coma for two weeks, since just after supper one Friday night. I was sitting with her when it happened—he'd been sick for a while, pieces of his body just eaten away by the disease—and she grabbed his hand, and cried out, "Edgar, don't you *leave* me!" in such a heartbroken voice that I had to go home and cry about it later.

The hospice workers and the nurse who came in every day kept saying they didn't know what in the world was keeping him alive. But I knew. So did Roberta.

The cry comes again, a wild piercing wail, the sound of her soul tearing in half. I put down my book, put my hand to my chest, and let it move through me. In a minute, I will stand up and go to her.

In a minute.

In between, I let it swell in me, the freshened sorrow that her grief brings. My husband is not dead, just in love with somebody else, but I'm mourning him all the same, and my heart joins in Roberta's howl, as if we're a pair of coyotes. My wrist, out of the cast now for a couple of weeks, starts throbbing, and I put my other hand around it protectively.

Roberta. I put on my shoes and coat and hurry over to her house.